LINDA MITCH̶̶̶̶̶̶̶ ̶̶ began writing in the late 199̶̶̶̶ ̶̶̶ ̶̶er a late starter – when she lost her hearing due to viral dam̶̶̶e. To begin with she buried herself in magazines and books and then decided to have a go at writing. She found it a way of communicating. And it paid! She has now had over 300 short stories published, worldwide. Linda has had four full-length novels and two novellas published with Choc Lit, *Christmas at Strand House* is her second novel with HQ Digital, following *Summer at 23 The Strand*.

Linda has lived in Devon, beside the sea, all her life and wouldn't want to live anywhere else. She walks by the sea most days, or up over the hill behind her house where she has fabulous views out over Dartmoor. In summer she can be found on the pillion of one of her husband, Roger's, vintage motorbikes, or relaxing in the garden with a book and a glass of Prosecco. Life couldn't be sweeter.

You can follow Linda on Twitter: @LindaMitchelmor

READERS LOVE LINDA MITCHELMORE

'The perfect book to take on holiday.'

'It's inspired me to go on a little holiday of my own.'

'By the end of the book I wanted to sit on the veranda with a glass of wine, eat fish & chips and visit the local café.'

'A wonderful summer read.'

'Charming and uplifting.'

'Such a delightful, uplifting and heartwarming read.'

'A lovely book to read on holiday.'

'Fabulous.'

Also by Linda Mitchelmore

Summer at 23 The Strand

This novel is entirely a work of fiction. The names, characters and incidents portrayed in it are the work of the author's imagination. Any resemblance to actual persons, living or dead, events or localities is entirely coincidental.

HQ
An imprint of HarperCollins*Publishers* Ltd
1 London Bridge Street
London SE1 9GF

This edition 2018

First published in Great Britain by
HarperCollins*Publishers* Ltd 2018

Linda Mitchelmore asserts the moral right to be identified as the author of this work

A catalogue record for this book is available from the British Library

ISBN: PB: 978-0-00-832704-0

MIX
Paper from
responsible sources
FSC™ C007454

This book is produced from independently certified FSC™ paper to ensure responsible forest management.

For more information visit: www.harpercollins.co.uk/green

Typeset by Palimpsest Book Production Ltd, Falkirk, Stirlingshire
Printed and bound in Great Britain by
CPI Group (UK) Ltd, Croydon CR0 4YY

Christmas at Strand House

LINDA MITCHELMORE

ONE PLACE. MANY STORIES

For my son, James. And for my daughter, Sarah, and my grandchildren, Alexander and Emily Rose.

With my love always, and forever.

23rd December

Chapter 1

Lissy

Alicia – Lissy to her friends – was the first to arrive. Strand House, the far end property in a small cul-de-sac, stood majestically on the headland, large and imposing with its startlingly white walls and flat roof, very Art Deco, and, Lissy had always thought, more suited to the South of France, or maybe Miami, than a quiet Devon coastal town. The early morning, low winter sun was glinting off the huge windows, and the mimosa she remembered helping her late godmother, Veronica, to plant was just coming into bud. It never failed to surprise Lissy that mimosa flowered so early in the year, often when there was frost around, although frost rarely tinged the gardens of Strand House, situated as it was, quite literally, a stone's thrown from the sea and warmer air. The first sight of Strand House always took her breath away, even though she'd known the house since childhood. And now that Veronica had left it to her, it was hers. A large, square, black-and-white tiled hallway led up to six bedrooms, all with en suites. The sitting room ran the full depth of the house and the dining room could seat twelve with ease. The kitchen was so large and well-appointed it would do any high-end hotel proud.

And later, three of her friends – Xander, Bobbie, and Janey – all single and alone at Christmas, and brought together by her so they would be less alone, less lonely, would be arriving at Strand House.

Xander – now sadly a widower – she'd first met fourteen years ago when he'd married Lissy's childhood friend, Claire. God, how she missed Claire. They'd been friends since they'd met when Lissy came down to stop with her godmother; Claire's family lived just a few doors along from Strand House and geography had made them instant playmates. All through college and university they'd kept in touch, meeting up when they could. Lissy remembered how excited Claire was to have met Xander, how her voice had buzzed with the romance of it all when she rang Lissy to tell her that he'd asked her to marry him. 'You won't believe this, Liss, but he's lived just a mile away from my house all these years and I've not met him until now! You and me, we've probably been in the same café as him, or the same pub, or on the same beach as Xander at some stage. If that's so I don't know what we were thinking not registering how gorgeous he is! You'll just love him!' Claire had said. And Lissy had found that yes, Xander was easy to love, accepting her as his friend because she was Claire's. He'd never minded that Lissy took Claire away for a long weekend once a year when they did some course or other, some activity that would teach them new things; time when they loved and laughed and had fun, cementing their friendship further. But that friendship had been cut short with Claire's tragic death. Xander's phone call telling her Claire had died in a road accident had played on repeat in her head for days afterwards. The shock of it. The tragedy of a wonderful, vibrant, friend's life cut short. She'd kept in touch with Xander by email and the occasional phone call, but they hadn't met up since Claire's funeral; Lissy had let Xander grieve in his own way, as she had grieved in hers. Between then and now, Lissy had had her own life-changing moment and had got divorced.

4

Thank goodness, she thought, that she had Janey and Bobbie in her life. Neither were life-long friends as Claire had been but there'd been an instant bond between them from the moment they'd walked into the art studio for a life-drawing weekend workshop in Dartington four years before. Now without Claire to share sad news with it was to Janey and Bobbie that she'd turned, emailing them both, and getting an instant response from that they were there for her whenever she needed to talk. Mostly she didn't because it was Lissy's way to fight her own battles, but there were times when it had been almost too much to bear because she'd honestly thought she and Cooper were happy – well, she was. 'The wife is usually the last to know,' Bobbie had said. 'And the first to make a better life for herself once she's over the shock. Mark my words.' Lissy had flinched at those words at the time, but it was just Bobbie's forthright way. Janey, bless her, had been less forthright, but no less supportive. She'd painted Lissy a card – an exquisitely executed, busy picture filled with birds and flowers and clouds – and inside she'd written, *'Birds and flowers and clouds are always around you, take time to look and 'be' among them'*. And so, every day, Lissy looked at birds and flowers and clouds and just let herself 'be' among them, and it helped, more than she ever thought it would when she'd got Janey's card.

Lissy steered the car into the drive of Strand House. She couldn't wait to see them all again, even though her mother had poured scorn on the idea.

'But, darling,' her mother had said when Lissy had divulged her Christmas plans, 'why don't you come to us? Mark was only asking this morning if you would be.'

'No ferries?' Lissy had replied, the hint of a question in her voice. Perhaps her mother had forgotten the ferry didn't run at Christmas. She doubted that her stepfather had said any such thing – largely he avoided her whenever they were in the same place.

'Flights, darling?' her mother had replied, whippet-fast. Lissy's mother, Carol, was one who liked to have her own way.

'Too problematical. I'd have to catch a flight to Paris and then get a train or hire a car.'

'Goodness, but you're making it sound as though you don't *want* to come. Please do, darling, Christmas is for families.'

Lissy had heard her own deep intake of breath like a pistol shot in her ears because hadn't her mother fractured their family when she'd left Lissy's father, Ed, for another man? And hadn't her father died of a broken heart? Well, 'heart disease' was the official term but Lissy had always believed differently.

'Some people don't have families. At Christmas or otherwise,' she'd replied wearily.

'And these *friends*, darling,' her mother had gone on, unwilling to let the subject drop, 'how well do you know them?'

'Mum, I am thirty-six years old. I've been married and divorced. I am a chartered accountant with my own practice. I took the very brave step of joining a choir with a bunch of people I didn't know and who could have been axe murderers for all I knew, and I was fine. It would be nice if you could give me the grace to choose my own friends.'

And the call had ended a little frostily as almost all calls to her mother did these days, and with Lissy on the verge of tears that her relationship with her mother wasn't better than it was.

But her mother had a point – how well did she know Janey, Bobbie, and Xander?

Feeling a little uneasy now with the memory of her last conversation with her mother still ringing in her head, she drove along in front of the house, reached for the radio-control fob on the keys in the ignition and opened the automatic garage door. There was room enough inside for at least four cars; her Mini was going to look a little lost, wasn't it? Janey would be coming by train, and Xander possibly on foot because he lived just half a mile away in a cottage behind the harbour. Bobbie, too, had said only

6

that she wouldn't be driving down to Devon, not in the Christmas rush to escape London and the chaos of the M25.

'Gosh, but Cooper is going to be so cross when he discovers Strand House is now mine,' Lissy said aloud as she let herself in. 'And mine alone.'

Not hers and Cooper's to divide between them. It had been Cooper who'd asked for a divorce because he'd fallen in love with someone else.

'Do I know her?' Lissy had asked, knowing instantly how analytical the question was, and that she must be in shock. Her heart had jolted in her chest, missed a beat, and her breathing became erratic as she took longer breaths which took even longer to let out again. Sometimes, even now, she woke in the night remembering that feeling, fearful that that scenario had only just happened, and it wasn't until she'd sat up, turned on the light, and seen that the bedroom was different now to how it had been when Cooper had shared it with her, with new everything, that she knew she was making a new life for herself now.

'You're making that sound as though you don't care.' Cooper had sounded more than miffed.

'Really? What did you expect me to say? To beg you not to leave?' Her mouth had been dry with nerves and she'd struggled to get the words out but get them out she had.

'I'd still leave,' Cooper had said. 'Her name's Nina.'

Lissy struggled to remember if he had mentioned anyone called Nina working in the same bank as he did; if, perhaps, he'd dropped that name into the conversation a few too many times and she'd failed to pick up on the clues. She felt her forehead furrow in concentration, and a pain arrowed through her head like gunshot.

'Don't worry your pretty little head about it,' Cooper had said, almost with a snigger. 'I can almost see the cogs going around. You don't know her, I met her at the gym.'

And then Cooper had begun throwing clothes into black bin bags. And shoes. And all his motor racing magazines. He'd even

7

had the audactity to take two pork chops from the freezer for his and Nina's supper. It had been that last act that had told Lissy there was no saving her marriage now.

'I'll be in touch,' Cooper had said after he'd carried the last of the sacks out to the car.

'So will I!' had been Lissy's reply. 'Through my solicitor.'

The divorce had been acrimonious, if swift, Cooper insisting everything was scrupulously divided in two. Lissy often thought he would have cut their friends in half if he could. What luck then, for Lissy, that the decree absolute had arrived a week before her godmother's fatal heart attack.

'And you are not going to give Cooper any more thought!' Lissy strode purposefully across the black and white tiles of the hall and up the stairs to the large, master bedroom with its patio doors that opened onto a narrow balcony overlooking the sea she had already bagged for herself. She could fetch her luggage in later. Lissy went over to the bed, covered in pristine white bed-linen with broderie anglaise trim, and lay down. How fresh it all smelled. She was glad now she'd gone to the expense of paying a cleaner to come in once a week after Veronica had died, even though there was no one to clean up after. The hall tiles had gleamed the way they always had, welcoming her in, as they had when Veronica was alive. The teak banister rail smelled faintly of polish as she ran her hand along it on the way up, as it always had. Lissy rolled over onto her side and sniffed the pillow. Yes, the pillow still held the fragrance of the fabric conditioner – sea breeze – that Veronica had always used.

'Oh, Vonny,' Lissy said into the pillow, using the pet name she had always called her godmother. 'Thank you for this wonderful gift, but I miss you so.'

She missed the warmth of her greeting and the scent of Shalimar on her godmother's skin, and the depth of her loving. She knew she would miss always the myriad little ways Vonny found to spoil her – making shortbread biscuits on rainy days;

filling a bath with what Lissy had discovered, when she was older and able to buy it for herself, was hugely expensive bath oil, and frothing it into a cloud of bubble so that only the tip of Lissy's nose and her mouth had been visible; and letting her pick the first yellow peony from the bush even though they both knew it looked better on the bush than in a vase.

But this was a bedroom that needed to be shared. A bedroom that begged for her to wake up beside someone she loved and who loved her. They would sit up, propped against the huge hessian-covered headboard, and watch the sun rise over the water. And then they would make love, with no need to pull the curtains because no one could look in. There was nothing between Strand House and the continent.

'And I have got to stop talking to myself! I've got three friends arriving soon and lots to do before then.'

The house had yet to be decorated for Christmas. There'd probably be some decorations of Vonny's in a cupboard somewhere but Lissy didn't want to use them. She had a fancy for a theme of some sort – silver and blue, or maybe gold and green. There was bound to be a shop in town somewhere that sold decorations and surely they wouldn't all have been sold already. And flowers. Strand House had always been filled with fresh flowers when Vonny had been alive. White roses had been a favourite and Lissy decided that she would try and find some to honour her godmother's memory. So many would be needed in a house this size – one little bunch of ten or so stems would look lost. Vases – she'd need lots of vases. And some smaller pots because she intended to put small posies in each of the rooms for her guests, something her godmother had always done for her, often picking buds of things, and interesting leaves from the garden – daisies even – to welcome her. Lissy looked around the room. Yes, that's what she missed the most, perhaps ... the little pot of hand-picked flowers on the bedside table in welcome. There probably wouldn't be much in the garden in the way of flowers at this time of year but there'd be ivy and some evergreen shrub somewhere she could use with a few buds taken from shop flowers. Just as soon as Janey arrived she'd suggest they go into town and see what they could find, but they'd need to be back in time for her 2 p.m. Waitrose delivery.

She leapt from the bed and went to fetch her luggage.

Yes, perhaps the decision to ask Janey, Bobbie, and Xander to join her had been the right one. Maybe she was the loneliest one of them all.

Chapter 2

Janey

'Morning, sweetheart,' the taxi driver said as Janey approached the open window of the passenger door.

'Good morning. Are you free?' Janey wasn't in the habit of taking taxis but she knew the drill. The three taxis in front of this people carrier were already filling up with passengers who'd got off the train and were beginning to pull away.

'Well, I'll expect you to pay your fare, sweetheart. But I'm free as a bird at the moment and at your service. Sam's the name.'

'I don't know that I need such a big taxi,' Janey said, feeling a smile twitch up the corners of her mouth a little. 'I can wait for the next one.'

She only had a small wheeled suitcase. It had been packed for ages with a few essentials like a change of underwear and some nightclothes, a dress and a spare pair of shoes. Her emergency exit luggage she always called it, all ready in case Stuart's drinking and his temper put her in fear for her life. Up until now she'd been able to calm a situation, get herself out of danger by escaping to the bathroom or with the promise of a steak dinner when Stuart had sobered up. But she'd always known there'd be a time

11

when she'd need that exit luggage and she'd come to her senses and was getting out before that time came, before a thump on the arm became much more, before a restraining hand went from her wrist to her neck.

'Same charge, love, whether there's one of you or half a dozen. Now you stay right there and I'll come round and help you. I'm guessing you're not a famous film star, or that Kate Moss, or foreign royalty or you'd be filling this taxi up with luggage.'

'No,' Janey said. 'None of those.'

Janey knew she ought, perhaps, to wheel her case to the back of the taxi so the driver could load it but she felt frozen with fright at what she had done.

The taxi driver had reached her now. He loomed over her – at least six foot four inches to Janey's scant five feet two. Standing facing him Janey, was just about level with the badge pinned to his jacket: *Sam Webber, Ace Taxis.*

'Are you going to let that thing go, love, so I can get it in the boot? Or are you one half of its Siamese twin? You seem very attached. Your knuckles have gone white you're gripping on that tight.'

And she could still keep on gripping it tight and go back into the railway station, find the other platform and take the up train back to Totnes, and home. It wasn't far. Stuart was probably still crashed out on the couch and wouldn't even have noticed she wasn't there.

Janey had left before dawn, the previous night's phone call still fresh in her mind.

'Who was that?' Stuart had asked when Janey put down the phone. He made it sound as though she ought not to have answered the phone in the first place.

'Suzy.'

'I might have known. That sister of yours is a total waste of space. What crisis is she having now?'

Yes, Suzy did seem to have more crises in her life than anyone else Janey knew, but then her health wasn't as good as most people's either. And Suzy's son, Daniel, had learning difficulties and problems with mobility, while her six-year-old twin daughters needed a lot of attention as well. Janey wondered how she coped sometimes.

'I might need to pop over there tomorrow,' Janey had told Stuart, her voice a wobble with the lie she was telling. Would Stuart be able to detect that or was he too drunk? She hoped the latter. 'Give her a hand with all the last-minute Christmas things.'

Janey had looked around the room, the only nod to Christmas by way of decoration was a few cards on the mantelpiece and a faux Christmas tree about a foot tall in a plastic pot. Janey hadn't even bothered to put any tiny glass baubles on it this year. Or the miniature fairy on the top. Her sister's house, she knew, would be full of colour and glitter and delicious smells of mince pies and brandy. And laughter. Despite all Suzy's problems her house was always full of laughter. But then, Suzy didn't have a husband like Stuart. And Janey wasn't going there anyway.

'Be her slave more like,' Stuart had said.

And it was the word 'slave' that had made Janey's decision for her. The only person she was a slave to was Stuart. And he didn't exactly have her chained up so she couldn't leave.

'I've had more than a bit of practice,' Janey said, her voice no longer wobbly.

'And what's that supposed to mean?'

'Whatever you want it to,' Janey said, a snake of fear rippling up her spine – a spine that seemed to be straightening as she stood there in front of Stuart challenging him, possibly for the first time. 'There's plenty to eat in the fridge, and more than plenty to drink seeing as the spare room has got cases of wine and twelve packs of beer from floor to ceiling.'

'Won't even miss you then, will I?' Stuart said, opening yet another can of Foster's.

And now here she was, on her way to spending Christmas

with Lissy and Bobbie. And Xander. She'd only ever met Xander at his wife, Claire's, funeral, which was sad. She wondered what she might talk to him about, or he her. The only thing they had in common was the fact they'd both known Claire. And that they were all alone at Christmas. Well, that was the story she'd told Lissy who had invited her to Strand House for the festivities. Festivities! How Lissy had got hold of her landline number Janey had no idea and wasn't going to ask but she was glad that she had. She might not have left otherwise. That phone call had been just the push-come-to-shove that she needed.

Janey fingered her mobile in her coat pocket, feeling for a vibration which would probably mean Stuart had woken up and found the note she'd tucked beside the tin of teabags on the kitchen counter. *I'VE LEFT AND I'M NOT COMING BACK.*

'I don't know where you are, sweetheart,' the taxi driver said, 'but it sure isn't here with me on a bit of tarmac that needs replacing, because doesn't it almost wreck the tracking of this taxi every time I drive over it.'

'I know. I'm sorry.' Carefully, Janey unpeeled her fingers from the grip of her wheelie case and flexed her fingers. Her knuckles cracked, like popping corn. 'Lots on my mind. Christmas and that.'

'Oh gawd, yes, Christmas. Right old fandangle, isn't it? The wife starts preparing back in September and heaven help me if I don't make all the right noises when she shows me what she's bought for this one and that. I expect you're the same. Most women are.'

Not me, Janey thought. As her marriage had slowly died so had her joy in any sort of celebration. But all that was about to change, wasn't it?

'Right then, sweetheart,' Sam said when he'd got Janey's case on board and had closed the huge, hinged, rear door. 'Where's it going to be? Paris? Rome? Or maybe Moscow if you've got your thermals in that case?'

Usually, Janey hated anyone she didn't know calling her 'sweetheart'. But right now, it was welcome. It was as though this tall, kindly, man who reminded Janey of her long-dead granddad, knew she needed that familiarity. His cheery chatter was a balm for her bruised soul. Bruised, not broken, she told herself.

'Strand House. It doesn't seem to have a number,' she said, taking the piece of paper from her pocket on which she'd written the name of what was to be her home for the next five days, and Lissy's mobile phone number. 'TQ5 1QS if that helps.'

'Cor, blimey,' Sam said. 'That's posh, sweetheart. Strand House. But then, there's lots of posh around here.'

'You know it?'

'I do. So, sweetheart, will you ride there in style beside me in the front or do you want to queen it in the back? You'll rattle around a bit but you could practise your regal wave.'

'In the front, please,' Janey said, getting in. 'Is it far?'

'No journey's long with good company, sweetheart,' Sam said, getting in the driving seat and doing up his seatbelt. 'Well, that's what they say. You can tell me to belt up and that you like your journeys the way Oscar Wilde liked his haircuts – in silence – if you like. Or I could keep wittering on because the old boy that's me, who's been around the block a bit, thinks you might be needing a bit of company.'

'I do,' Janey said. 'Need a bit of company.'

Sam started the engine and indicated he was pulling out.

'So, you've come away from somewhere else for Christmas, then? That's my guess because you don't know where Strand House is.'

'You guess right.'

'Well, Strand House is pretty big so there'll be company once you get there. Rich old biddy used to live there, ran it as a sort of upmarket B&B – boutique hotel or somesuch – for years but she's dead now. I got a lot of trade ferrying guests to and fro back in her day. And her as well when she wanted to go into

15

Torquay for a bit of shopping and the like. I have no idea who owns it now.'

'I do. She's called Lissy. She's a … a friend.'

Janey had few friends – well, none unless you counted Megan who ran the newsagent with whom she'd been at school – because Stuart discouraged it. Friends with bigger incomes than hers would only fuel jealousy, was what Stuart had said. And he hadn't wanted her to go out to work either because that only put ideas in people's heads and encouraged extra-marital relationships. Janey had her suspicions that Stuart had had one of those with a colleague at the school where he worked. When she'd challenged him, Stuart had cut her down to size – with his words and with his fists. Why, oh why, hadn't she left before? What was she going to do now that she had? Another shiver snaked its way up her back and over her shoulders. She felt for the phone in her pocket again. No vibration. She was safe for the moment.

'Well, I hope she's a friend, this Lissy, if you're spending Christmas with her. I mean, most of us spend Christmas with family who we'd never in our right minds choose as friends, but there we are, all shackled up together, for the duration. We all might have a better time of it if we could spend it with friends. And I hope this blooming taxi isn't bugged because if the wife gets to know I said that she'd strangle me.'

Janey didn't think for a minute that Sam had a hard time of it with his wife and family at Christmas. He was just being self-deprecating and trying to make her laugh in the process, wasn't he?

'I could be a private detective for all you know,' Janey said. A giggle escaped, fizzing up from inside her somewhere where giggles had long been buried, like bubbles in a glass of lemonade. It made her cough a little. 'You know. Hired by your wife to check up on you.'

'Yeah, and I'm that Richard Branson, moonlighting to make a few bob.' Sam indicated he was going to overtake a bus, and

Janey breathed in because there was hardly any space between it and an oncoming car. She was still holding her breath when Sam said, 'You can breathe out now, sweetheart. I've done that before you know. Not killed anyone yet. Anyway, this Lissy, got a family, has she?'

Had she? Janey had no idea. When they'd met at the art weekend in Dartington none of them had got around to sharing histories. She knew only that Lissy had been married then and wasn't now. And that Claire had been married to Xander back then but wasn't now because she'd been killed in a road traffic accident. And Bobbie, who had been the model for that life-drawing art class – she didn't know much more about her other than that she was good fun and impossibly glamorous, and she saw Bobbie's face in a magazine or a Sunday supplement sometimes. Bobbie put up Facbook blogposts dripping with glamour shots that were a world away from Janey's experience but sometimes, when she was more down than usual, she'd look at Bobbie's page and be transported to her world if only for a little while. Lissy had still been married to Cooper when they'd all gone to Claire's funeral and the opportunity for asking if they'd left children in the care of grandparents hadn't arisen. But then none of them knew much about her either, did they? They probably knew she was good at art. Xander had popped up on Janey's Facebook page a couple of times asking to buy a painting from her, but she'd said no, it wasn't for sale. She wondered why she'd said that because if she'd sold a few paintings she'd have had some savings instead of the nothing she had now.

'A family?' Janey said, her brain being dragged back to the present with great difficulty, as though it was being pulled through treacle filled with bits of gravel. 'I don't know. I don't think so.'

'What does she do then, this friend of yours?'

'She's an accountant. With her own practice.'

'Now there's a useful friend to have!' Sam turned to Janey and smiled broadly. 'Help you fiddle your taxes and that. You'll have to give me her details.'

Janey didn't pay taxes. She had no income on which to pay them, and the cheerful banter she'd been having with Sam seemed to be leaching out of her. Perhaps she'd already said too much, divulged too many confidences.

'Oh, I don't know that I can. It might not be professional or something. I don't really know about these things. We've only met up a couple of times although we do pop in and out of one another's lives on Facebook and an email now and then. We went to an art class together and a funeral and that's about it really.' The words seemed to be gushing out of Janey, like water through a crack in a lock gate.

Janey took her mobile from her pocket, checked it quickly and slid it back in again.

'Oh dear, do I suspect someone's telling porkies?'

'I ... I—' Janey began.

Sam cut her short.

'You don't have to explain yourself to me, sweetheart, but I've had an uncomfortable feel about you since the moment I saw you there like a rabbit caught in headlights, not knowing where it was you were going. Got a daughter your sort of age, and I'd like to think someone would be concerned for her if she was in a spot of bother. I know I'm a soft touch but I'm a bit worried about you. Anyway, here we are. Strand House coming up.'

Chapter 3

Lissy

Lissy heard a car pull in the drive. Janey had arrived. She went to the door to welcome her. There'd been no one to welcome her to Strand House, arms outstretched in greeting, but she could welcome the others the way Vonny had always welcomed her, couldn't she?

'Oh, is that all you've brought? One small case?' Lissy asked as the taxi driver carried it up the three shallow steps to Strand House, Janey doing her best to keep pace beside the man's long legs. Lissy thought her friend looked tired and anxious. She stepped closer to Janey and gave her a hug, and could feel the thinness of her despite the thick, wool coat she was wearing; it smelt slightly damp and musty as though it had been in a cupboard until now. Janey stood still, accepting the embrace but not responding and Lissy wondered what might have happened to make her like this because at the art workshop where they'd met Janey had been relaxed and happy, immersing herself in her art. In the evenings, a glass of wine in her hand, Janey had joined in the conversation easily enough, everyone hugging one another goodnight at bedtime. But now …?

'No Kate Moss, is she?' the taxi driver said and Lissy gave him a look that said 'you have over-stepped the mark, mate.' 'Shall I carry it inside?'

'I'll take it,' Janey said, as though suddenly realising she was in charge of the situation. Taking a ten-pound note from the pocket of her coat she paid the driver. 'Keep the change.'

'Thanks, sweetheart,' the driver said. 'Now, you've got the card I gave you, yes? In case you need picking up after? And here's one for you.' He thrust a card in Lissy's hand and then the taxi driver turned to go, Janey turning back to look after him as he went, before turning back to face Lissy. To Lissy's alarm Janey had gone very pale, as though she might faint. And she'd begun to shiver.

'Come on in,' Lissy said. 'I know it's sunny but there's a bit of an east wind today. Look at the waves!'

'It's beautiful. Really beautiful. The sea in all its moods is beautiful,' Janey said looking back over her shoulder before Lissy grabbed her free arm and pulled her gently into the house.

'Room first, or coffee first?' Lissy asked once they were in the hall and she'd closed the front door. She put Janey's small case – so light Lissy wondered if there was anything more than a toothbrush and a nightdress in it – down on the floor. She'd let Janey choose which of the sea-facing bedrooms she wanted. Three of the bedrooms in Strand House faced the sea, and three were at the back of the house looking out over rooftops with Dartmoor in the distance. 'I'm so glad you could come. If you hadn't put that remark on Facebook I'd never have known you were going to be on your own for Christmas. Now, you know, you and Stuart have separated.'

Lissy knew she was gabbling and had probably just said the wrong thing mentioning Stuart, because she saw Janey stiffen at the mention of his name, but she felt she had to say something, get Janey to open up a bit because she seemed frozen to the spot, frozen inside somehow.

'Yes, yes we have,' Janey said.

Lissy gave Janey another, quick, hug.

'It gets better. I know it's hard in the beginning. Very hard. You don't know which way to turn and there's no one there at night when the curtains are closed, to talk to about things. But you can always ring me, you know. And before I forget, that card you painted for me with the birds and the flowers and the clouds, well, it helped me more than you'd believe. I kept it by the front door and looked at it every time I went out and remembered to look at them all. Every day.'

'Did you?' Janey said.

'Yes,' Lissy said, a lump in her throat now. All sorts of memories of her split from Cooper were flooding back but Janey didn't need to know that. Janey needed her support now – Lissy's turn to return the favour. 'So, what's it going to be? Room first, or coffee first?'

'Coffee, I think. Please.'

'Coffee it is, then. That's about all I've got in the house at the moment until the Waitrose delivery arrives. I think I've ordered just about everything we need to get us through four days of merrymaking, but if I haven't then there are a couple of small supermarkets within walking distance up on the main road to Torquay. Follow me.'

'The house is a lot bigger than I thought it would be,' Janey said, once they were in the kitchen and seated at the island on high, black leather, bar stools. 'I mean, the hall is vast, like something from a Dutch painting with the black and white tiles. We could play chess or draughts on those tiles.'

'Now there's an idea!' Lissy said. 'If only I could find an outdoor chess set to play it with!'

'And this kitchen, Lissy. Words fail me almost.'

'A bit big for one, isn't it?' Lissy laughed. 'When Vonny was alive we used to joke that we needed a map to get from the larder to the kitchen sink! And there's a bit of an echo when I'm in here on my own.'

She was finding the conversation, if not stilted, then hardish work. As hostess she felt the onus was on her to make her guest happy, make her laugh, and Janey most definitely wasn't happy in Lissy's view, and neither was she laughing. They had a shared history, if a very small one, and one that Lissy hoped they could expand on because she liked Janey. The words 'timid' and 'mouse' sprang to mind and Lissy was cross for herself for thinking them because she couldn't know what had happened in Janey's life – apart from the split from her husband but she didn't know the reasons for that, not yet and she'd wait for Janey to tell her. Hopefully Christmas and a few drinks with the others, and some good food inside her – how had Janey got so thin? – would change the dynamic of their friendship, of all their friendships. Janey had taken off her coat and it had been all Lissy could do not to gasp when she saw how thin her friend was; how her collar bones stuck out making it look as though the navy jumper she was wearing was still on its hanger. She didn't remember her being that thin.

'An echo? Ooooh,' Janey said, with a shiver. 'I'd find that a bit creepy. I'll have to remember never to be in here on my own.'

The kettle came to the boil and Lissy poured water onto the coffee grounds in the cafétière, depressed the plunger and filled two mugs that had shells and pebbles and seaweed fronds painted on them.

'Here we go, then,' Lissy said. 'Once we've drunk this – no biscuits yet, I'm afraid – you can come and choose the room you'd like and then we'll go into town and see if we can hunt down some Christmas decorations.'

'Okay. Fine,' Janey said. She sipped tentatively at her hot drink.

'If I haven't left it a bit too late to be thinking about Christmas decorations. I mean, how rubbish am I? Christmas Eve tomorrow and not a bauble up yet.'

'You're not rubbish, Lissy,' Janey said in a very quiet voice. 'I couldn't quite believe it when you asked me to spend Christmas with you. It's more than generous of you and I … I can't contribute much. Towards the food and drink or anything. I did say.'

Janey looked as though she was on the verge of tears so Lissy slid off her bar stool and stood beside her friend, putting an arm around her shoulders and squeezing firmly.

'And I did say the whole Christmas period is on me because I've been left this very generous gift of this very wonderful house, and enough money for us to have a very lovely time. And that is what we're going to do. I'm not saying a bit of help setting the table and filling the dishwasher wouldn't go amiss but other than that all I want of you is that you have a happy time. Deal?'

Lissy placed a hand under Janey's chin and turned her face so she was looking at her.

'Deal,' Janey said, her powder blue eyes glassy with unshed tears.

Chapter 4

Bobbie

God, but this journey was taking forever. Not the taxi driver's fault, of course. Coming out of London he'd known every shortcut known to man but still they hadn't been able to avoid the stand-still that was the M25 much of the time. Okay, so it was an indulgence taking a taxi all the way from London to Devon. But Bobbie had done the costings, and with price of the train fare both ways, first class – because Bobbie had so much luggage that would have been her only option – there'd only been a few pounds difference between that and the taxi fare. She'd paid for the taxi in advance. How she was going to get back home again she'd sort later. Anything could happen between now and 27th December, couldn't it?

'Are we nearly there yet?' Bobbie asked leaning forward and opening the communication window.

The taxi driver laughed, a deep and full-throated laugh, to go with the size of him. The boxer Anthony Joshua came to mind the second Bobbie had set eyes on him – big and black and handsome with a smile on his face.

'What are you, madam, six? My kids ask that all the time even when I'm taking them to school and they know exactly where the school is and how long the journey takes!'

They'd spoken little on the journey – just the way Bobbie liked her journeys. Bobbie liked to catnap, something she'd learned to do early in her career as a model when there were often long hauls to exotic locations to shoot bathing costumes or high-end dresses, or shampoo even. Mercifully she still had that career although there were fewer exotic locations these days.

'So, are we? Nearly there yet?'

Bobbie checked the time on her watch. And that, Bobbie reminded herself, showed her age – sixty-two should anyone ask although she did her level best, often at huge expense, to make herself look at least five years younger than that.

'Twenty minutes or so now.'

'We should be there by one o'clock, then?'

Bobbie checked the time again – just after twenty-five to one. All the young things these days only ever checked the time on their mobiles, didn't they? Bobbie couldn't understand the logic in that because you had to find the thing in your pocket or your bag, switch it on if it wasn't already and then remember to switch it off afterwards and put it away again. All so, well, time-consuming. Bobbie liked a good watch – designer for preference. Modelling spoiled a girl, that was for sure. It wasn't enough to wear a designer dress or jacket or shoes – accessories had to be designer too or it could spoil the whole look. The journey had taken just over five hours now. The last twenty minutes couldn't go quickly enough for Bobbie. She was getting more than a little stiff. Only idiots decided to travel the day before Christmas Eve. So that made her an idiot then, Bobbie chided herself. Lissy's invite had come out of the blue. She'd seen a Facebook post Bobbie had put up of a designer-clad woman sitting in an otherwise empty high-end restaurant, a glass of champagne in her hand, and a doleful expression on her beautiful face – an image Bobbie had captioned 'Me on Christmas Day'.

And so, here she was, just minutes away from seeing Lissy again. And Janey, too. She'd only ever met both of them in person twice, the first time when they'd come, with Lissy's friend Claire, to the life-drawing art weekend at Dartington at which Bobbie had been the life model, and the second when they'd all attended Claire's funeral. What a sad waste that was. Claire had been a stunner. Fun, too. She'd had them in stitches each morning of that weekend, when they'd met up in Claire's room for an impromptu exercise class – Claire's toned body evidence that she practised what she preached as a fitness instructor. Claire had dusky skin, eyes like chocolate Minstrels, and a head of shoulder-length café au lait curls. Bobbie remembered asking Claire if she'd ever considered modelling because she had such unique looks. Times had changed, Bobbie had told her, and there was a call for older models these days, not just sixteen-year-olds. Claire had laughed and said that at thirty-four she was hardly old and that no, she hadn't ever considered modelling, but she might now. But with clothes on, not life-modelling as Bobbie had been doing that weekend. A lump lodged in Bobbie's throat remembering Claire and what a great weekend they'd all had together and how surprisingly quickly they'd all bonded as a group – the four Musketeers, Claire had joked – despite their differing ages and life styles … just one of those happy, serendipitous moments in life that happen sometimes. How Claire's husband, Xander, must miss her, Bobbie thought. How almost unbearably sad he'd been at Claire's funeral. And how sad it was that the first time of meeting someone it should be at a funeral. Bobbie didn't think she'd ever be able to rid herself of the image of him, standing with his hand on Claire's coffin as though it was glued to it, and he couldn't bear to let his wife go, after the service as everyone filed out. One of the funeral attendants had had to prise Xander's hand away, and Bobbie – who almost never cried – cried then. Xander would be at Strand House too.

'Strand House!' the taxi driver called out, reaching to open up the communication window. He pointed at a large, flat-roofed, house at the top of a steep drive. 'I'll pull up as close to the front door as I can, madam.'

'Oh, just up my street,' Bobbie said. 'It looks wonderful. My friend didn't say it was quite so grand.'

Lissy had told Bobbie she'd inherited Strand House but no other details, except there'd be plenty of room for all of them to stop for Christmas. Bobbie could hardly wait now.

The driver carried all Bobbie's luggage – in three trips – to the front door, while Bobbie stood and sucked in the view. She hadn't expected Strand House to be quite so close to the sea although, had she thought about it, the clue was in the name, wasn't it?

'Right then, madam, I'm off,' the driver said. 'My kids will be driving their mother mad, modifying their Christmas want list a thousand times and expecting her to get it all by the day after tomorrow. Christmas is for kids, eh? You got children, madam?'

Bobbie hadn't been expecting that question.

'No!' she snapped.

It was what she told everyone who asked that question. It was easier that way. How could you say to anyone, especially, a stranger that you'd had a child – a boy; a child you'd washed and dressed and fed, and held close, and watched in sleep as he snuffled and sighed, if only for a short while – before you'd given him away? But every time that question got her, made her heart beat faster and often she would also feel a little faint with the holding of such a secret. It had got to her now. This perfectly nice and kind taxi driver, who had children of his own he hadn't had to give away, had asked the simplest of questions, a question one might expect to get at Christmas because Christmas was all about children, wasn't it?

It was her secret. The only person still alive who knew her secret was her cousin, Pamela, and her cousin's husband, Charles. And they were in Australia, half a world away; half a world away where they'd taken Bobbie's baby, Oliver, never to return with him. In her bag, safe inside the zipped section, was a letter. It had an Australian postmark. Bobbie had received it in with a letter from her own solicitor in London just a week ago now; just a short note to say he was passing it on as instructed by a colleague in Sydney. Bobbie had been afraid to open it, fearful of what she might read. Was it from Pamela and Charles to say something had happened to Oliver? Was it a letter from him filled with hate for abandoning him? Perhaps, here at Strand House, with friends around her she'd have the courage to open it? Perhaps.

Chapter 5

Lissy

'So, Bobbie, will this room be all right for you? It's the last one free that's facing the sea – Janey and I have bagged the other two, I'm afraid. En suite.' She hurried across the room and flung wide the door to the en suite, and immediately felt stupid and gauche because Bobbie would sure as eggs are eggs know what an en suite was. 'Help yourself to toiletries. Shout if you need more towels. There are bigger rooms at the back of the house. Views out over the town to the moors if you prefer. If it's windy it'll be less noisy at the back, and warmer. And there'll be more room for your luggage in any of those. Xander's not here yet but I doubt he'll be fussed which room he has.'

And I am sounding like a landlady or a chambermaid or something, so bloody formal. This is my friend for goodness' sake. Relax, for pity's sake. This was your idea to invite everyone. No one was holding a gun to your head.

What had taken Lissy by surprise was how utterly glamorous, how very London, Bobbie was. She'd stepped from the taxi, fresh as a daisy, her long silver hair barely moving in the breeze off the sea, and wearing a calf-length scarlet coat over an ankle-length

29

paisley dress, the background of which was an identical shade of red. A floral bag – mostly shades of red – was hooked over one shoulder. Claret-coloured heels completed the look.

Standing in the hall in faded jeans and a blue-and-white striped shirt with her ancient but comfy Ugg-boot slippers on, she'd been hanging Christmas decorations with Janey when Bobbie rang the bell. Janey had excused herself and rushed upstairs saying she'd leave Lissy to welcome her guest. Lissy had never felt so frumpy in her life.

'Darling, do relax,' Bobbie laughed. 'It's only me. This room will be more than fine. I'm just glad to be here, to be honest. Christmas almost always is a solo affair for me.'

'Oh, any reason?' Lissy asked.

'A few,' Bobbie said, the smile sliding from her face. 'But you don't want to hear them. I promise to be full of ho-ho-ho and good cheer, and – hopefully – a few glasses of something seeing as it's Christmas. But before you even think about getting the violins out and feeling sorry for me, the reason I'm usually alone at Christmas is choice, mostly. Work sometimes. That is all!'

'Okay,' Lissy said. 'Violin is back in its case.'

Bobbie was being so very Bobbie, able to take control of a situation in the blink of an eye. Lissy had a feeling there was another reason Bobbie chose to spend Christmas alone but she wasn't going to ask.

'Good. And lose the bow!' Bobbie said with a giggle.

'Already have,' Lissy joked back. 'But if, you know, there's something you want or need to say then … well, you can guess the rest and …'

'I'll keep you posted.' Bobbie shrugged herself out of her coat, and Lissy marvelled at how even that was a glamourous, catwalk sort of gesture. 'This room really is fine and I don't expect to be fighting Xander for it when he turns up because you are absolutely right – men usually aren't fussed about what room they have or the view.' She lifted the smallest case onto the bed. 'I have brought

30

rather a lot of luggage, haven't I?' Bobbie laughed. 'But you did say to stop for four nights so I've packed accordingly. I hope it didn't give that rather scrumptious taxi driver a hernia carrying it all in.'

'Oh God,' Lissy said. 'I ought to have invited him in for a cup of tea or something before he started on the return journey.'

'He had a couple of flasks of tea and a packet of sandwiches. We stopped a couple of times for comfort breaks as well, so don't worry. He was keen to get back to his kids.'

'Yeah, Christmas is for kids really, isn't it? Anyway, we haven't got any, have we? None of us has, you or me, Janey or Xander. We'll have to play at being big kids for a few days, won't we? So if this room is okay, I'll leave you to unpack. Join Janey and me when you're ready. Ah, is that the gentle tones of my Waitrose delivery arriving?' Lissy went to the window and peered down onto the drive. 'It is so. So now we'll all be able to eat!'

And in a minute I should have relaxed a bit and begun to sound more like me and not someone out of a film out of the Fifties – all perfect diction and political correctness. It's only Christmas for heaven's sake and you've cooked enough Christmas dinners and made enough mince pies and poured enough cocktails to know how to do it properly.

'I'm glad you like the room, Bobbie. Really glad.' She was glad now she'd taken the trouble to pick a few bits and pieces from the garden that had berries on and add a white rose bud from the bunches she and Janey had bought in town. In a rush of affection for her friend she enveloped her in a big hug, a hug Bobbie returned with rather less pressure than Lissy. And when Lissy pulled back and looked at her friend there was something about the guarded look in her eyes, and the way she nodded instead of answering her question – as though she couldn't trust herself to speak at that moment – that told Lissy she had said the wrong thing. But what?

31

Chapter 6

Xander

'Christmas, Felix, who'd have it? It's a woman's thing. Claire loved Christmas, didn't she?'

Xander reached to fondle the soft fur of Felix's head, smoothing the palm of his hand over it, gently circling the cat's ears with his fingers. Sometimes Xander wondered how he would have managed after Claire's death if he hadn't had Felix around – another body to touch, someone to talk to.

'Not a very original name I gave you, is it?'

But Felix had seemed appropriate at the time when Claire had come home with him. One of her students – Sandy, if Xander's memory served him well – in the fitness classes she ran had come in with a kitten that her father said he put down if no one wanted it because they already had too many cats in the house. Sandy had begged someone to give it a home. So Claire had. She'd arrived home with it in a cardboard box sealed with masking tape, and some holes punched in it so the cat could breathe, that old Arthur from the newsagent on Manor Corner had given her.

Xander remembered, still stroking the cat, how he'd laughed because the cat had looked like a living version of the cartoon cat in the Felix cat food adverts. So Felix he had become. And now Xander was reluctant to leave him for four days even though it was only a mile along the prom from his cottage to Strand House.

'I could pop home every day to see you, old boy, if you like.'

Felix purred, pushed his head further into Xander's hand as if to say, 'How could you give up on all this affection I'm dishing out, man? Abandon me if you must. Leave me to Eve Benson's ministrations if you must.'

'I know it's no hardship having Eve look after you. And don't think for a second, I don't know you spend half your day in her house anyway, because I do.' Xander increased the pressure of his hand on Felix's head and then ran it along the full length of the cat's back. Felix stirred, stood up, stretched. 'Had enough of that then, have you, old chap?'

Xander stood up too and began clearing his lunch things. There was no need for him to be at Strand House until five o'clock. And what a surprise that had been, to get Lissy's invite to spend Christmas there with her, and Janey and Bobbie. He knew Lissy, of course, because she'd been of Claire's oldest friends, but Janey and Bobbie he'd only met the once – at Claire's funeral. It had been kind of them to come but in all honesty, he couldn't remember them. He'd probably pass them in the street as though they were strangers. Had he, he wondered, made a grave mistake accepting Lissy's invitation? What did any of them have in common? What would he talk to them about? It wouldn't add anything to the festive spirit, would it, if he said he'd been mourning Claire so long he never thought he was going to feel like himself ever again and that his building business was suffering. Really suffering. A few days ago, he'd been called in to see his bank manager and been told that his overdraft could not be increased. It was only a small business and if he'd been the sole workforce then he could sell his cottage, find a flat somewhere for him and Felix, pay off his debts. But he wasn't the sole workforce; there were Tom, Josh, and Ethan in the equation too. Each with families to support. Ah yes, families. How he wished now that he and Claire had had one because then he'd have someone who looked like her around, someone who had her genes, the essence of her. But Claire hadn't wanted children.

'I wouldn't have minded a couple of kids, Felix,' Xander said as Felix lapped noisily at his saucer of milk. 'Christmas is for kids really, isn't it?'

Felix looked up at him and walked towards the catflap.

'Oi, you!' Xander shouted after him. 'I hope you're going to say goodbye.'

But Felix – as the cartoon of old had it – kept on walking and went out.

With a sigh Xander put his dishes and the saucepan he'd used to heat the soup he'd bought from the supermarket in the dishwasher, found a tablet – the last, so he'd have to remember to buy some more as soon as Christmas was over – and switched it on, even though the thing was only a quarter full.

He had some Christmas cards still to write and hand deliver. He'd driven down to Kingsbridge to see his mother at the weekend and hand-delivered that one, along with a bunch of roses and a silver bracelet he knew she'd like because he'd been with her when she'd pointed it out in the window of Silver Dollar the previous week.

'I don't like to think of you on your own, Xand,' his mother had said in Bailey's Bistro where they'd gone for coffee.

'I won't be on my own. Lissy will be there. And two of her friends, Janey and Bobbie. They all came ...'

'Don't think about that time,' his mother said, cutting him short. They'd both known how he was going to finish the sentence – to Claire's funeral. 'It doesn't help. I know it hurts you still that she's not here but, well, don't you think it's time to date again?'

'Date?'

Such an old-fashioned word, date. Did people still use that

34

term? Xander supposed they did because wasn't there a programme on TV called *Blind Date* or something like that?

'Yes. Date. You know, you see someone you like and you invite them to the cinema or for a meal. And …'

'For God's sake, Ma, I'm forty-one years old, not fourteen!' He'd looked at his mother's crestfallen face and felt bad about snapping at her like that. Felix and his mother, he wouldn't have survived without either of them back then. His mother had let herself in, cleaned the house while he was at work, taken his dirty laundry and brought it back the next day, ironed and in a neat pile. She'd left meals too – single portions of cottage pie, or fish pie, or a stew. Single portions that, as kind as it was for her to have made them, had only accentuated his one-ness.

'I know, Xand, I know,' she had said. 'But you're young still and have a lot of life yet to live. I'm going to play the "mother card" now and say I think it's time, now Claire's been gone three years, that you start to live it again. And …'

'Ma! Leave it!' Xander's turn to interrupt this time.

'See,' his mother said, nonplussed this time at Xander's reaction. 'I said we shouldn't have brought up the subject of Claire and the funeral … it always sparks a bit of a falling out, doesn't it? Anyway, how well do you know Lissy? I know Claire talked about her a lot and they used to go away for girly weekends.'

That was so like his mother to spark a bit of a disagreement and then move the subject on to something else.

'Lissy?' he said. And it was then that there was a sort of screen play going backwards in his mind. Dancing with her at his and Claire's wedding. She'd been wearing a strappy dress the colour of a kingfisher's breast, and long dangly earrings that glittered under the lights of the dancefloor. He remembered being slightly the worse for wear after more than a few glasses of champagne and a couple of glasses of real ale. And Lissy had been rather tipsy too. In his head, Xander saw the lights dip, saw himself pulling Lissy closer to him, feeling the warmth of her against the powder blue shirt he'd been wearing. Smelled the fragrance in her hair. They'd sort of pressed even closer together until their lips had all but touched before Xander pulled away. There'd been a connection, something almost primeval, in that moment. A sort of what-might-have-been realisation for them both. He'd danced with just about every woman at his wedding reception, as Claire had with the men. But none of them had given him that rush of feeling that Lissy had. He'd put it firmly to the back of his mind and whenever Lissy fetched Claire when they went off on a girly weekend or brought her back he was careful not to hug too close, not to let his lips linger on Lissy's cheek when he leaned in to kiss it, in case those feelings came back. Too dangerous for a married man to have those feelings. And besides, Lissy probably didn't even remember that dance.

'What a flipping ego, thinking that she might!' Xander shouted to himself now. 'This won't do. A right bundle of misery you're going to be at Strand House if you turn up in this mood, aren't you?'

And that was another thing. Xander had found that being alone he spoke to himself far more than was probably healthy, just so he could hear a voice, even when that voice was his own. And thoughts. He couldn't remember thinking as much when Claire had been with him. But that was all he seemed to have done lately – think. All sorts of random things came into his head: things they'd done, things they'd argued about, things they'd made up about, as all couples do at times. Too many thoughts.

Well, he'd try and banish those as of now. Cards to write and deliver, a small case to pack because he could run back home in fifteen minutes or so if he needed anything, Eve Benson to pop in and see and give the Christmas hamper that he'd bought her for Christmas in thanks for her ministrations to dear old Felix, and then he'd shower and change and present himself at Strand House. Lissy had emailed to say 'Strictly no exchange of Christmas presents, and the entire weekend is on me, celebrating my unexpected windfall' but some champagne would probably be welcome and unlikely to be in excess of requirements if the memories of his and Claire's wedding in particular, and women when they got together in general, were anything to go by. Funds could still run to a couple of bottle of fizz, but after this Christmas break Xander was going to have to give some serious thought to an overhaul of his finances. And his life.

Just a few minutes before five o'clock, Xander rang the doorbell of Strand House. It was answered almost immediately.

'Nearest the church door, last one in, I see,' Lissy said, smiling widely, her eyes gleaming, and looking just as beautiful as Xander remembered. Perhaps his mother had been right after all? She leaned forward to kiss his cheek. 'Come on in.' And it was probably just as well that his hands were full and he wasn't able to put his arms around her and hug her tight. She had no idea how much her invite was starting to mean to him.

Chapter 7

Bobbie

'Could I take a look at that one, please?' Bobbie said to the assistant in a shop called Silver Linings opposite the railway station.

Still in her travelling clothes, but having changed her stilettos for low, wedge-heeled black leather ankle boots, Bobbie had walked the half-mile into town. Xander was yet to arrive but she didn't think for a second he'd mind that she wasn't at Strand House when he did get there. She told Lissy and Janey that after an almost six-hour journey in a taxi she was sorely in need of exercise and fresh air. And the air was certainly fresh, colder than London, but then there was always a heat to London from the lights of buildings and the traffic and the general thrum of the place.

'I'll open the case for you,' the assistant said. 'I'll just find the key.'

Bobbie had spent a good half hour browsing the shop and the assistant had left her to it, not pressured her at all to hurry up and choose because – Bobbie, realised now – it was almost closing time. Bobbie liked that – the space to be left to make her own choices. Okay, so Silver Dollar wasn't Oxford Street or Regent

38

Street, but this little shop in a typical seaside town had some good things. She'd been spoilt for choice really. There were watches in a number of styles, hip flasks, and medallions (necklaces for men really) and quirky little desk ornaments but in the end Bobbie had settled on a watch. It was hardly Philippe Patek but she hoped Oliver would like it, or at least accept it for the love in which it was given. Whenever that giving might be. Certainly not over the Christmas period while she was at Strand House.

Lissy had said there were to be no exchanges of presents at Strand House but that didn't mean Bobbie didn't have a present to buy. She did. For Oliver. Like she'd done every Christmas for the past forty-four years. Forty-four!

'A good choice,' the assistant said, unlocking the cabinet and lifting out the watch Bobbie had pointed to. 'Timeless design but with a slightly quirky edge. For someone special?'

'Oh yes. Someone very special,' Bobbie said, her voice suddenly husky. It still surprised her that it always went husky, and her heartbeat quickened, and sometimes she even felt a little faint, whenever she voiced that she'd had Oliver in her life for forty-four years, and while she'd not seen him for almost all of those forty-four years he was never far from her mind. He came to her in odd moments: in a supermarket queue when she might see a man around the age Oliver was at that time and wonder if her son wore his hair like that, or had a fancy for a pink shirt, or brogues; when she was washing up a few dishes and imagining Oliver reaching for a teatowel to help – such a companionable thing to do, washing up and drying dishes with someone; when she saw a pregnant woman, holding hands with her man, who was proudly carrying a bag from Mothercare or some other baby clothes shop.

'Gift wrapped then?' the assistant said. She turned her head slightly to glance at the clock over her desk. 'Oh, I'll just close up. But I'm not hurrying you. Gift-wrapping won't be problem. You can browse a bit more while I do it if you like.'

'I will,' Bobbie said. 'Thank you.' Her voice and her heartbeat returned to normal now.

But there was nothing else she wanted or needed really. She had enough jewellery – precious and costume – to stock a shop of her own.

Chapter 8

Janey

'This feels a bit strange, doesn't it?' Janey said now she was alone with Xander. Bobbie had gone for a walk saying she needed exercise and fresh air after the journey, but Janey had the suspicion she'd gone present-buying for them all, which Janey hoped she hadn't as she had no money with which to reciprocate. Lissy was in the kitchen, putting the finishing touches to the evening meal, so she said, and she'd also said she didn't need help doing it. She'd told Janey to sit with Xander and chat. She'd given Janey a bottle of Pinot Grigio and two glasses to chat over. 'That'll loosen my tongue,' Janey had said nervously. She wasn't used to small talk, or very much talk at all to be honest.

'Would that be good strange, or bad strange?' Xander said. 'Hey, give me that bottle because you're in dire danger of snapping the neck off. Your knuckles have gone white.' He reached towards her for the bottle that Lissy had already uncorked. 'And the glasses, Janey. They look like rather fragile, quality glasses from where I'm standing.'

Janey did as she was told. She was used to doing what she was told around Stuart because to resist only exacerbated whatever terrible situation she was in.

'I think, Janey,' Xander said, setting the glasses down on a side-table in the sitting room and filling them, and handing one to Janey, 'that Lissy won't mind if we sit down.' He patted the couch nearest him, but there were four in the vast room from which to choose, plus a single arm chair by the window. All were covered in some sort of white linen, like the boiled and bleached teatowels Janey remembered from visits to her grandmother when she'd been small.

Janey sat on the nearest one.

'So, back to strange – what's strange, Janey?'

'Us being here,' Janey said, taking a sip of wine. 'I mean, we've been friends on Facebook and you've messaged me about my paintings, so we sort of know one another, but not really.'

'Time to make amends, then. And four days to do it in.'

Janey pressed her lips together, fearful emotion would spill out. Xander was being so kind, so courteous of her, and doing his best to put her at her ease when ease was the last thing she felt at that moment – she was tense, everyting pulled tight, wondering if Stuart had found her note yet and what his reaction would be when he did.

'I only had four days getting to know Claire, but it felt as though I'd known her forever,' Janey said. 'She was so kind inviting me to join her and Lissy for a drink after the first class. Bobbie came, too, because Claire said the others seemed in awe of her, how beautiful she was to paint. People were going off in little groups to go for a meal or a drink or a walk or something and Claire said Bobbie looked lonely so she invited her along too and … oh God, sorry. It must hurt to have her name brought up at every turn and now I have.'

Janey took a huge gulp of wine so words that perhaps ought not to be said didn't come splurting out.

'It's okay. People around me, who knew Claire well, and who

break their necks not to mention her so that it seems for them, and me, she never existed, upset me more. You've mentioned her name for the first time and I haven't gone to pieces, have I?'

Janey shook her head.

'And I expect, over this Christmas break we're all on, her name will be mentioned a few more times as well before we all leave again on the 27th. Shall we have a little toast, you and me?' Xander sat down beside Janey and raised his glass. 'To memories of Claire, whatever form those memories take.'

God, how kind he was. His kindness was like some sort of balm to Janey's bruised soul. She hadn't known men as kind as this existed.

'To memories of Claire,' Janey said, as they clinked glasses. Her memories of Claire were all good ones. How vibrant and full of life she'd been. How beautiful. How she was absolutely rubbish at art on that weekend workshop but it didn't seem to matter. She was with her friend, Lissy, and learning something new, and she was having fun. And laughing. It seemed to Janey that Claire had laughed constantly that weekend, her head thrown back with the weight of her laugh so that her café au lait curls rippled. And she'd been generous in her praise of Janey's life-drawing, urging her to do something with it. Sell her work, or teach, but – Claire had said – Janey had to do *something*, or Claire would come and shake a big stick at her … that last over more than a few glasses of wine in the White Hart. But now she could never come and shake that stick, could she? And Janey was yet to do something with her art.

'Now, tell me about you. What have you been doing since I last saw you?'

'Um …' Janey said and then clammed up.

'Which was at Claire's funeral. So, now we've got that word out of the way as well.' Xander smiled gently at her. 'And that was three years ago. It's a myth, you know, that men only ever want to talk about themselves. I know you're good at art because

Claire was full of how good you are when she got back from the workshop, or whatever it was.'

'Was she?'

'She was, indeed. And it must have been fulsome praise if I've remembered. So, how's that going? I'd like to buy something but you'll never sell me anything. Any reason?'

Because Stuart says it's no better than a six-year-old could do. Because stupidly I let myself believe that. Because to go against his wishes would have meant another tirade of abusive words and possibly some fists thrown in as well.

Janey couldn't tell Xander any of that, could she? And neither should she. She blinked back tears, but one escaped and she brushed it away hastily with the back of her hand.

But Xander saw.

'Hey, it's okay. You don't have to tell me a thing. I must be right out of practice at talking to women if I'm making you cry. I'm sorry. Here, have a top-up.'

Xander reached for the bottle and topped up her glass.

And then Bobbie came breezing in, filling the room with her vibrant clothes and her even more vibrant personality and Janey had never been so pleased to see anyone in her life. She felt herself relax. For now.

Chapter 9

Lissy

Lissy was thrilled with the way the house was looking. Everything had been left to the last minute – the buying of decorations and the catering – but it was all coming together now, looking Christmassy. Janey was at one end of the kitchen island making a wreath for the front door, and she was at the other. Xander and Bobbie were in the sitting room doing a catch-up. She could hear Bobbie laughing now and then at whatever it was Xander had said.

'We ought to have bought a wreath from the greengrocer in Parkside when we were in town, Janey,' Lissy had said when they got back and she realised that although they'd bought bags and bags of baubles and four packs of lights, six bunches of white roses that she'd put in one huge vase on the dresser in the hall, there was nothing with which to dress the door.

'They'd have been too small anyway. Your front door's huge – only Westminster Abbey's got a larger door.' And she'd giggled, and with that giggle Lissy hoped that a little of the Janey she'd got to know three years ago was coming back.

'I could make one,' Janey said. 'If there's any greenery in the garden. But you can make a wreath out of anything really.'

45

'Really? Scarves?' Lissy asked. She'd cleared a lot of Vonny's old clothes, keeping just a few classic, designer pieces, and all her scarves, pressed and neatly folded in the bottom of the chest of drawers in the room that was now hers. 'Costume jewellery?'

'Perfect,' Janey had said.

'How's it going?' Lissy asked now. She had her hands in a large aluminium bowl rubbing fat into flour – a huge labour of love because Lissy hated the feel of it under her fingernails. It was the only part of cooking she didn't like because the rest of it she absolutely loved … the smell of fresh ginger never failed to lift her spirits, and the fresh green of basil leaves made her think of sunny afternoons lying in Hyde Park on lush grass when she'd been a student in London; the texture of orange and lemon peel, like some sort of aromatic skin eruption; the lush softness of roasted sweet potatoes. After Cooper left she didn't cook much for a few months because she had no personal appetite and no one to cook for. But then she began experimenting and eventually it had led to putting up photos of what she'd cooked on Facebook and Instagram – experimenting with foods that Cooper had never liked and refused to eat, like Jerusalem artichokes and anchovies and pineapple rings dipped in batter, fried and sprinkled with sugar. It had been cathartic then, but it had opened her mind to the fact there were other things in life apart from running her accountancy business – such as making pastry for savoury whirls she intended to serve as nibbles before dinner.

'It's going fine,' Janey said, dragging Lissy's thoughts back to the present, to the room she was in with her friend, with two other friends in the sitting room and making food for them she hoped they'd like but which she knew they'd appreciate for the effort she'd put into it for them. 'You?'

'Getting there,' Lissy said.

She had the filling to make – sundried tomatoes, mozzarella, and spinach – but she could do that while the pastry was resting in the fridge. Once she'd made it! She was running late with dinner – salmon she'd already cooked, with new potatoes she'd yet to cook and salad that would only take five minutes to put together – but it didn't matter much. None of them had a time schedule, after all. And besides, she hadn't said what time she'd be serving dinner so none of them would know it was late anyway, would they?

'There!' Janey said, picking up the huge wreath she was working on and turning it this way and that.

'That is so good, Janey,' Lissy said. 'That's not going to go out with the Christmas rubbish ... you know the ripped apart crackers and the festive napkins and so on.'

'It's not finished yet,' Janey said. 'Another ten minutes should do it and then I'll ask Xander to help me hang it. Anyway, what are you going to do with all this jewellery?'

Lissy looked up as Janey wound an amber necklace around a plaited red and gold scarf, the whole thing glinting under the overhead downlighters.

'I haven't given it a thought, to be honest. Not my thing any of it but it seemed too good to take to the tip. Charity shop? That's where I took most of her books and some ornaments, not that Vonny had much of either.'

And what a horrid job that had been, throwing Vonny's shoes and most of her bags, and clothes that had seen better days into the relevant skips at the community tip. She shivered, remembering how she'd felt a traitor almost doing it.

'Well, let me know which charity shop you take them to and I'll go and buy some back. These scarves are gorgeous. Fabulous colours. I've picked out all the scarves that are Christmassy ... anything with red in it, or green, with a bit of gold thrown in.'

'Good. Lovely,' Lissy said, awed at how deftly Janey had plaited and twisted and woven the scarves around old wire coat-hangers she'd cut to shape with some pliers Lissy had found in a drawer in the kitchen. How talented she was. 'But take what you want once Christmas is over. You're welcome.'

The two women carried on working at their respective tasks in silence. How peaceful it was, Lissy thought.

'You like cooking, don't you?' Janey said in her gentle voice as though, perhaps, she'd been reluctant to break the silence.

'I do.'

'Did Coo ...' Janey began but then didn't seem to know how to go on. Lissy saw a flush on the side of Janey's neck.

'Did Cooper like my cooking? Is that what you were going to say?'

'Mmm' Janey said, nodding. 'Oh, God, sorry. I shouldn't have even thought it.' Janey began twisting another string of beads around the scarves as though her life depended on it.

'Yes, you should. We're friends. Friends can say things to one another that sometimes even family can't say. And besides, it's said the way to a man's heart is through his stomach and all that. But to answer your unasked question,' Lissy said, 'yes, he did like my cooking. In the beginning. But if he didn't like it enough to stop him going off to exchange it for third-rate, reheated Chinese takeaways with radio-active coloured sauces, then that's up to him.'

'Oh!' Janey said, putting a hand to her mouth.

'It's okay, you can laugh, you know,' Lissy said.

So Janey did.

'It's all coming back now. The time we spent together at Dartington doing that course. We laughed a lot, didn't we Lissy?'

'We did. And we'll laugh some more this Christmas. Deal?'

'Deal,' Janey said. 'There!' Janey held the wreath out in front of her, twisting her head this way and that to look at it. 'That's just about done. Mustn't over-gild the lily. Less is more sometimes.'

'It's beautiful,' Lissy said. 'Once it's on the door it will feel like Vonny is here welcoming us back in from wherever it is we've been.'

Initially full of misgivings that she'd made too rash a decision inviting them all for Christmas, she was changing her mind by the minute. This house needed people in it. It needed laughter, and friendship, and … and love.

The doorbell rang then.

'Oh, blast. Who can that be?' Lissy said, her hands, covered in raw pastry. An Amazon delivery perhaps? Her mother always sent presents via the internet and she'd not received anything from her yet. To run her hands down the sides of her apron and answer the bell or not? Janey had that second picked up a pair of dangly crystal earrings and was attaching them to the bottom of the wreath. 'Can one of you get the door!' Lissy yelled in the direction of the sitting room and Xander and Bobbie.

She heard movement. Good, they'd heard her.

'Will do!' Bobbie yelled back.

Bobbie's heels clacked on the hall tiles as she hurried to the door. And then Lissy heard them again as she scurried back towards the kitchen. She stood in the doorway.

'For you, Janey. There's a man at the door asking for you. He …'

'No!' Janey said, cupping her hands over her mouth. She swayed on the high stool, slumped forward.

'Oh my God,' Bobbie said rushing to catch Janey as she slid towards the floor. 'I was going to say,' she went on, turning to look, shocked, at Lissy, 'I asked what he wanted but he said he had something of hers and he needed to see her. Who the hell is he and what has he done to this poor woman?'

'You see to Janey,' Lissy said. 'Xander and I will sort this out.'

'Xander!' Lissy yelled, tearing across the hall. 'I need you.'

There was a very tall man – sixties? – in her hall, the front door shut behind him. He was holding something in his hand. A smartphone?

'Who are you?' Lissy asked as Xander came to stand by her. He put an arm on her shoulder as if to say, 'I'll protect you, don't worry'. That simple gesture put a lump in Lissy's throat. 'Oh, I remember you now. You're the taxi driver.'

'The very same. Sam. Ace Taxis. Forgive me for taking liberties closing the door but you were paying to heat the street with it wide open.' His smile was broad and, Lissy decided, genuine. But he looked embarrassed now.

'I don't think anyone's ordered a taxi,' Lissy said, the hint of a question in her voice.

'Not me, anyway,' Xander said. He put slight pressure on Lissy's shoulder as though to remind her he was still there.

'No, no they haven't. But the thing is I brought a young woman here earlier today. Before lunchtime it was. Fairish hair down to here.' He put the side of his left hand halfway down his right arm to show where her hair had come. 'Wearing a black coat, she was. Swamped in it. Anxious. I've got her phone.'

'Oh,' Lissy said, a massive sigh of relief taking the tension from her. 'Is that all?'

'Well, not entirely,' Sam said. 'I need to make sure I give this phone to the right person because ...' He lowered his voice, looked into the distance behind Lissy and Xander and then towards the staircase. 'Where is she?'

'Janey,' Lissy said. She could see this man – Sam – meant Janey no harm now. 'She's in the kitchen.'

'Yes, that would be the name,' Sam said. 'I sensed there was something up with her the second I picked up the fare. She looked lost in that coat of hers like it was two sizes too big in the first place or she'd shrunk two sizes since buying it. And scared, she looked scared. This confirms it.' He waved the phone towards Lissy. 'She must have dropped it down beside the seat. I was just parking up for the night when I heard its ringtone. Frightened the life out of me it did. On and on it went. I know I should have switched the thing off but curiosity got the better of me. Anyway, whoever it is was was threatening her with all sorts. Filthy language like you wouldn't believe. Sounded drunk to me.'

'Oh, poor Janey,' Lissy said.

'Got a daughter the same sort of age, I have,' Sam went on, as though he was in no hurry to leave. 'Stuff's happened to her over the years, poor maid.'

Lissy couldn't help smiling at Sam's use of the Devonshire term 'maid'. Vonny had used it all the time when Lissy had been younger. 'You're more drowned than a drowned rat, maid,' was what she always said when Lissy had come back dripping and covered in sand from the beach.

'I'm sorry you've had to deal with this, Sam,' Lissy said, aware now how Xander's arm was still around her and how good it made her feel. Safe. Cared for. But it was only the sort of gesture anyone would make to comfort another in a time of stress. 'But I'll take over now. Thank you for your concern. Not many would have bothered.' She reached out a hand for Janey's phone and Sam handed it to her.

'Some Christmas it's going to be for her, poor woman,' Sam said. 'I'll let myself out.' He turned to go. Then he turned back again. 'Got it lovely in here, you have. All it needs, in my humble opinion, is a stonking great floor-to-ceiling tree, decorated to within an inch its life, in this barn of a hall. Maybe two. And that's me sticking my nose in where it's not wanted.'

'D'you know,' Xander said. 'I think you're right. We'll go and get one tomorrow, shall we, Lissy?'

'I think we must,' Lissy said.

'Happy Christmas anyway, you guys,' Sam said.

'Happy Christmas,' Lissy and Xander said as one.

Chapter 10

Janey

'I lied,' Janey said. 'Stuart and I haven't separated. Well, not legally. I've left him. I left a note under the tin with the teabags in it.'

'When?' Bobbie asked gently. She sat beside Janey on the couch – one of Janey's hands held between both of hers – where Xander had half dragged, half carried her, after she'd come round from her faint. 'When did you leave?'

'This morning.'

'Does he know you're here?' Lissy asked.

'No. Not unless he's hacked into my emails and found the details but I doubt it. He was still in a drunken stupor from the night before. As always. Well, not always. He drinks moderately in the week in termtime. He can hardly turn up drunk at nine o'clock for his first maths pupils, can he? But he goes on benders at weekend and in the holidays. I couldn't take any more. I should have left him years ago.'

Janey felt her shoulders drop down from somewhere near her ears just saying the words – words she'd thought for years but never thought she'd utter.

52

'Lots of us stay in relationships longer than is good for us. Sometimes it's just too scary to go it alone,' Lissy said.

Is that what it had been like for Lissy, Janey wondered, surprised at Lissy's comment, because the emails they'd exchanged after Cooper had left Lissy had suggested otherwise … that Lissy had been heartbroken. Maybe she was seeing things in a new light now she was divorced. Divorced. Oh my God, Janey was going to have to deal with all that. She was going to have to see Stuart at some stage but she wasn't going to be alone with him ever again. She'd ask her brother-in-law to be with her. Or a solicitor.

Janey looked at Xander and then Bobbie and they were both nodding, as though they agreed with what Lissy had just said.

'Have you listened to Stuart's call?' Xander asked. 'Sam said, well, he said it wasn't the nicest Christmas message.'

A bubble of laughter fluttered inside Janey – Xander was trying to lighten the mood, trying to comfort her.

'No. I'm not going to,' she said. 'He wouldn't have said anything I haven't heard before. He's a fair bit older than me,' Janey went on. 'Did I say?'

Her three friends shook their heads. There was so much none of them knew about each other.

'Sixteen years.'

'Really?' Lissy said, eyes widening in surprise and leaning forward as though wanting to hear better. And more.

Lissy sat on the couch beside Xander, opposite her and Bobbie. Lissy had crossed her legs as though holding herself, and her emotions tight, but Xander was sitting, legs sprawled and Janey thought he looked so comfortable, the house might have been his not Lissy's.

'My mother warned me about the age difference,' Janey said.

'Oh, mothers!' Bobbie laughed. 'They don't always get it right, you know, Janey.'

'I know. But mine sort of did. She warned me that the age difference would throw up all sorts of issues, if not in the beginning but as time went on. She said that Stuart and I had been brought up in different eras with different music and different politics. We'd had a different education – Stuart went to uni, I didn't – and been subjected to different morals in our upbringings. That's what my mother said.'

'And your father?' Lissy asked.

'I must have had one,' Janey said with a shrug. 'But he was never mentioned. My mother married Grant when I was six and then they had Suzy. If I bought up the subject of my real father my mother swiftly changed it. So I stopped asking. It just wasn't worth the hassle.'

'And does your mother know? About Stuart? How your marriage has been for you?' Lissy again. Janey could tell she really cared, and that she wasn't being nosy, just trying to get the fuller picture.

'I told her once. I went to her, covered in bruises, and all she said was I'd made my bed and I'd have to lie in it. She and Grant are living in Spain now.'

'Oh, God,' Lissy said. 'All these mothers swanning off to live abroad, leaving their children!'

'With respect, Lissy,' Bobbie said, rather sharply Janey thought, 'sometimes people – even mothers – have to do what they have to do. And what's more, you and Janey are hardly children anymore.'

If Lissy was taken aback at Bobbie's comment, she covered it well, although Janey noticed Xander turned sharply to look at her, checking she was okay.

'You're right, of course.'

'And,' Janey said, unable to let the subject of Stuart go although she knew she had to or it was going to spoil this whole Christmas break, wasn't it? 'He liked Freddie Mercury. So Eighties' music and I was only a child then listening to *Postman Pat*!'

'Postman Pat and his black-and-white cat,' Xander said in a sing-song voice.

And then there was what was possibly the most bizarre moment Janey had ever had, or would have, when they all sang the *Postman Pat* song. Bizarre, but heavens how it lightened the mood.

'Freddie Mercury was one helluva performer,' Bobbie said. 'It's an age difference thing. There's quite a gap between my age and you three.'

'Yeah, yeah, so there is,' Lissy said. 'It didn't seem to matter much at the art workshop though, did it?'

'No. And it doesn't matter now really,' Bobbie said. 'I was just saying.'

Bobbie was right – the difference in their ages didn't matter at all, not back then and not now in Lissy's beautiful house with Christmas to look forward to together. Janey's head was a mishmash of thoughts and she struggled to find something to say – she was finding it slightly embarrassing now that all the attention was on her.

'Thanks,' Janey said. 'All of you. For being so kind ...'

'Stuff and nonsense,' Bobbie said, giving Janey's hand a squeeze. 'It's what friends are for.'

'Oh my! Gosh! Is that the time?' Lissy said jumping up. 'Janey, will you be okay here with Bobbie while I get on with supper?'

Janey nodded.

'No one's going to harm you anymore, Janey,' Lissy said, her tone softening. 'Not if the three of us have anything to do with it. You're safe here. Right, gang?'

'Right,' Xander and Bobbie agreed.

Janey hoped not, but surprised herself with what words actually came out of her mouth.

'I won't let anyone hurt me. Not anymore.'

Bobbie let go of Janey's hand and put an arm around her shoulders, gave her a squeeze, but when Janey turned to look at her she saw there were tears in Bobbie's eyes. What, she wondered, had Bobbie had to put up with in her life?

Again, a silence fell over them all, soft as gossamer, not uncomfortable.

'I think it's time we had some Christmas music. Vonny loved Christmas music, the carols and the classical stuff.' Lissy went over to a dresser, opened a drawer and brought out a handful of CDs. 'Player's over there, Bobbie. Can I leave you in charge of light entertainment?'

'You can.'

'And help yourself to drinks.' Lissy waved an arm towards the drinks trolley. 'Oh, and Xander, could you put the wreath Janey made on the front door?'

She marched over to the couch, the hostess taking charge of the situation again, and reached out a hand to help Xander up, although he didn't exactly look reluctant when he took it.

Well, well, well … what might happen there, Janey wondered, as Bobbie put a CD in the player and Bing Crosby began to croon.

Chapter 11

Xander

'I hope it's not all going a bit Pete Tong,' Xander said.

'What?' Lissy asked. 'This savoury swirl filling? It firmed up a bit when we were in there with Janey. I'll need to loosen it, fill the pastry, and then whack it in the top oven.'

Xander watched as she lobbed in a tablespoon of mascarpone and gave it a vigorous stir. He began to salivate, thinking about supper. A side of salmon sat in a dish, covered in some herb or other and slices of lemon ready, he supposed, to go in the oven when these swirl things were done. Claire had never made swirls. Or cooked salmon for that matter. Cooking hadn't been Claire's thing and the few times she'd attempted it had been total disasters so that they'd had to go up to the Boathouse to eat or get a takeaway.

'No, not that,' Xander said. 'I meant your plan for a jolly, ho ho ho, Christmas break. All Santa hats and stockings and champagne and mince pies.'

'The plan is still on track, if running late a little,' Lissy said, smiling warmly at him. Her cheeks looked like little crab apples glistening with the effort of her cooking under the downlighters of the kitchen island. 'Although I'm right out of stockings, I'm afraid. The felt variety with Christmassy logos on, I mean.' She pressed her lips together and gave him a cheeky look.

Was that a wink? Xander gulped.

Before he could think of how to reply that wouldn't have been 'I bet you'd look dead sexy in stockings' which would be sexist and inappropriate in anyone's opinion, Lissy filled the conversational gap.

'If you mean Janey having the shock of her life and a bit of a wobble, then it's not spoiling anything for me. Is it for you?'

'No. I was a bit out of my depth with what to say though. Poor Janey. I'm right out of my comfort zone with men who abuse women, and I've met a few. Employed a few before I found out their true colours and then got rid of them again. It's a mercy that was the taxi driver at the door and not Janey's husband or I'd have done him over. Anyway, I'll get this wreath Janey made on the door and then I'll come and give you a hand. I'm a fairly domesticated example of the male species.'

Xander picked up the wreath along with a ratchet screwdriver and a couple of screws Lissy had put ready. Crossing the hall, he could hear Bobbie and Janey laughing. He let out a sigh ... thank goodness for that.

He had the wreath fixed in minutes and now, with the front door firmly closed, he stood with his back to it looking out to sea. The moon was up, casting its beam towards him. How strange it was that wherever anyone stood looking out to sea the moon's beam always came directly at them, putting them in a sort of lunar spotlight. In high summer, on hot nights when it was too clammy and uncomfortable to sleep in their bed, he and Claire had often walked along the beach in the moonlight, when all the holidaymakers were tucked up in their holiday accommodation or in a club somewhere. Hand in hand. Until Claire always raced away from him shouting back at him that the moon's beam was on *her* which was a cue for Xander to race in the opposite direction and yell that no, she'd got that wrong, the beam was on *him*. And then they'd run towards one another colliding in a slightly wobbly fashion as the sand shifted under their feet, their lips eventually meeting. On more than a few occasions those kisses had led the way to other things, the way kisses do, and they'd thrown caution – and the possibility of a conviction for a breach of the peace – to the wind and made love under the pier, tucked under the overhang of the ice cream kiosk.

Xander stood and let memories of Claire wash over him but he was struggling these days to remember the scent of her, the feel of her skin on his, the exact depth of the brown of her eyes, and that scared him at times.

'I hope you're at peace,' he whispered into the night before turning and going back into the house. Memories wouldn't bring Claire back. He still had a future and it was time he got on with having one. Everyone he knew said so.

'Do you need any help?' Xander asked, when he went back in to join Lissy.

She was washing down the evidence of pastry making and savoury swirl mixture that had spilled out onto the worktop. There was a delicious smell filling the kitchen now.

'Please. You could pour me a drink. Glasses in the cupboard over there.' She pointed to a floor-to-ceiling range of shelves and cupboards. 'Second row of cupboards down on the far left. There's a bottle of white open in the fridge. Have one yourself unless you'd prefer beer. That's in the larder.' Lissy waved an arm towards a door Xander deduced was the larder.

'I'll join you with the wine,' Xander said, fetching the glasses. He took a bottle of Viognier – the only bottle in there that was already opened – and poured two glasses. 'This is one vast kitchen you've got. I reckon the whole floor plan of my cottage would fit in here!'

'Most people's would, I expect,' Lissy laughed. 'It was quite a

59

surprise when I was told Strand House was now mine. And everything in it.'

'Claire spoke very fondly of this place,' Xander said, a tad cross with himself that just a few moments ago his thoughts had told him it was time to move on and now he was going back again.

'We had some good times here.' Lissy had finished wiping down and was now taking plates and bowls from a cupboard in the island. 'Vonny was very welcoming. She never minded that we came back from the beach covered in sand with bits of shell sticking to us. Or seaweed between our toes. I've got a ton of photos back in Exeter. I was going to thin them down because if there's one of Claire and me with our arms around one another's necks, making stupid faces at the camera, there must be dozens, if not hundreds. But, well, after she died I just couldn't.'

'Yeah, yeah,' Xander nodded. He knew the feeling. He'd kept all of Claire's clothes for two years before dealing with them – charity shop donations mostly. But still there was a pair of socks – neon pink with yellow butterflies on them – that he couldn't bear to part with. Claire had always worn them in bed on cold nights. Xander still slept with them under his pillow.

'Claire always came here. I rarely went to her house, even though it's only a couple of houses down the road.'

'She said. Her parents still live there.'

'Hmm,' Lissy said. She was rather noisily searching out cutlery now. 'I've thought about calling to say hello. Do you think I'd be welcome, or ...'

'I'm not,' Xander cut in. 'They've more or less cut me off. There was the funeral that we organised together and I gave her mother all Claire's jewellery, except her wedding and engagement ring, but after that if I rang to say I was thinking of popping over they always said they were busy or going out or it wasn't convenient or something. I got the hint in the end.'

'Oh, that's so sad for you. I'm sorry. But I suppose people grieve in different ways, Xand,' Lissy said.

Xand? Only Claire had ever called him Xand, and his mother sometimes, and he'd always resisted letting anyone else call him that. Hearing Lissy say it gave him a good feeling.

'Yeah, I suppose.' *And I'm being bloody gracious saying that because I was a very supportive son-in-law to them.* He'd even done any jobs they'd needed doing around their house for free. Because they were family. But not anymore, it seemed.

Lissy took a tea towel from the airing rack of the cooker and began polishing the cutlery with it. She sniffed the air. 'Ah, the savoury swirls are done, I can smell them.'

She took them from the oven, placing the hot baking tray straight onto the granite working surface. Xander had put in more than a few granite worktops for people. Horrendously expensive stuff, granite. And heavy. It always took at least three of them to carry and fit it.

'Salmon in next,' Lissy said. 'Then there's the salad to throw together and the potatoes to boil. Shouldn't be long now until we're all sat down. My stomach's beginning to rumble and I dare say Janey at least will be wanting something to eat – something to sort her blood sugar levels after her shock. I was going to set the table in the dining room but I'm thinking maybe in here, around the island, might be best. Less formal. What do you think?'

Xander thought Lissy was sounding slightly anxious now. Worried perhaps that she wasn't being the perfect hostess or something. From where he stood, Xander thought she looked pretty perfect to him with her long, slim nose, full lips, and flaw-less skin. Lissy had a slight Mediterranean look about her and somewhere in the depths of his mind Xander remembered Claire saying once that Lissy's great grandmother had been Italian. Yes, that was the look – Sophia Loren in her younger days.

'I think eating here would be best. I'm hardly dressed for formal dining. However, before you throw me out for having the wrong kind of clothes, I have brought new chinos and my very best Paul Smith shirt to wear on Christmas Day.'

61

'I'm not going to throw you out,' Lissy said so quietly Xander only just caught her words. 'I'm glad you're here. Really glad. Okay?'

'Very okay,' Xander croaked out. Something was happening here between him and Lissy, he could feel it. He cleared his throat, pushing back an emotion he wasn't sure of. That getting to know a new woman feeling? He hadn't felt that in a long time. 'I'll set the cutlery out while you see to the rest of it, shall I?'

'Please. Christmassy napkins are in the end drawer of the island. Any ones will do. There's loads in there.'

Xander was glad of something to do as he rifled through the end drawer that did, as Lissy had said, have loads of napkins in there, because what he really wanted to do at that moment was put his arms around Lissy, bury his head in her hair. The slightly tipsy dance they'd shared at his wedding came back to him. The feeling he'd had then that the chemistry between them could lead to other things, was threatening to overwhelm him now. Not that there was anything to stop him letting it take hold now, was there? He so wanted to kiss Lissy.

Too soon, man, too soon.

Xander mentally brought himself to his senses and got on with the job in hand. He settled on some napkins that had black and grey fir trees on a white background. Those should do. They matched the black and white of the kitchen floor tiles. Almost.

'Right,' Lissy said. 'That's the salmon in.' She opened the fridge and pulled out the chiller basket, brimming with salad stuff. Then she lit the gas under the potatoes. 'I'm going to have to shift if we're going to sit down to eat this before midnight.'

'Right,' Xander said, although he wouldn't have minded being alone with Lissy a bit longer. Until midnight. And after. And …

'Going back to what we were talking about earlier,' Lissy said, turning from the stove to look at him. 'I wrote to Claire's parents as soon as you told me what had happened, and then again after the funeral. They didn't respond. I found that sad and I admit to being a bit put out because Claire had been in my life since I was six years old, as had they. But then I gave it some thought and I can't imagine anything in the whole world that's worse than losing a child, and I haven't got any to lose. But I know a couple of people who have been in that living nightmare of a scenario and it looks like the scariest, saddest place.'

'Did you want children?' Xander asked. 'From your marriage? No, scratch that, that question is way out of order. Sorry.'

'Don't be. The short answer is I wouldn't have minded children, but Cooper wasn't keen. Maybe having them with Cooper wasn't the right thing for me?' Lissy shrugged in an I-don't-know sort of way. Her eyes had widened as though she was asking his opinion on whether children with Cooper would have been a bad idea.

'Now that you've split, maybe not,' was all Xander could think of to say.

'I think you're right,' Lissy said. 'I'm a child of a broken marriage and it still hurts like hell so … anyway I went on the pill – which is probably too much information!'

All information received and stored, Xander thought, but didn't say.

'Anyway,' Lissy went on when Xander didn't respond to that comment, 'my practice is hyper-busy, so it was perhaps a blessing in a way that children didn't happen for us. I don't know how I'd have coped running a business and looking after children. And this conversation is getting a bit deep as Christmas conversations go! Shall we change the subject?'

'Knitting?' Xander joked. 'Twelve-box sudokus? Neither of which I do, by the way.'

'Phew!' Lissy laughed. 'Something else we have in common.'

'I'm feeling a bit spare part,' Xander said, quietly thrilled that he and Lissy seemed to be laying their cards in front of one another as it were. Trading information. Getting to know one another just a little bit more. 'Anything else I can do to help?'

'There is. Could you get four large glasses and four small out of the cupboard and give them a buff up with this?'

Lissy reached for another tea towel and threw it towards him.

Xander found the glasses and began polishing vigorously. Neither spoke for a few minutes, each getting on with their respective tasks. But Xander found he didn't like the silence. He needed to hear Lissy's voice again.

'I often wish Claire and I had had children,' he said. 'I'd have something of her now around me always. A little girl that looked like her and a little boy I could have done boys' stuff with. But she …'

'I know, Xand,' Lissy said. 'She said. All the tests and everything. I'm sorry …' Lissy's voice trailed away as though she'd decided she'd said too much.

Of course Claire would have told Lissy about the tests they'd both had when children just didn't happen for them. Women talked about stuff like that – more than men did. He swallowed hard. Well, he was a man and he was talking now. He had to know so he had to ask?

'Did Claire tell you that after so many tests we began to wonder if we were on the payroll at the hospital, the only option for us was egg donation?'

'Yes,' Lissy said.

'And that Claire didn't want to go down that road?'

'Yes,' Lissy said again.

'She said the child would be mine but would never be hers and I said that that was rubbish because she would be carrying it for nine months and it would absorb the foods she ate and what she drank and feel her heart beating next to it.' Xander had to stop speaking because he was almost choking with emotion now.

'I know,' Lissy said. She reached out a hand to touch him gently on the arm. 'Look, Xand, I'm really sorry that you're hearing all this now but in a way it's a relief for me that you know that I knew because, well … I don't like secrets, and that was a big one I was carrying. I was sad for Claire but now I'm feeling really sad for you as well. We tend not to think how it is for the men.'

'Thanks,' Xander said. 'We didn't argue much, Claire and me, but we did debate that one long and hard. In the end I decided it had to be Claire's decision.'

'I know,' Lissy said sadly.

'We slept apart for the first time in our marriage that night and … oh God, we were going to change the subject and now …'

'I know that, too,' Lissy said. 'Claire called me that last morning …'

'When?' Xander interrupted. A thought had just struck him – had she been talking on her mobile to Lissy when the accident had happened?

'About nine o'clock. She was putting fuel in the car and talking to me at the same time. I could hear the pump whirring, and traffic noise. Does that put your mind at rest?'

She knew what he'd been thinking, didn't she? How heart-warming a thought that was.

'What did she say?' Xander asked.

'What you've just said, and that she was going to give it some more thought, read up on egg donation and see if there was a way she could accept it.'

'You're not just saying that?' Xander asked. 'To make me feel better about it?'

'No. Why would I?'

'Sorry. Scratch that. Heart's on my sleeve at the moment.'

'Best place sometimes,' Lissy said. 'We all know where we are then, don't we?'

And where are we? Xander wondered. *You and me, Lissy?* Were they ready yet to start a relationship that goes from being friends because Claire was Lissy's friend, to something more?

'You okay?' Lissy asked.

'Yeah, yeah. Fine. Well, getting there. Thanks, you know, for

65

your understanding and being so honest. We've cleared the air a bit, haven't we?'

'We have. I don't know if we'd have had this conversation if poor Janey hadn't had the terrible shock she had and opened up about her truths, so …'

Lissy left it at that, spreading her arms wide as though to say that's all been done and dusted and nothing else needs chewing over now, as it were.

'So,' Xander said, 'before those two women in your sitting room starve to death is there anything else I can do to help get dinner on the table?'

'In a sec, yes.' She opened and closed a few cupboard doors until she found what she was looking for – a huge glass bowl into which she began tipping bags of mixed leaves. 'Could you slice the cucumber, very thinly, while I skin the tomatoes? I can't abide tomato skins.'

Now there's a thing! Xander couldn't bear tomato skins either. Could people bond over their mutual hate of tomato skins? Hmm.

Chapter 12

Bobbie

'That, Lissy, was wonderful,' Bobbie said. 'No one would know you're not a professional chef, Cordon Bleu trained.' She didn't think she was going to be able to move for at least half an hour and she hoped no one would suggest she did. She rarely ate a quarter of the portion size Lissy had put in front of her that evening – each plate of food more delicious than the one before. It was a mercy she didn't have a modelling assignment to go to until after the New Year, but she couldn't be certain of that. Sometimes another older model booked for a magazine shoot or an advert would pull out at the last minute and Bobbie would step in. It was what she was known for – her availability and her reliability. Well, with no one else in her life to consider it was all too easy for her to drop anything she was doing and fly off to Paris or Barcelona or drive down to Kent or wherever. She crossed her fingers that she wouldn't get one of those calls until she'd worked off whatever weight she was going to put on here in Strand House.

'Cordon Bleu?' Lissy laughed. 'More Giorgio Locatelli and Jamie Oliver! And recipes ripped from the cookery section of Sunday newspaper supplements.'

'Wherever,' Bobbie said. 'You're a dark horse, hiding your light under a bushel. No one would know looking at your Facebook page and your Instagram and all the foodie pictures you put up that make me drool just to look at them, that you were an accountant.'

'And that's the way I want it to stay,' Lissy said. 'It's not the most exciting of professions, is it? I mean, we aren't doctors saving lives. We're not singers of soul music that soothes people's minds. Besides, people want favours done once they find out I'm an accountant sometimes. I'd like a ten-pound note for every time on a first date, once I've said what I do for a living, that it suddenly seems okay for me to offer my services for free in exchange for the meal we're eating. Besides, social media is all smoke and mirrors. Few of us are our true selves on there, are we?'

'I'm not!' Bobbie laughed. 'You've all been kind enough not to say you've noticed but my avatar photo was taken in Bali when I was thirty-five. I've not revealed my age, so who's to know?'

'I know what you mean, Lissy, about smoke and mirrors,' Janey said. 'I only use one of my paintings or a photo of flowers or something as my avatar. I'm going to have to … no, forget it.'

'Forget what?' Bobbie said. They'd had a conversation earlier in the sitting room while Lissy and Xander were getting supper ready and Janey had said she'd consult a solicitor once Christmas was over and get her brother-in-law to go with her to fetch her computer and any other things she wanted taken out of the house she'd shared with Stuart. She had her smartphone if she wanted to access the internet or get in touch with her sister. But she wasn't going back.

Janey shrugged.

'Look, sweetheart,' Bobbie said, 'you're doing fine. So much has happened to you since this morning.'

'I know. I'm trying to stay positive, I really am. But it's hard.'

Bobbie had realised that. Every time there was a sudden noise, like a car backfiring, or a firework going off as had happened about an hour ago, Janey had jumped. She'd even jumped when Xander slid the plate with the pavlova Lissy had made across the table and it squeaked like a trapped mouse.

'It'll get easier,' Lissy said. 'I promise you it will.'

'I hope so. Anyway, thanks all,' Janey said, raising a now empty glass towards the others. 'To friends and delicious food. And wine.'

'To all of that,' Xander said. 'Hey! I've got an idea. We could play a game. Where we want to be in ten years' time.'

'Ten?' Bobbie said. 'Make that one, given my age! And even at that I think I'd like to still be able to stand on my four-inch heels. Yes, that's where I'd like to be – still standing basically!'

The others all laughed and Bobbie was glad because Janey had been in danger of killing the good mood of the evening.

'You next, Janey,' Bobbie said. 'One year from now.'

'One year from now,' Janey repeated, her voice firm, and Bobbie was glad to hear it after the whisper-like shakiness of it of earlier. 'One year from now I'd like to be able to say I've sold some paintings. I'd like to travel further afield to paint. I mean, I must have painted Totnes castle at least twenty times and there's another castle at Berry Pomeroy that I've never visited even though it's only a couple of miles down the road from where I live. Now I'm by the sea I'd like to paint it in all its moods and in all seasons. And I'd like to be able to say I am making a living at it. And that I'm half way to being divorced.'

Bobbie reached for a bottle of Prosecco that was still half-full. She topped up Janey's glass.

'That's my girl.' She took a swig of her own drink and swallowed hard. That was the thing – she, Bobbie, was old enough that Janey *could* be her girl. 'We'll drink to that. Who's next for future dreams?'

'I'll go next,' Lissy said. 'One year from now I hope I've been brave enough to follow my heart and do what I really love which is cooking, and not what I'm doing now to please my dear, late dad. Not that he said I had to become an accountant and take over his business, although he was pleased I did. So … one year from now you could be eating at my restaurant. The House on the Strand has a nice ring to it, don't you think?'

'Book me in,' Bobbie said. 'As long as you've got those savoury swirl things, and that salmon. What was the topping on that?' Not that she was going to replicate it any time soon. She barely had time to put something in the microwave some days.

'Pesto, breadcrumbs, fresh basil, and a dash of olive oil.'

'Keep that recipe, then, because that will be a big seller on the menu. And the pavlova. It was to die for. That leaves you, Xander. Where, my darling, do you want to be?'

'Me?' Xander looked suddenly stricken that the spotlight was now on him. Or was it that she'd called him 'darling'? Calling people 'darling' or 'sweetheart' was something people in the world she moved in did all the time. Perhaps only Claire had ever called Xander 'darling' and the memory had pierced his heart somehow.

'You don't have to if you don't want to,' Lissy said before Bobbie could. She reached out and laid her hand on top of Xander's. 'Does he?'

'No,' Janey said.

'Not one bit,' Bobbie agreed. 'But this game *was* your idea, Xander.'

'So it was! So I'll play fair. In one year's time I'd like my business to be on a better footing than it is now. A much better footing. And I'd like to be able to socialise more because at the moment all my social life consists of is one night a week for quiz night at the Pier Inn. And, with a following wind, I'd like someone in my life to socialise with. And … this is probably too much information, but I'd be made up completely if there was a baby on the way. That last, of course, could be the wine talking!'

Well, well, well. This was a turn up for the books. Lissy's hand was still on Xander's and he'd turned to look at her as he spoke. Had she missed something? Had there been a subtle clue dropped here and there that Lissy and Xander knew one another rather better than Bobbie had thought they did, and she'd missed them?

'Right, everyone,' Lissy said, snatching her hand back. She began gathering the debris of the meal together. 'I'll just get this lot in the dishwasher and then make coffee.'

'Not for me thanks,' Bobbie said. She slid down off the bar stool, a tad wobbly from all the wine, but she hadn't fallen over.

'Nor me,' Xander said. He held out an arm towards Bobbie inviting her to take it. 'I'll escort you to your room, madam.'

'I'll help you load the dishwasher and clear up,' Bobbie heard Janey say as she and Xander left the room.

Chapter 13

Lissy

'You don't have to sleep in this room on your own, Janey,' Lissy said, 'if you'd rather not. There's another room with twin beds at the back and I'll be happy to share if it will make you feel more comfortable. You know, after everything's that happened today.'

Janey had chosen the smaller of the two rooms she'd been offered. It had been Lissy's room whenever she'd come to stay with Vonny.

'I don't think Stuart will come after me,' Janey said. 'He's probably still not sober enough anyway.'

'He wouldn't be able to get in if he did,' Lissy told her. 'There are two bolts on the front door and a chain. All the windows have locks and the patio door is alarmed.'

Janey shivered.

'Are you cold? I can turn up the central heating if you are?'

'No. Not that. I was running a sort of scene in my head about Stuart trying to get in and me being frightened, and everyone going downstairs to sort him out.'

'Blimey,' Lissy said, 'your thought processes run fast! You should be a writer with thinking like that!'

'I've never thought of that,' Janey said, smiling. 'But I could. A revenge novel perhaps?'

They were keeping their voices low mindful that both Bobbie and Xander weren't far away. The landing was wide and the ceilings high but sound carried at night, Lissy always thought. A Christmas tree on the landing would add to the festive atmosphere as well. She'd ask in the morning if Xander knew where she could get Christmas trees – if there were any left.

'Something else to add to your list of things to be doing a year from now, then,' Lissy said.

'Yeah,' Janey said, perching herself on the side of the bed. 'God, this room is so big. It feels luxurious having so much space. And all for me.'

'For as long as you want,' Lissy said. 'I didn't say anything in front of the others but, well, I've not decided what I'm going to do with Strand House yet. I'd like to keep it, but I've also got a business …'

'Which,' Janey said, wagging a finger playfully at her, 'you might not have one year from now because you might be cheffing for a living. The House on the Strand has a nice ring to it, so you said!'

'I did, didn't I?'

But was she brave enough to take that step?

'Did you mean it? What you just said? About me staying here?' Janey asked, looking serious again. She put her hand over her mouth as though she couldn't quite believe she'd said what she had. Lissy got the feeling Janey didn't ask for much, afraid of what reaction she'd have got from Stuart if she had.

'I did. Even if I manage to sell my practice …'

'Not if! When!' Janey butted in.

Lissy thought it was still the wine talking, as Xander had said earlier it was for him. But many a true word spoken in jest, and all that. Her heart ached for him and Claire, and the baby of theirs that had never been.

'When,' Lissy agreed.

Janey's luggage was still on the end of the bed. One small, rather tatty, brown, very old-fashioned case. Had that been Stuart's, brought to the marriage along with his Freddie Mercury records? And a tote bag that had seen better days.

'Wouldn't it be good,' Janey said, 'if we all were to meet up in one year's time to see if any of us have achieved our dreams?'

'It would. We could. But I think it would be a good idea if we got some shuteye now. I'll help you unpack, shall I?'

'There isn't much,' Janey said. She leaned over and sprung the catch on the case and pulled out a jersey nightshirt – navy with pale pink spots and a bit of lace around the neck. She laid it out, almost reverently, on the bed beside her. 'There's this, a wrap dress I got from the charity shop on the High Street, underwear, and a different jumper. These jeans,' she said, patting her knees, 'will have to see me through.'

'Oh, Janey, I hope I didn't put pressure on you about this Christmas invite.' She reached out to pat her friend's arm. 'It's just that I picked up from your Facebook response to Bobbie's post about being alone, that you would be too, and I suppose I must have assumed you and Stuart had already parted.'

'I know. You said it yourself earlier – social media is all smoke and mirrors. And you didn't put pressure on me. You were, if you like, a catalyst to me doing something about sorting my life out. But I'm going to look like the poor relation here what with Bobbie being so glamourous.'

'It's what she does. Glamour. Second nature to her, I should think. It's never good to compare ourselves to others, though. But I've just thought of something. I've still got a few of Vonny's things here. Some cashmere jumpers, and her silk nighties. Some dresses. Vonny was one smart and sassy lady. Not in Bobbie's league but then not many are. They're too small for me but you're about the same size she was. If you don't mind wearing second-hand?'

'Mind? I live in it!' Janey giggled.

'Sssh,' Lissy said. 'The others are probably just about nodding off.'

'As must I,' Janey said with a wide yawn. 'Thanks for everything. The invite, the delicious supper, the offer of somewhere to stay while I get myself sorted.'

'You were supportive of me when I told you Cooper had left me. I didn't tell many people. Not even my staff or my mother until I had the decree absolute.'

'Really?'

'Really.'

'Then I feel privileged and honoured that you did tell me.'

'Sometimes the fewer people know, the better it is. One of my clerks – Sasha – told the whole world, I think, and she was plagued something rotten by blokes wanting to, er, comfort her.'

'I bet,' Janey giggled, putting a hand to her mouth again to stifle the sound. 'Tip taken. Keep quiet. Thanks.'

She got off the bed and flung her arms around Lissy's neck and hugged her – not a bear hug as such but the giving of affection – and the receiving of it, Lissy decided, was probably more needed right now. She hugged her friend.

'Night, night,' Janey said. 'Christmas Eve tomorrow.'

'Yep, so it is. Night night.'

Lissy kissed her friend's cheek before she turned to leave. How good it felt to be giving something back to Janey.

'Oh!' Lissy said, startled.

Xander was on the landing doing press-ups when she left Janey's room. Why here and not in his room? she wondered. Was he drunk?

'Ah. Sorry. Should have asked,' he puffed. 'There's a bit more space out here. Hope you, er, don't mind?'

'Of course not.' How could she mind when he looked so healthy, so sexy, in dark grey boxers and no top? Building obviously gave a man muscles like an athlete. 'I said to make yourself at home and you obviously are. Do you do press-ups every night?'

'Forty-two, forty-three,' Xander said. 'Yes, mostly. I'm being as quiet as I can. Nearly there. Forty-six.'

'I'll leave you to it,' Lissy said. She didn't think she was going to be able to stay there a second longer without throwing herself on him. Had he meant it about wanting to have another woman in his life to love again, and to be loved? To have a child in his life? And if he did, could she be that woman?

'Twenty more to do,' Xander said, and he seemed to have got a second wind now. 'Before you go, what time's breakfast?'

'Whenever you surface,' Lissy told him.

'Ah. Right. Good. Only I'm thinking of going for an early morning run. If it's not raining.'

'Fine. Great,' Lissy said. 'Do that.'

'Feel like joining me?'

'Not tomorrow,' Lissy laughed. 'Good night. Sleep tight.'

And she hurried, her heart rate having gone up a few notches, to her room.

Christmas Eve

Chapter 14

Xander

It was still six-thirty when Xander let himself out of Strand House. Still dark although the sky was lightening a little. And chillier than he'd thought it would be given there was no breeze. The meteorogical office had murmured about the possibility of snow over Christmas at some stage. Xander shivered, then jumped up and down on the spot to get his blood going around a bit faster. He wished now he'd worn more than shorts and a sweatshirt. But he couldn't go back to Strand House just yet as it would mean ringing the bell and waking Lissy up to let him in. They'd all been rather late to bed the night before. Not that Xander had slept much. He'd listened out for every creak and groan in case Janey's husband decided to turn up. Xander began to run along the promenade. It was just under a mile between Hollacombe and his cottage in Cliff Road – not as far as he usually ran. He decided he had time to run around the green which was, roughly, a mile as well. That would be enough for today. Hardly anyone was about yet as he quickened his pace.

'You fickle creature,' Xander said when he got to Cliff Road. Felix was sitting in Eve Benson's window. Not that he minded.

Eve needed the cat's company as much as the cat liked a lap to sit on.

He let himself in and went in search of Christmas tree decorations which were in the spare room somewhere. He remembered packing them away the Christmas before Claire was killed but he hadn't bothered to get them out since. Did anyone living alone put up Christmas decorations or get a tree?

Ah, there they were. Rather a large boxful, but Lissy would probably need far more than that if she was going to get two trees as the taxi driver had suggested the day before.

Eve would be up, he knew that. He often heard her putting out her recycling before it was light. He tapped on her door.

'Oh dear. Total disaster is it?' Eve said opening the door and ushering him in.

'Quite the contrary,' Xander said. 'I've just come back for some Christmas tree decorations. And my lorry. I thought I'd better tell you I've taken the lorry in case you notice it's missing and ring the police or something, seeing as you can't ring me.'

Eve Benson was yet to embrace mobile phone technology, but had found out somehow that it was expensive to use a landline to ring a mobile number and had declined Xander's offer of his mobile number.

'Your lorry for a few decorations?' Eve said.

'Well, not just that. I'll take Lissy to the Christmas Tree Farm to choose a tree or two later on today. If they've got any left.'

'Oh, they will have,' Eve said. 'A veritable forest it is up there. I went once when my Ed was alive, and didn't he moan we had to walk miles to choose one! Anyway, you don't want to hear all that. I just want to say, though, that I'm glad you've got a reason for using those decorations again. No doubt they'll bring back memories, and so they should, but you'll be making new ones as well. And now you can tell me to shut up and stop supplying my opinions where they're not wanted.'

'I'll say no such thing,' Xander said.

Eve was right … memories would come flooding back and he would be making new ones. He'd hold decorations in his hands that Claire had held and that thought pleased him. Claire couldn't be part of Christmas this year but he could honour the Christmases they'd spent together by using the decorations she'd bought and loved and wrapped so carefully in tissue fully expecting to be able to take them out again. A lump rose in his throat and he swallowed hard. Tears were forming, too, so he blinked them away.

'Time for a cup of tea, I think,' Eve asked.

She'd noticed, hadn't she?

'A quick one,' Xander said. He knew Eve would be going to Brixham in the morning to have Christmas lunch with her nephew, but as far as he knew she'd be on her own, as per usual, until then. Felix notwithstanding, of course.

He closed the front door behind him and followed Eve into her cluttered, if welcoming, home in direct contrast to the clean, sparsely – but elegantly – furnished, Strand House. His own lay somewhere in between but he'd have to give it a thorough clean and a tidy up before he invited Lissy, or the others.

'Felix is here,' Eve said.

'I know. I saw him sitting in your front room window. More or less ignored me.'

'Sulking,' Eve said. 'The second you left yesterday he was out of your catflap, over the fence, and miaowing at my door. What could I do but let him in?'

'What indeed. Most cats have at least three homes, so they say.'

'So, how's it going with your harem up the posh end of the seafront?'

'Harem? One divorcee, one who ran out on her husband yesterday, and one who is a fair bit older than I am. Single. Lissy's a great cook – she's the divorcee.'

'Oh, that's good. That she's a good cook. That'll do you good, some proper food, your recycling being full of pizza boxes and takeaway cartons as it is.'

'You've been spying on me!' Xander laughed. Not that he minded. Eve was a good neighbour and looked out for him, took in Amazon parcels and the like, and after Claire had died she'd brought round pasties or a couple of slices of cake more than a few times, simply knocking on the door and handing them over and not engaging him in any sort of conversation that would have brought his – and her – emotions to the surface.

'Better get back,' Xander said. 'Someone should be up by now.' Before he could take Lissy to look for Christmas trees he'd promised he'd take Janey to see Berry Pomeroy castle. He stood up. 'Happy Christmas Eve, Eve.'

'Ha ha, very funny,' Eve said. 'Happy Christmas Eve yourself.' She reached up on tiptoe and kissed Xander on the cheek.

Chapter 15

Janey

'There are two approaches,' Xander said. 'We can either park at the top of the drive, hop over the stile, and walk down – which is the better first view of the castle, if a long way back up again seeing as the carpark's closed at the moment. Or we could drive to the bottom of the road that runs to the Duke of Somerset's humble little abode and walk up through the woods which is shorter but not such an impressive first view.'

'Won't he mind?' Janey asked.

'Nope. It's a public road up to his front drive.'

'Oh. Are we allowed in the castle?'

'Not in the castle, no. That'll have the portcullis down for the winter. But the footpaths in both directions are public. So, what's it going to be? Left for the steep walk, right for the woodland walk?'

'Left,' Janey said. How unused she was to being given options, being allowed to choose. And how very good it was feeling.

When Xander had got back to Strand House after his run and dumped his big box of Christmas decorations on the kitchen island with a huge grin, Janey had been alone, eating toast and

83

marmalade. Lissy was still in the shower – Janey had heard it running for ages – and Bobbie was yet to surface.

'You,' Xander had said, 'are just the person I want to see.'

And then he'd gone on to say if she wanted to paint castles then there was no time like the present. Berry Pomeroy Castle was just ten minutes away by road and there'd hardly be a soul there given it was Christmas Eve and the rest of the world would be making mince pies or icing cakes.

'I don't think so,' Janey had said. 'Lissy will probably need help preparing for tomorrow.'

'She might,' Xander said. 'But my guess is if she wants help she'll ask for it. From where I was standing last night I'd say she was more than capable of throwing a meal together. A delicious meal I might add in case you think that was a facetious remark.'

Janey hadn't considered it a facetious remark at all and now here she was, sitting beside Xander in his builder's lorry. How much more a person could see from being so high up. Over hedges. Across the fields to Dartmoor and Haytor in the distance. Into fields where pheasants were pecking at something on the edges of what had had some crop or other in it.

'Right, then, Tracey Emin,' Xander said. 'Here we are.'

Janey laughed. Tracey Emin? She wouldn't mind earning the money from her art that Tracey Emin did, but she doubted that was likely.

'We'll park up here.' Xander pulled over against the end wall of a barn. No yellow lines here telling him he couldn't.

Xander came round and opened the door for her and she slid down onto the road. For her five feet two height, it was a long way down.

'Landed safely,' Xander said. 'You've got your smartphone?'

'Yes,' Janey told him. 'And a sketchbook and a couple of pencils I brought with me.'

'That'll do for now,' Xander said. 'Right, over the stile we go.'

Xander threw his long legs over the stile and stood on the

other side as Janey got herself more gingerly onto the path that led down to the castle.

She could sense the history of the place already. Most of the trees had lost their leaves but they were so tall they were casting skeletal shadows. There was a still, silent atmosphere. Not threatening, but otherworldly somehow. And it was cold. Colder here than down by the sea. Cold enough for snow? Janey hoped so. She'd never known snow at Christmas but there should always be a first time for everything. She did up the top button of her coat. Thank goodness she'd thought to ask Lissy if she had a hat and scarf she could borrow before she came out. She ought to have put a second jumper on as well but she couldn't do anything about the fact she hadn't now. She'd be warm enough on the walk back up.

'Tell me if I'm walking too fast for you,' Xander said. 'I tend to forget some think I've got lampposts for legs.' He pulled his beanie hat further down over his ears and hunkered down into his builders' reefer jacket. 'Brr. Bit nippy. I always forget how cold it can be up here. Creepy. One of the most haunted castles in the UK. Did I say?'

'You know you didn't!' Janey laughed.

'Would you have come if I had?'

'Wild horses wouldn't have kept me away.'

With each step she took beside Xander going down the steep and twisty lane she felt some sort of strength propelling her onwards.

'I can't believe I've lived so close to this place all my life and never visited,' Janey said.

'It happens. I've got a neighbour – Eve – who was born in the cottage she still lives in and if you were to spit out a cherry stone it'd land in the sea, and yet she's never even dipped her toes in it.'

'Really!'

'Really. Nearly there. Get your smartphone ready. The first sight is always impressive.'

Janey did as she told, pulling the smartphone she'd had her hand around since she got out of Xander's van from her pocket. She switched it on.

'Oh my God!' Janey said, as the rounded the bend. She stood stock still in awe. She hadn't expected it to be quite so big even though she'd seen photos of it and when she'd been at school there'd been a term when they'd studied local history but the day of the castle visit Janey had been ill and hadn't been able to go. If only she had.

'Perfect lighting as well,' Xander said. 'Now the sun's decided to break out from the clouds. Hollywood has missed a trick not getting me for a locations manager, eh?'

'Definitely!'

It was more perfect than perfect to Janey's artistic eye and she began taking photos.

'Come on. It's even more awesome when you get to the bottom of the path. Café's closed at the moment, as are the loos, and the ticket hut's boarded up, but we can walk around the perimeter and peer in.'

Janey was glad of Xander's company, of course she was, and grateful to him for bringing her here and being so kind, but part of her also wanted this experience on her own. Already ideas were forming in her mind how she would paint this castle.

She followed Xander on down the path, and he led her to the huge gate with the portcullis.

'It's like something out of a film,' Janey said. 'Or *Game of Thrones*.'

'Better than that,' Xander said. 'All hands-on, touchy feely.' He took a hand from his pocket and placed his palm against the stone. 'Bloody fantastic builders built this. Wish the blokes I employ could make half a good as job of their stonework as those guys did way back then when they had very little to help them do it by way of tools or technology.'

'I think that's what so impressive,' Janey said. She took a few steps backwards and took a photo of the doorway.

'When I was a lad, which wasn't a million years away in case you're wondering …'

'Ha ha,' Janey interrupted. How good it felt to be able to do that and know she wouldn't be yelled at for doing it.

'When I was a lad,' Xander repeated with a mock-sigh, 'me and my mates used to cycle up here. At night. We'd bring sleeping bags and a can of coke and whatever grub we could nick from our mums' fridges and we'd sleep out under the stars waiting for ghosts to appear.'

'Crikey,' Janey said. 'It's a bit steep from sea level up to here.'

'We were younger then. Invincible as youngsters think they are. The Eighties were quieter on the roads than they are now. Mothers used to fret less about what their kids were up to.'

Janey had been in junior school in that decade and by the time she was a teenager kids were kept on a tighter rein. Too many dangers. Too many predators of young children, although there always had been more than likely.

Janey turned her back on the castle and took photos of the path she'd just come down and the skeletal trees that had lined her way. It struck her then, given her last train of thought, that she felt quite, quite safe here with Xander who she barely knew. Far safer than she had ever felt with Stuart, who she'd thought she'd known. 'D'you want to see how me and my mates used to get into the castle at night?'

'Please,' Janey said.

'Down here, then,' he said. 'Dungeons this way.'

Janey followed.

'Oh, and if you see a lady in white walking across that battle-ment up there, pretend you haven't. She means—'

'Death,' Janey finished for him, laughing. 'I remember that much from school!'

'Good. Here we are. All barred now so little oiks like I was can't get in and light barbecues and drink themselves stupid on alcopops.'

'I'm sure you didn't!' Janey said.

'I'm sure I did.'

Janey took yet more photos, most of which she knew she'd delete but there would be a fair few in there she knew she would be able to turn into paintings. An idea flash-forwarded in her brain that she could go on to produce birthday cards or art postcards with these sorts of images on. People would buy them. People who were members of the National Trust, or English Heritage, would.

'It'll be another half hour's walking or so to get down through the wood into the lane and back again,' Xander said. 'Are your shoes up to that?'

'They'll have to be. They're all I brought with me. Oh, and a pair of slippers but I haven't felt brave enough to put them on yet, preferring to walk around in my socks. You can't imagine Bobbie in slippers, can you?'

'I'm a gentleman,' Xander quipped. 'I won't answer that.'

'Of course. Sorry. Fishing for compliments, I expect.' Janey thought she'd forgotten how but perhaps now with a kind and handsome man wanting to be in her company her mind was rememberin. 'Lead the way.'

The path was stony and steep for the first part and Xander, very gentlemanly, offered Janey his hand to hold for support. Again, she got nothing but a safe feeling being with him, being offered such an intimate gesture. As soon as the path levelled out, though, Janey took her hand from his.

'Five minutes down the lane and past the pond,' Xander said when they reached another lane, 'and the castle will come into view. Get ready for another photo opportunity.'

'Ready,' Janey said. 'Oh, larch.' It never failed to surprise and delight Janey – who loved to paint nature – that larch which was coniferous changed leaf colour in the autumn. The larch further down the lane were glowing a sort of reddish bronze in the morning light.

And then, there were the ruins of the castle, high up on the hill above. What Janey thought might have been the remains of chimney stacks or what was left of higher buildings stretched high from the castle wall into the pale, clear blue December sky.

'Thank you so much for bringing me here, Xander,' Janey said as she took photo after photo. A heron flew across in front of her lens on its way to the pond no doubt. It felt ethereal and yet so very right for what her soul needed now. There was a lump in the throat with the beauty of it all and she swallowed back tears; tears of happiness and not the aching fear and sadness of tears she'd cried far too much over Stuart. 'Thank you so much.'

'My pleasure,' Xander said. 'But we're going to have to get back. I've promised Lissy I'll take her to go and fetch Christmas trees after lunch. Hence the decorations and fetching my lorry.' He put an arm on Janey's shoulder and gently steered her around to start walking back the way they'd come before taking it away again. 'What will you, and Bobbie, do you think this afternoon while Lissy and I are out denuding the pine forests?'

Janey had no idea what she'd do yet although there was an idea forming in her mind that it couldn't be too early for her to start on her painting, now she'd given herself permission to do some and belief in the fact she was good at it. She didn't have a clue what Bobbie would do. What she had worked out, though, was that Xander was ever-so-not-so-subtly letting her know he didn't want either of them on board while he took Lissy on a Christmas tree hunt. He wanted them to be alone.

Even though a new romance wasn't on Janey's radar, and wouldn't be for some time, she felt a warm glow of something flow through her – much like the brandy Lissy had given her for the shock the night before – that she was being warmed by the first flames of someone else's.

'I'll think of something,' Janey said, quickening her pace.

'Are you coming, Janey?' Bobbie called out to her from the hall doorway. They'd all finished lunch and now Xander and Lissy had just left to go and look for Christmas trees. Janey was sitting, legs curled under her on the couch by the window, looking through the photos she'd taken up at Berry Pomeroy castle.

Bobbie stood in the doorway in a knee-length white coat with a funnel neck, black buttons and a very wide black patent belt. On her feet she wore vertiginously – well, they were vertiginous to Janey – high-heeled black boots that disappeared up under the hem of the coat.

'Coming where?' Janey said. She didn't know she wanted to go anywhere. Not at the moment, without Xander's protection, she didn't, although she knew she couldn't have that for long.

'Town. Lissy's given me a key so we can let ourselves in and out.'

Bobbie was pulling her long, silver hair into a ponytail on the back of her head with one hand. Janey watched, mesmerised, as Bobbie took the black cloche hat she had in the other hand and pushed her twisted hair up into it. It was like that thing some actresses do when they go for a part, where they turn up wearing a hat, sit down, then remove the hat and all their fabulous locks come tumbling down. Like that, only in reverse; Bobbie's hair was like a sheet of molten silver. Or mercury. Janey hoped she might be able to re-create the exact shade in a painting some day.

'There, that's me done,' Bobbie said. 'So *are* you?'

'I don't know that's there anything I need.'

Bobbie sighed theatrically.

'And I don't know that that's a reason for not going into town. Any town. I know this one isn't exactly London or York or even Paris, but I happened to notice a stationer's shop when I was in there yesterday. And I happen to know you have been out sussing out views to paint. And Xander informed me while you were upstairs and we were waiting for lunch that you've only got a sketchpad and a couple of pencils with you.'

'Not a lot you don't know about me, then,' Janey laughed, getting used now to Bobbie's very forthright manner.

'Quite the opposite, darling,' Bobbie said. 'I'm sure there's loads about you I don't know and probably never will, just as there's an awful lot about me you don't know either.'

'Yet!' Janey said. She got up off the couch. She did need some art supplies because she badly, badly wanted – and needed? – to start on some new work. And she had a suspicion Bobbie was suggesting they go out so she could get some. The problem was she only had a credit card, very little cash, and her card was getting dangerously close to the max.

'And if,' Bobbie said, 'you're worried about that tedious little facility we call finance, I can stand you the wherewithal. A present.'

Janey wondered with a slight panic, if she was so transparent? Bobbie was reading her mind.

'Lissy said no presents,' Janey said firmly. 'That's the rules.'

'And rules are there to be broken. Good God, girl, where would we be if we didn't break rules now and again! Anyway, that aside, you can pay me back when you're famous if you're not accepting gifts. So what's going to be your medium of choice – watercolours, oils, acrylics, pastels, pen and ink? See, I know about this stuff.'

'Blackmailer!' Janey said.

First Xander and now Bobbie taking control of her but in a kindly way – wanting the best for her. But she still wasn't sure she wanted to go into town. She pulled her jumper, which had ridden up while she was sitting down, over her jeans, and tugged on it a little.

'Two options,' Bobbie said. 'You come with me and choose or I choose for you and you have to make do. I can see those fingers of yours are itching to get creative the way you're fiddling with the end of that jumper.'

Janey wondered for a moment if Bobbie had been on the bottle all morning while she and Xander had been at the castle and had had more than the one glass Lissy had poured for them all at

91

lunchtime. But she didn't think so. Not really. Bobbie was unwinding now, getting used to the new dynamic of the four of them, relaxing and beginning to be more her true self. As they all were a little.

'They're not,' Janey said. 'It's just that, well, Totnes is only seven miles away and Stuart could … although it's hardly likely … have come over this way. If he's hacked into my email details and found out where I am. I wouldn't want to put you in any danger if he came flying at me or something.'

'And do you think I'd let him get away with that? See these spikes on the end of my feet?' Bobbie said, lifting one leg and twisting it round so Janey could see the stiletto heel. 'He'd have that run right through him if he did. It's not only big beefy men like Xander who can protect anyone in need of protecting, you know.'

'I know,' Janey said. 'Okay, I'll come.' How could she not after that little display of solidarity and support? 'I'll just get my coat.'

What a surreal day so far. An interesting one. A day that was making her feel an entirely different Janey somehow.

Chapter 16

Bobbie

'I can't walk across the beach in these boots,' Bobbie said once they were outside and walking along the promenade towards the town. Janey kept looking down onto the sand as though she was eager to be on it.

'Shame,' Janey said. 'The tide's out. The sand's firm enough.'

'You can go if you want,' Bobbie said. 'I'll catch up with you again by that café that sticks out over the prom on the other side of the pier.'

'No, it's okay. I'll stay with you. I've only got this one pair of shoes with me and I wouldn't want to slip in a puddle or something and get them soaked.'

Janey only had one of everything as far as Bobbie had been able to tell. Same jeans, same jumper, same shoes for the last twenty-four hours. She wondered if Janey had anything special to wear on Christmas Day, and was beginning to doubt she did. How different their lives were and yet how very fond of the younger woman Bobbie was becoming. She felt protective of her somehow which was a first because Bobbie had had to watch her own back, and only hers, most of her life.

93

Bobbie had had to work hard to get Janey to agree to come into town with her but was glad she had. There was a gentle smile playing around Janey's lips – the first time Bobbie had seen it for any length of time – as they walked along.

What was the cost of a few art materials to her if Janey would get so much pleasure out of using them? Wasn't that what Christmas was all about – the giving?

'I think you've worked it out, Bobbie,' Janey said, 'that I'm more than a bit strapped for cash at the moment. I'll pay you back whatever you spend on art supplies for me. I won't want much because I've got loads at … well, back in Totnes … when I can get around to fetching them.'

Janey had been on the verge of saying 'home'. She'd only just stopped herself and Bobbie was glad she had because it showed she was thinking forward and not back.

A gaggle of young people came – arm in arm and very noisily – along the prom towards them. They were all wearing Santa hats with bells on and most of them had strings of tinsel around their necks. Bobbie wondered what bar they'd all just tumbled out of – there were enough of them on the ground floor of huge Victorian buildings that had once been select hotels. But times changed, and these kids were probably getting more fun out of them than any Victorian ever had.

'Merry Christmas, ladies!' one of them shouted.

'Merry Christmas!' Bobbie and Janey said as one.

Bobbie put her hands over her ears.

'Hard to hear yourself think, the row that lot were making!'

'Happy though,' Janey said and the way she said it told Bobbie that while she was definitely moving forward, Janey hadn't hit the happy note just yet.

'Those drawings you did of me at the Dartington Art workshop,' she said. 'I know it was a few years ago now but have you still got them?'

'And the little terracotta sculpture I did although it's started to crumble a bit because it was only fired. It's not had any patina put on it. They were in the shed which is where I go to draw or paint but when I was forming the idea in my mind that I would try and leave Stuart somehow I was afraid he'd trash them if I did. Well, *have*. I *have* left him now.'

'You have indeed,' Bobbie said. 'I also happen to have noticed that there is a little cocktail bar in town – *PLAYERS*. It looks a tad out of place amongst all the tripper shops and the one-armed bandit machines, but no matter. It does cocktails. And when I peeped inside yesterday it had by far the classiest decorations I've seen around here. We'll have one on the way back to celebrate your leaving. But that still leaves the question of where your artwork is now if it's not in the shed.'

'In another shed. Fred and Annie's next door. They – and their dog, Guinness – will guard them with their lives until I fetch them. They know what Stuart's like, they've heard …'

'Well, they won't hear anymore, darling, will they?' Bobbie said quickly.

'No, no they won't.'

Bobbie caught, out of the corner of her eye, Janey balling her hands into fists and stuffing them in the pockets of her coat.

'Thank you, you know, for being so kind to me. It's not as if we knew one another all that well.'

'But getting to know one another better by the minute, eh?'

Bobbie reached for Janey's arm as they neared the pelican crossing. Two cars went past lit up like Christmas trees. One of them even *had* a fully decorated Christmas tree about a foot high strapped to the radiator grill. The lights changed to red and Bobbie steered Janey across before letting go of her arm again.

'I'm not entirely philanthropic offering to buy you art materials, Janey,' Bobbie said, brightly. She didn't want Janey to think she'd brought her out under false pretences or as part of some sort of devious plan.

'Oh,' Janey said.

'You made by far the best fist of drawing and sculpting me that weekend. I'd like to buy what you did. Or swap for art materials we will soon be purchasing if you wish.'

The two women turned the corner into Torbay Road and the long walk up to the art supply shop.

'I was going to say before but didn't like to,' Janey said. She was grinning broadly now, giggling. 'Only I almost didn't recognise you at Claire's funeral with your clothes on. I'd only ever seen you nude before. Well, that's what's always been in my mind whenever I've thought of you and seen your Facebook posts. You, nude.'

'I have never been nude in any of my Facebook posts I'll have you know. Facebook wouldn't allow it for a start.'

'No,' Janey giggled, 'but you know what I mean.'

'And what's more I had clothes on in the evenings,' Bobbie said, giving Janey a mock-offended look. 'Unless, of course, you were so rat-arsed you didn't notice.' Oh, God, what a crass comment. She doubted Janey had ever been rat-arsed in her life. Not with a husband like hers she hadn't because she'd have had to keep her wits about her, always. 'Sorry. Ought not to have made that glib comment.'

Janey waved it away.

'No worries. But I've often wondered why you did life modelling. I mean, you do the other sort all the time – I've seen you in *YOU* magazine and *Good Housekeeping* and other places – and it seems such a contrast.'

'It is. That's what I like. The contrast. When I'm modelling clothes, or bags, or shoes, or being part of a feature of some sort there are always people around talking nineteen to the dozen, poking me here, poking me there, telling me how to stand or sit, how to breathe, how to smile, and I can get more than a bit fed up with it. When I'm life modelling there's silence in the room as the students concentrate. I know I cease to be me to them and I'm just a body. I like that. It gives me the space to let my mind wander. To remember things. To wish for things.'

'What things?' Janey said.

'Oh, look, there's that cocktail bar I was telling you about. *PLAYERS*. We'll stop on the way back. And maybe pick up some boxes of fairy lights in that ticky-tacky shop next door. A house as big as Lissy's could always use another set of lights, I should think. More is more and all that.'

Bobbie was more than glad of the diversion. There were lots of things Janey need never know about her. Things she didn't want her – or anyone, for that matter – to know.

'And besides, back to the life modelling topic, it pays well. A mews house in London, just your proverbial stone's throw from Marble Arch, doesn't come cheap. I've worked my butt off – quite literally sometimes – to get it and I intend to hang onto it.'

'Yeah, yeah,' Janey laughed. 'I bet you have! Have you paid for it *all* on your own? Has there never been anyone in your life – a man – to share all that?'

'Nor a woman either,' Bobbie said. 'And that's all I'm saying on the subject. This trip out was supposed to be all about *you*, not me. Come on. It's Christmas Eve and we don't want this art shop to be closed by the time we get there, do we?'

Then, linking her arm through Janey's, Bobbie quickened their pace.

And I'm going to have to accept that maybe I've got to the age when walking a couple of miles in stiletto boots isn't the best idea I have when I wake up in the morning. Bobbie's insteps and her calves were beginning to throb.

Chapter 17

Lissy

'Phew! Made it! They're still open,' Xander said as he drove his lorry into the Christmas Tree Farm and it bumped and rolled over the tracks, tossing Lissy this way and that, falling into Xander at one stage before she was able to pull herself upright again.

Lissy hadn't known there was even one here. 'Established 1985', it said on a board by the gate. But then, she'd only ever spent a couple of Christmases with Vonny after her husband, George, had died, and she couldn't remember there being a Christmas tree in the house then.

'Three, I think,' Lissy said. 'One very big one for the hall. One a sort of middling size for the sitting room, and a smaller one on the top landing. Something to greet us when we get out of our beds tomorrow.'

Xander had fetched a large box of Christmas tree decorations from his house – decorations that had been his and Claire's. He was happy for her to have them for Strand House he'd said. She could keep them, he'd said, and Lissy wondered if he'd really meant that or was just putting a brave face on things. She, and

Janey and Bobbie, were constant reminders of the fourth corner of the friendship that was missing, weren't they?

'Will you have enough decorations for three?' Xander asked. 'This is your typical builder, who knows how many bricks and planks of wood he needs to finish a project, talking of course. I'm not being a bossy bloke, in case that's what you're thinking.'

'I'm thinking no such thing,' Lissy said. And she wasn't. She was thinking only how nice it was sitting beside Xander, feeling safe and more than a little happy, as they trundled along in their own little world. She had a hunch Xander felt the same because he kept turning his head to look at her and smiled although he hadn't said much on the drive up from the sea front. 'But there'll be plenty. I found two boxfuls that were Vonny's in a cupboard in the laundry room. We could always buy some more, though, if you think we need them.'

'We?' Xander said, just a hint of a question in the word, as he turned to grin at her. 'Here we are.'

Lissy and Xander were told by the proprietor to walk around and see which trees they liked best. He gave them some bits of yellow ribbon to tie on to whichever ones took their fancy so they could find them again easily, and then the proprietor would come along with his mini tractor and his cutting equipment and take them out for them.

'I had no idea it was so vast up here,' Lissy said. 'We could be in Switzerland, couldn't we?'

'Or Austria,' Xander said. 'Parts of the US look like this as well. So I'm told. Not that I've ever been. Have you?'

'Austria once, when I was about seven,' Lissy told him. 'With my parents. *When* they were still together.'

'Ooh,' Xander said, pulling a face as though he'd just sucked on lemons 'There was acid in that comment.'

Lissy chose not to respond. She walked on ahead of Xander instead of beside him as she had been. Yes, it still wrankled that her mother had left her father and all the heartache that had caused, but Xander didn't need to hear it.

'You can see Haytor very clearly from here,' she said, pointing. 'Oh, all the bigger trees are down there. How tall a tree do we want?' She began hurrying down the slope towards the taller trees, stopping in front of a tree so tall she had to crane her neck to see the top of it.

'Your ceilings are about twelve feet high. So, the builder in me used to measurements and making things dovetail fit tells me you'll need one about ten feet.' He took a retractable tape from the pocket of his jacket, extended it, and held the end – in a rather wobbly fashion – as near the top of the tree as he could get it. 'Never travel without one of these.' He turned to Lissy, quite serious-faced, she thought, given the quip.

'I'm glad now you don't,' she said. She'd quite forgotten to check how high a tree she'd need for the hall.

'This one should do it,' Xander said, checking his measurements. 'If you're going to put a fairy on the top.'

'Definitely a fairy,' Lissy laughed. 'I'll tie a bit of yellow around this one and then look for the smaller two.'

'Not too small,' Xander said. 'All your ceilings are the same height so a tiddler would look a bit lost. Oh, God, hark at me telling you what to do. Forget I said that. It's a bloke thing, thinking we know best always. That's what my mum and old Eve next door tell me all the time anyway. Sorry.'

'Sorry? What for? For giving me the benefit of your experience?'

'Your house, your trees, Lissy,' Xander said. 'But thanks for the compliment. I've got duct tape also in my jacket pocket. Perhaps I need to use a bit across my mouth so I don't come over all bloke-bossy.'

Lissy couldn't help a bubble of laughter escaping.

'You took a brave step agreeing to have Christmas with three women you hardly know and ...'

'I know *you*,' Xander said. He swallowed hard. 'I know we shared a dance and how it made me feel having you in my arms, and ...'

'I remember that too,' Lissy said. 'We could have, you know ...'

'Kissed?' Xander said.

'That,' Lissy said, feeling nervous now. 'But we didn't. So we're not carrying any guilt on that score, are we?'

'No.'

Lissy put her top teeth down over her bottom lip and pressed hard. Xander was standing on the rise of the hill and she below him. All of her ached to follow that moment through to what could have been its ultimate conclusion, right now, in the middle of a pine plantation, when she had two friends waiting for her back at Strand House, and a million things to do before Christmas Day. Lissy hadn't expected those feelings to resurface, surprised at the depth of them.

'It comes to me in dreams sometimes,' she finished almost in a whisper. 'That moment. What might have been. But wasn't.' She wasn't sure this was the place to follow that feeling through. Then she raised her voice and said, 'One tree down, two to go.' She could hear a tractor being started up over by the shed where the trees got put into green netting carrying sacks. 'I think they're waiting to shut up shop.'

'Whatever you say, Lissy,' Xander said. 'But I hope that wasn't the big brush off. I've got one of those – a brush – on the lorry.'

Again, Lissy got that bubble of laughter inside her, making her stomach flutter.

'Of course it wasn't,' Lissy told him. She began to walk back towards the smaller trees, knowing Xander would follow. 'Still not our time perhaps?' she said turning back to look at him and Xander shrugged and pulled a mock-sad face. She got the feeling their time would come though. This was all getting a bit deep a bit too soon maybe. A change of subject was required now, for both of them. 'There are decorations in the shop, so the man said. I might choose a few more to go with the ones we've already got.'

'The ones we've already got,' Xander repeated behind her and Lissy realised that was the second time she'd used the word 'we'. Perhaps her sub-conscious was telling her something?

'I've got some large buckets on the lorry,' Xander said when they got back to Strand House. 'And a couple of bags of gravel. The trees will stand up better in that than they will mud.' He hoiked the larger tree off the back of the lorry. 'I'll get this one in first, then the others, then I'll sort the buckets. Could I come over all bossy bloke again and ask you to put the kettle on while I do it?'

'You could,' Lissy said, finding her key. Far from thinking he'd been given the brush off it seemed that Xander was more comfortable with Lissy than before they'd gone up to fetch the Christmas trees. That, Lissy told herself, as she let them in, was a good feeling. 'Come on through to the kitchen when you're ready. Or I could bring it out to you if you prefer?'

'Best not stop the workers,' Xander said. 'I'll drink it in the hall while I work.'

'Best not!' Lissy laughed.

She walked on towards the kitchen, listening out for sounds that Bobbie and Janey might be back. She couldn't hear them and her heart gave a little whoop of joy that they weren't. She hoped they were having a good time in town, she really did, although it would be noisy and busy, and full of light and colour, along with the Festive atmosphere. But she was glad she wasn't there, and that it was just her and Xander for a while yet, if not for long. The light was beginning to drop now, and it would be dark soon.

'Ladder?' Xander said when she got back with the tea. 'I know I'm tall but even I'm not going to be able to reach the top of this tree to plonk the fairy on it.'

He had the tree in a huge builders' bucket that had bits of cement stuck all over it, and was pouring in gravel from a big bag, holding it as though it was feathers he was pouring it in.

'In the laundry room. One of those A-frame things. Vonny used to scare me half to death climbing it to change lightbulbs sometimes. Will that do?'

'Perfect. Show me to it.'

Lissy put the tea down on the hall table.

'Follow me. I'll be getting on with some mince-pie-making while you get the ladder,' Lissy threw back over her shoulder as Xander followed her through to the kitchen and the laundry room.

He fetched the ladder and was gone again while Lissy found a bowl and the ingredients for mince pies. She made them the way Vonny had always made them, with a teensy bit of cream cheese on top of the filling, and some flaked almonds on the pastry lid, letting the flaked almonds catch a little to give them an even nuttier, smoked, taste. The sausage rolls she intended to make were Vonny's recipe too – ordinary sausage meat mixed with a grated apple, some finely-sliced spring onions, and chopped sage. Rough puff pastry. Sausage rolls and mince pies after the candlelit Christmas Eve service up at St Paul's was the tradition. Lissy would go out of respect to Vonny who had always gone although she wouldn't force the others to.

And it was as though Vonny was with her still as she made them. She could hear Xander out in the hall seeing to the Christmas trees. There was a bit of banging going on and a bit of cursing now and then as something obviously hadn't gone the way he'd wanted it to. He was singing snatches of songs but nothing all the way through. And humming – he hummed a lot.

'Put a CD in if you want to,' Lissy shouted through to him

'Don't you like my singing?' he shouted back.

Lissy went to the doorway and leaned against the jamb studying him for a moment. He'd taken off his shoes and was padding about in his socks. The largest and the middle-sized trees were in their pots and he was turning the smallest tree this way and that, sliding it around on the floor to check he'd set it squarely in the middle. He looked, Lissy was surprised to even be thinking, as though he belonged there. But did she? Would she keep Strand House after this Christmas break? Looking at the scene in front of her it would be a crime not to, wouldn't it?

'Love it,' Lissy told him making him jump because her voice was closer to him now. 'Just thought we could have it all Christmassy in here for when the other two get back. They should be here soon.'

'Hmm,' Xander said. 'I thought they'd be back by now. The light's quite gone. Hope they're not lost. Or that Janey's scumbag husband hasn't turned up and there's been trouble.'

'Oh, God,' Lissy said. 'I'd quite forgotten that might happen. You don't think ...'

And with that the door opened and Janey and Bobbie stood in the open doorway, red-cheeked, arms full of bags, and smiling.

'Mmm,' Bobbie said, taking a deep breath and holding it. 'It's beginning to look like Christmas in here.'

'And feel like it. Very like it,' Janey said.

'We thought,' Lissy said, 'we'd wait until you both got back before we decorate the trees.'

There it was again, that 'we', although she hadn't discussed such a thing with Xander.

'So we did,' Xander said, grinning at her.

He'd been in implicated in her fib and he hadn't minded a bit.

'We come bearing gifts,' Bobbie said. 'And before you start reminding me about the no presents rule, Lissy, these gifts are for the house. Boxes of Christmas tree lights, practically given away in one of those ticky-tacky shops in town. The tripper shops, I mean. We thought the house deserved a present didn't we?'

'Oh, that's so nice,' Lissy said. Everything in the house had been Vonny's. All beautiful and tasteful and stylish, but hers. She hadn't even brought so much as a cushion herself to make it her own. Bobbie, with her gift for the house, was making her think she'd have to think of a way she could keep it now.

'Well, I'll leave you to it,' Bobbie said, handing the bag with the fairy lights to Lissy. 'If I don't go and put my feet up for half an hour they're going to drop off! I hope no one's going to fall out about it?'

No one had fallen out about anything yet but these things sometimes happen when people – especially people who barely know one another – were thrown together for any length of time. Lissy hadn't given a thought as to what she might do if that happened.

'Of course we're not,' she told Bobbie. 'Take as long as you like. We won't be eating until about eight o'clock. I've got soup and then quiche and salad followed by a trifle for dinner.'

'Yum,' Janey said.

'Are we,' Bobbie said, unzipping a boot and pulling it off over her foot, 'dressing for dinner?' In one swift moment she'd dealt with the other boot.

'Are we?' Janey asked. She looked stricken.

'Bloody hell, I hope not,' Xander told her. 'I'm saving my best for tomorrow.'

Was this the moment Lissy hadn't even thought about? Was there going to be a falling out between them or, at the very least, a clash of interests? It happened, even amongst the best of friends, sometimes. Bobbie obviously lived in different circles and played to different rules from the rest of them.

'It's not a country house weekend, Bobbie,' Lissy said as brightly and as politely as she could.

Lissy left Janey and Xander hanging decorations on the tree, Janey doing the lower branches and Xander on the ladder doing the top. They were going to add two more strings of lights now that Bobbie had bought some.

She went upstairs, tapped gently on Bobbie's bedroom door. She waited a few seconds and when there was no answer she tapped again, a little louder this time. Perhaps Bobbie had fallen asleep?

But then the door opened and Bobbie stood before her, looking a lot shorter and more vulnerable somehow in her stockinged feet.

'Can I come in?'

For answer Bobbie opened the door wider, then shutting it behind Lissy when she stepped inside.

The two women stood facing one another and neither spoke for a moment.

Bobbie took a couple of steps backwards and held out her hands in supplication towards Lissy.

'I know. I know. I'm sorry. It was a throwaway remark. A rotten attempt at humour. I wouldn't have wanted to upset anyone by saying what I did. I should have kept my trap shut. I've been putting my foot in it all afternoon with Janey. I actually asked her if she'd been rat-arsed. With a husband like she's got, what was I thinking?'

Bobbie looked genuinely contrite, her words coming out in girly, tumbly, rushes. Lissy thought Bobbie could be dangerously close to tears. And this close up, Lissy noticed more lines beside her eyes than she'd noticed before, even though they were heavily kholed, with – possibly – more eyeliner than Lissy had ever owned.

Lissy moved towards her, held out her arms and then gave her a brief hug – which Bobbie didn't return, so she moved away a few inches. Perhaps she was uncomfortable having her personal space invaded. She tried to remember if there had been hugs and kisses on parting after the art workshop weekend but couldn't.

'It's okay. We all say things we shouldn't sometimes. Our

mouths go ahead of our brains a bit. Well, mine does. But I haven't come up here to tear you off a strip if that's what you're thinking. I've come to apologise. My response was snippy in the extreme. Country house weekend indeed! I'm getting ideas above my station with this house, I think.'

'Who wouldn't?' Bobbie laughed. 'The second I saw it from the back seat of the taxi rising so large and imposing in front of me my mind was fast-forwarding to cocktails on the terrace, and walking down a staircase dressed to the nines for dinner. I don't know where you've lived until now but I'm betting it's nowhere near as big as this and that this is also the most wonderful surprise.'

'You always dress to the nines, Bobbie,' Lissy said. 'And yes, it was – is – the most wonderful surprise. I have to keep pinching myself so I know I'm not dreaming.'

'Well, dream on a bit. But back to basics, if you haven't come up to tear me off a strip, how can I help?'

'You can dress for dinner for a start, if it makes you happy. I'll probably change out of these clothes I wore to go trudging around a pine plantation looking for Christmas trees, and baking sausage rolls and mince pies when I got back.'

Lissy looked around the room. There wasn't a single thing out of place. Bobbie's bag was on the bed but apart from that everything had been put away; all the wardrobe doors neatly shut, all the drawers tightly closed, so she'd taken no time in hanging up her coat and putting away her hat and her boots, had she? She didn't have a hair out of place either and Lissy would have bet the contents of her bank account that that was a fresh lick of fuchsia lipstick on Bobbie's lips too. Did Bobbie ever look less than her immaculate best? Did she ever let her guard down? Lissy was pretty certain now that Bobbie had a guard.

'I've had a bit of a nap,' Bobbie said, 'and I'll come and help you. There must be still loads to do for tomorrow. Not that I know the first thing about hosting Christmas because I've had Christmas lunch in a restaurant for decades!'

'No need. I'm on top of things,' Lissy told her. 'But thanks. There is something you can do though.'

'Anything,' Bobbie said. 'I'm a bit of a freeloader here at the moment!'

'You're not! Honestly. But the thing is I'd like you to help me to help Janey if you can. She told me she's brought hardly anything with her and I told her I had things of Vonny's here that would probably fit. Well, they will fit, but they're far too old-fashioned for her. A bit drab in colour. I'm a size or two bigger than Janey so my things would swamp her.'

'You're hardly big,' Bobbie said. 'But you're right. Janey's rail thin. A size eight, I'd say. I'm a ten these days, alas and alack.' Bobbie pulled a mock sad-but-resigned face. 'I'll take a look and see if there's anything that will suit.'

Bobbie padded over to the wardrobe and threw wide the double doors.

'Good grief!' Lissy laughed. 'I've seen fewer things on the racks in Monsoon!'

'Which is where a fair bit of this has come from,' Bobbie said. 'Here, how about this?'

Bobbie pulled out a taupe-coloured skirt on a hanger. It seemed to have a lot of material in it gathered at the waist, and a wide waistband with a large faux bow on the front. Lissy wouldn't have minded that one for herself but could hardly say so.

'It's got slight elastication on the waist.' Bobbie put her fingers in the waistband to demonstrate.

'Looks perfect to me,' she said.

'It'll be nearer calf-length on Janey than just below the knee as it is on me, but the fullness will be good on her, I think. There's a navy and taupe striped jumper in the drawer she can wear with it. Boat neck, three quarter sleeves.'

Bobbie brought the skirt over to the bed and laid it down as gently as one would a baby, Lissy thought.

'What about shoes?' Bobbie asked. 'I'm a seven.'

'Fives,' Lissy said. 'I took a sneaky look in her shoes just now after she took them off in the hall when she came in. Janey wears a five so I'm certain there'll be something of mine that will fit. She's only got the loafers she came in, I think.'

'What a team we are!' Bobbie said.

'Yeah, but just wondering how I'm going to broach this. I feel sure Janey would like to dress up but I don't want to appear like a charity.'

'I shouldn't worry about that,' Bobbie said. 'We're all here for Christmas on your charity.'

'Don't say that. You're my guests. My friends. People I've chosen to spend time with ...'

'Oh God, me and my big mouth again,' Bobbie said. 'But why not leave Janey to me? We were getting on really well in town. I felt she was relaxing more than I thought she would given the events of yesterday and what she's got coming ahead over her once we've all packed away the tinsel and the mince pie tins and the rest of it. I think she's getting use to my, um, forthright ways.'

Yes, and I need to get used to those as well because I'm being a bit thin-skinned here, Janey thought. *The nervous hostess maybe? Or the nearness of Xander? That little bit of shared past almost-naughtiness?*

Lissy felt herself flush at the thought of him and how she'd have liked to have stayed leaned against him when the lorry had rocked and rolled on the track at the Christmas tree farm.

'Yes,' she said. 'You might be the better person to offer the clothes to Janey.' She put hands to her cheeks which seemed to be glowing now. 'Gosh, but it's a bit warm in here. You can turn the central heating down if it's too hot for you.'

'Ha ha,' Bobbie said. 'I might be cabbage-looking but I'm not green. Those rosy crab-apples of yours have nothing to do with the central heating and everything to do with something you were thinking about. Something naughty. I could tell. You had a faraway look in your eyes then. Hmm?'

'Golly, Bobbie,' Lissy said, grinning at her. 'What a vivid imagination you have!' She walked to the door, then turned around and said, 'I'll send Janey up, shall I?'

She didn't wait for a response but hurried on down the stairs.

Chapter 18

Bobbie

'Lissy did say we could help ourselves to drinks, didn't she?' Bobbie said.

She came into the sitting room and closed the door behind her. Xander was winding a string of lights around the sitting room Christmas tree. He'd finished the one for the landing because that had been outside when she and Janey had sorted what clothes Janey wanted to borrow. Well, not *wanted* exactly, but Bobbie had been able to persuade her that she was on the cusp of a new life so why shouldn't clothes she'd never have considered wearing before be part of that life? Janey had taken them to her room and was now helping Lissy in the kitchen. Janey had probably seen enough of her for now which was why Bobbie had decided to join Xander in the sitting room. Besides, she'd not spent much time with him alone.

'That was yesterday,' Xander laughed. 'But I don't think for a minute she'll throw you out if you do.'

'I don't suppose she will. She needs us here, I think, as much as we – well I – need her. She'd rattle around in here on her own. Some of the rooms have got an echo they're so big.'

'I noticed that,' Xander said. 'Probably the hard flooring. Ceramic tiles. Parquet.'

'And the stripped boards in the bedrooms. Well, there is in mine. Rugs, as lovely as the ones in this house are, don't really soak up much sound.' Bobbie walked over to the dresser where bottles stood on silver trays. Glasses, up-ended, were on a folded tea-towel beside them. 'Are you joining me? Whisky? G&T? I see Lissy's put out some cans of Fever Tree.'

'Not for the moment, thanks. Despite what people might think, not all builders drink pints to cool down. Besides, Lissy will probably serve wine later. That'll do me.'

'What do you build, then?' Bobbie asked. She'd poured herself a G&T – no lemon she noticed but beggars couldn't be choosers – and went and sat in the middle of the largest couch to admire Xander's handiwork with the Christmas tree decoration. Very artistic as it happened.

'Extensions. I do a lot of those. People like to enlarge a kitchen downstairs and then put a bedroom on top while they're at it. Squeeze in a downstairs loo if I can fit it in and it doesn't contravene building regulations and has the required number of closing doors so it's hygienic. Fitted kitchens. Garden walls. Flights of steps. Anything anyone wants really.'

'Right,' Bobbie said. 'So, let's have a flight of imagination here, Xander, and say Strand House were yours, what improvements would you make?'

'Have you been reading my mind or something?' Xander laughed.

'Might have,' Bobbie said. She took a sip of her G&T – a double but who was counting? 'But quite possibly not reading the things you think I am.'

'Meaning?' Xander said.

Meaning that I am picking up on the fact you are falling in love with Lissy even if you don't realise it yourself yet. And she with you.

112

The air positively crackled between them sometimes when they looked at one another or brushed in passing.

Bobbie shrugged.

'A woman has to keep a bit of mystery. So, back to the building. What improvements could you part Lissy from her cash over?'

'Look, Bobbie,' Xander said. He put down the box of silver stars he'd been hanging and turned, fully, to face her. 'I don't know what sort of bloke you think I am but that thought – parting Lissy from her cash – has never entered my head. Yes, this is a very valuable house, as is just about everything in it. I have no designs, no designs whatsoever, on it. Okay?'

Oh God, she was doing it again. First Janey, then Lissy, and now Xander.

'Sorry. I can't stop opening my mouth and putting my foot in it today. It's a bit of a lame excuse but I'm feeling a bit stressed at the moment. It wasn't easy offering someone clothes. I didn't want Janey to be insulted by the offer, but we all know she came with next to nothing. I'll take a big swig of this drink and come and help you with that tree.'

'We're all feeling a bit stressed in our own ways, I think,' Xander told her. He reached for a box of decorations he'd put on a footstool beside the couch Bobbie was sitting on. 'Take this. This is one Claire bought the Christmas before she died.'

He held up a glass angel about three inches high. It glittered in his hand under the overhead light. There was a lump in Bobbie's throat thinking about that.

'An angel,' she said.

'I don't believe for one minute that's what she is, though,' Xander said. He came and sat on the arm of the couch.

'She had her faults?' Bobbie asked. She got the overwhelming feeling that Xander needed to talk and perhaps, her being older, he would find it easier.

'Plenty,' Xander said. 'As we all do.' He was turning the glass angel over and over in his hand and it seemed to Bobbie as though shards of light were being emitted from it, like lasers.

'You can tell me if you think it might, well, help. No one's expected you to get over losing Claire in five minutes.' She wondered if Xander might be referring to the baby issue he'd mentioned at supper the night before but didn't want to ask.

'Thanks.' Xander waved his free hand around the room and said, 'She'd have had this place trashed in no time. Messy, that was Claire. Housework was so not her thing. Or cooking. If I didn't investigate the laundry bin now and then the stuff would have been up over the top and making its own way to the washing machine. And she got a bit wrapped up in her fitness classes as well. Three a day sometimes. She was working her way up to being paranoid about what she ate because she was so conscious of putting on too much weight which wouldn't have been a good look for the business she ran, would it?'

Ah. Xander was waiting for an answer here, wasn't he? Bobbie knew all about not wanting to eat – not even so much as a lettuce leaf sometimes – in case she put on a nano-gram and lost a booking for being overweight.

Xander wouldn't want to hear all that, would he?

'But you loved her?'

'Yes. Unreservedly. But I think,' Xander said, back now to turning the glass angel over and over in his hand as though he was glad he had something to do, 'Claire must have told her parents things I thought were just between us. Or told her mother anyway. I could get cross sometimes about Claire's messiness and I'm not proud of that now. Her parents have barely spoken to me since she died. It's like Claire had never done a thing wrong in her life and I've become the baddy because I didn't look after her well enough and she was killed.'

'Xander,' Bobbie said, getting up. This was all getting a bit heavy. 'I am going to get you a drink whether you want one or not. You only need to sip it. I need another anyway.'

She poured a Scotch for Xander and topped up her glass with gin, then came and sat back down.

'I liked Claire,' Bobbie said. 'I liked her very much from the get-go. She was full of fun and so beautiful. She had such a dirty laugh, didn't she?'

'Oh, God, yes. Yes to all of that.'

Xander took the Scotch from Bobbie and sipped at it.

'I didn't know her well enough to comment with any authority but I will say this … from the benefit of having a few more summers under my belt than you have and, probably, having been around the block a few more times. When people die young – think Marilyn Monroe, Judy Garland, Princess Diana, and for the blokes, JFK – they tend to achieve some sort of sainthood in the eyes of the public. They never got old or fat or ugly – well, maybe Judy Garland went to seed a bit, but the others didn't. And it was all about the voice with Judy, not the looks, I'd say. Anyway, they remain in people's minds as they were in their heyday, beautiful and talented. Claire's parents will have that sort of mindset about it all.'

'Yeah, yeah, you're probably right.'

'And what remains in people's minds, long after the people they love or admire have gone, is the youth and the beauty, and the future that was snatched away, leaving only sadness and the sheer bloody unfairness of it all.' Bobbie took a deep breath. In for a penny, in for a pound. 'And then, added to all that, is the fact – in Claire's case – she didn't make them grandparents. Most people hold a lot of store by that.'

'And they're blaming me for that?' Xander said. He looked stricken.

'I'm not saying they are, but they could be. Especially if, as you said, Claire used to talk to them about personal stuff. But you can take it from me, you are not to blame for anything. It takes two to tango.'

Xander spluttered into his Scotch.

115

'Christ, Bobbie,' he said, 'but you have one hell of a way with words!'

'Not always the right ones or in the right order though.'

'Those will do for me,' Xander told her. 'Thank you.' He leaned down and kissed Bobbie on top of her head. I'm glad you're here.'

'Me too,' Bobbie said, relieved she hadn't offended Xander by anything she'd said although she'd have stood by her reasons for saying it. If, Bobbie had always believed, people share their intimate feelings with you then they have to be prepared to hear the truth sometimes.

'Claire talked a lot about you after that weekend. She was in awe of you, I think. She said although she was body conscious and body aware she'd never have been able to take her kit off in front of people. Especially ...' Xander put a hand to his mouth.

'At my age,' Bobbie finished for him.

'You'd still get wolf-whistles from my lads,' Xander said.

'Which are a bit sexist these days, but I'm not likely to be bringing a prosecution against anyone if they did. Shall we get this tree finished, now we've sweated all the heavy stuff?'

'Yeah, best had,' Xander said.

He put down his now empty glass and went and hung the little glass angel at the top of the tree.

Good. Bobbie liked to think by hanging it there he was letting Claire go a little bit more. Well, not letting go, but making a bit of space for someone else to come into his heart.

The door opened then and Lissy came in, stopping with the door frame making it look as though she was the subject of a painting, Bobby thought. Lissy had changed for dinner, dressed now in the most amazing pair of wide-legged dog rose pink trousers and a creamy satin blouse. She'd piled her hair on top of her head and stuck some sort of diamante ornament in it. Bobbie heard Xander's deep intake of breath at the glorious sight of her. Well, well, she'd been right – Xander was on the point of letting someone else in. He just needed a bit of help to do it.

'Hope I'm not disturbing anything,' Lissy said.

'Nothing I wouldn't do or say in front of a vicar,' Bobbie said, and Xander laughed.

'Good, good. Only I'm thinking we could eat in the hall underneath the chandelier. With the tree looking stunning reflecting in all the mirrors it's the perfect place. Less formal than the dining room, not as casual as the kitchen. I'll need a bit of help carrying the table in though. Good idea or not? What do you think?'

'I think it's your house. Your decision,' Bobbie said.

'Xander?' Lissy asked.

'I think, Lissy,' Xander said, 'you are utterly, utterly amazing in every way.'

Chapter 19

Janey

'It's me,' Janey said, the second her sister, Suzy, answered the call. She kept her voice low. The others were down in the hall setting up the table ready for supper and she'd escaped to change into the clothes Bobbie had loaned her. And ring Suzy. Someone had just put 'Do you think they know it's Christmas' in the CD player.

'Where the hell are you?'

'I can't say.'

'Why not? Are you in trouble?'

'No.'

Troubles don't go away just because it's Christmas, was on the tip of Janey's tongue but she couldn't say it.

'What then?'

Janey hadn't thought through what she was going to say next. She was still thinking about it when Suzy said, 'Oh, I can hear music. Are you in a bar?'

'No.'

'Well, wherever it is come back. Stuart's making our lives hell here, ringing every hour or so – day and bloody night.'

'Has he been over?'

118

'What do you think? Any more points for drink-driving and he'd lose his licence, right? And probably his job as well once the school found out. But as it's the holidays and there's no school he'll be drunk, as per usual. Don't tell me that whatever's got into your head with all this madness you've forgotten that little item of importance? I wonder sometimes how well you know that man, Janey.'

Gosh, but her sister was cross, and Janey knew she had to take some of the blame for that because she hadn't informed her at all about what she'd done.

'Too well.'

'That's up for debate,' Suzy said. 'What isn't in question, is that Gary's getting more than fed up.'

So, Stuart had been in touch. Nice of Suzy to contact her – *not*. Janey was hurt that her sister hadn't called to to see how she was, seeing as she'd known for years what Stuart was like. She decided to give her sister the benefit of the doubt. It was, after all, Christmas and Suzy had a lot to do.

'What's he been telling you?'

'Well, after he found out you're not here like you told him you were, he's been calling you all sorts of delete-expletive liars. He said you're having an affair. He said whoever it is must have a bloody big van or something because all your painting stuff had gone. He'd have trashed it if it hadn't.'

'Well, he won't be able to,' Janey said.

It was all safe enough with Fred and Annie, with Guinness on guard. And besides, Stuart hadn't spoken a word to either of them since the day, six years ago, that she and Stuart had moved in next door to them.

'That music's bloody loud, Janey,' Suzy grumbled. 'I can tell what's playing – 'Do you think they know it's Christmas'. Talking of which, it *is* Christmas. I'm guessing here you've left Stuart for person, or persons, unknown. What a time to leave anyone! Christmas!'

Yes, it was loud, and Janey had a hunch Lissy – or maybe one of the other two – had turned it up loud aware that she might be needing to phone home. Not that she was going to do that.

'Is there ever a right time?' Janey asked, suddenly feeling bold. The scales were falling from her eyes now. While she'd supported her sister over the years, buying things for her nieces and her nephew when Suzy couldn't afford to, and helping look after them for weeks on end when Suzy had been ill or simply been unable to cope, she hadn't had a lot of support in return. She needed it now but a few more scales fell off and a sadness, like a particularly wet and soggy woollen blanket, swamped her soul that maybe her sister wasn't going to be there for her in her hour of need.

The three people downstairs in Lissy's hall, happily setting up a table for Christmas Eve supper had given her more support in the past twenty-four hours than she could ever have thought they might.

What was it people said? You can choose your friends but you can't choose your family. A lump lodged in Janey's throat thinking about the little baby that had been Suzy and how she'd been like a second mother to her. What fun she'd had making dolls' house furniture for Suzy and how proud she'd been of her little sister when she'd taken her to school on her first day.

'I don't want to choose between you,' Janey said in a whisper. 'But you're making me.'

'Eh, what was that? What with that din going on wherever you are and the kids racing up the stairs in some mad game of Festive *Star Wars*, I didn't catch that.'

'I said, say Happy Christmas to everyone. I'll be in touch.'

And then Janey killed the call. She didn't know what she ought to be feeling. No one could tell her which was the right thing to be feeling, could they? But all she felt was blessed relief that she'd got away from Stuart. The skirt and jumper Bobbie had loaned her was laid out across her bed. And now there were some shoes stood neatly to attention beside it. Lissy had slipped in and left them for her.

Janey pulled off her socks, then got out of her clothes. She stood in front of the full-length mirror. The last lot of bruises Stuart had given her were looking less dark. She touched a finger to the one above her left breast – it had lost its purple lividness now and had a greeny-yellowish tinge; it had been why she'd had to refuse Lissy's offer of sharing a double room the night before – she couldn't risk Lissy seeing. She wouldn't have been able to face the shame that she'd let Stuart do that to her. *'No one can hurt you without your permission'*. Janey remembered seeing that once in the doctor's waiting room when she'd plucked up courage to go and ask for some help before she'd chickened out and asked the doctor instead for a prescription for migraines she didn't get.

'It doesn't hurt anymore,' she said to her reflection.

Stuart had been careless when the abuse had begun, giving her bruises that showed – her face, her arms in summer. He'd got cannier lately. But these were the last. The last! There weren't going to be any more. Not ever. From anyone. Didn't everyone know it was normal for people to repeat bad patterns? Well, not her. It had taken too long to come to this point and where she was going from here she really had no idea but she knew that one, or all, of the three friends downstairs would help and advise her. They were helping already.

She went over to the dresser and picked up one of the towels that Lissy had left for her. Lissy had also left some toiletries, quality stuff from the Body Shop.

'For sensitive skin,' Janey read.

Had she known all along? Or guessed?

Janey showered and dried her hair, dressed in Bobbie's clothes and Lissy's shoes but instead of feeling alien as she thought she might, when she looked in the mirror she saw only a woman who had forgotten how to be pretty, but was.

Chapter 20

Xander

Xander knew it was hopeless for him to consider competing – or even matching – the women for smartness at supper. They were all upstairs now putting finishing touches to whatever it was women put finishing touches to. He didn't think Lissy could perfect how she'd looked standing in the doorway asking him and Bobbie to help her move the table. His heart had missed a beat there.

So, he decided to go for the 'fun' element Lissy had hinted at about eating in the hall. It still looked pretty classy in there to him; the black-and-white tiles, the oversized mirrors on opposite walls, the floor to ceiling tree loaded to the gunwales with glittery bits, and the double-width staircase curving from one corner to the level above. Xander had been to a friend's wedding at one of the big hotels in Torquay and the foyer of that hadn't looked a million miles away from the one at Strand House.

'Right,' he said, opening and closing drawers in Lissy's kitchen. He'd dressed in black jeans and the tightest white T-shirt he owned. He'd given himself a centre parting, wetted down with a slick of styling gel he'd had in a Christmas present from his mother a couple of years ago, part of a set he'd not used until now. He considered finding something black to draw a moustache with above his top lip but decided against it in case it was more semi-permanent than he wanted it to be. And now he was looking for the biggest white tea towel he could find.

'Ah, got one.' He shook it out. It looked more like a starched small tablecloth than a tea towel but at least it was big enough to go around him. He didn't think Lissy would mind him borrowing it.

He could hear them coming as he tied it around his waist, picked up a tray – no time to find glasses or a bottle but they'd get the drift he was going to be waiter for the night – and hurried out into the hall.

They were coming down side by side, arms linked, Janey in the middle as though the other two had decided she needed a bit of support.

'You look … incredible,' he said as they all stepped onto the hall floor and burst into spontaneous giggles. 'All of you.'

'And you,' Bobbie laughed, 'look what the Irish would call a "right eejit".'

'No, he doesn't!' Janey laughingly remonstrated with her. 'He looks like that TV chef. The French one. What's his name? He's got a big garden. Well, him, in his younger days.'

Raymond Blanc. Xander knew which one Janey meant because his mother was a massive Raymond Blanc fan, watched all his programmes, had all his books, but was yet to cook a masterpiece from it. Certainly she'd never cooked anything from that, or anything else, that came anywhere near the deliciousness that Lissy was serving up. Not that he was going to risk his life by telling his mother that though.

'I'm grateful you mentioned the younger day bit,' Xander said.

He was waiting for Lissy to comment, but she looked like a rabbit caught in headlights, just standing there looking at him, sort of frozen to the spot with shock. But beautiful. He hadn't thought she could perfect how she'd looked when she'd stood in the doorway half an hour ago asking him to help move the table but she'd added some dangly earrings – crystal or something – and proved just how wrong he'd been. When Lissy made no attempt to move he wondered if, perhaps, he'd made a mistake taking the liberty of doing what he had.

'If you ladies would care to take your seats,' Xander said, desperate to break the ice a little, 'I'll fetch your drinks. As you see I'm new to this game and I've only managed to find the tray so far.'

With that, Lissy pulled away from Janey.

She walked over to Xander and linked her arm through his.

'You can't get the staff these days, can you?' she giggled, grinning up at him. Then she turned to Janey and Bobbie and said, 'It's his first night, girls, go easy on him. Sit where you like, we'll be back in a mo.'

'Don't rush it,' Xander heard Bobbie say as Lissy steered him towards the kitchen.

Schemer!

Lissy pulled the door to a little but didn't close it.

'Thanks,' she said, taking her arm from his and he wondered why he suddenly felt bereft. He'd liked the feel of it there, liked the closeness of her, the scent of her. 'I know she didn't say, and I know she's putting a huge face on it, but I could feel Janey shaking beside me. It can't be easy doing what she's done, then coming down to supper in a house she's never been in before and wearing someone else's clothes, so your mad antics have lightened the mood. None of us was expecting that.'

'I did it as much for you as Janey,' Xander said.

'Did you?'

'I just said.'

There was just a nanosecond of something between them. Some sort of understanding. Something that if one had leaned towards the other for a kiss then the other wouldn't have resisted. He'd had that feeling with Lissy before, hadn't he?

124

'Anyway,' Lissy said, the first to break the spell, 'there's a bit missing though. Hang on, I've got something here that will rectify matters.'

She went over to a drawer in the dresser beside the window and brought out a make-up bag. Xander knew what a make-up bag looked like. Claire had had at least half a dozen of them around the house and he was beginning to suspect Lissy did, too.

'I am not wearing lipstick if that's in your plan,' he said.

'Not that.'

She took out a mascara wand – Xander knew what one of those looked like, too – twisting off the lid.

'Stand still,' she said, coming to stand in front of him, so close. Oh, so deliciously close. 'Pouty mouth.'

It was all Xander could do not to put his arms around her, kiss her. Don't rush it, Bobbie had said. She'd be waiting for supper a long time if Xander were to follow his instincts right now. But maybe now wasn't the right time.

'Oooh ...' It was tickling like the very devil.

'And no talking,' Lissy said, as she drew a moustache. 'There. Perfect. There's a mirror on the windowsill above the sink.'

'I think I'm probably best not knowing!' Xander laughed. 'Now if you'll show me what needs to be brought to the table and in what order, I'll be waiter for the night.' He noticed it was all laid out on the long kitchen island anyway and he wouldn't have needed a BTEC in catering to work it out, but thought it best to ask.

'But you'll eat with us between courses,' Lissy said.

'If I'm invited.'

'Open invitation. Always.' Again that nanosecond of hesitation as though she wanted to say – or do – more but wasn't going to. 'There's a bottle of white chilling in the door of the fridge. Another in the rack in the larder. Red wine will need to be uncorked. Can you manage that?'

'Or die in the attempt,' Xander told her, struggling to look serious, get himself into waiter mode.

'There won't be any need for that. If you spill it all over our gorgeous selves I might need to rethink that, though.'

'You're a hard task-woman,' Xander said. 'I'll watch my step.'

'Glasses over there where you found them yesterday. Don't keep refilling mine because I'm intending to go to the candlelit service up at St Pauls.'

'Yes, ma'am. No ma'am,' Xander said. He gave a little bow, one hand behind his back. He'd seen someone do that on TV in a play once.

'The Reverend Mason would take a dim view of that. As would the rest of the congregation, many of whom will probably recognise me from when I went to church with Vonny when I stayed with her.'

The Reverend Mason? Xander had been really enjoying this bit of play-acting with Lissy and he knew she was enjoying it too. But the vicar's name brought him right back down to earth. Right back to the past. The Reverend Mason had officiated at Claire's funeral. At St Pauls. He hadn't been inside the place since.

What if Lissy asked him to join her? Would he go? Could he go?

'Yes, I expect the Reverend Mason would,' Xander said. 'But I'll rustle up my best waiting skills to make sure that doesn't happen, ma'am.' He picked up the tray. 'Now if you'd like to take your place at table I'll be with you all shortly.'

He had a fun evening to get through, an evening he had taken the liberty of suggesting, so he was going to do what Janey was doing and put a brave face on it. He'd worry about being back at St Pauls if he had to.

Chapter 21

Lissy

'Vaseline, Xander,' Bobbie said. 'Wonderful for getting make-up off that's stuck a bit. I've got some upstairs, I'll go and get it. We'll have you back to your normal handsome, macho self in no time.'

'God, I hope so,' Lissy giggled as Bobbie went upstairs, although if she were honest she quite liked the seven o'clock shadow look the smudged mascara was giving Xander.

Janey had excused herself after supper saying she was going to have a rest until Lissy and Xander came back from the candlelit service at St Paul's because she'd had a long day, and laughed so much her stomach ached. Xander had taken on a terrible French accent and they'd all laughed their way through supper.

Xander had rubbed a hot, wet flannel over his gelled hair and got rid of his French waiter's centre parting, but soap and water had failed to remove the dark shadow of his faux moustache.

'If it doesn't work, Lissy,' Xander said, 'it doesn't matter. I'll still come to church with you.'

'Sure?' Lissy was having misgivings now. How she'd forgotten that Claire's funeral had been at St Paul's she couldn't imagine, unless it was being caught up in all the Christmas preparations and her friend coming to stay.

'Positive,' Xander said. 'It's a candlelit service, right? It's hardly going to be spotlight bright.'

'No, no it's not,' Lissy said, although that wasn't what she meant by her question.

Bobbie came back then and set to work with the Vaseline removing the mascara moustache. Then it was a mad rush to find a torch so Lissy and Xander could use the public footpath that ran from the end of the cul-de-sac up to the tip of the headland, and across the railway bridge. It was only five minutes then to the main road and the church.

'I've never been up here at night,' Xander said, as they hurried along. Xander had taken Lissy's arm and threaded it through his. A gentlemanly gesture in the dark.

'Not many do I don't think,' Lissy said. She had the torch in her other hand, shining it from side to side on the path as they walked. 'I used to sometimes. I like the darkness of it with no street lights or houses once you pass Strand House. I like it when it's a clear sky and the moon is so bright you could read a book almost.' And then, before she thought about what she was saying, 'I brought Cooper here once but he couldn't wait to get back to Vonny's,' came tumbling out of her mouth like a dam breaking almost. Cooper was in her background just as Claire was in Xander's.

Xander put his hand on Lissy's where it rested on his arm.

'You don't mention him much,' he said.

'No. I don't know why I did now.'

'Memories, of whatever sort, are just that and that was one of yours I reckon. I'm guessing your divorce was acrimonious?'

'A shock really. Acrimonious come the end. Cooper asked for it. He'd found someone else. Blamed me that I'd pushed him to it for all sorts of stupid reasons. The fact I earn more than he does was one of them. He even tried to claim part of my earnings in the settlement, but I was able to pay for a good solicitor and he lost that little battle.'

'God. Really? I'm so sorry. That must have been hard to take,' Xander said. He patted Lissy's hand in a 'there-there-everything-will-be-all-right' sort of way. 'It's a well-known fact that people find it easier to blame someone else rather than accept their own bad behaviour. Tell me to mind my own and stop asking questions if you like but how did he take the fact you've inherited Strand House?'

'It's okay, I don't mind you asking. I brought his name up. And the answer is he doesn't know yet. Well, I haven't told him. But seeing as we were divorced before Vonny died and I inherited then he can't do a thing about it. Before that and he'd probably have got half.'

'That's a mercy, then,' Xander said. 'End of subject or do you want to talk some more about Cooper?'

'End of subject!' Lissy said. 'Definitely.'

'Right, turnstile coming up,' Xander said. He gently removed Lissy's hand from the crook of his elbow. 'I'll go first, shall I?'

'Okay. But you do know the tradition of turnstiles, don't you?'

'Nope. What would that be, then?'

Lissy took a deep breath. She knew exactly what she was going to say.

'The folklore name for them is a kissing gate, and you have to kiss in a turnstile. For luck. That whoever you kiss going through a turnstile you will come with this way again.'

Her arm through Xander's and his hand on hers and the near-ness of him in the dark – just the two of them under the moon and the stars – was making Lissy more relaxed, happier, than she had in a long time. Making her bold. This was the twenty-first century, for goodness' sake, and women could make the running if they wanted to. And she'd just told Xander all he needed to know about Cooper – he was out of her life and she was a free agent once again. She'd dealt with her personal elephant in the room.

'Ah, a kissing gate. Is that so?'

'Yes. So folklore has it.'

'And we, Lissy, have a service to get to and we're never going to make it if I stop to kiss you now.'

Xander stepped ahead of her, then swung the gate across so Lissy could step in.

'Not that I don't want to,' Xander said.

Lissy stepped on through, feeling a little foolish now. Perhaps that second glass of wine at supper had been a glass too much? She noticed Xander had merely sipped at the one glass he'd poured himself.

Xander took Lissy's hand as she stepped out of the turnstile.

'I've got a ghost to lay tonight, Lissy. I haven't been in St Paul's since, well, since the last time we were both there; you and me and a lot of other people. For the first year after Claire died I wouldn't even drive past it. I'd drive two miles around just to avoid looking at it.'

'You don't have to go now,' Lissy said.

'Yes, I do,' Xander said, quickening his pace, guiding Lissy along with him. 'Little by little I've been letting Claire go. St Paul's has been a bad memory for me and it wasn't her fault, and it isn't yours. This isn't a step back for me, though, in case you're wondering, it's a step forward. Moving on. Understand?'

Yes, Lissy thought, she understood. Xander was trying to tell her he was ready to move on now. Ready to begin a new relationship, and with her perhaps. God, but she hoped so.

'Besides,' Xander said as they reached the door of the church lobby. 'We can always uphold the folklore of the kissing gate on the way back.'

Lissy hadn't expected to see Claire's parents at the service. She and Xander were given a lighted tea-light in a glass dish in the lobby and guided to seats at the side of the church. The organ was playing something slow and gentle, not at all Christmassy.

And then, as Lissy looked towards the altar where the Reverend Mason was walking towards the pulpit, she saw Claire's parents, four rows in front of where she sat, but on the other side of the church.

Had Xander seen? Not yet she didn't think. She knew they'd barely spoken to Xander since their daughter had died. None of that was Xander's fault. Or hers.

The organ stopped playing and the Reverend Mason stepped towards the lectern but didn't speak. There were a few moments of total silence, apart from the flickering of tea-lights and someone clearing their throat. And then a lone voice from the balcony at the back of the church filled the void. *Silent night*. A voice so pure that it brought a lump to Lissy's throat and a shiver of something up her spine.

The service had begun.

Lissy didn't think Xander had noticed Claire's parents and she hadn't told him that she had. He seemed to have enjoyed the service, singing the carols with gusto. He had a fine voice. Tenor. More than able to carry a tune, and unafraid to use it.

Lissy held back, fiddling about with the order of service sheet and the hymn book on the ledge that ran on the back of the seats in front. Claire's parents must have left while she was fiddling because when she looked up again they'd gone.

But only as far as the lobby. As she and Xander made their way out, Claire's parents were stood talking to another couple. Kisses and 'Happy Christmas' greetings were being exchanged between them.

'Oh,' Xander said. 'Claire's mum and dad.'

'I know. I saw them earlier. Did you?'

'No.'

And with that Claire's mother spotted them and the happy smile she'd had on her face dropped. She looked shocked.

There was nothing for it. She and Xander would have to

131

walk towards them now. And they'd have to stop and say something.

Claire's mother got in first.

'Alicia,' she said. 'What a surprise. And you, too, Xander.'

Xander extended a hand and Claire's mother took it, her arm extended and rather stiffly, making it more than obvious she was fending off any thoughts Xander might have had about a cheek kiss. Then there was a polite exchange of handshakes all round.

'I heard that Strand House is now yours, Alicia,' Claire's father said.

Alicia, and not the more friendly Lissy that they had always called her by. How alien it sounded, how cold somehow.

'Will you be selling?' Claire's mother asked.

'That,' Xander interjected, 'is a decision for Lissy to tell, I think.'

He placed a hand in the small of Lissy's back. An I'm-here-and-supporting-you-in-every-way sort of gesture.

'Yes, I'll let you know when I've made my decision,' she said. There really didn't seem to be much point in prolonging this conversation and Lissy wondered where the Christmas spirit had gone, where the remembered happy memories had gone, and the feeling of love and sharing that they'd all, presumably, felt at the service. 'Happy Christmas,' she finished.

There was an exchange of rather half-hearted 'Happy Christmases' and then Lissy linked her arm through Xander's and they left the church.

When they were well clear of being in anyone's earshot Xander said, 'Crikey, that was cold enough to freeze an igloo. I think my hand's still got frostbite!'

Xander extricated Lissy's arm from his and held her hand instead. It was indeed quite cold, but then it had been cold in the church and they'd had a chilly walk from Strand House with the wind coming in off the sea.

'It was my heart that got frostbite,' Lissy said. 'Are you sad you came with me now?'

'No. Two ghosts have been laid tonight, although I was only expecting one. Did you say there were sausage rolls and mince pies waiting for when we got back?'

'I did.'

Lissy wondered why the sudden change of topic. She soon found out.

'How do you feel about walking back the road way? More of a stretch of legs after all that sitting?'

It was nothing of the sort and they both knew it. Xander was avoiding the kissing gate scenario but couldn't actually say the words. Lissy could understand that. It didn't seem appropriate somehow after seeing Claire's parents and the more than cool reception they'd got. Perhaps now just wasn't the right time.

Chapter 22

Bobbie

'Happy Christmas, you two,' Bobbie said.

She and Janey had been peering out from time to time to see if Lissy and Xander were coming back yet. She'd expected to see the bobbing torchlight lighting their way as they came back down the path they'd gone up but they were coming from another direction. Then she noticed their faces. Serious would sum it up. What the heck had happened there? A solemn service or something else? The matchmaker in her had imagined them coming back hand in hand, rosy and glowing from a few kisses under the moonlight but that had so obviously not happened. It was one of the reasons she'd declined the offer to go to the candlelit service with them – to give them time alone, so they could hold hands and kiss without her and Janey cramping their style. Not that Bobbie was overly religious, but this was Christmas for goodness' sake – even the most hardened heathens entered into the spirit of the festivities, didn't they?

'Did you enjoy the service?' Janey asked.

'Yes,' Lissy and Xander said together, looking towards one

another as if joined by some sort of invisible thread. 'The Christmas Eve candlelit service is always special,' Lissy finished.

There was a flatness in Lissy's voice and Bobbie picked up on it.

'But?' she said. 'There's always a "but", isn't there?'

'Two,' Xander said. 'Claire's parents were there and they made it rather obvious they wished Lissy and I hadn't been.'

'Ah,' Bobbie said. 'I'm tempted to tell them to "get over it".'Oh God, me and my loose lips again,' Bobbie said.

'It's okay,' Xander told her. 'I was thinking much the same. They were quite rude actually. I'm not sure all of it was grief over Claire.'

'But let's not let it spoil Lissy's Christmas, eh?' Bobbie said, rather desperate now to lighten the mood for Lissy who had worked so damned hard for them all. 'I don't know about you lot but I might die if I don't get my sausage roll and a mince pie and a glass of sherry to go with them. Brings back memories of my old gran, that – a bottle of Emva Cream sherry from the off licence and mince pies. She only ever had that one bottle at Christmas.'

She was desperate now to make things better for Lissy and there was a crumb of comfort when Lissy laughed at what she'd said.

'Nothing but the best here,' Lissy said. 'Choices, too. Dry, sweet, or medium sweet. Follow me. The kitchen all right for you guys?'

No answer was needed really so Bobbie didn't give one.

'Lead on,' Bobbie said.

The last thing she wanted or needed was a sausage roll or a mince pie. She'd got on the scales in her en suite that morning and had already put on half a kilo. But just mentioning her old gran a moment ago had made her realise how much she'd enjoyed her Christmases with her late grandmother. Family. And she had so little of that now.

There was a stupid lump in her throat threatening to choke

her. Christmas was about families and it seemed more than sad that the four of them in Lissy's kitchen – about to tuck into sausage rolls and mince pies and drink sherry late at night which was probably bad for them all, if traditional – were a makeshift family here in Devon, not a proper one, none of them related. The wind seemed to have got up and Bobbie could hear the crash of waves and the clack, clack, clack of whatever it was on top of yacht masts that spun in the wind. It seemed to echo in the nighttime.

'Name your poison,' Lissy said, waving a hand towards the selection of sherries on the dresser.

'Dry for me, please,' Xander said.

'And me.' Bobbie had always thought there were fewer calories in dry drinks than sweet and she wasn't likely to change her opinion any time soon at her stage of life.

'Sweet for me,' Janey said. 'A little one. Please. I want to get up early tomorrow and draw the sunrise.'

'Not too early making a racket sharpening pencils though,' Bobbie joked.

'You're safe there,' Janey told her. 'You use soft pencils to draw.'

'That's me told, then,' Bobbie said. 'Shall I make myself useful and pour the sherries?'

'Please.' Lissy fetched the sausage rolls and then took a glass dish of mince pies from the far end of the counter top and put them in the microwave to warm a little. 'Cream, anyone?'

'Devonshire clotted, I hope,' Xander said. He tilted his head to one side looking at Lissy as he spoke and pulled a mock-sad face that there might not be.

'Good God, man,' Bobbie laughed. 'Where do you stash it all? There's not a spare ounce of flesh on you? Not that I'm showering you with compliments or anything.'

'The builder's metabolism,' Xander told her. 'If you can lay a thousand bricks in an hour you can eat all the fat you want.'

'That's so not going to happen for me, then,' Bobbie told him.

A makeshift family they might be, but they were bickering good-naturedly as many proper families do, knowing when it's a joke and when there's, perhaps, a deeper and nastier side to a comment. And goodness, how wonderful it felt at that moment to be part of it.

Bobbie finished pouring the sherries and handed them around just as Lissy brought out the warmed mince pies, and then fetched the cream for Xander who was the only one who wanted any.

'I'll get this down me and then it's bed for me,' Xander said. 'This little boy has hung up his stocking and if he's not asleep when Santa calls then he won't be getting anything.'

What, Bobbie wondered, was it like to watch a little boy hang up a stocking in anticipation and then to see the delight on his face when he woke to find it filled with all sorts of things he'd play with on Christmas morning and then discard? Well, that was how it had always been for Bobbie, the not knowing, the wondering.

'Shall I tuck you in?' Bobbie asked, quite literally tongue in cheek.

'Is that an offer I can't refuse?' Xander spluttered into his sherry.

'Not at all,' Bobbie said, hands on hips in mock-outrage. 'It's just that it seems to me I'm turning into a mother hen around here and I thought I might fulfil that role as well.'

'I think I can manage, thanks,' Xander said, taking a paper napkin from the holder on the kitchen island and wiping a crumb from the corner of his mouth. 'I'll say goodnight everyone.'

Then, to Bobbie's surprise, Xander kissed them all good night in turn, leaving Lissy to last.

'I'm glad I went to the church,' Bobbie heard him whisper against Lissy's hair as he added a small hug to the kiss he planted on her cheek.

And then he was gone, and within seconds Janey followed.

137

Bobbie got up and closed the kitchen door behind them.

'In my role as mother hen, is there anything you'd like to talk about? Anything that would make you sleep a bit easier if you spoke about it? Only it seems to be that there might.'

'Probably,' Lissy said. 'Oh, I don't know. I don't think you have to be Einstein to work out I really like Xander, do you?'

'Nor he, you. But what started out as possibly the beginning of something lovely for you both under the moon and the stars, went a bit pear-shaped when you found Claire's parents were at the service?'

'That!' Lissy said. 'We were getting on so well, cheekily flirting with all the banter, but in the doing laying our feelings out, sort of on a plate, for the other to choose if we wanted. And then it all went pff, frozen in the chill of seeing Claire's parents. It was as though Xander felt guilty being with me.'

'Well, sweetheart,' Bobbie told her, 'there's never ever going to be another first time for that horrid scenario, is there? You've already done it. They've seen you as a couple and they're jolly well going to have to get used to it, aren't they?'

'A couple?' Lissy said.

'You've just more or less admitted as much, or the hopes that you will be. And from where I've been standing I'd say that was happening by the minute. A woman could get fried in the cross-fire of looks and feelings between you, you know.'

'That vivid imagination of yours running wild again, Bobbie. But ...'

And then Bobbie saw huge pools of unshed tears in Lissy's eyes. It didn't seem appropriate to ask why.

'Come here,' Bobbie said, holding her arms out wide.

Lissy walked into them, her tears running now so that they dampened the silk of Bobbie's lounge-wear kaftan.

Bobbie let Lissy run her tears until they dried up and she pulled away, wiping her face with a towel hanging from a drawer rail.

'The kiss you seem so keen for Xander and me to share? It wouldn't be the first time our feelings almost got the better of us,' Lissy said.

'Ah.'

'That was at his and Claire's wedding. I was, I admit, a bit tipsy. We had a dance – Xander danced with just about every woman in the room the same way Claire danced with all the men. But when Xander and I danced it just felt so right, more right than it should have been given the occasion. Our bodies sort of gravitated close than they should have done, an almost magnetic connection. And then Xander pulled back.'

'But you didn't?'

'No.'

'And did anything develop from there?'

'No! That's the ultimate betrayal, isn't it? Nicking your best friend's husband.'

'But you could have?'

'Yes. I'm not sure Xander would have though.'

'I'd say you're probably right there. He seems a very moral sort of bloke. Not that I don't think he hasn't come down off his shelf a time or two since Claire died.'

Lissy made a sort of snorting laugh sound and put a hand to her mouth.

'You say the most outrageous things, Bobbie,' she laughed.

'Maybe. But do you think I'm right? About the coming down off his shelf bit?'

'Did he tell you that? You know, when you were in the sitting room yesterday?'

'Of course he didn't. There's only so many things a forty-something man will tell a much older woman, and that's not one of them. But would you mind if he has?'

'No. After Cooper left I had inappropriate sex a couple of times, just to prove to myself someone would find me attractive, and that I hadn't forgotten how to do it.'

139

'So, there you are then. Level playing field again, I'd say, for the two of you.'

'It's still feeling a bit like the ultimate betrayal even though Claire's not here.'

'Stop that,' Bobbie said, wagging a finger at her in what she hoped was a playful and not a full-on bossy fashion. 'It's no such thing and I think you know it.'

Lissy shrugged. Yawned.

'And we've discovered that neither of us has forgotten that almost-kiss moment,' Lissy said. 'And ...' Lissy's eyes met and held Bobbie's and she smiled a sad sort of smile.

'And you don't know why you're telling me all this stuff because we hardly know one another really. Is that what you're thinking? Am I right.'

Lissy nodded.

'But maybe that's why?'

'The comfort of not quite strangers, eh?' Bobbie said. 'Okay, so things didn't go as you'd hoped they'd go tonight and I'd bet my Jimmy Choo collection – which is not inconsiderable by the way – that Xander feels the same. Right?'

'Right,' Lissy said. She yawned again.

'So, how about you sleep on things,' Bobbie said.

'Good idea,' Lissy said. 'Thanks, you know, for listening.'

Lissy checked all the knobs on all the appliances were off and then opened the kitchen door, and turned off the lights.

'Thanks for talking,' Bobbie said, linking her arm through Lissy's as they walked across the hall. 'Sometimes a girl likes to be needed. Come on, up the wooden hill we go. As Scarlett O'Hara was wont to say, tomorrow is another day.'

'So it is,' Lissy said. 'So it is.'

Christmas Day

Chapter 23

Janey

Janey wrote a note for Lissy and the others. *'Popped out to draw. You'll probably be able to see me if you look out of one of the bedroom windows. I'll be back for breakfast. Happy Christmas'*
It was six-thirty when she reached the top of the steps that led down to the beach. The tide was way out. Lots of rocks had been exposed during the rough seas of the previous tide because Janey remembered it being a flat expanse of sand when Sam had driven her up the road in the taxi and now it wasn't. Now it looked, Janey thought, like Badlands in the US – sandstone pillars of rock of varying heights, some straight and some leaning. Only not as big of course. She just had to draw that. The beach in winter, after a rough sea.

Janey had taken the liberty of borrowing the hat and scarf Lissy had loaned her when Xander took her up to Berry Pomeroy to see the castle. That seemed so long ago now but it had been like a light switching on for Janey – Xander had given her permission to follow her art. Not that she needed his permission but the knowledge that he approved of what she did, admired her for it, had shifted something in her.

Janey took the notepad and a pencil she'd brought with her from a plastic bag she'd taken from Lissy's kitchen. She didn't think Lissy would mind her taking that either. She would take copious photographs in a minute but first she wanted to feel the energy of the rocks and the sea being absorbed into her work tools – eye to mind, mind to hand, hand to pencil, pencil to paper. If she could have drawn the smell of the sea as well then she would have done. She inhaled deeply, that iodine seaweedy smell. There was a ribbon of dark green, almost black, seaweed on the tideline, encrusted with shells and stones. Janey walked on down the steps to get a closer look. Sitting down on the bottom step she began to sketch. Strong strokes, almost cartoonish in their execution. The scene in front of her seemed to want that style even though Janey had never drawn like that before.

'Less is more here, I think,' she said as the sky lightened.

Not quite dawn, but nearly, and there was more than enough light for her to see by already. A few gulls were already pecking about in the seaweed, some of them scrabbling over some tasty morsel or other. She heard a dog bark over the other end of the beach although she couldn't see one. Or it's owner.

She was not afraid. She, Janey, who'd been afraid throughout her marriage – if you ignored the honeymoon period when Stuart had been doing his best to impress her – was not afraid now, sitting on a beach where no one could see her at that moment. She felt safer than she had for years. A Christmas gift in itself and what a gift!

'It's going to be a beautiful day,' Janey said. She could feel that. There was no wind.

And then the sun suddenly popped up on the horizon, a small arc of light to begin with and then rather more quickly than Janey had thought it would. Well, she'd never sat on a beach and watched the sun rise before so how would she know? And then there it was, a perfect orb resting on the horizon like a tightrope walker.

Putting down her pad and pencil, Janey took her phone from her pocket and began taking pictures. The scene in front of her seemed to be changing by the second – the colour shifts from palest, pearl grey to a sort of muted saffron was, she thought, like a kaleidoscope. If you took your eyes off it for a second you'd miss something. So she didn't.

And then she changed from photograph to text.

Stuart, it's me. Janey. I will be filing for divorce. I've probably got grounds for that but I'll settle for irreconcilable differences. As soon as Christmas is over I'll be contacting a solicitor. Do not try to make me change my mind.

She pressed 'send'. She'd told Stuart she wanted a divorce before. Many times actually. But always he'd begged her to stay. Promised he'd change his ways, but he never had, not for longer than a fortnight anyway.

'Men like that never do,' Janey said into the new day. Christmas Day.

Suzy had been quite wrong the day before when she'd questioned how well Janey had known Stuart, because she *had* known, she'd just been in denial for far too long, that was all.

'Suzy next,' Janey said, scrolling down for her sister's number. She knew Suzy would be up – would probably have been up for a good hour or more.

She pressed 'call'.

'Janey!' Suzy said, almost instantly. 'Thank God.'

The relief in her sister's voice that she'd called her was almost tangible and Janey was glad she had now.

'Happy Christmas,' Janey said. 'And sorry, you know, for not keeping you in the picture about my plans. I didn't really have one apart from always having a small case packed so I could escape, and then I did, and I thought if I stopped to tell you then you might have tried to persuade me to change my mind …'

145

'I might,' Suzy interrupted. 'But I'd have been wrong to do it.'

'And I'm sorry if I was a bit on edge yesterday.'

'Me too,' Suzy said. 'Are you okay to talk?'

'Fine.'

'No eavesdroppers?'

'Only a gull or two?'

'Oh my God! You're never living rough?'

'Far from it!' Janey laughed. She wouldn't tell Suzy about Strand House just yet, but she would eventually.

'Good,' Suzy said. 'I'm glad you've rung, really glad. I've got a second in the madness that's the usual family Christmas Day, to say I'm sorry I didn't offer more support yesterday. Stress probably. I never think I've bought enough presents for the kids – well not as many as others do. And I worry that I'll run out of food or I'll poison us all with the turkey not being cooked properly. I was running around chasing my tail with it all and I wasn't thinking straight. Like I said, Stuart had been ringing and my mind was going through all sorts of worst-case scenarios about what might have happened to you and where you've been. It's like when one of the children runs out into the road and I just manage to grab him or her and then I yell at them like a banshee when really I'm just so relieved they weren't run over, and I should be hugging them close, comforting them. My friend, Sarah, calls it the shock-adrenalin cocktail. So, I'm sorry … I didn't mean to add to your troubles.'

'Thank you,' Janey said. It felt good, what Suzy was saying. 'I know you didn't.'

'So where are you? I'm guessing the seaside if there are gulls?'

'You guess right,' Janey said.

As if it understood its name a gull came and landed on the step just yards from her. Looking for scraps probably. It began pecking at shells, turning some over, flicking its head from side to side with one in its beak. How magnificent they were up close, gulls. How sleek. Saffron-coloured eyes. Janey had exactly the

146

shade in the box of watercolours Bobbie had bought her. She'd try a bird study later.

'So where? Do you want Gary to come and fetch you? He said last night that he will. You can come here ...'

'No. No need for that. I think I've probably already spoiled your Christmas Day. I wouldn't want the children to have their dad disappear when they're opening their presents or something. And I can't say where I am. Not yet.'

Janey heard her sister sigh loudly on the end of the phone. Then she heard a long intake of breath.

'Janey? I need to say something.'

'Go ahead.'

'We should be having this conversation face-to-face not over the phone with me sitting in my dressing gown on the back doorstep so no one can hear me, but I'm really sorry I've not been a better support to you. Over Stuart. I suppose it was that not-wanting-to-get-involved thing most of us do, and then also wanting you to sort it for yourself rather than have someone sort it for you which is always the best way. You've always been so good to me helping out and everything.'

'Because I wanted to,' Janey told her. With her phone to one ear she was doing quick sketches, with her free hand, of the gull in all its different stances as it pecked away. 'Not because I felt I had to.'

Janey heard a little sob on the other end of the phone. And then Suzy gulped.

'It's just,' Suzy said, 'I never realised how awful it must have been for you with Stuart until we started getting his terrible phone calls when you went missing. If he's been saying half the things to you he's been saying to Gary and me, then it makes me shudder to think of you standing there listening to it. And ... he's hit you, hasn't he?'

'Many times,' Janey said.

'You never said.'

147

'Abuse victims rarely do,' Janey said.

'And often it's too late for them,' Suzy said. 'Oh, God, Janey, I'm so glad you've got out.'

'Me too,' Janey said.

'Does Mum know?'

'I haven't told her. Stuart might have found her number and called her, but let's just say she's not been in touch.'

'That doesn't mean he hasn't though, does it?' Suzy said.

'No.' Janey couldn't remember the last time her mother had been in touch. The last she'd heard she'd been holed up in some Spanish resort with yet another rich man funding her. 'I'm still not expecting her to call any time soon.'

'Mothers, eh?' Suzy said. 'Who'd have 'em!'

She was making a joke of it but Janey knew Suzy was probably more hurt than she was by their mother's indifference. The children needed a grandma in their lives. Well, Janey thought so.

In the background Janey could hear one of Suzy's children calling her.

'Sounds like you're wanted!' she laughed.

'Seems so. Anyway, I'm so glad you rang. I've been awake all night thinking what a complete shit I was reacting the way I did yesterday.'

'Forget it, Suze,' Janey said. 'And you'd better go and begin the day. Happy Christmas. I'll ring you to let you know what my plans are after tomorrow. Okay?'

'Okay. Happy Christmas, Janey. I hope it will be. Happy. And that you've got kind and supportive people around you.'

'I have. The best. Now go.'

'Love you,' Suzy said.

'Back to you,' Janey said, and then Suzy killed the call.

When was the last time they'd said those words to one another? Possibly never because Janey couldn't remember saying them herself. Or hearing them. Maybe it took a crisis for people to open their minds to what was in their hearts.

A lone tear escaped and slithered down Janey's cheek. She let it roll all the way to beside her ear and down under her chin.

Janey slid her phone back in the pocket of her coat and carried on sketching until she began to feel chilled. Half an hour? An hour? The sky was quite light now and there were more early morning dog walkers on the beach, throwing balls for their pets, some of them even running into the sea to fetch them.

'I might get one of you,' Janey said as a woman with three retrievers tried to protect herself from her dogs' frantic shaking of their fur as they came back to her on the beach.

A retriever. Something to snuggle into. Something to make her go out and face the world every day, be part of it, when she no longer had Lissy, and Bobbie, and Xander around. Stuart had refused to even discuss having a pet.

'Well, I don't have to ask him now, do I?' Janey said. 'About anything.'

She stood up and turned back towards the road that Strand House was in. It was bathed in the soft dawn light, like a candle glow.

She couldn't wait to be back there now and ran up the road.

Chapter 24

Lissy

Lissy's Christmas Day plan was running like clockwork. That was the thing about being an accountant – she was good with numbers, whatever form those numbers took.

She'd made croissants for everyone's breakfast. They were on a baking tray under a tea-towel having their second prove. As soon as everyone was up then she'd pop them in the oven. And she'd prepped all the toppings for the bruschettas she planned to serve with drinks about an hour before they all sat down to eat the Christmas meal. That, she planned to serve about four o'clock, just as the light was going. The turkey crown, with its apricot and pine nut stuffing, was in its tin ready to go in the oven later. She'd made a chocolate brownie studded with cranberries in lieu of a Christmas pudding because the others had said they weren't great fans of that tradition. A half-kilo tub of clotted cream sat at the back of the fridge waiting to go with that. She was glad she'd bought it, now that she knew Xander was such a huge fan of it.

And then as though just thinking about him had conjured him up, he came into the kitchen. He was carrying two bottles of champagne by their necks in one hand, and he had two boxes of orange juice in his other arm, cradled like a baby.

'This,' he said, lowering them gently onto the kitchen island, 'is about the total limit of my festive cookery.'

'That'll do me,' Lissy laughed. 'Too many cooks spoil the broth. Bucks Fizz more than acceptable. Thank you.'

'You look like you've been busy,' Xander said. He lifted up a corner of the tea-towel. 'Oh, croissants. How did you know they're my guilty pleasure?'

'Aren't they everybody's?' Lissy laughed.

'If they're not then they should be,' Xander said. He was wearing shorts and a polo shirt and Lissy wondered if he would be going for a run. 'Am I the first up?'

'No. I heard the door go earlier. Janey. She left a note. I looked out and could just pick her out walking towards the top of the steps.'

'Ah. I'm glad she's done that.' Xander peered into the dishes covered in clingfilm that held the bruschetta toppings. 'This all looks a bit yum. And this,' he said, pointing at the brownie cooling on a rack 'is the stuff of gods. Never had it when Claire … well, you know. Sorry.'

'Don't be,' Lissy told him. 'None of us can expect you not to mention her when memories come flooding in for whatever reason. Claire and I shared more than a few as well and I'm thinking about her much of the time being here.'

'But she didn't do brownies,' Xander said.

'No,' Lissy said. She knew that. Claire had rarely eaten anything that had more than a hundred and fifty calories in it. 'Not good for the figure, is it? And she needed to present the perfect body when she stood in front of her students. Not that I was ever one of those, however many times she tried to persuade me that I should be.'

If Xander needed to talk about Claire on Christmas Day then she'd listen.

'You look pretty good to me,' Xander said, his voice a bit husky. 'Nice dress.'

Lissy was in one of Vonny's housecoats – such an old-fashioned word, but then Vonny had been a throwback from a different era. She'd bought the house for its Art Deco looks. Anything from the Thirties was good to have around in Vonny's opinion. There were mirrors and little side tables all over the house that were from that era.

'This "dress", I'll have you know is vintage. Silk. It's a housecoat, or sometimes known as a peignoir. I'll change in a minute.'

'Oh, are we dressing for breakfast?' Xander pulled a mock terrified-he-might-have-to-face. 'As you see I'm a bit of a beach bum at heart.'

'Good look,' Lissy said. 'Do you sport it winter and summer?'

'Mostly. Lots of blokes my age around here do. Unless it's cold enough to freeze the hairs on your legs off then we sport shorts, as it were.'

'Shorts at breakfast will be fine by me,' Lissy said.

Fine any time at all, she wanted to say. Xander was taking her breath away a bit standing there looking so, well, so damn sexy. He'd always been a handsome bloke but a few years on him since his wedding had brought improvements, if any were needed. A few silver threads in his hair only added to the look, in Lissy's opinion. They seemed – she and Xander – to be back to the happy banter they'd enjoyed before that fateful encounter with Claire's parents up at St Paul's.

'Great,' Xander said. He came round to the same side of the kitchen island as Lissy. 'Anything I can do? I'm an ace potato peeler I'll have you know. Ditto carrots, parsnips, and swede. Not so hot on the sprouts and my cabbage-shredding leaves something to be desired, but they remain edible. My mother trained me well. And I've just rung her to wish her Happy Christmas should you be thinking I'm a neglectful son.'

'She obviously trained you well, then. And I was thinking no such thing.'

'So there's nothing left for me to do apart from give you a Happy Christmas kiss?'

Lissy gulped. She'd been thinking along exactly those lines. And she was going to have to summon up all her willpower here not to let that kiss deepen, not to throw him over the kitchen island and beg him to make love to her, wasn't she?

'How neglectful!' Lissy said, turning to face him. She put her hands on his upper arms, stood on tiptoe and offered him her lips to kiss.

When Xander's lips touched hers she was in no doubt about her feelings for him.

And then the doorbell rang.

'Saved by the bell!' Lissy quipped. 'That'll be Janey. Can you let her in? I'll go and get dressed.'

'I hadn't got to that bit,' Xander said. He took Lissy's face between his hands and kissed her forehead. 'Instigating the need for you to get dressed.'

'But …'

'But the thought wasn't a million miles from my mind.'

'Nor mine,' Lissy gulped.

She stood there, her head still being held so tenderly, and her legs had taken on the consistency of marshmallow. Her insides seemed to have turned to melting toffee.

'If only we were here alone,' Xander said in very theatrically wistful way.

'Well, we're not,' Lissy laughed. She put her hands up to prise Xander's from her face and ran for the kitchen door. She turned to look back at him. He blew her a kiss. 'And I am in dire need of a very cold shower!'

Chapter 25

Bobbie

'Happy Christmas, everyone!' Bobbie said coming into the kitchen, thinking she was the last down because she'd heard all three different voices not long ago. 'Oh, where is everybody?' Only Xander was there sitting at one of the bar stools at the kitchen island drinking coffee. 'Have I missed breakfast?'

'Happy Christmas to you, too. And to answer your question, not yet,' Xander said. 'Janey's back from a stupid o'clock visit to the beach making sketches and has gone upstairs to start on something. Lissy must have been up for hours preparing this little lot.' He waved an arm towards bowls and trays covered with cloths or clingfilm. 'She's just gone upstairs to get changed and we have these little delights to come.' He lifted a tea-towel to reveal pastries waiting to be cooked, and grinned like the cat that had got the cream.

'I don't know about you,' Bobbie said, 'but I'm starting to feel a bit guilty that we're not doing anything to help Lissy.'

'She's pretty organised,' Xander told her. 'I'm pretty sure she'd ask if she wanted us to do anything, though. I think she just wants us to have a great Christmas. No angst about buying the right present for the right person or any of that stuff, and no standing in the queue for hours at the supermarket waiting to be served.'

'Hmm. Part of me thinks we ought to have liaised beforehand and got her something as a thank you.'

'Yeah, I thought that. But what? I mean she probably doesn't need another parmesan grater or a bread knife, or a set of dinner plates, does she?'

'Probably not!' Bobbie laughed. She looked around the kitchen, which was vast by anyone's standards. 'The trouble is, though,' she said, 'that the more space one has the more stuff one needs to fill it up.'

'Precisely why I live in a shoe box,' Xander said.

'Me too. Mews cottages don't come big.'

'But valuable?'

'Fairly.'

Bobbie rarely talked finance with anyone but it seemed perfectly normal to be mentioning the value of things with Xander. Somehow, they always seemed to fall into a conversation about something easily and comfortably enough whenever they found themselves alone together.

'Listed?' he asked.

'Yes.'

'Ah. And that will give you no end of problems if you need to make any sort of alteration.'

'Tell me about it! Putting a shower in took a whole ream of paperwork to sort. One builder gave up completely and pulled out because he just wasn't prepared to put up with all the waiting and the form-filling. I'm afraid I got on my high horse a bit and told him he ought to think about changing profession because London is full of listed properties.'

'Not a problem I'm likely to have down here. Listed buildings are rarer than hens' teeth in the bay.'

'Plenty of other work though?'

'So so. I let things slide a bit after Claire died. I stopped answering enquiry emails and texts and people went elsewhere. I had to lay off one of my workers. There's barely enough to keep me, and the three blokes still working for me, ticking over. This time of year is a bit lean for work as well. Anyway, it's Christmas morning and you don't need to hear my woes. Coffee? I made a fresh pot a moment ago, hoping someone would turn up to help me drink it.'

No, I don't want to hear your woes, Bobbie thought. She wanted to hear something a bit more positive, more forward thinking. She wanted to hear that he would always keep a place for Claire in his heart but that he was ready to open it up to someone else now. Someone like Lissy. She wanted to hear that that kiss that didn't happen between them last night after the candlelit service had happened now, or would later today. But part of her was secretly pleased that Xander felt able to talk to her about his feelings. Would he do that if he were her son? Or was that a totally different relationship – mother and son?

Xander obviously thought she was being slow to respond because he waggled his coffee cup at her to remind her of what she'd just been offered.

'Please. Coffee will be good.'

Xander stepped off his bar stool and went over to the worktop that had the coffee pot on it. He opened a cupboard over it and selected a mug.

How at home he looked here, Bobbie thought. And that grin he'd given her when she'd first come in told her that something had passed between him and Lissy before she'd gone to get changed. Something good.

Xander lifted the lids on various pots on the counter top, then he opened the fridge and peered inside.

'As your barista for this morning I can offer you sugar – brown or white. Milk with three differently coloured lids – red, green, or blue.'

156

'Black, please,' Bobbie said, smiling at him. 'No sugar. I'm cheap to keep.'

'That,' Xander said, filling the mug for Bobbie and bringing it over to her, 'I do not believe. What's the phrase … high-maintenance?'

'Hey you!' Bobbie laughed. 'If I were your mother I'd wash your mouth out for that remark!'

'It was meant to be a compliment,' Xander said. 'Honest.'

'Then I'll take it as one, thank you.'

'Friends again?' Xander said, sitting himself back on his bar stool.

'Always,' Bobbie said. A shiver of something shot up her spine. A tingle of something otherworldly. A snapshot of being in the lobby of the art workshop when they'd all said goodbye, she and Janey and Claire, and they'd all said how great it was to have met and how they hoped they'd stay in touch, remain friends and Claire had given them all high fives and said 'Always!', flashed up in her mind. She didn't believe these things but in that second it was as though Claire was in the room with them somehow.

Lissy and Janey came in then.

'Happy Christmas!' they called in unison.

Bobbie slid down over her bar stool and rushed over to embrace her friends.

'Happy Christmas both of you,' she said, kissing first Janey's cheek and then Lissy's.

'Let the day begin,' Lissy said, disentangling herself from Bobbie's hold. 'I'll need to get the pastries in the oven. While they're cooking I'll prep the scrambled eggs. With smoked salmon this morning because it's a special morning. That okay with everyone?'

Everyone said it was so she went to the range of double ovens, lit one, then fetched the pastries.

Janey and Xander exchanged Happy Christmas kisses.

'Hey!' Janey said. 'What about Xander, Lissy? No kiss for him?'

'We've already done that,' Lissy said, reddening.

Well, well, well. Bobbie smiled to herself who'd have thought it! She looked at Xander who gave her the merest vestige of a wink. Yes, that kiss had happened, and if she were a betting woman she'd put money on it that it wasn't the air kiss variety.

Chapter 26

Lissy

It was gone ten o'clock before they all finished breakfast. Lissy told them that lunch would be whatever they could find in the fridge whenever they felt hungry or the various tins that were filled with Christmas goods. She would be serving the Christmas meal at about four o'clock.

Janey told them about the text she'd left for Stuart ending things for ever with him, and the one to her sister that had opened up new avenues of communication. She was, she said, still feeling a bit fragile seeing as it was only two days since she'd made her momentous decision to leave her marriage. She wanted, she said, to stay at Strand House and do some watercolours from the sketches she'd done on the beach after dawn. Lissy said that was fine by her. She was going to go for a long walk, along the beach to Goodrington and back seeing as the tide was way out, before she holed herself up in the kitchen cooking again. Did anyone want to join her?

'Count me out,' Bobbie said.

'Count me in,' Xander said which was exactly what Lissy had wanted him to say.

And now, here they were, Lissy having closed the front door behind them. Xander held out his hand for her to take. Lissy took it and together they walked down the steps to the road.

'What are you going to do with it?'

'With the house?' Lissy said, knowing instinctively what he meant.

'Yeah. Sell? It'd be a shame to see developers get it. You know, turn it into holiday let flats or something. This, of course, is a property developer speaking!'

'Do you want to buy it?' Lissy asked.

'I'd love to, although I'd more than rattle around in it. My bank manager would have something to say about that, though.'

They'd reached the steps that led down to the beach where Lissy had seen Janey sitting sketching as the sun rose. Lissy wondered what sort of cashflow problems Xander might have but wouldn't ask – she'd wait to be told. When people found out she was accountant many of them thought she would give free advice over a drink in the pub or a lunchtime meal in a café somewhere.

'Beach or prom?' Xander said.

'Prom first, I think,' Lissy said. 'All the little kiddies will be riding their new bikes or be on their skateboards. I remember doing that one Christmas morning when we stopped with Vonny. I had a chopper that year.'

'Prom it is, then,' Xander said. 'Watch your ankles with little girls getting to grips with their dolly pushchairs.' He pointed to a gaggle of children and grownups about two hundred yards ahead who were walking towards them.

'It was prams in my day,' Lissy laughed. It had taken her a while to get the hang of steering one and she'd taken lumps out of various skirting boards at Strand House the Christmas Vonny had bought her one, not that Vonny had minded. Lissy was, she knew, the daughter Vonny had never been able to have. 'Buggies

160

were only just beginning to be popular. God, that makes me feel ancient, saying that?'

'So, how ancient is ancient for you?' Xander asked.

'A man should never ask a lady her age.' Lissy laughed before adding, 'I'm thirty-six.'

'Ah. So how do you feel about going out with an older man? I can give you five years.'

Two little girls on scooters came hurtling towards them and Lissy and Xander were forced to let go of hands and weave around the children.

On automatic pilot their hands reconnected within seconds. How good it felt, her hand in Xander's.

'Hardly an age gap,' Lissy said. 'But does it matter if there is? Vonny's husband was a good ten or more years older than she was but they couldn't have been happier.'

'And you can feel that happiness in the house, I think. I never thought I'd hear myself say something like that. A bit of a hippy thing for a builder to be saying, but there it is.'

Xander gave her hand a little squeeze, and Lissy squeezed back.

'I've always felt it,' Lissy said.

'So, back to my earlier question. What are you going to do with it?'

'Keep it. Somehow. In just two days with you all being there I know it's the right thing to do. I've been unhappy running my practice for a while now. It'll probably take time to find a buyer and sell my flat in Princesshay but time is what I have at the moment.'

'And do what?' Xander said.

They'd got as far as the pier now. The lights were flashing on the helter-skelter and Lissy could hear the beep of the one-armed bandits up above them as they walked underneath. There was even a queue at the ice cream stall and anyone could have been forgiven for thinking it was midsummer, except Lissy was bundled up in a coat and boots and had a beanie on her head, and Xander

161

was wearing a donkey jacket and a scarf around his neck, although he was still wearing shorts.

'I could do what Vonny did and run it as an upmarket B&B. I'd need to make myself a totally private bolthole though. Somewhere guests couldn't find me to ask for more teabags for their hospitality trays, or if they could hang wet bathing costumes on the line.'

'I could help with that,' Xander said. 'The builder in me – well, frustrated architect really – has been making plans. You know, the old if-it-were-mine-this-is-what-I'd-do-with-it scenario.'

'Which is?'

'I'd put an L-shaped conservatory around the kitchen. And then I'd extend the laundry room out into the garden to butt onto the end of it and make that a sort of den. The kitchen's so vast you could carve out a bit to make another laundry room, easy peasy. I'd put in a woodburner in the sitting room for the winter – central-heating radiators always seem totally lacking in warmth and atmosphere to me. My sitting room faces the sea so I know how cold it can be sometimes, even with central heating. Out the back you'd be cosy in the winter and then it would be a bolthole in the summer.'

'Gosh, you have thought all this through! But am I guessing correctly here that you need the work?' Lissy said. She could feel Xander's professional enthusiasm for a project and yet there was something deeper as well.

'Got it in one.' Xander took a deep breath. 'But you've missed a trick?'

'Which is?'

'I want you to stay. I like to think we're at the start of something that could be very special between us. I like to think you'll be on one end of the curve of the bay and I'll be on the other in our own spaces until, well … until I've got something to offer you.'

'I don't need you to offer me anything, Xander,' Lissy said.

'Let's not get in too deep, eh? Why don't we just enjoy the moment? I feel the same as you – that we're at the start of something that could be very special. I've come more alive just being around you these past two days than I have in ages. There's a sort of fizz inside me.'

'Me too,' Xander said. Again, a little extra pressure on Lissy's hand. 'But I need to lay my cards out. I don't want you thinking that my eyes have suddenly gone off like cash registers knowing you've inherited Strand House, and that I'm trying to cash in because I'm not.'

'I think I'm a better judge of character,' Lissy said, 'than to think that.'

'That's a nice thing to say. Thank you. Anyway, here it is … confession time. I've got big decisions to make in the New Year. I'll need to lay my blokes off, hopefully only for a short time. I should have done it before but I couldn't ruin their Christmases. They're family men, all of them. Good blokes.'

'I like your idea for the conservatory and the makeover of the laundry room,' Lissy said.

'I hoped you might,' Xander grinned at her. 'So, you're considering going with the B&B option?'

'Not completely. I don't think that would be all that challenging. I mean, how many different breakfasts can a girl make?'

'Today's was awesome,' Xander said. 'Made a change from cornflakes and a couple of rounds of burnt toast because I always forget to check it under the grill and get side-tracked feeding the cat or something.'

'I'll see what I can find for you tomorrow, then,' Lissy said.

And the day after, and the day after that.

'You put all sorts of mouth-watering photos up on your Facebook page,' Xander said.

'And Instagram,' Lissy said.

'Ah, I've yet to embrace that. I only got into Facebook when

I had to close down Claire's account. I looked you up and then, after the funeral, I found Janey's and Bobbie's pages. I love Janey's art. I've offered to buy a couple of things but she always says she's not selling.'

'I think she's coming round to a change of heart on that,' Lissy said.

She'd have to now she'd be funding herself. She must remember to mention again that Janey could stay on at Strand House after Christmas if she wanted or needed to. It could be a mutually useful arrangement – a safe haven for Janey while she thought through the rest of her life, and a house-sitter for Lissy while she sold her practice. Gosh, had she really said that – sold her practice? It was starting to feel like more than a reality.

'Yeah, she'll have to, poor woman,' Xander said.

Xander bent to pick up a mussel shell, the two halves still joined. It had a mother-of-pearl glow to it, and Lissy suddenly had a vision of a pot of steaming mussels, with herbs and white wine. Crusty bread. A glass of Chablis. Oh yes, her thoughts were all going in the right direction now, weren't they? This walk with Xander was just what she'd needed to clear her head.

'She'll get there,' Lissy said. 'Bobbie, too. I'm beginning to read between lines there. I'm not sure what I'm reading but there's a sort of sadness, I think, despite her cheery, and very fast, way of talking.'

'Yeah, I'm thinking that, too. But Bobbie's Facebook pages are off my radar really with the clothes and the shoes and the bags and the hats and all the stuff she puts up, but there's something about the constant joy she gives the people who follow her. I read all their comments but never comment myself.'

'We shouldn't be talking about them behind their backs,' Lissy said. She was beginning to feel a bit uncomfortable about that. It was something she'd always made a conscious decision to avoid because running a business she knew how dangerous it could be to share a confidence only to have that confidence passed on as gossip.

'No. It's not mean stuff though, is it? And I'd say it to their faces. I think, the bottom line is that we both want the best for them, that's all. It felt sort of right to keep you all in my life seeing as you'd been in Claire's. I haven't noticed you taking photos of what you've served up for us, though. Have you?'

'No,' Lissy said. 'I decided to keep off all social media over Christmas. Besides, the photos I put up are impersonal – just food I've been experimenting with, and only for my own consumption, although sometimes I take the bakes into the office and share them around. Cooking for you all has more … well, more love in it, I suppose.'

'Aw, that's a lovely thing to say. We certainly love eating it. Had enough of the prom?' Xander asked, steering Lissy towards the next set of steps coming up that led down onto the beach.

She was happy to be steered. The steps were steep and uneven, worn away by centuries of footsteps and the tides, covered in places in barnacles and the traces of fossilised egg cases. Xander let go of her hand, and took her elbow instead, the better to steady her. Such a gallant gesture and Lissy couldn't help but make a comparison between him and Cooper who had only ever put himself first, although she knew it was more than stupid to make comparisons.

'My humble abode coming up,' Xander said, as they neared the harbour. 'Would you mind if I stopped off to check on Felix?'

Lissy had been there before, of course, when she'd dropped Claire off after one of their girly, learning new things, weekends. She'd never stopped for long – just a cup of tea or coffee before she drove back to Exeter. But she couldn't remember anyone called Felix having been there.

'Felix? A lodger?'

'No. My cat.'

'I love cats,' Lissy said, pulling Xander along now towards where she knew an alleyway went up to his cottage.

Would they, she wondered, make it to Goodrington now? Would they?

Chapter 27

Xander

The second Xander opened the door to his cottage and began to usher Lissy in, he knew he was making a massive mistake. His father's advice to his teenage self came back to him, echoing loud in his mind. So loud he thought for a moment that Lissy could probably hear it.

'Don't even think about making love to a woman, Xand, unless it's in a place that looks as though you've taken trouble over it. Especially the first time. Round the back of a pub will not do. Remember, your brains are not in your bollocks, son.'

Xander had been hugely embarrassed over that conversation at the time. Amused, too. His father had always called a spade a shovel and his sex advice had been no different. Short and to the point. By and large, Xander had stuck to those rules, the times he and Claire had made love on the beach in the darkness excepted. But those times had been her choice as much as his own.

So, what was he thinking now, bringing Lissy here? Upstairs in his bedroom he knew the bed was unmade from when he'd got out of it. There were probably socks lying about somewhere.

The socks of Claire's he'd felt unable to throw away were still under his pillow. If they were to make love on the couch he knew it would be liberally sprinkled with Felix's fur. Lissy deserved better than that.

'Um,' Xander said, closing the door gently behind Lissy. 'I'm not sure about this now.'

Another of his father's favourite sayings had been that honesty was the best policy. His gut feeling when they'd been walking along, their hands firmly clasped together, fit together like two pieces of a jigsaw, was that Lissy wanted to make love as much as he did. Making love and being in love weren't the same thing. He'd done a fair bit of the former before Claire and after, but he'd only ever been in love with Claire. In lust a few times, and there was an element of that in his feelings for Lissy but, back to that honesty thing, he was beginning to fall in love with her. He was beginning to accept that now.

'Nor me,' Lissy said.

She was looking at an enlarged photo of Claire, bare feet, long floaty skirt pulled up over her knees, running out of the sea. The sun had caught the splashes of water she'd been kicking up and there seemed to be a halo of light around her shock of loose curls. Xander loved that photo but Lissy didn't need to be seeing it now, did she?

'Beautiful photo,' Lissy said.

'I'll never part with it,' he said, knowing now that whoever he shared his life with in the future – and he hoped with all his heart that that would be Lissy – she would have to understand that Claire would always be with him.

'Nor should you,' Lissy said.

'Coffee?' Xander said. 'Tea? The milk might be a bit iffy though.'

God, he was sounding like a pimply teenager now and not the assured lover he'd been told more than a few times that he was, although he found that hard to believe.

'Or we could carry on with our walk?' Lissy said. 'I didn't think it would affect me quite so much coming in here and Claire not being here.'

'No,' Xander said.

'I'll never have to do this for the first time ever again though,' Lissy said. 'You know, come in here and see all Claire's photos because I couldn't expect you not to have them around, and neither would I want that. Bobbie said that about meeting Claire's parents at St Paul's – I'd never have to do that for the first time again. There'll be other times for us.'

Xander felt like punching the air at her words.

'God, I hope so,' he said.

Lissy turned and smiled up at him. She stood on tiptoe and kissed his cheek.

'So, back to the walk? Probably the better idea because, well, there are two ladies back at Strand House expecting dinner this afternoon and goodness knows what state of exhaustion we'd be in if we … well, you know.'

Oh yes, Xander knew. And then an idea came to him at the mention of Janey and Bobbie. They – and Lissy – would be dressing for dinner, wouldn't they? He was a right scruff bag by comparison. He couldn't play the comedic French waiter again either. But he did have a dinner suit upstairs, still in its polythene wrapping from when it had come back from the dry cleaner's after a business dinner he'd attended.

'Be with you in five,' Xander said. 'Just got to fetch something.'

Chapter 28

Janey

Janey came downstairs – wearing a pair of randomly splashed leggings, like someone had used them to paint walls and rubbed the brushes off on them, and a powder blue, cowl-necked, Angora jumper that Bobbie had loaned her – to find Bobbie sitting on the largest couch, her legs tucked up underneath her, reading.

'Ah, there you are Bobbie.'

'The very same,' Bobbie said, putting down her book and sliding her reading glasses up onto the top of her head.

Even that gesture looked elegant and worthy of a photograph in Janey's opinion. Or a painting. Now she was thinking about it more she was seeing opportunities everywhere.

Bobbie straightened her legs from under her and groaned.

'Oh my God. When do we lose the ability to do that without being stiffer than an ironing board?' Bobbie grimaced.

'I'm a bit stiff myself,' Janey said.

She'd been sitting so long, her paintings resting on the window sill to get the maximum light. She'd done four. Quite small. More impressionistic than photographic. All of them a different aspect of the seaside. They'd need a bit of refining but the essence of them was there, the feel of the place. She couldn't quite believe she'd hardly ever come here, and certainly never as far around the coast as Hollacombe, but she hadn't. She was here now, though, and loving it like she'd never have believed she could just forty-eight hours earlier. Her stomach rumbled. 'I think I've missed lunch.'

'Me too,' Bobbie said. 'Although mine was by design rather than accident. I'm going to have to do some serious dieting when I leave here.'

'I'm not!' Janey laughed. 'Lissy's been teaching me, albeit unknowingly, to love my food again.'

'Yeah, I can understand that.' Bobbie rubbed her bare feet to get some life back into them. 'Fear robs us of an appetite. Been there, done that over the years. For me now, it's fear there won't ever be another job that makes me watch what I eat and tell myself I do not like pastries filled with chocolate shards and cranberries, or chocolate brownie.'

'Except you do!' Janey laughed.

'Too much! Thank goodness this Christmas lark is only a few days long. My work is my ongoing pension … well, not that I'm pension age yet, of course.'

As she spoke she looked away from Janey and Janey wondered what untruth she was covering up because Stuart had never been able to look her in the eye when he'd been lying about something. And now she was looking at Bobbie, really looking at her, she could see there were rather a lot of crows' feet at the corners of her eyes, and her hands had a few freckles … age spots her old granny had always called them.

'No, of course you're not,' Janey said. 'Anyway, thanks for loaning me this stuff. It was far comfier to work in than my jeans would have been.'

'Keep it,' Bobbie said, 'It looks better on you, I'm aware sometimes that I go too far down the mutton-dressed-as-lamb road.'

Janey couldn't think how to answer that so she didn't.

'Thank you.'

'And I've got a dress you might like to wear for dinner later. *If* we get some.'

Janey laughed.

'I thought they'd have been back by now,' she said.

'I didn't!' Bobbie said. She tapped the side of her nose with a finger.

'You've lost me,' Janey told her. 'I realise they got on quite well ...'

'Very well, I'd say.'

Bobbie stood up and did some sideways stretches, then bent down to touch her toes with the tips of her fingers. Stretching again she tipped her head from side to side. Then she raised each knee in turn hugging it hard. Six on each leg. That was followed by swinging her arms like a windmill, and she took deep breaths in and out as she did it.

'Claire made an exercise plan for me. That was part of the daily routine. I've got to keep supple for my job, even though it looks as though models have been wired up stiffly in very unnatural poses sometimes. The camera lies because it takes an awful lot of core strength to do all that.'

Janey was still feeling a bit fragile, weak, but she wasn't going to be starting a fitness regime any time soon. Her mind needed nurturing first. Her soul. And painting was doing that for her.

She walked over to the window and looked out. It had clouded over and everything had taken on a greyish hue, like old-fashioned mens' flannel trousers. Could she replicate that shade from the small box of watercolours she had upstairs? When might she be able to go over to Annie's and Fred's to collect all her things? Lissy had said she could stay on at Strand House and she hoped that offer still stood. She'd ask again tomorrow. Just so she knew where she stood and if she'd need to think again or not.

'Can you see them yet?' Bobbie asked from behind her.

Janey could tell she was still doing some sort of exercises and could only think it was jolly hard work staying as slim and as fit and as glamorous as Bobbie was.

'Not yet.'

Bobbie came over to stand beside her.

'This is an odd sort of Christmas Day, Janey, don't you think?'

'Hmm. Yes. Different. Breakfast was rather wonderful. Christmas Day breakfast was never special for me before.'

'Nor me.'

'That's going on the list of things to make my life better – fabulous Christmas Day breakfasts from now on.'

'Good for you,' Bobbie said.

'And then we've been doing our own thing here, you and me, while Lissy and Xander have gone out walking, but it's been with the promise of wonderful things to come ... the food and the company and the conversation. I don't want it to end if I'm honest.'

Bobbie put an arm around Janey's shoulder.

'If there's something to upset the plans and Lissy changes her mind about you stopping on, you can come back to London with me if you'd like to.'

'Really?' Janey said, twisting around to look at her.

'Really. London's heaven for artists. You see them all over the place with their easels or their sketchpads, and the place is awash with art galleries. And don't forget, when you get around to fetching your art stuff from your neighbours there's a painting that's got my name on it. I'd pay serious money for that in a London art gallery.'

'Consider it yours,' Janey said. 'For, you know, being so kind.' There was a lump in her throat now. She didn't think for a moment she'd take Bobbie up on her offer because, well, their worlds were just so different, but it was nice to have it all the same. 'Oh, look! There they are.' She pointed to the top of the steps where Lissy and Xander had just appeared, like a jack-in-a-box popping up. 'Oh, they've got their arms around one another.'

'I should flipping well hope so!' Bobbie said. 'Or all my pep talks have been for nought!'

'You matchmaker!' Janey said.

'But lovely with it,' Bobbie laughed. She linked her arm through Janey's. 'Come on. I've got a feeling it's going to be all hands to the pump to get this meal on the table for four o'clock.'

Janey saw Lissy and Xander – who had something in a big black bag dangling from his free hand – stop to share a kiss. And then another. And then another.

'I think,' she said, 'you might be right.'

'Come on,' Bobbie said. 'Let's make ourselves scarce. We don't want them to think we've been spying on them, do we?'

'Try this for size, Janey,' Bobbie said, standing in the open doorway of Janey's room.

She was dangling a black dress, with Chinese-style pink strands of blossom randomly printed on it, on its hanger at her. It had a scoop neck and slashed shoulders, and an asymmetric handkerchief hem.

'I wore this once for a shoot for one of the bigger high street chains. Some idiot got cream from a bun they shouldn't have been eating on the shoot over it so I was told to keep it. It wasn't worth the maker's while to get the thing dry-cleaned and they wouldn't be able to sell it on afterwards if they had.'

Janey couldn't imagine wearing something only once.

'More you than me, this one, I think,' Bobbie said. 'Comes into the mutton-dressed-as-lamb category for me but it'll be perfect on you. I've got some hair product you can use as well if you want. A wash-in, wash-out thing. Won't take you long. But it'll, you know, brighten it. If you blow dry it afterwards and then brush it slightly forward over your shoulders instead of ... oh God, listen to me. Bossy boots is at it again.'

174

'A bit,' Janey said, standing up. She noticed that as well as having the dress on its hanger in one hand, Bobbie was also clutching a bottle of something in the other. 'But I really don't mind. It's great that, well, you care. Come on in.'

'Only for a moment,' Bobbie said. 'As you've probably worked out by now I take more time than the average woman getting ready. Can't let the catwalk go, really. As Xander told me, I'm high-maintenance.'

'He never did!' Janey laughed taking the dress from Bobbie and holding it against herself. She caught a glimpse of herself in the mirror on the wardrobe door. Not something she'd have chosen for herself but she liked it. She would wear it.

'He did so! Cheeky blighter. Said it was a compliment, so I took it as one. Anyway, do you want a bit of help with your hair?'

'Not if it's self-explanatory on the bottle, no,' Janey said. She'd use that as well. She was beginning to feel like a butterfly emerging from its chrysalis in this house, sloughing off her old, dark, clothes. 'But have I got time before we eat?'

She was starting to feel really hungry now.

'Plenty. Those two down there probably don't want us on board for a moment. I've been hearing lots of chat and then silence for a few minutes. Kissing time, I'd say.'

'Good for them.' Janey wasn't remotely jealous but she hoped there might be someone new for her some day. Someone like Xander who was funny and kind. And very easy on the eye as well.

'You've just blushed,' Bobbie said, wagging a playful finger at her. 'What naughty thought were you thinking?'

'Not going to tell!' Janey laughed.

'Stash your naughty little secret away, then,' Bobbie said. 'Most of us have got them.'

'I'm slowly revealing mine,' Janey said. She'd told them more about how things had been with her and Stuart and her mother and sister than she'd ever told anyone. It had felt raw to do it, but also cleansing somehow, as though her soul had been scrubbed with a bath brush.

'Oooh, listen,' Bobbie said. She cupped a hand, shell like, to one ear. 'I can hear silence. They're at it again. I don't know about you but I'm beginning to feel a tad wallflower around those two.'

'I honestly don't think they meant that to happen, or even thought that it would. I think it's come as a lovely surprise to them both, don't you?'

Bobbie shrugged.

'Picking up where they left off.'

'Really? Has Lissy said?'

Janey didn't want to think that there might have been something going on between Lissy and Xander when Claire had been alive but also knew they wouldn't be the first to go down that road if there had been.

'No,' Bobbie said, sharply, which told Janey that Bobbie did know something but wasn't going to trade a secret. And she wasn't going to try and prise it from her. 'But don't worry your pretty little head about anything. Go and do the deed with this bottle of magic and then get into that dress. We need to keep up appearances because I've got a sneaky feeling that bag Xander was holding in the hand that wasn't tenderly clutching Lissy, had a dinner suit in it.'

'Dinner suit?'

'You know, black with a satin trim to the jacket. Bow tie. Pristine white shirt.'

'Oh, that,' Janey said. 'I know.'

She'd been to a black-tie event at a school do with Stuart once. He'd started to drink too much, slurring his words, being aggressive. She'd managed to get him out and into a taxi before he embarrassed himself. They'd not been to another since.

Bobbie left the room and Janey wondered just how long it would take to get Stuart out of her mind. She had a feeling getting him out of her life was the easier part.

Heading for the bathroom she decided she was going to make more of a concerted effort to do just that. Her friends here deserved more of her mind to be in the room with them, and not elsewhere.

Chapter 29

Lissy

'Can you give them a shout, Xand?' Lissy asked.

She'd toasted the sourdough, put the bruschetta toppings on and had only to put them under the grill and that was the canapés ready. The boned and rolled, stuffed turkey breast was in the oven and browning nicely. Trays of roots – sea-salt crusted potatoes, parsnips with a honey and thyme rub, and carrots tossed in balsamic vinegar and olive oil were on a tray roasting in the fast, top oven. The obligatory Christmas pigs in blankets also had a Lissy twist – she'd added apple to the pork and wrapped them in pancetta with a sage leaf inside. Chocolate mousse – made with the very best Green and Black's and locally sourced double cream – with raspberries was waiting in the fridge for dessert.

'Anything for you, madam,' Xander said.

That, I think, will have to wait, Lissy thought but didn't say. It had been the right decision not to make love in Xander's cottage, although that was what had been their intention in going there and they both knew it. She had a feeling that when Xander turned up shortly in his dinner suit she'd get those intentions all over again. There was something about a man in one of those, wasn't there?

'You've already done loads,' Lissy said.

Xander had set the table in the hall, lit the candles, laid out the crackers, and selected music to play gently in the background while they ate. He'd played sous chef stirring gravy – with a dash of balsamic vinegar and cranberry juice for pep – and uncorked a couple of bottles of red so they could breathe should anyone want red wine with the six varieties of cheese Lissy had bought if anyone had room for it after they'd eaten their way through everything else.

'All that remains, then, is for me to turn the pig's ear that is my usual self into the silk purse you lovely ladies deserve for the occasion. Back in a jif.'

And then Xander was gone, shouting out to Janey and Bobbie that dinner was all but ready and where the heck were they, they were already perfect enough and their lilies didn't need over-gilding.

Lissy chuckled to herself. She'd already nipped upstairs while Xander had been polishing glasses with a tea towel and setting them out ready for the meal – red wine, white wine, water – and changed. Nothing fancy, just a plain royal blue jersey wrap dress, beige heels, and a thick rope chain gold necklace that had been Vonny's.

Practising, that's what she was doing with the setting out of things just so, Lissy told herself, for when … for when she'd no longer be making lots and lots of money being an accountant, risking everything in a new venture. A risk she had to take. She had to be true to herself and she knew it now, more than helped by the fact her friends were so encouraging and complimentary about her culinary efforts. Strand House and everything in it, Lissy couldn't claim any credit for because that had all been Vonny's taste. Good as it was, it wasn't Lissy's entirely. While she'd been putting veg ready to roast, Xander had sat on the end of the kitchen counter with a couple of sheets of paper Lissy had fetched from her printer when he'd asked for some, making some architect's drawings of how a conservatory might look, how a snug might look, for when Lissy moved in to Strand House full time.

He was more than good at it, and Lissy had asked if he'd ever fancied retraining, studying to take his building to the next level. He might, he'd said, and then he'd put down his pencil, got up from the bar stool, and gone over to Lissy. Turning her round to face him, he'd kissed her gently. 'Thanks for asking. I'll sleep on it.'

Lissy could hear movement upstairs now, and then footsteps on the wooden treads of the stairs. She put the tray with the bruschettas on it under the grill to heat through.

Janey and Bobbie were laughing about something. Good. And then, there they were, framed in the kitchen doorway.

'Oh, my! Janey!' Lissy said. 'You look wonderful.'

Janey's hair seemed a few shades lighter than it had been when she'd gone upstairs earlier. She'd combed one long curtain of hair over her left shoulder and the other was behind her right one. She was wearing lipstick – Bobbie's at a guess because this was the first time Lissy had ever seen Janey wear any. She was also wearing the nude heels Lissy had loaned her and leaned against a door jamb crossing one leg behind the other in a slightly nervous way. This was all so new to her, wasn't it? Lissy couldn't help but notice how slender Janey's ankles were. How beautifully shaped her legs were too. And her shoulders. She looked as much a model in that moment as Bobbie – who actually was – did. Not, Lissy knew, that it was looks that mattered to Janey. But surely, looking good in herself would make her feel better too?

'Scrubbed up well, hasn't she?' Bobbie said, putting an affectionate arm around Janey's shoulder.

Bobbie was making a joke of it, in a bid to make Janey feel less self-conscious perhaps, but Lissy hoped it wasn't having the opposite effect and making her feel as though she needed to improve her look.

'Oh!' Lissy said. She could smell toast just beginning to catch. The already-cooked edges of the bruschetta had been rubbed in olive oil. In the moment of taking in the vision that was now Janey she'd forgotten them for a moment. She rushed to rescue them just in time, dropping the hot tray with a clang on the granite work top.

'Come and get it, girls,' Lissy said. 'Help yourselves to drinks.'

It was a second or two before Janey was able to move, but Bobbie propelled her on. And Lissy was glad they were forming a stronger bond, albeit having been thrown together by her invitation.

'You can take them through to the sitting room if you want,' she said after Bobbie had poured all three of them a glass of white wine.

'We'll wait for Xander,' Bobbie said. 'Ah, I hear footsteps. I think we might all be in for a visual treat if what was in the black bag he was carrying is what I think it was. An improvement on last night's waiter look – although, that said, I've seen more badly-dressed maître D's. You might need to hold on to your breath, girls, 'cos I've got a feeling he's going to take it clean away.'

And then there he was, looking – Lissy thought – very Pierce Brosnan in his younger day. Bobbie was right, the sight of him had taken her breath clean away.

'Very smart,' Janey said.

Lissy couldn't think of a thing to say except perhaps that if it was the last sight she saw on this earth she'd die a happy woman. She was waiting for Bobbie to say something witty and pithy to fill the gap. All she heard was a strangled sort of cry, a half sob. When she looked Bobbie had grabbed the edge of the kitchen island and was struggling to hold herself upright, her legs sort of buckled beneath her.

Xander came rushing forward to grab her before she fell.

'I've never had that effect on a woman – any woman – before,' Xander laughed. 'Hey! You okay?' He righted Bobbie, and Janey slid a bar stool under her so she could sit down.

Lissy wondered just what it was about her kitchen that had made two women now go weak at the knees over something. Xander was having that effect on her as well but she was hardly in danger of collapsing.

'Low blood sugar,' Bobbie said. 'I missed lunch.'

'Bruschetta coming up,' Lissy said, offering her the tray.

Somehow she didn't quite believe that explanation of events and she had a feeling Xander and Janey didn't either.

Chapter 30

Bobbie

'If I don't eat for a week,' Bobbie said, 'it'll be too soon. That, Lissy, was Michelin star. More than. And trust me, I've had more than a few Michelin-starred meals in my time.'

Everything about the meal had been perfect – the fabulous setting of Lissy's hall, the food itself, and the company. She couldn't remember ever having had a better Christmas.

She was feeling stronger now, but it had been a momentary struggle to recover from her panic in the kitchen. The sight of Xander, standing there so tall, so handsome, so very like the man to whom she'd given her heart – and who had changed her life so dramatically – had thrown her momentarily. He was dead now. She knew that beyond doubt, because she'd read his obituary in *The Times*. But she'd thought quickly and blamed missing lunch and low blood sugar for her sudden loss of self control. Yes, got away with that one, she smiled to herself, scraping up the last of the chocolate mousse and popping it in her mouth.

'And this stuff is pure ambrosia. Gods never had it so good in my opinion. This has to be, for me anyway, the best Christmas Day ever. Nothing could better it.'

'Oh, Bobbie, that's a lovely thing to hear. I'm just glad you're enjoying it,' Lissy said. 'It was getting a bit sad, cooking up all this stuff just to take photographs of it and post them on social media and then throw most of it away. Thanks, you know, for all joining me so I can show off.'

'It's not showing off,' Janey said. 'If you're good at something why shouldn't you let others know?'

'Precisely,' Bobbie said, wiping delicately at the corners of her mouth with a paper napkin decorated with silver stars on a black ground. Very classy. Very chic.

'Hands up for coffee,' Lissy said, and then three hands shot up in the air.

Bobbie would need something to sharpen her mind after so much food and a glass or two of wine more than she would normally have drunk, but hey, this was Christmas.

And then she felt her mobile tremble in the pocket of her palazzo pants. Lissy had said she'd prefer it if no one used their phones at the table and they'd all adhered to that request. But she hadn't said she couldn't have her phone on her, had she?

'So, so sorry, everyone,' Bobbie said, getting up. 'I've been expecting a call about work so I need to take it. Sorry, sorry to be breaking up the party. I'll take it in the sitting room, okay?'

That wasn't strictly true. None of the outlets she worked for were likely to be calling her on Christmas Day, were they? There was a flutter of something under her breastbone – who could it be?

'Okay,' Lissy said. 'I'll get coffee when you come back. No worries.'

Bobbie threw her a kiss for her thoughtfulness and hurried across the hall floor to the sitting room, closing the door behind her. She heard the volume of music go up in the hall – another of Lissy's kindnesses, drowning out any possibility of eavesdropping.

'Is that Roberta?' someone said before she got the chance to say hello. She didn't recognise the number coming up, but answered anyway.

A man's voice. Deep.

'Yes. Roberta. Bobbie.'

'Are you a relative of Pamela and Charles?'

'Pamela, yes,' Bobbie said. She pushed herself back in the couch, snuggling into the cushions. She kicked off her shoes and pulled her feet up to one side. She was getting all sorts of funny sensations running through her now, but she couldn't afford to go to pieces as she had in the kitchen earlier. 'We're cousins. Has something happened?'

'I think,' the voice continued, 'and there's no easy way to say this … I think you're my mother.'

Bobbie's mouth went wide with shock and her intake of breath seemed to rush through her, as far as the bottoms of her feet. Her fingers began to tingle. Oliver?

'Oliver?' she said.

'I'm called Olly – with a y – these days.'

'Where are you? Olly with a y?' Bobbie was thinking fast – if he'd called her he must want to be talking to her, but why now? On Christmas Day of all days.

'So, are you my mother?'

'Yes. But—'

'Is it okay for you to talk right now?' Olly interrupted. 'I mean, it's Christmas night and you're probably with family.'

'I'm not with family, no.'

No family. She'd given Olly away, under family pressure, and had made a conscious decision not to have another child. How would it be for Olly now if she had to say, yes, she was with family – three or four children on whom she'd lavished love and cash, when she'd given him away.

'Did you get my letter?'

'Your letter?' Bobbie had received a letter with an Australian stamp on it via her solicitor – the one she'd purposely not opened in case it contained bad news about Oliver. Olly – with a y now. She must remember to call him that. 'I haven't opened it yet.'

'Ah, that might explain things. Are you alone?'

'At the moment, yes.'

She had so many questions she needed to ask him, but where to begin? And besides, she was aware that her three friends were sitting around the table still amongst the detritus of a fabulous meal, and all waiting for her to come back and join them.

'I have news,' Olly said. 'Whether that's good or bad I'll leave to you. Okay.'

'Mmm,' was all Bobbie could manage.

'Pamela and Charles are both dead now. Charles two years ago, and Pamela last September. Clearing out their effects I found stuff.' Olly's voice seemed to be breaking now.

'What stuff, Olly?' Bobbie asked. There was a sick feeling in the pit of her stomach that she knew what the answer to that would be if he was asking if she was his mother.

'First up, that they weren't my parents.'

'And you didn't know until last September?'

'No.'

'But were they good to you?' Bobbie asked. She had to know. She'd been promised they'd care for him as if he was his own. That he would want for nothing. She wasn't surprised that Pamela had kept the fact she wasn't Olly's mother from him because appearances were all to her, and being childless was, to her, a failing in her somehow.

'Yes. I can't deny that but I'm feeling short-changed now. I couldn't find any adoption papers though.'

'There weren't any,' Bobbie told him. There was no need for that, her parents had said. Pamela was family, wasn't she? It happened all the time in China, people who weren't a child's parents bringing them up. Grandparents, aunts and uncles, cousins, whoever. And she'd believed Pamela when she'd said

186

she'd see that Oliver always knew about her being his birth mother. It hadn't taken Pamela long to renege on that one. 'All future communication will be via solicitors,' Pamela had said in a letter when Olly was eleven, or maybe twelve, years old. 'It will be for the best.'

'Ah,' Olly said.

'How much do you know?' Bobbie asked. 'You know, about why ...'

'I'm learning,' Olly said and Bobbie could see in her mind the wry look he'd have on his face – understatement was probably the word for how it was for him right now. 'I've found a whole trunkful of letters. Cards. Presents. Small boy presents. You sent them, didn't you?'

'Always. Until you were about eleven or twelve.'

After that Bobbie had had no idea what boys growing up would like or need so she'd stopped sending presents on Oliver's birthday and at Christmas. The parcel she'd sent for Oliver's thirteenth birthday had been returned – 'Not known at this address' – and then she'd got that solicitor's letter so she'd stopped sending them. But she hadn't stopped buying presents for him. She had a trunkful of things relating to him back at her mews house in London.

'I never got those presents,' Olly said.

Bobbie was beginning to work that out for herself. Her mind was uneasy mix of anger at Pamela and Charles for not giving Olly the presents she'd so lovingly bought, and sadness for Olly that they hadn't and also the fizz of joy that he had called her.

'I am so sorry.'

'Why did you stop sending them? Or just a card?'

'I didn't stop,' Bobbie said. This conversation was so surreal – one she'd had many times in her head and she had to pinch herself that she was having it now, sitting on someone else's couch in someone else's house.

As quickly and as briefly as she could, she told Olly about the solicitor's letter she'd received. And then she said, 'Where are you? Australia?'

She'd begun to detect a slight Australian accent.

'London.'

'Oh my God!' The first Christmas she'd ever had away from home and now …

'I thought I'd surprise you. Pamela and Charles's solicitor put me in touch with your solicitor and he gave me your address. It was all in that letter you haven't opened. I'm a big boy now and while I felt like a small boy who'd had all his toys taken away finding out this stuff, I realised pretty quickly that I wasn't the only one short-changed and lied to. You were too.'

'Yes. I was,' Bobbie said, a smile creeping to her face that Olly seemed to have the same sort of humour as she did. 'I left instructions that you were to be told where to find me. If … you wanted to.'

'I want,' Olly said. 'Surprise?'

Bobbie gulped and it was difficult to swallow for a moment. She felt a little faint.

'It's a surprise, all right,' she managed to say at last.

'That's both of us then, Bobbie,' Olly said. 'So now you know where I am and that I'm not angry about anything you did in the past, where are you?'

'Devon.'

'Ah, that will explain why no one answered when I knocked. Are you there alone?'

'No. I'm with three friends.'

And boy, wasn't she glad of them. She didn't want to think now how this call would have been had she been on her own with no one to share the news with. All three of them were going to get a surprise but she didn't think it would faze any of them. Already so much was happening this Christmas to them all.

'Perhaps,' Olly said, 'now I've dropped this news you might want to get back to them. There's so much more I want to tell you, so much more I need to know but hey, it's Christmas Day, you were having a jolly time until I called so …'

'I'm having an even jollier time now, Olly,' Bobbie laughed, or perhaps it was more of a nervous giggle and she was that gauche, unworldly, eighteen-year-old again who had made not the best choices ever. She hung onto the thought that Pamela and Charles had been good to Olly, if economical with the truth.

'So, can we meet? I'm curious to meet. I've discovered you're quite a famous face for followers of fashion! My daughters are made up!'

'Granddaughters?' Bobbie said. 'I've got granddaughters?' She was still struggling to get more than a word or two out at a time, afraid if she said too much she'd dissolve into tears of pure joy, and not a little guilt as well.

'Three. Grace, Martha, and Emily.'

Bobbie had never factored having granddaughters into the equation.

'Ages?'

'Eighteen, sixteen, and twelve. In that order.'

Eighteen – the same age Bobbie had been when she'd given birth to Olly, held him in her arms for so short a time. Loved him. And then given him away.

'Can I meet them, too?' she asked, fearful that Olly would say maybe not yet, or no, or that it would be up to them and then they'd more than likely – being teenage girls – decide it was uncool for this to be happening …

'Of course,' Olly said, cutting into her wayward thoughts.

She'd always been such a clear thinker! Now her thoughts were fractured, all over the place. There were thoughts and ideas rushing through her mind like a reel of film. What welcome presents could she buy for girls of that age? Where could she take them in London that would impress girls of that age? Where would they all stop? With her? Her house had four bedrooms, over three floors. There'd be room. But would they want to?

189

'Are you still there?' Olly asked. 'I know this is a shock, and maybe not the best day to have dropped all this on you …'

'Any day would have been the best day,' Bobbie said. 'But this is *the* best.'

'My wife said you'd say that!' Olly laughed. 'She said it was a mother thing and that's how she'd feel if she was in your position.'

So, Olly had a wife.

'What's her name?'

'Beth. Bethany really but everyone calls her Beth.'

'Beth,' Bobbie said, feeling the sound of her daughter-in-law's name on her tongue. That made her a mother-in-law, something else she hadn't factored into the equation of future possibilities.

'She can't wait to meet you. I think she's got fed up of me talking about you constantly since I found out you exist. So, when will you be back? Or shall we all come down to Devon? I've hired a car.'

Bobbie had planned on returning to London the day after Boxing Day. There'd be more chance of getting a taxi all the way to London then. Taxi drivers worked on public holidays but she doubted there'd be one free to drive her all the way to London tomorrow. Besides, it would be rude to break up Lissy's party too soon.

'The 27th,' Bobbie said. 'I'll be home then.'

She looked at her watch. She'd been on the phone talking to Olly for over half an hour now. How easy this conversation had been after all. After all the imaginary conversations she'd had with him in her head – angry conversations, blaming conversations, tearful conversations. Olly, she was fast discovering was more like her in the direct way he spoke, than she could ever have wished he might be. She could happily talk to him long into the night but he had a family to be with and she had three of the kindest, dearest, friends a person could ever have waiting for her so they call finish their Christmas meal.

190

'Safe journey,' Olly said. 'I'll let you get back to your friends now. And if I'm honest I need Beth and the girls too. I've only just held it together in the tears department. I'm a blubbering wreck inside.'

'Me too,' Bobbie said.

'Until the 27th, then?' Olly said, and Bobbie detected just the sliver of doubt in his voice that she might pull out.

'Of course.' Bobbie couldn't trust herself now to say much more without breaking down and Olly didn't need that. 'Goodnight.'

'Goodnight,' Olly said, his voice still firm. But then on the end of it, Bobbie heard him whisper, 'Mum.'

Bobbie only just had the presence of mind to save his number before going back to the others.

Very slowly she opened the door into the hall. All three turned to look at her, their faces anxious, not knowing what it was they were about to hear. Bobbie took some slow deep breaths and Xander got up to turn off the music.

'I am so sorry,' Bobbie said, 'to have taken so long.'

'Bad news?' Lissy said, getting up to come to her.

'Absolutely not,' Bobbie said, her face breaking into a wide grin so strong and sudden that her jaw cracked. 'That was Oliver. Olly now. My son.'

Chapter 31

Lissy

After they'd all got over the shock of Bobbie's reveal, Lissy said they were all in dire need of coffee, possibly with brandy in it for the shock, and she got up right away and went into the kitchen to make it. Never in her wildest dreams had she even considered that this Christmas would turn out the way it had. First there was the very deep attraction she realised now she'd always had for Xander, and the delight that he felt the same. And Janey – so much there for her to be dealing with after this Christmas break was over and Lissy could only be pleased that she had been able to provide Janey with such a safe haven.

And now Bobbie with her secret lovechild. There was going to be a story there and she had a feeling it was going to unravel over coffee and brandy. Lissy added some mince pies and some leftover slices of brownie – not that any of them needed any more food but sometimes it helped to be doing something in a difficult situation – to the tray and carried it in.

'I've waited until you got back,' Bobbie said. 'It's going to be a struggle saying it all once, so I thought I'd wait.'

'Only as much as you feel you can or want to,' Lissy said, setting down the tray.

Xander set out the cups and poured the coffee, while Lissy laid the plates out on the table. Janey took the top from the brandy bottle and picked up the measure Lissy had put beside it on the tray. A team – they were a team.

'Everyone?' Janey said.

'Make mine a double.' Bobbie laughed nervously. 'I'm shaking like a leaf.'

'So are we!' Janey said.

The group fell silent for a few moments while Xander handed round the cups and everyone helped themselves to something to nibble at should they need it.

Lissy gave Bobbie what she hoped was an encouraging smile.

Bobbie picked up on it. She reached out a hand and laid it on Lissy's for a moment.

'Thanks,' she said. 'Well you're all ears now so I'll begin.' She picked up her cup and took a sip. 'It is, of course, the age-old story. I was seventeen. I met him at a car promotion for Ford. The latest model – the name of which I've now forgotten. I was starting out in the world of modelling and took just about anything that was offered to get my name out there back then. I was hired to wear a bikini and drape myself over the bonnet. I'm not proud of it now but you do all sorts of stupid things when you're seventeen and think you know it all, don't you?'

She looked from one to another around the table inviting confidences, needing them perhaps. Lissy could have taken the title 'Miss Goody Two Shoes' at that age because all she'd been able to think about doing was pleasing her father – whose heart her wayward mother had broken – by studying hard to become an accountant and join him in his practice. Janey merely nodded. It was Xander who picked up the baton.

'God, yeah. Berry Head was nearly the end of me. Despite all the warning signs not to dive off the cliffs or climb them, no prizes for guessing what I did. There was a bottle of whisky that nearly put me in hospital as well. An older woman who turned out to be toxic came into it as well.'

He looked at Lissy, wondering perhaps if he'd said too much. If this was something she didn't want to know, but all she could think was how kind he was helping Bobbie out when she needed someone to – and maybe he was just saying those things to make her feel better and none of it was true anyway.

'Got it in one, Xander,' Bobbie said. 'He was older. Much older. My local MP as it happened. Going through a divorce. So he said. Very, very handsome with it. He began inviting me to dinner in expensive restaurants. He asked me to be his escort at functions a few times. I think he liked having me on his arm – a younger woman who knew how to dress. My hair was jet black in those days. And I was as thin as a reed. Catsuits were the rage, and I was wearing a black one. This is probably too much information but after one particular function where the wine had flowed even more freely than it usually did, we had a little bet, him and me – how fast he could get me out that catsuit if I were to go upstairs with him. There were rooms. I said I was going to win that one because there was no way I was going to sleep with him, not that sleep was on his agenda.' Bobbie sighed, then took a sliver of brownie, pulled off a few crumbs and ate them.

'I've always thought that was a strange expression,' Janey said. 'Sleeping together. A contradiction in terms if ever there was one.'

'Quite,' Bobbie said.

The joy in Bobbie's face that she'd spoken to her son who, Lissy was guessing, she'd not heard from before, was sliding now.

'If it's too painful recalling all this,' Lissy said, 'you can stop now.'

'What was it Bamber Gascoigne used to say?' Bobbie said, pulling her back up straighter. 'I've started so I'll finish?'

Everyone laughed and Bobbie took another sip or two of her coffee.

'Of course, the inevitable happened. We did go upstairs and it was me who got myself out of the catsuit. I found out in quick succession that he a) wasn't going through a divorce at all, b) that he had no intention of facing up to any sort of responsibility for his child and c) my parents thought more about the neighbours' feelings than they did mine.'

'They threw you out?' Janey asked.

'Ultimatum time,' Bobbie said. 'If I was even considering keeping the baby then they'd disown me. That's what happened back then. There were mother and baby homes all over the country bearing that out. You didn't go to the one nearest where you lived, of course, but got sent to one thirty miles away or so where no one was likely to see you at the hospital keeping antenatal appointments. Anyway, somehow my cousin Pamela got to hear about "my condition" as it was called, like it was a nasty bout of flu or something. She was childless but not by choice. So she offered to take the baby and bring it up. It seemed the best solution at the time. I had no way of earning a decent living – modelling didn't make the money then that it does now – and my parents weren't going to step in and do the caring of my baby for me.'

Bobbie reached for the coffee pot and topped up her cup. Lissy realised it was probably just for something to do rather than the fact she needed it. She was buying time while she thought about how she was going to tell the next bit, wasn't she?

'I can't imagine what it must be like to give your child away,' Xander said.

Lissy's heart skipped a bit, remembering how Xander had said recently, and with such sadness, that he wanted children.

'I didn't think of it as that,' Bobbie said. 'Pamela was family. She was just child-minding to my naïve mind. I would see Oliver – as I eventually called him – now and then. Pamela would keep me informed of all his milestones. There would be regular photos. I could send birthday and Christmas presents, and cards, and he'd be told they were from his birth mother and in my innocence I thought he would write me little notes and thank me for them. Except ...'

'Except that didn't happen,' Lissy said, giving Bobbie time to compose herself.

'No. They went to Australia instead. I've no idea how because I imagine there might have been a passport issue for Oliver or something. I suspect they changed his surname pretty quick.'

'There are always ways and means,' Xander said. 'If money changes hands.'

'Probably,' Bobbie said. 'Pamela and Charles had plenty of that, far more than I did for a very long time. I still sent things, of course, but then they moved and didn't give me any forwarding address. So I stopped sending presents and cards at Christmas and on Oliver's birthday. But I didn't stop buying them. Every year since then I've bought Oliver something and stashed it away in a cupboard. Madness, I know.' She looked from one to the other and Lissy's heart went out to her.

'Not madness at all,' Lissy said. 'How do any of us know what we'd do in the circumstances?'

'And now,' Janey said in her quiet, calm voice, 'you can give them to him.'

'I'm not sure he'd want a T-shirt with *Dr Who* on it,' Bobbie said, her voice breaking.

'Of course he will,' Xander said. Lissy saw him swallow hard – fighting back tears of his own at a guess. 'Because you bought it for him. Because all those cards and presents will tell him how deeply he's been in your heart and your mind, and now you can give them to him.'

'My guess is he won't be taking it all back to Australia with him when he finds out. Anyway, that's for the future, for when we meet.'

'If he's not in Australia anymore, where is he?' Lissy asked.

'London.'

'London!' the other three said in unison, in joint disbelief.

'I know. The irony of it. He thought to surprise me. Actually he wrote me first. I had a letter with an Australian stamp on it via my solicitor a week ago and was afraid to open it, so I didn't. I thought it might be from Pamela and Charles telling me something bad had happened to Oliver – I'd always been dreading that – and I didn't want to find that out before coming here and being with you all because it would have spoiled things, rained on your parade, Lissy.'

'Oh, Bobbie,' Lissy said. 'How did you bear such anguish?'

'I did what many people do … filed it away in the part of my mind that's got a lock and key on it. Out of sight, out of mind.'

'Except it never was, not really,' Janey said.

'Got it in one,' Bobbie said. She sighed. 'And now he's been to my house and I'm not there when I could have been, all because I was too scaredy cat to open his letter.'

'And, perhaps, you should have been,' Lissy said.

The time without Bobbie wouldn't have been the same, but that didn't mean that she and Janey, and Xander, couldn't have had a perfectly lovely time without her.

'No. I think it's been for the best. I wouldn't have had anyone to share the news about getting the letter – and what it contained – with. How lonely that would have been!'

'Did you bring the letter with you?' Xander asked.

'Yes.'

'Do you want to read it? Now, I mean?' Lissy asked.

'No,' Bobbie said. 'Olly said he was telling me just about, word for word, what he'd written in the letter. I'll read it later, in my room. But I'm just so glad you three are here to share the news with me.' Bobbie's smile was wider than the proverbial Cheshire Cat's. 'His daughters have found me on Google and know all about my career now. They're made up, Olly said.'

'I bet they are!' Janey said.

'Are you going to go home? Now?' Lissy asked.

She hadn't envisaged the party breaking up quite so soon but if it had to, it had to, and what a wonderful reason for it.

'I thought about it. I sat there looking at the phone for ages after the call ended as though just thinking about Olly would make him appear in front of me. I have no idea what he looks like.'

'You didn't think to look for him on Facebook?' Xander asked. 'I mean, that's how I found you guys.'

'No. There's that element of spying, or stalking, that would have come into it. I would have been deeply uncomfortable about that.'

'You could do it now,' Janey said. 'Now you know. Then you'd know what he looks like. I mean everyone's got some sort of internet profile these days. Even me!'

Bobbie pressed her lips together, closed her eyes briefly before opening them again.

'I could but I think I need another day to let it all sink in a bit. And I think Olly does too. So,' Bobbie went on, 'when Olly was eleven I got a letter to say any further correspondence would be through our respective solicitors. And it was. My solicitor has always been given any changes of address and phone numbers. First Charles died and then last September Pamela died too. It was then that Olly found the contact details.'

'So that's what's brought about today's phone call?' Xander asked.

'Yeah, that and a trunkful of stuff telling him he wasn't exactly who he'd thought he was.'

'Poor you, poor Olly,' Janey said.

'I can't quite believe I invited you here and he's come to London and you're not there.'

Part of her wished she hadn't done that now. Inviting her friends hadn't been entirely altruistic – she'd need the company too, but all the same …

'Don't for God's sake beat yourself up about that, Lissy,' Bobbie said. 'I've had a million scenarios about just this moment going through my mind and in all of them I've been alone with no one there to tell, and maybe after having an angry Olly on the phone, or in an email. I know I'm developing a bad dose of verbal diarrhoea here,' Bobbie laughed, 'but ...'

'Better out than in,' Xander said.

'Yes, oh yes,' Bobbie said. 'Seeing you in that dinner suit, Xander, threw me a bit. You looked so like Olly's father had the last time I saw him; same outfit, same sort of age, same insouciant stance leaning against a doorjamb. I had a sort of mini time travel to way back then. But never in my wildest dreams did I think that before Christmas night was over I'd be talking to his son.'

'Did Olly ask who is father is? Was?' Janey asked.

'No. But I'll tell him. I've got photos. He was well-documented.'

'How old is Olly?' Xander asked.

'Forty-four. I was a child non-bride.'

Everyone laughed. What a trooper. What a survivor. Such a Bobbie comment, Lissy thought.

'Hey! We haven't pulled the crackers yet,' Janey said, picking up her cracker from beside her plate and waggling it in the air.

'So we haven't,' Lissy said. 'Ready guys?'

Lissy giggled as they all began that sort of arm and cracker origami, so each had someone different with whom to pull a cracker, and there was a simultaneous pulling and tearing and cracking.

'Right, here we go,' Xander said, pulling the joke from his now broken cracker. 'What goes "Oh! Oh! Oh!"?'

'Give up,' Bobbie said with a theatrical yawn.

'Father Christmas walking backwards,' Xander said.

'Oh, this is good,' Lissy said. 'Listen. What do you call it when you get a sore throat at Christmas?'

'Tell us!' Janey said. 'I can't bear the suspense!'

'Tinsellitis!'

Xander groaned.

'I've heard worse,' he said.

Everyone put on the paper hat that came with their cracker and there was an exchange of plastic rings and miniature set squares and bagatelle games, and Lissy realised it had been a good idea to pull them after Bobbie's surprise reveal because she was joining in and laughing. She was even wearing the silly paper hat on her usually pristinely presented head. It was as though Bobbie had physically and mentally relaxed following the phone call from Olly.

'But, guys,' Bobbie said, 'I'd be lying through my expensively fixed teeth if I said I wasn't bone-achingly tired right now.'

Lissy couldn't help a giggle erupting at Bobbie's comment – she might have been down a few times in her life but she'd obviously always bounced back, just as she was bouncing back now. Having Oliver back in her life might be good for them both, or not – who could tell? Sometimes these things worked wonderfully and sometimes they didn't.

As if to prove how she was feeling Bobbie yawned.

'Up the wooden hill with you, then,' Lissy said.

Bobbie got up, and went around the table, hugging them all in turn.

Just twenty-fours ago Bobbie had said to her that – in the famed words of Scarlett O'Hara – tomorrow was another day. Her hug for Lissy went on just a little bit longer than it had for the others. Was she remembering that?

But just in case she wasn't Lissy whispered into Bobbie's hair: 'Tomorrow is another day.'

'So it is,' Bobbie whispered back. 'So it is.'

Chapter 32

Xander

After Bobbie went upstairs Lissy said she'd tidy up and that no, she didn't need any help thank you. Xander had protested saying he was a fairly civilised member of the male sex and could do dishes and wield a J-cloth with the best of them, but Lissy had remained firm. She obviously wanted to be alone with her thoughts. She said Xander and Janey could go into the sitting room and put the TV on if they wanted to. Or some music. Xander's thoughts were all over the place now. How would he feel if he'd found out just a short while ago that the mum and dad who'd brought him up weren't his birth parents? Would he love them less? He didn't think he would but how could anyone who hadn't been in that position know? He thought about going up to bed himself but he wanted to talk to Lissy before he did. And Janey didn't seem to want Christmas night to end either.

So there they were, both nursing cups of now quite cold coffee, in the sitting room. He could hear Lissy in the kitchen putting things down rather noisily, but then granite worktops were hard, and the kitchen was massive and sound echoed in it.

'I've been thinking, Xander,' Janey said. 'The Christmas story is all about a baby. Right?'

'Bobbie's?'

'No!' Janey said. She gave Xander a mock exasperated-at-his-stupidity-in-thinking-that look. 'Not Oliver. Jesus. I know we don't all believe or if we do we rarely go to church these days but it's still the birth of a baby at the centre of all this ...' Janey waved an arm towards the Christmas tree and the string of lights Xander had hung at the window. There were some glass angels and a big fat glass snowman on the coffee table in front of them. 'Well, all this decoration and the traditional food and, well, everything really. It's kind of surreal, don't you think, that this has happened for Bobbie today?'

'I know what you mean. If my mum's reading a book and things like this happen she says she throws the thing across the room because it would be just too farfetched.'

Xander felt a sudden flush of tenderness, thinking about his mum. He felt a bit bad about not accepting her invite to spend Christmas with her but he'd had to do his own thing this Christmas instead of going with the flow of what others wanted for him. He was so glad he had because now he was on the cusp of something very special with Lissy.

'I do that!' Janey said.

'Do what?' Xander said, having momentarily lost the thread of the conversation. 'Sorry, been a long day.'

And it had. First that rather fabulous breakfast and then the walk to the harbour along the coast with Lissy. Holding hands. Being physically close and getting emotionally closer. Then had come that rather embarrassing – well, for him it had been although Lissy seemed less so – moment when they'd reached his cottage and he'd assumed they'd go up to his bedroom and make love and then he'd chickened out.

No, chickened out wasn't the right expression – he'd come to his moral senses. How could he have even thought it would be okay to make love to Lissy in the bed in which he'd made love to Claire so many times?

'Hasn't it just!' Jancy said, bringing him back to the present. 'Not that I've done a lot apart from eat and drink, probably more than is good for me. I've done some drawing and a bit of painting. You wouldn't believe how good it is to be able to do that and know I'm not going to be interrupted, know that I'm not ...'

Janey clasped her hands together, squeezing so tightly Xander saw her knuckles had gone white.

'Not what?' he encouraged.

'Not going to find that Stuart's found out where all my art things are and made trouble for Annie and Fred, and trashed it all, trashing their shed in the process. I really, really want to take up this opportunity I've got now for doing something with my art. Both Lissy and Bobbie have said I can stop with them until I sort somewhere else to live. And some sort of income because I don't think Stuart's going to support me. I've never worked. Well, not since the day I got married. Stuart ...'

Again, that hand-wringing.

'I'll stick my head above the parapet here and say that's because Stuart didn't want you to.'

Janey nodded.

'He was jealous. I used to work for an estate agent before and I loved it; meeting people, going to some fabulous houses with potential buyers, and some awful ones too, but that was life. He thought I was having an affair with my boss. He accused me of it on our honeymoon. When we got back he said I was to ring and say I wasn't going to be working for him anymore. As a maths teacher in a grammar school his earnings could keep us both.'

'But they didn't keep you happy, eh?' Xander said.

'In the beginning, yes. I was flattered, I suppose, that he put me on a pedestal in his way, and that he thought I was so attractive others would be attracted to me.' Janey smiled at him, a sad sort of smile and yet there was light in her eyes, a glimmer of something he couldn't quite define, like the way the sun shone across the sea sometimes making it look like it had been sprinkled with diamonds perhaps. 'And that,' Janey laughed, 'isn't me fishing for compliments in case you wondered!'

Xander hadn't thought anything of the sort. He was happy to talk to Janey, of course he was, but he'd rather it was Lissy sat opposite him right now. He fished around in his mind for something to say, sticking with the piscatorial vibe.

'I've had a thought, Janey,' he said. 'This stuff of yours you've got stashed in your neighbours' shed. How safe is it really? For it, and for them?'

'Probably not very, why?'

'Well, I've been thinking. We've all had a long day today and I doubt anyone will be up with the lark although I could be. If you like, and if you could get hold of your neighbours to let them know we're coming, I could drive you over there in my lorry at the crack of dawn. We could load your stuff onto my lorry and be back here before anyone's put the kettle on. What do you think?' Xander bit his cheeks to stifle a yawn.

'Would you? Really? Gosh, don't answer that because you wouldn't have offered if you didn't mean it. I want to say yes but I'd need to run it past Lissy first. I mean, she might not want it all here on Boxing Day.'

'I'm pretty certain her invite for you to stop runs to the materials you need to make a living, but if she doesn't then you can leave it at mine. I've got a spare room. So, what do you say?'

'I say yes.'

'And there's more,' Xander said. He didn't know where all this stuff coming into his head and out of his mouth was coming from but it seemed to be the right thing to be saying, just to see the joy on Janey's face. All the tight lines he'd seen there when he'd turned up the day before Christmas Eve were ironing out. She looked younger. Calmer. Safer. 'If you need to go back and fetch stuff like clothes and books or whatever and you don't want to face Stuart on your own then I can gather the heavy gang and take you.'

'Heavy gang?'

'The blokes who work for me. And a few of their mates. Rugby players, all.'

Janey's mouth went big and round with surprise, and then she laughed.

'That I would have to see. He wouldn't put up a fight with them,' Janey said.

No, he just picked on you, the bloody coward, Xander thought but wasn't going to say. Janey knew it anyway, didn't she?

'So, that's a yes to that as well, then?' Xander said.

'It is. I know Annie and Fred don't go to bed until the early hours. I'll go up to my room now and ring them. They'll probably be glad to get it off their premises, to be honest.'

Janey leapt up off the couch, suddenly energised at the thought of having her things around her again. She came over to Xander and put her arms around his neck, and kissed his cheek.

'Thank you so much for what you're doing. I don't know I'll ever be able to repay you.'

'Just be happy,' Xander said. 'That'll do me. Oh, and safe.'

'Night night, then,' Janey said. 'I'm sure it'll be okay with Annie and Fred. What time shall we say, you and me?'

'Eight? Totnes isn't far. We can be there and back before the other two surface and still be in time for breakfast.'

There was a charity Boxing Day walk into the sea to go to later but that wasn't until later in the morning. His name was down to do it. He hadn't mentioned it to the others yet and he was hoping at least one of them would join him, but he wasn't holding his breath about that. The forecast for tomorrow was dry but cold. He had a wetsuit but he didn't think any of the girls would have one, not even Bobbie who seemed to have travelled to Devon with the entire stock of a branch of Marks and Spencer.

'Let's do it!' Janey said, giving him a high five. She went to the door and opened it. 'Oh, the kitchen light's out. Lissy must have gone to bed. We'd better turn all the other lights off.'

Damn, damn, damn and blast. Xander had wanted to give Lissy a goodnight kiss at the very least.

Chapter 33

Lissy

Lissy tiptoed across the tiles of the hall and up the stairs. She wanted to catch Bobbie if she could – tell her she was fine about it if she wanted to go back to London in the morning. She had Sam, the taxi driver's card. If he wasn't up for driving Bobbie all the way to London then he'd probably know someone who was.

She tapped on Bobbie's door.

'Bobbie?' she called, quietly. 'It's me. Lissy.'

The door opened almost at once, as though Bobbie had been waiting for her.

'Can I come in?'

'I hoped you would,' Bobbie said, reaching for Lissy's arm and drawing her into the room. She was still fully dressed even though it had been a good half hour or so since she'd come upstairs. She was still fully made up. And she still had a huge grin on her face.

Lissy closed the door with a soft click.

On the bed was a sheet of paper taken from an envelope, and face down on the bed. Olly's letter.

'You've read it?' Lissy said.

'Yes. And I'm in shock somewhat at the coincidence of things. Someone else must have written the envelope but Olly's hand-writing could be mine – the same slope to it, the same quirky way we write the letter "r" and the same straight downstrokes of "p" and "y" and "g", without curls to them.'

'Genetic,' Lissy said. 'Not coincidence at all.'

'Bless you for saying that,' Bobbie said. She gave herself a little shake and then said, 'Where are the others?'

'In the sitting room. I heard them laughing. Oh …' Lissy heard footsteps coming up the stairs. 'I think that's them now.'

'They'll be going into their own rooms, don't fret,' Bobbie said, drawing Janey over towards the window and the two bucket chairs that were placed there. She tapped the side of her nose in an 'I know something that you don't' sort of way.

'I don't know what you mean!' Lissy said, knowing she was colouring up, knowing exactly whose room she wanted to be going into.

'Oh yes, you do,' Bobbie said.

They were both instinctively lowering their voices now so as not to be overheard.

'Oh, all right. You win. I might do,' Lissy told her, suppressing a giggle.

'Next question,' Bobbie said. 'Am I right in thinking that things didn't quite go according to plan this morning when you went out with Xander?'

'Yes, and no.'

'The "yes" bit being the hand-holding bit Janey and I witnessed and the arm around your shoulders bit?'

'That,' Lissy said.

'And the "no" bit being you didn't make it into Xander's cottage? Right?'

'Wrong. We got there.'

'But there was a but?'

'A big one.'

'Called Claire?' Bobbie said.

'That's not a very nice thing to say, or think, but yes. It just didn't seem right. Xander knew the second we stepped into his hall actually. I would have gone for it … God, I don't know why I'm telling you all this especially after the news you've had – it seems a bit self-indulgent.'

'Rot,' Bobbie said. 'No one could have been more self-indulgent than I was an hour ago. And you three listened, and you three said all the things I needed to hear. So, I'm going to say something now …'

Lissy wasn't sure she wanted to hear. She'd come up here to tell Bobbie she really didn't mind if she wanted to jet off in the morning and now she was getting a gentle lecture of sorts.

'Bobbie,' she interrupted. 'I'm telling you stuff I wouldn't even tell my own mother.'

'And that's precisely why you're telling me. I'm not your mother.'

'The very best of friends, though,' Lissy said. 'Our instincts were right when we chummed up at that art workshop, weren't they?'

'Precisely.'

Bobbie yawned.

'Sorry, I'm keeping you from your shut-eye. But I just wanted to say that I really won't mind if you want to go back to London tomorrow. If it were me with that sort of news then I'd probably go. So …'

'You're not me,' Bobbie said. 'But thanks for the offer.'

'You'll sleep on it?'

'Maybe.'

Lissy got the feeling Bobbie had already made up her mind about not going back in the morning and wasn't likely to change her mind any time soon. But she didn't want Bobbie to feel bad about it if she did.

'If you change your mind, I dare say Xander would even

209

volunteer to drive you back although I'm not volunteering him. Or I can. Janey would be safe left here with Xander.'

'Hmm, yes. It's all well and good looking out for others, but Auntie Bobbie has some advice. Put yourself first for once, Lissy, that's all I'm saying. I know I talk a lot but I hear a lot as well. And I see a lot. I see you've always been a good daughter, and you're a good friend. You've offered Janey a place to stay, you're offering to get me back to London, and you were showing great interest in the conservatory plans Xander was drawing up earlier so you can give him work which, I'm guessing, he needs. So ...'

'So, what does Auntie Bobbie suggest,' Lissy said. She had a shrewd idea she knew what it was going to be.

'You don't need telling. I can see that in your face. And you don't need anyone's permission, especially not mine. Christmas Day is very, very nearly over, Lissy. Finish it off in style. Carry on where you left off with Xander this morning. You're a free agent, he's a free agent. The ghost of Claire isn't here for him, is it?'

Lissy shook her head. She'd thought it might be for her, but it wasn't, and the relief of that realisation was almost tangible.

'No.'

'You knocked on the wrong door just now, Missy Lissy,' Bobbie said. She stood up and then pulled Lissy to her feet. 'Now go and knock on Xander's. And make it loud enough so he hears.'

Bobbie propelled her to the door.

Lissy went. She knocked. And Xander opened it while her fingers were still in contact with the wood. He'd been waiting, hadn't he?

'Lissy!'

Xander, in nothing but boxer shorts that had seagulls printed on them that made Lissy want to laugh because they looked so funny and gauche somehow but oh so very endearing, reached for her hand and drew her in. He leaned over her shoulder and pushed the door to behind her.

'Who else did you think it would be?' Lissy tilted her head to one side, questioningly. 'Hmm?' she teased.

'No one I'd rather it was,' Xander said. He took both of Lissy's hands between his own and raised them to his lips, and they stood together for a few moments – quiet, still. Comfortable together.

Lissy wondered who should be making the next move. Her? She, after all, had made the first one by knocking on Xander's door and he'd have been left in no doubt as to why.

She looked around the room – easily the biggest in the house. The light was soft because Xander had only switched on the lamp on the dressing table and the two, smaller ones, either side of the bed. All had bulbous paper-covered wire shades. The kingsize bed, covered in a cloud-soft duvet patterned with white shells on a taupe ground, had been neatly made, and Xander's clothes placed on the chair against the wall.

'Room inspection time?' Xander said.

Obviously he'd noticed her looking.

Her hands were still being held gently, almost reverently and Lissy was unsure as to whether to pull away a little or not. Whether to reach up and put her arms around his neck and kiss him, or not? Or wait …

'We have unfinished business, you and me,' she said.

'Today's or previous?'

They both knew what Xander meant by previous – the day of his wedding to Claire when a spark had been ignited between them, a spark neither had fanned into something bigger.

'Both. Neither of those times was right for us, were they?'

'But it is now?' Xander said. He let go of Lissy's hands and cupped her face in his hands.

In answer, Lissy reached up and put her hands over Xander's resting oh so lightly on her cheeks.

'I've never forgotten it,' Lissy said. 'That feeling. It came to me in dreams sometimes.'

Her lips were so close to Xander's now.

'I think,' Xander said, 'that we had better stop talking. In a minute Bobbie's going to be yelling for us to keep the noise down.'

'I wouldn't put that past her,' Lissy said. A shiver ran through her thinking about what sort of noise they might make – later. 'And …'

But Lissy silenced him, her lips on his. Gentle, with barely any pressure, just the delicious feel of skin on skin. In one deft movement she placed her arms around the back of Xander's neck and he put his arms around the back of her waist before swinging her round, lifting her into his arms and carrying her over to the bed.

'Just following my father's advice,' Xander said, as he pulled back the duvet just enough to able to lay Lissy down.

Now that was a sentence she never expected to hear. She got the feeling that Xander wasn't feeling quite as confident about this as he looked.

'Which was?'

'That making love to a woman should look as though a man has made an effort. Comfort, warmth, caring.'

'Round the back of the bike shed just won't do?' Lissy suppressed a giggle.

'Something like that,' Xander said.

'So,' Lissy said. 'I'm comfortable. I'm warm. You care. Shall we begin?'

Everything began in slow motion after that. There was something rather wonderful in the way Xander helped her undress as though she was fragile, gently pulling her arms from the sleeves of her silk top, kissing the length of them as he went. There seemed no reason – for either of them – to be hurrying things. It was as if they knew there would be other times for that sort of sex but now it was a coming together of souls as well as bodies.

There was something rather wonderful and delicious in the way Xander was discovering her body as he caressed every part

212

of it. Respectful. This was so unlike how sex behind the back of a bicycle shed would be. This was so not going to be a one-night stand and they both knew it.

'Confession time,' Xander whispered in her ear, before nibbling it and setting off a chain of desire within her that Lissy thought she might explode with it.

'What?' she said, although she was beyond caring now what that might be. She wanted him, and badly.

'I'm not a very good Boy Scout. I've not come prepared.'

'But *I* have,' Lissy said. While Lissy had had only a few lovers since her split from Cooper she'd remained on the pill, although thinking about it now she couldn't remember taking any since she'd been at Strand House and she ought to have done. Ah well …

'Still okay with this?' Xander asked.

A gentleman to the last, Lissy thought as she reached down and slid his boxers off his bottom and he wriggled out of them.

'Very, very …'

And those were the very last words either of them spoke as they came together.

Boxing Day

Chapter 34

Xander

Janey was waiting for him in the kitchen. No one else was up. He'd left a note on the bedside table letting Lissy know where he would be. He'd promised Janey he'd take her to fetch her art materials and he wouldn't go back on that promise, as reluctant as he'd been to leave Lissy, curled on her side in a foetal position, her back to his when he'd woken up.

As Christmases go, Xander thought as he crossed the tiles of Lissy's kitchen to grab a cup of coffee, this had to be up there with the best.

'Merry Boxmas, Janey,' he said. It struck him then that Janey might have heard him and Lissy in the night. Not that they'd had swinging from the chandeliers sex, but deep and meaningful sighs had been expended. By them both. 'Sleep well?'

'Very. Surprisingly. I'm a bit anxious now, though. Annie said last night it'll be fine to come over but, well, what if Stuart's up and looking out of the window?'

'Is there only one way into their place?'

'Yes.'

'You can stop in the lorry if you like. I'll go in on my own if you let Annie know that's the new plan.'

Dressed now in the clothes she'd been dressed in when Xander had first seen her – jeans and a sweatshirt of sorts, with rather battered shoes on her feet – Janey was looking so fragile again, so scared. In Bobbie's clothes she'd been transformed, been who – he supposed – she could be as the self-help articles he read sometimes in the dentist's waiting room would have you believe. She still had a long way to go, didn't she? God, but how he'd like to punch the living daylights out of her swine of a husband, not that he'd ever resorted to his fists to sort things. Well, maybe once or twice when he'd been in his teens.

'No,' Janey said. 'I'll tough it out. He'll probably be drunk as a skunk as per.'

'Right.' Xander stifled a yawn. He was bone-tired now but he couldn't – and wouldn't – let Janey down. A promise was a promise. He hoped Lissy wouldn't get too big a shock when she woke up and found him gone. Found his note. He'd made it as funny as he could, given he'd had very little sleep. Something to bring a smile to Lissy's beautiful face to start her day. 'One coffee, then, and we'll go. A bit of caffeine to help us along. Okay?'

'Okay. And thanks, you know, for doing this for me.'

'It's what friends are for,' Xander said.

And they *were* friends now although just three days ago they'd only been acquaintances; had he seen Janey in the street, he'd never have remembered her from Claire's funeral.

He downed his coffee which was a bit hot and it made him cough.

'Come on,' he said. 'Mustn't wake the others.'

And then they were going out the door, Xander closing it as gently as he could.

'In you get.' He opened the passenger door of his lorry and helped Janey climb up into the seat. 'Long way from the ground, but there'll be great views as we bowl along.'

He went round to the driver's side and got in, put the key in the ignition.

'I think I'll let it roll down the hill before starting the engine. We all had a bit of a late night, last night.'

Well, I did. And Lissy. He couldn't quite believe what had happened, had happened. After Claire died he'd been propositioned a time or two. Well, five and counting actually. Friends of Claire's, and the wives of two of his, had all decided he must be missing sex more than he was missing his wife and had come calling, bearing gifts of homemade flapjack or a bottle of wine or something they decided he needed to 'get over it'. There'd been something brazen and a bit Eastenders in their approach though if he was honest now they'd been no different to how Lissy had been last night – knocking on his door 'with intention' was how his father had put it when he'd told him about being propositioned so soon after being widowed. Not long after that his father had had a heart attack from which he didn't recovered. Xander missed him like hell – thought about him every day. He'd have liked Lissy, Xander knew it.

But it hadn't felt like being propositioned with Lissy. It had felt the right thing to do although he'd been as nervous as hell. A born-again virgin.

'Good idea,' Janey said, making Xander jump.

'Good idea what?' he said, letting off the handbrake.

'To roll down the hill. You just said. Remember?' Janey grinned at him.

'Ah yes, that. Of course. I was thinking. Men do sometimes, you know.'

'Ha ha, very funny,' Janey said. 'You don't fool me. My money's on the fact your mind's not entirely on the ball here this morning.'

'You'd clean up,' Xander said. 'And that's all I'm saying.'

This would be a case of too much information – Janey didn't need to know. And besides, Lissy might not want him to tell. He could have shouted it to the world, of course. He felt like opening the cab window and shouting it to the gulls and the early morning dog walkers and the copper in his patrol car parked at the bottom of Seaway Road hoping to catch a few drivers still over the limit from the night before.

I have just had sex after a very long time treading water, as it were. I have found someone to love again, someone who has made it very obvious she doesn't find me too rat ugly either. I am, in therapists' parlance, ready to move on. My mother, in particular, will be very pleased to hear that news. But not half as pleased as I am.

'We'll go Berry Pomeroy way,' Xander said turning into Manor Road. 'It'll be quicker. We can skirt the castle.'

'Oh good,' Janey said. 'I can take a photo or two.'

She took her smartphone from her bag and switched it on. There were a few beeps and Xander wondered if they might have been calls from her husband. Best not to ask.

She ignored the beeps and began scrolling through the photos she'd been taking over the holidays. Hundreds of them from where Xander was sitting.

'I've blocked him,' Janey said. 'In case you were wondering who those beeps were from.'

'Not Santa, surely?' Xander quipped, then worried that it might have come across as crass, not appropriate. A bit of a bloke remark.

'Yeah, him as well this year,' Janey laughed. 'I meant Stuart.'

'I know you did.'

They'd reached the ring road now but there was little traffic about. Just an ambulance going towards the hospital but without the blues going. A couple of cyclists were heading in the opposite direction, heads down, bums up.

'I don't know about you,' Janey said, 'but it didn't seem at all strange that the four of us have spent Christmas together and not a single card or present was exchanged between us all.'

'Giving and receiving of another sort, I'd say, if that's not coming across a bit new age and all that.'

'Well, we *are* going to Totnes,' Janey said. 'Hippy capital of the world.'

'Yeah, weed on every corner,' Xander laughed. The time he and a couple of friends had cycled on into Totnes after a night spent ghost-watching at the castle, came to mind. They'd been offered weed when they'd stopped for tea and toast in a café on The Plains. Curiosity had got the better of them, but Xander decided, when he was throwing up into the River Dart, that weed wasn't for him.

'Stuart does that as well. Smokes weed, I mean. God only knows what the headteacher's going to think about that when he finds out.'

'When?'

'It'll all come out in the wash, I expect. Stuart's not going to take me leaving him quietly. I'd bet my last ten-pound note on that. Talking of which ...'

'That's about all you have?'

'At the moment.'

Well, although he might not be as flush for cash as he wished he was he could still run to a couple of hundred pounds, or however much it was, that Janey would charge for a painting. She'd put one of Totnes Castle up on her Facebook page that he'd been coveting and asking to buy for a while now.

'Here we go. Camera alert.' He turned off the main road into a lane. It wasn't the most direct route to be taking but he'd decided Janey needed to divert her thoughts from her problems if only for a few seconds. 'Castle coming up.'

And there it was, rising out of the early morning mist. A pheasant fluttered up at the side of the road as they approached, flapping its feathers as it tried to get purchase on the bank.

'Oh!' Janey said. 'This is going to make one wonderful painting.'

'With my name on?' Xander said.

'Could have,' Janey said.

He slowed down and stopped. Janey took photo after photo.

221

'I'll pay.'

'You won't. Okay, I think I've got enough now. Annie will be up and waiting and the kettle's probably been on since six o'clock.'

'Mustn't keep a lady waiting then, must we?' Xander said and drove on.

Chapter 35

Janey

Janey didn't need to knock on Annie and Fred's door because it opened wide the second Xander pulled up outside. She glanced nervously towards her own house – ex-house now – and all the curtains were drawn. There were a couple of bags of rubbish on the front doorstep.

'Here we go, then,' Xander said, opening the passenger door for her and helping her out. 'You'll be fine, trust me. I'd say that lady on the doorstep there might be small but I bet she's feisty when roused.'

'Oh, she is,' Janey said. 'We used to get problems with lads off their heads on cider of a Saturday night and she got fed up with it. Lay in wait. Didn't exactly tar and feather them but they had a lot of explaining to do to their mothers when they got home. Watered down treacle fired from water pistols topped off with wood-chippings makes a bit of a mess.'

'That your house?' he asked pointing next door.

Janey nodded. She was ashamed of the state it was in now. The garden was a wilderness of browned-off summer growth and things Stuart had thrown into it. She could have cleared it up, she knew that now. It shouldn't have been all down to Stuart but somehow she hadn't had the heart for it knowing it would be just as bad again in a few days. She'd had the back garden – more of a yard really – and the shed to retreat to which meant she'd avoided seeing it.

'Oh, my eye!' Annie said when Janey and Xander reached the front door. Guinness, beside her, barked a greeting and Janey bent to fondle his black and tan bony head.

'Hello, old boy,' Janey said. Guinness looked up at her with his chocolate eyes and pawed her leg – his version of a handshake perhaps. 'I've missed you.' And she had. While she knew Guinness was the softest dog on the planet despite his size – a German shepherd crossed with a Border collie – it had comforted her when Guinness barked sometimes when Stuart was in one of his aggressive moods, the noise obviously disturbing the dog somehow.

'Missed him?' Annie said in a totally disbelieving way. 'Not much, I'd say. You didn't tell me about *him* last night when you rang!' Annie fluttered her eyelids jokingly at Xander and they all laughed.

'He's not mine,' Janey said. 'I've borrowed him. From Lissy. That's where I'm staying – with my friend Lissy. Oh …' She looked at Xander and realised what she'd said. No one had said officially that Xander and Lissy were an item but she knew they were. They were now. In her room on Christmas night, getting ready for bed, she'd heard someone tap on a bedroom door, and then she'd heard voices. Xander's deep one talking for a few seconds and then she'd heard Lissy giggle. And then there'd been silence for a while. She'd lain awake for ages, going over the day, going over what the next day would bring and the one after that, and once or twice she'd heard them – low moans of pleasure … night-loving music she'd heard it termed once.

'Lissy's a very lucky girl,' Annie said, offering Xander her hand.

'I'm the lucky one,' Xander said, taking Annie's hand but leaning in to kiss her cheek.

''Ere what's all this, then?' Annie's husband, Fred, came down the hall. 'Someone making free with the missus?'

'You should be so lucky!' Annie said. 'Can't get rid of me so easy.'

'That's as maybe,' Fred laughed. 'Anyway, ain't you lot coming in? Never do business on the doorstep, I say.'

Janey made the introductions and they all stepped inside and Fred shut the door. How small it was in here compared to the vastness of Lissy's beautiful house. How cluttered. There didn't seem to be a spare inch of wall that didn't have a picture on it, or a surface without a knickknack. And so much colour – wallpaper, curtains, cushions on stools, rag rugs. If there was a colour not here then Janey had never seen it. But safe, it felt so very safe.

'Fred's brought all your stuff in from our shed, Janey,' Annie said. 'Timed it good and proper he did. The second that man walked down the path and off to The Lion, he was out the back bringing it all into our back room. Gawd, gal, but you're a threat to the rainforest all that paper you've been using up. But then, I suppose it were a bit of an escape, a release from *him*.' Annie jerked her head towards next door.

Janey was starting to think of it as next door herself now, rather than her house.

'I'll get it loaded up then,' Xander said. 'I assume he's sleeping it off?'

'Well, I don't know about sleeping,' Annie said. She was starting to look embarrassed now, all her cheeky chatter evaporating.

Janey had a feeling she knew what was coming next.

'Go on, Annie,' she said. 'Tell me.'

'Well, this ain't pretty but he came rolling up about one o'clock this morning making one helluva din. Scared the cats he did. Set 'em all off caterwauling like they do. I looked out the window and there under the light of the lamp I saw him. With a woman.'

225

'Right,' Janey said. It wasn't news to her that Stuart went with other women sometimes, especially any woman who was as drunk as he was down The Lion.

'Sorry, lovey,' Annie said, 'that I had to be the one to tell.' She patted Janey on the shoulder. 'You're well out of it.'

'I know,' Janey said. 'I should have done it ages ago.'

She should. She knew that. Launching herself, alone, into a different world had been too scary a thought for a long time.

'That's as maybe, lovey,' Annie said. 'But you could look at it another way. Maybe now was exactly the right time if you're stopping with this Lissy person and she's got this handsome feller in her life!'

Janey looked at Xander who had rather a bemused expression on his face. Annie was a one-off and Janey was used to her but she could see Annie was a whole new experience for him, standing there in her pinny and with three rollers in the front of her grey hair like she'd not moved on from the Fifties, which she probably hadn't.

'Calm down, woman!' Fred joked. 'Anyone would think you haven't seen a handsome man before when you've been married to one for nigh on sixty years! Are we going to stand here all day or is someone putting the kettle on? The stuff's in the back room.'

'I don't think we've got time for tea,' Janey said. It was lovely seeing Annie and Fred again and feeling the love they had for one another and the banter, but the sooner she and Xander got back now the better. She wasn't jealous of what Annie and Fred had but it did serve to remind of her what she didn't have. What she'd never had really.

'But you'll come again?' Annie said. 'There must be stuff inside you want.'

'There is. Not a lot. My computer for a start. To be honest I did wonder if I'd find it all thrown out in the garden smashed to bits.'

'I wouldn't put that past him,' Fred said. 'Look, I'll tell you what I'll do. You give me your key and then when he and his floozy go out later, I'll nip in and fetch stuff if you give me a list. Tell me where it all is. A plan?'

'A very good plan,' Janey said, overwhelmed now at Fred's kindness and the risk the old man was willing to take on her behalf. 'But Xander's said he'll come with some friends and do it. I don't want to put you in harm's way if he came back …'

'He wouldn't get one over on Fred, lovey,' Annie said. 'He's got a gun.'

'A gun?' Janey said, startled.

'What sort of gun?' Xander said.

'You don't want to know, boy,' Fred said. 'And you can pretend you didn't hear me say it but I wouldn't be afraid to fire a warning shot or two if I had to. Can't have men behaving to women like he's been, can we?'

'No, we can't,' Xander said, his expression more bemused than ever now.

Janey got a frisson of unease shoot up her spine thinking that she'd lived next door to a man with a gun and who wasn't afraid to use it for so long. But she wanted to giggle too. This was all so surreal and she wondered just what Xander might be thinking.

'So, Janey's artworks,' Xander said. 'Lead me to it.'

'Not before you have one of my mince pies – for which I am legendary even if I say it myself – and a nip of sherry. It's Boxing Day in case it's slipped your consciousness. Can't have a Boxing Day without a mince pie, can we?'

'Seems we can't,' Xander said. 'But a very small nip of the sherry for me. I'm driving.'

'Oh, drivel,' Fred said. 'You're a big bloke. You'd soak up a thimbleful of sherry in no time.'

Xander and Fred loaded the lorry with Janey's artwork while Janey set out the sherry glasses and Annie warmed the mince pies for a couple of minutes in the oven.

'Funny old Christmas you've had, Janey lovey,' Annie said setting a mince pie on each plate. 'But then I suppose bad stuff doesn't stop just because it's Christmas, does it? For every household that's all festive spirit and presents and tinsel and roast turkey dinners, there's probably another one with bugger all.'

'No,' Janey said. 'You're right. Bad stuff doesn't stop.'

She wasn't so stupid as to think she was the only one who had to deal with this sort of thing.

'We heard things, Fred and me,' Annie said. 'Through the walls and them times he forgot to shut the fanlights when he were, well, doing what he did to you. We saw the bruises sometimes too, no matter how you tried to cover 'em up. We should have done something. Said something. We're sorrier about that now than I can tell you.'

There were tears in Annie's eyes and Janey hugged her old friend.

'There, I've said it all now,' Annie said. 'Got it off me chest. Pass me that sherry. I need one if you don't.'

Janey filled a glass to the brim and handed it to Annie.

'Don't blame yourself for anything. I was the only one who could do anything about me.'

'And now you have. Are you going to be stopping long with this Lissy person?'

'I don't know yet. I've had another offer too. From Bobbie. She lives in London. Just until I sort myself out and find somewhere of my own to live.'

'And where does this Lissy live, then? I'm guessing it ain't far if you've driven here so early in the morning unless you got up at the crack of dawn.'

'I can't tell you. It wouldn't be good if Stuart got to find out somehow and went there and made trouble.'

'No. Walls have ears,' Annie said, flicking her head towards Janey's old house. 'All it would take was for me and Fred to be chatting, saying something like 'I hope Janey's all right over there in Torquay,' or wherever it is you are, with the window open and then he'd know. Can't risk that.'

'Can't risk what?' Fred said coming back into the kitchen with Xander looking so tall behind him.

'See!' Annie said. 'Just what I was saying! Walls have got ears! Proves I've got a brain or two up there still.' She laughed and tapped her forehead.

'I wouldn't go as far as that,' Fred said. He picked up a mince pie, put it whole into his mouth and then washed it down with a glass of sherry.

Janey handed Xander the very small measure she'd poured him.

'Ready?' Xander met Janey's eye and raised an eyebrow.

'I am. Thanks for the mince pie, Annie, it was delicious. And the sherry. I'll ring you and let you know when I'll be back for the rest of my things.'

'You do that,' Fred said. 'And I'll be on hand, riding shoTgun just in case.'

Everyone laughed, although Janey's was probably more nervous than the others because she was in no doubt that Fred would use it if he had to. And then it was hugs and kisses goodbye, and Merry Boxmas, and Janey and Xander were back in the lorry and bowling back to Strand House, laughing all the way.

'Another surreal Christmas experience under the belt,' Xander said, as he brought the lorry to a halt outside Lissy's house.

'But a belter!' Janey laughed. Things could only get better for her now.

Chapter 36

Lissy

Lissy was just finishing whisking the batter for the Scotch pancakes – which she liked to serve with blueberries and maple syrup and some rashers of crisply friend pancetta if people liked it – when the doorbell rang.

Xander and Janey back at a guess. The note Xander had left her was on the kitchen counter beside the box of blueberries. She must have read it at least a dozen times, couldn't take her eyes off it. And every time it made her laugh.

> *'There's no easy way to tell you this but I've left you for another woman. I know, I know … too soon. It was hard to leave you lying there looking so beautiful in sleep, so very desirable all over again, but a man can't perform on an empty stomach. And besides, a promise is a promise and I told Janey I'd take her to fetch her art things. I hope you'll be able to find it in your heart to forgive me. Love Xander xxx'*

She folded the note carefully, put it in the pocket of her jeans, and went to let them in.

Janey stood there with a large portfolio in one hand and a jug of brushes in the other. Xander was coming up the steps carrying the rest of Janey's things – boxes of paints at a guess. He made kissy gestures at Lissy behind Janey's back, making Lissy laugh.

'Is that all?' Lissy said.

Somehow, she'd been expecting it to be much more. She'd been thinking about which room Janey could have on a semi-permanent basis. The one she was in at the moment, or one at the back where it would be quieter and there was view out over the town to the moors beyond? The back of the house faced west and Lissy knew that gave a good light for artists, beautiful sunsets. She'd give Janey the options and let her choose.

'It is,' Janey told her, stepping into the hall. 'Nothing's framed so it won't take up too much space. Is it okay to put it all in my room for now?'

'It is. Breakfast in about fifteen minutes. Okay with that, both of you?'

'Very okay,' Janey said. She told Lissy about Annie and the mince pies and Lissy grimaced to think of having either of those so early in the morning.

'Fred had a gun and I'm in no doubt he'd have shot us if we'd refused his wife's hospitality,' Xander said.

'A gun?' Another of Xander's jokes, surely?

'That's exactly what my reaction was, Lissy, when he said it!' Janey laughed. 'I had no idea he had one!'

'See?' Xander laughed. 'You didn't believe me there, did you?'

Oh, I did really, I did. That's what she admired so much about Xander – his honesty. It might not always be what she wanted to hear but far better that than all the lies she'd had to hear from Cooper.

And damn and blast him for creeping into my thoughts with someone who is so the opposite of him standing in front of me looking so adoringly at me, and with whom I am falling less in lust but more deeply in love with by the second.

231

'How could I not?' Lissy said.

'Hey, you two,' Janey said, grinning from one to the other, 'I'm beginning to feel a bit two's-company-three's-a-crowd around here.'

Oh, was it that obvious, Lissy's feelings, her desire for this man standing there so early still on Boxing Day morning and wearing shorts! Probably.

Lissy couldn't quite believe Xander was wearing shorts. There'd been a frost on the shrubs in the front garden when she'd looked out earlier which was unusual being so close to the sea, although she could remember stopping with Vonny once when it had been so cold that the beach had frozen – what fun they'd had stamping about on the crunchy sand.

'I'm off,' Janey finished. Then she turned to Xander and said, 'See. I wasn't so far off the mark with what I said to Annie, was I? Anyway, don't answer that because no answer's needed. I'm off. If you can tear yourself away, Xander, to bring up my stuff …'

Janey walked towards the stairs and Xander began to follow, but Lissy laid a hand on his arm to detain him a moment.

'What was all that about?' Lissy asked. 'What did she say to Annie?'

'Well, don't let this go to your head at all but when Annie assumed that I was the new man in Janey's life she told her in no uncertain time that you and I are an item, as the saying has it. So, are we? An item?'

'I think we must be,' Lissy said. 'After last night it would be rude not to. And now, I think, before we embarrass ourselves in the hall I think you'd better get that stuff up to Janey's room. And thanks, you know, for doing that for Janey.'

'And for you,' Xander said. 'I did it for you, too. Any friend of yours is a friend of mine. I'll be going back for things she's got in the house still – well, me and the blokes who work for me and some of their mates. She says it's not a lot.'

'Doesn't matter if it is,' Lissy said. 'There's plenty of room here.

It's a double garage as well so some of it could go in there. See, I've thought it all through.'

'Ah,' Xander said, 'but have you taken on board that time is ticking away and you told Janey fifteen minutes to breakfast, and that I am absolutely ravenous?'

'I have. Double quantity Scotch pancake batter is ready and waiting.' Lissy tapped her jeans pocket to let him know the note he'd left her was in it. 'Five-star performance-worthy batter, no less!'

And then Lissy blew him a kiss and hurried back to the kitchen, her body still throbbing and glowing from the night before, her heart fit to burst with a happiness she'd never have believed could be hers ever again. Had there not been two other people in the house she knew that she and Xander would have spent the whole of Boxing Day in bed, emerging only now and then to nibble at Christmas Day leftovers, and make coffee. But she could wait. Deep down she'd been waiting for him a long time, hadn't she?

Lissy set to making a fruit smoothie – mango and apple with some grated fresh ginger in it – because she thought their bodies had probably been overloaded with Christmases excesses and needed a healthy-eating fix, although no one had complained of being bloated or been tipsy. Just mellow. Would she have gone into Xander's room last night if she'd been stone cold sober?

Yes! A resounding, stonking great yes!

'And what, madam, are you grinning so broadly about at what, to me, is such a ridiculously early hour?' Bobbie said, coming into the kitchen, looking as though she was just off on a photo shoot wearing wide black palazzo pants, a white shawl-coloured jumper, and her trademark teeteringly high heels.

'You've got one guess,' Lissy said.

'You took Auntie Bobbie's advice?' Bobbie tapped the side of her nose knowingly, making Lissy giggle.

'I did.'

'Wise, very wise,' Bobbie said. 'What I didn't say last night was that I didn't want you to let what I could see was meant to be for you, slip through your fingers. There was someone – when Oliver was about fifteen or sixteen – I met who was right for me. He was free, I was free, and we loved one another. But I let my past experiences cloud everything and I couldn't bring myself to tell him about Oliver. The shame and the guilt were with me still. It was too big a secret to keep and I knew I'd fester keeping it from him, so I evaded the issue altogether by ducking out. There was never anyone who came close after that.'

'Oh, Bobbie,' Lissy said. 'That's too sad. Could you find him again?'

'I could. I might,' Bobbie said.

She looked away from Lissy, unable to meet her eye for some reason. Lissy wondered what that might be. She gave the batter another whisk and waited for Bobbie to tell her – if she wanted to.

'I've done what just about everyone does when they go on Facebook, however much they might deny it and pretend they don't, and I've searched for him.'

'And?' Lissy prompted.

'And he's newly single. Divorced. I must be getting devious in my old age because I searched his ex as well and she's all cosied up in Hampstead with the new love of her life. No children it seems.'

'So, the coast is clear? You could …'

'Not just yet. I'll get to know Oliver first. And his family. He's sent me photos of them all on my phone. His eldest is the spit of me when I was that age, so much so I thought he'd got hold of a photo of me from Pamela and Charles at first. And the youngest, she's got her grandfather's blonde hair. They were there waiting for me when I woke up. Not that I slept much. Too much noise …'

'Stop it!' Lissy said. 'You're side-tracking!'

Bobbie had heard her and Xander in the night, albeit they'd

both been conscious of not shrieking from the rafters how wonderful their love-making was.

'I am. I'm still in dizzy shock over Oliver. But now, well now I don't think the fact I've got a lovechild … far preferable to that other phrase, illegitimate child, I always think and mostly it's true, a baby conceived of great love - is likely to ruffle any feathers for anyone, is it?'

'You mean the man you let slip through your fingers? What's his name?'

'Sebastian. He's Swiss. Speaks four languages. And he told me he loved me in all of them.'

'Don't then—' Lissy began. She heard Xander and Janey talking to one another coming down the stairs and went to switch on the kettle for coffee. 'Don't, then, let him slip through your fingers a second time if there's a second chance to be told in four languages again that he loves you. Just do it, okay? And soon. For me. For you. And ultimately it could be for Oliver and his family as well.'

'Darling, girl,' Bobbie said, rushing over to put her arms around Lissy from behind, and hug her, lean around to one side and kiss her cheek. 'Thank you. You may not be my daughter but you're beginning to sound like me.'

A massive swell of emotion threatened to swallow Lissy up. Bobbie was as far removed from her own mother as it was possible for two women to be and that saddened her and thrilled her in equal measure. She couldn't imagine not having Bobbie in her life now.

'That,' Lissy said, 'is the loveliest thing to hear.'

Chapter 37

Xander

'Okay, ladies, here's the thing. It's not raining. The frost's gone. The sun is making a hazy appearance. We have all been more than well fed.'

Lissy had said, after breakfast, why didn't they go into the sitting room because there was yacht racing in the bay and they might like to watch from the comfort of an arm chair.

So, there they were. Janey – delighted to have yet another subject to draw and take photographs of for future art projects – had dragged the single arm chair to the window and turned it round so she now had her back to them all, looking out. Bobbie was lounging, feet up on a footstool, on the smallest couch and Xander was sitting on the same couch as Lissy, but not touching.

'Is this a trailer for something?' Bobbie asked. She was pretending not to look at her phone which they all now knew contained photographs of Oliver and his family, but she was.

'Could be,' Xander said.

'Spit it out, sonny,' Bobbie laughed.

God, but Oliver was going to love her, wasn't he? How could

he not? She was such a character. It would be only too easy to take Bobbie on looks alone and see her as somewhat narcisstic – his mother had a cousin like that, always having some treatment or other searching after the elixir of youth – but they would miss so much; her humour, her caring, her understanding. And, as now, her insights and her ability to read between lines.

'Right, guys,' Xander said. 'It's like this. It's ten o'clock now and in another hour I'm due on the beach by the pier for a charity dip.'

'Dip?' Lissy said.

'In the sea?' Janey said turning around, so obviously she wasn't totally focused on her art at that moment.

'I would assume he means the sea,' Bobbie said. 'Hardly likely to be champagne, is it?'

'Now there's a thought,' Xander grinned. A vision of pouring a bath of champagne for Lissy in the en suite of his room upstairs popped into his head. How she'd look, stepping into it, her long legs, her mane of dark hair flowing down her pearly back. He glanced at Lissy quickly to find she was looking at him and smiling. Hmm ... he had a feeling she was reading his thoughts because she wagged a finger playfully at him. 'I'll file it away for future reference Bobbie, if I may. But, yes, the sea. I've rather recklessly put myself down for ten minutes, fully submerged. For the Children's Hospice.'

There had been three choices; a local youth group so they could go on a trip to Italy, kayaking; a group of pensioners who knitted toys for orphaned children; and the Children's Hospice which wasn't exactly local but in the county. Xander had been in school with a girl called, Hannah, whose baby son had been in the hospice with a string of problems no medic could ever put right. It had seemed the right choice for him at the time when he'd first started doing these swims, ten years ago. Today's would be the first since Claire had died.

'Are there any other categories?' Bobbie asked. She'd switched off her phone now and had slid it underneath a thigh. 'Like dipping a toe in?'

'A bit more than that is required. If memory serves me well the lowest category is to walk in up to your knees and stay there for thirty seconds.'

'How cold is it?' Janey got up and turned her chair around to face them all.

So, that's two potential partners in crime he had now, Xander thought. Bobbie and Janey were showing interest, if gingerly.

'Not as cold as you might think,' Xander said. 'It was a very warm summer, and autumn was pretty good, too, for sunshine. The sea's had time to warm up and it's not been that cold yet to cool it down.'

'You're selling it,' Bobbie laughed. 'I'll do the up to the knees bit.'

Crikey, would she really? Xander hadn't expected Bobbie to be the first to volunteer.

'And me,' Janey said. 'How much do we have to give in sponsorship for that?'

'Not sure, but I'll pay it,' Xander said, which wasn't true because he did know – he was down for £50, the next category was five minutes, fully submerged, which came in at £30, and then it went down in increments to the walk-in for various lengths of time, £10 being the least anyone could pay. The thinking was that participants would get sponsorship from family and friends but most just paid up – a charity donation they were happy to pay. 'We can sort it out later.'

'They do it every Boxing Day,' Lissy said. 'The Lions Club or something like that. Vonny used to do it.'

'So,' Xander said, 'in her honour you'll join me then, Lissy?'

'Not for ten minutes,' Lissy said. 'Five. I've still got a wetsuit in the garage.'

'That's for wimps,' Bobbie said. 'I don't suppose there's a bathing costume hanging around here somewhere, is there, Lissy?'

'You're considering going in the sea, in December, in just a bathing costume? You're joking!' Lissy said.

'Not,' Bobbie told her. 'It's for the Children's Hospice, right? I've got a healthy son and three granddaughters who have never needed its services as far as I know. That's a lot to be grateful for, I'd say. I wouldn't want to risk saltwater damaging any of my clothes because, well, they're my stock in trade, but I've got enough life left in me to be able to cope with standing up to my knees in sea water if I had a bathing costume to do it in. And besides, it's going to look good in photos for my granddaughter's, isn't it? Trendy Grandma tames the waves, and all that. So are there any costumes we could borrow?'

'There are,' Lissy told her. 'Vonny's. Rather old-fashioned now but good. Classic, I suppose you could say.'

'Meant to be then, isn't it?' Bobbie said.

And so it was as easy as that. Xander had felt a bit guilty about not mentioning the charity dip before, maybe changing Lissy's plans for the day, but it seemed there were no firm plans.

It all got a bit manic after that, digging out the costumes for Bobbie and Janey – who said if Bobbie was going to brave the elements then so was she – and for Lissy to turf out her wetsuit in the garage and see if it was presentable enough to get into it, and if she could actually get into it if it was; she hadn't, she said, worn it since she was nineteen or so. It turned out that that was a yes on both counts, not that Xander had doubted it for a moment, having held a very lithe Lissy in his arms the night before until they eventually slept.

'And another thing,' Xander said, 'that I forgot to mention.'

Xander had Lissy on one arm and Bobbie on the other, with Janey's arm linked through Lissy's on the other side. A unit. A team. Xander had been surprised at how emotional he felt at that thought and he could see now how Claire had bonded with all three women so easily. Although they were all different heights, somehow they were now all walking at the same pace, Xander and Bobbie having shortened their strides to match the other two.

They were nearing the pier now and quite a crowd had turned up. Some were already in costumes with towels over their shoulders, others in wetsuits, and a few spectators were in fancy dress.

'Here we go,' Bobbie said, laughing. 'It's skinny-dipping after all. All this other stuff about categories was just a blind.'

'It's been known,' Xander said. 'But not that. For all those who complete their categories satisfactorily there are discount vouchers for breakfast butties, in variety, up for grabs in the Port Light. Take it from me, they are second to none in the area. Oh, and coffee, tea, hot chocolate. Ana, who runs the place, doesn't have a drinks licence but she'll turn a blind eye should anyone want to tip a tipple in their drink.'

'Sherry before breakfast,' Janey giggled, 'brandy before lunch. You're turning me into a dypso, Xander.'

'Only at Christmas,' he said. 'Right, here we are.'

A handful of people came up to Xander saying how pleased they were to see him there again and he made the introductions. Bobbie had already got out of the jogging pants and sweatshirt Lissy had loaned her and was wrapping a huge towel around her shoulders. Janey was stripping off more gingerly, while Lissy wriggled deliciously into her wetsuit.

Everyone taking part was assigned a second with a stopwatch. Bobbie had instructed hers on how to operate her smartphone so she could have evidence for her granddaughters. Xander went to the official sign in area – someone's summer gazebo weighted down with piles of stones to stop it blowing away – and paid the fees for everyone.

Just a few short weeks ago he wouldn't have thought in his wildest imagination that he'd be doing this; being here with three women with whom he'd just spent Christmas, and whom he'd come to love, although being *in* love with only one of them which was a totally different, wonderful thing.

The man with the klaxon walked across the prom and Xander rushed to join the others. Once the klaxon sounded it would be a mad rush for the sea.

Wearing trunks – and no T-shirt as some blokes were – Xander reached for Lissy's hand. How good it felt, her hand in his.

'Best to run in as far as we can without stopping. Armpits for preference. The cold will take your breath away for a few seconds, but if you don't open your mouth in shock you'll recover quickly enough.'

'Now you tell me!' Lissy said as the klaxon went and everyone ran to the water's edge.

'Keep striding,' Xander said, the force of the water giving his leg muscles a workout. He was dragging Lissy along now and worried she might duck out. 'It gets easier, trust me.'

And then they were up to their armpits.

'Ready?' Xander said, letting go of Lissy's hand. 'Dip your shoulders under the water. Now.'

Lissy dipped, her mouth closed despite the shock of the cold water as he'd advised her to.

'That's my girl,' Xander said, stealing a quick kiss. 'See you in ten.'

And then he began a front crawl, powering away to join the other ten-minute swimmers, knowing Lissy would be perfectly fine, as would they all.

Xander was a strong swimmer. He'd kayaked in his youth, and sailed, and been tipped into the sea doing both, more than a few times. He couldn't imagine living anywhere else but by the seaside and he hoped with all his heart that Lissy would stay here now. Now she was in his life he didn't want to let her go.

On and on he swam towards Hollacombe – once a small fishing village but now swallowed up by the bigger town. The summer chalets at beach level, all in ice cream colours, were boarded up for the winter against any rough seas. Strand House stood out on the highest part of the headland way above them. In the low winter sunshine it shone, its whiteness accentuated by the rusty-coloured sandstone cliffs on which it was built, and standing out like a beacon against the pale blue of a cloudless sky.

Claire seemed to be with him as he swam. But when he tried to remember the feel of her skin on his, he was shocked that he couldn't. All he could remember as his arms powered him forward at that moment was Lissy's skin on his, her lips on his, and how that had felt, and how it would feel in the future if he gave her space to make her own decisions about selling Strand House or not, about moving here permanently, or not. And about them.

He turned and began the swim back and Claire wasn't with him anymore. He'd never forget her, but she was his past and now he had a future. As he neared the pier he saw Lissy – his future? – waving her bright turquoise towel at him. He raised a hand high in the air above him and waved back.

Chapter 38

Bobbie

'Oh, this is nice,' Bobbie said. There were tables and chairs set up outside the Port Light, with a pile of fleecy throws in a huge log basket for people to help themselves to. Outside heaters too, spreading their warmth and hissing slightly as though they were some sort of benign beast. Bobbie helped herself to a fleecy throw, sat down at a table, and draped it over her knees even though she wasn't cold. The water had been chilly enough but hadn't been as icy as she'd thought it might be, despite Xander's selling of it as unseasonally warm. It had been invigorating, adrenalin coursing through her, awakening all her senses. Afterwards, having dressed again in the makeshift changing cubicles she'd been warm again in no time. 'It's very Med here, I think. I sat outside something very like this many years ago. Cannes, I think. Could have been Nice. Or maybe Antibes. South of France anyway.'

'Name dropper!' Xander said.

'Oh, I can do more … Acapulco, Genoa, Marseilles, Venice … shall I go on?'

Everyone laughed and then Janey said, 'You're like a different person this morning, Bobbie.'

243

'That would be the sub-zero temperature my legs were subjected to,' Bobbie said. It wasn't, and she knew it. It was Oliver's phone call and everyone's reaction to it. How kind they'd all been, how understanding. People's attitudes to anyone having a baby out of wedlock were so different these days to how they had been back then. Not all change was for the better, but so much was and that had to be the biggest thing. Well, it was for Bobbie. She looked from one to the other of her friends who were all so very dear to her now, all sitting down, draped in fleecy throws, waiting to have their vouchers collected and to place their orders.

The Port Light had fairy lights draped in the windows and a huge HAPPY CHRISTMAS banner over the door. Lots of other people had obviously completed their categories because the tables were filling inside and out now. There was lots of chatter, lots of laughter, and the air was electric almost. How glad she was that she'd accepted Lissy's invitation to be part of her Christmas. They might have to wait a bit to be served but no matter. Bobbie felt her shoulders drop down another notch. She even allowed her stomach muscles to relax a little, not holding them in every waking hour as she usually did. It felt good.

'Do we have to take our tickets inside and order?' Janey asked.

'I don't think so,' Lissy said. 'Vonny always said everyone just waited patiently, invigorated by their dips. Is that right, Xander?'

'Yep. And here's Ana now.'

A young woman with chubby rosy cheeks – like little crab apples, Bobbie thought – and very dark hair brushed through with red streaks of colour, arrived at their table.

'Good morning, everyone,' she said. 'Congratulations that you finish your swimming tasks. Vouchers?'

She held out her hand for the vouchers Xander had collected

for them all and they gave their orders – soup for Bobbie and Janey, a fried egg roll for Lissy, and the full Monty breakfast roll for Xander.

They all ordered cappuccinos.

'Me? A cappuccino?' Bobbie said when Ana had left with their order. 'This will be an absolute first.'

'Too many calories?' Lissy said.

Yes, far too many calories for Bobbie who had always counted every single one she'd taken in. In control of earning her own living from the day she'd given Oliver to Pamela and Charles, she couldn't afford to be anything less than perfect when she went for jobs where she was given clothes that were a stock size eight to get into and be photographed in from every angle.

'Not now,' Bobbie said. 'I know I'm hardly likely to turn into a cuddly mum at this stage of my life but, well, I feel I need to knock off a few of the hard edges I've had all my life before I meet Oliver. Well, meet him again because obviously I was the first person to see him.'

'You're not hard,' Janey said. 'A bit spiky maybe … oh God, sorry. I shouldn't have said that.'

'Yes, you should,' Bobbie said.

She'd put up a sort of fence around her emotions for the past forty-four years, rarely letting anyone in – apart from Sebastian – afraid to get close to anyone, physically as well as emotionally. If anyone was the mistress of the non-touching air kiss then she was!

'And I'm being self-indulgent again, talking about me and Oliver and …'

'Stop it!' Lissy said. 'I think if I'd been through what you have and if I'd had the phone call you had yesterday then I wouldn't be showing the patience you are in still being here. I'd have got the first train back to London. Or a taxi. I might—' she paused, reaching out to pat the back of Bobbie's hand '—I might even have walked!'

'I wouldn't put that past you,' Xander said.

A look passed between them, Xander and Lissy, and Bobbie had a fast-forward moment pop into her mind to how she might – might – be sharing looks like that with Sebastian, if she got back in touch with him. If.

Their food and drinks arrived then and it was only at that moment that Bobbie realised she had neglected to ask what the soup was.

Leek and potato as it turned out – something else she'd always rejected as being too calorific. But not now. Now it was just what she needed. The after-glow of the swim was beginning to wear off a little. She pulled the fleece more tightly around her neck.

'Cold?' Xander asked, noticing.

'Not really. It's clouding over a bit now though.'

'Yeah,' Xander said. 'I checked the Met Office site this morning and it seems snow could be on its way. Dartmoor will take the brunt of it.'

'Really?' Janey said. 'Gosh, how romantic that would be! Snow at Christmas. Just like on the Christmas cards.'

'Don't hold your breath!' Xander said. 'We might see a few flakes.'

'That would do me!' Janey said.

Bobbie listened to their banter, happy that a gesture from her had sparked yet another happy conversation between her friends. But she was beginning to feel the cold now. She wasn't as young as the others although part of her had stopped at eighteen – the length of her hair for one thing, which she'd not had cut short since that day, only trimmed. That was, she knew, a psychological barrier she'd put on herself. It had become her *look*, especially now that she was older and still getting work because of it and she had to be grateful for that, but still … she'd never been who she could truly be, had she? She'd been preserved in some sort of mental aspic, hadn't she?

The others were tucking in to their food, heads down, concentrating.

Would she enter the portals of fast food places like McDonald's or Pizza Express with her granddaughters? Would she bring them here to the Port Light? She hoped the latter at least. So many possibilities and Bobbie felt dizzy with them.

But she was ready for all that now.

'Guys?' she said and waited a few seconds for them to look up. 'Do you think it's time I cut my hair short?'

'Goodness,' Janey said. 'You're a surprise a minute, you are! You ask the most unexpected questions!'

'Doesn't she just!' Lissy said. 'But I can see you're feeling the cold a bit now, Bobbie. Am I right?'

'Yeeees,' Bobbie said with a dramatic shiver for effect, but warmed by the thought that Lissy had noticed, as Xander had when she pulled the fleece closer around her neck.

'Everyone done?' Lissy asked, gathering her plates and mug together, and reaching for the bag with her swimming things in.

There was a chorus of 'yeses'. Bobbie looked up and saw that the blue had almost disappeared from the sky now, replaced by rather strange coloured clouds – a sort of dog rose mixed with beige mixed with a yellowish hue. She shivered some more, and sent up a silent prayer that if it did snow it wouldn't prevent her from going back to London in the morning.

'I'll just nip home and check on Felix,' Xander said. 'I left a fanlight open for him but the temperature's dropping by the minute and I know the old boy won't go out if it's too cold for him.'

How kind Xander was, how caring of his pet, and of all of them around this table too. She wondered if Oliver had had a pet as a child, or if his granddaughters had, which was something she'd not even considered before – so many things to ask her son, so many years to catch up on. She could hardly wait. She'd have to sit on her hands to stop herself texting Oliver to ask question after question when they all sat around the table again at Strand House for the Boxing Night dinner.

'Can I come with you?' Janey asked. 'I could suss out future painting projects.'

'Be my guest,' Xander said.

Chapter 39

Lissy

Lissy and Bobbie were lounging – a couch each – at Strand House waiting for Xander and Janey to come back. How comfortable it felt, just the two of them, at ease in one another's company and to think Lissy had had second thoughts at times about asking Bobbie in the first place!

'Did you mean it, Bobbie?' she asked. 'What you said earlier, about cutting off your hair?'

'Yes and no,' Bobbie said, reaching back with an arm and running her hand from the top of her head, down over the long length of her exquisitely cared for silver locks. She fanned it out over a shoulder. 'More hypothetical, I think. When we were in the Port Light I had one of those flashes of insight. I've kept it like this all these years because that's how it was – long, if black and not grey like it is now – the day I gave birth to Oliver.'

'And that's how you wanted him to see you? The mother you were then?'

'Exactly that.'

Bobbie kicked off her shoes and swung her legs up onto the couch. Lissy couldn't imagine doing that in anyone else's house, unless it had been family, but it felt good now seeing Bobbie do it. She must have got the welcome right.

Lissy got the feeling that Bobbie wanted to say more but was probably conscious of being too self-indulgent as she'd said down at the Port Light. She waited a moment or two for Bobbie to continue and when she didn't, she said, 'You must have felt so cheated when your cousin reneged on her promise.'

'Betrayed,' Bobbie said. 'Pamela was family. I thought you could trust family. My parents told me I could but … well, I don't need to tell you again, it isn't any prettier for saying it a second time.'

'No,' Lissy said.

She got up to switch on the tree lights, and light a candle – tuberose, one of Vonny's she'd found in a cupboard. It was starting to get darker outside, the sea like a sheet of platinum, and she wondered if Janey was busily making sketches somewhere – from the harbour wall perhaps. She closed the vertical blinds and went back to sit down.

'You've not said much about your divorce,' Bobbie said suddenly.

Lissy hadn't been expecting that. She'd scoured Cooper from her mind, very effectively she thought, but it only took the mention of his name to bring the bad stuff back. The lies, the rows, the humiliation that he'd been unfaithful more than a few times.

'No,' Lissy told her. 'I did the opposite of you with the hair, though.' She couldn't help but giggle at the memory. 'This,' she went on, flicking out her loose curls with her fingers, 'is the natural look. No amount of hair straightening can get rid of them, but I tried. Blonde was so not a good look for me either! I had to cut it all off very short in the end. I looked about fourteen.'

'Cleansing, though. Maybe fourteen was a good time for you and you needed to get back to that.'

God, but this woman knew how to home in on things, didn't

she? When Lissy had been fourteen it had been the last time her parents had been together, the last time they'd been a proper family. For her fourteenth birthday they'd taken her up to London for the weekend. They'd stopped in a hotel near Marble Arch and done the sights. They'd eaten in the same Italian restaurant both nights and that's when Lissy had been introduced to a different cuisine to school dinners and her mother's roasts. Squid, olives, courgette fritters, anchovies and slivers of blood red lamb that had barely touched the heat but which melted in her mouth – Lissy had been in culinary heaven with it all. Her love affair had begun with food then.

'How insightful you are,' Lissy said.

'It comes with experience,' Bobbie said. 'You're not so dusty yourself. I'd say you've got the instinct about when to say something and when to wait for the other person to get off their chest whatever it is they need to say.'

'Hmm, yes,' Lissy said. 'Maybe.'

Yes, there was something she needed to get off her chest. Something she needed to tell Xander. She went into his room on Christmas night intending to tell him before they kissed – which she'd known they would – that Claire had told him she was going to leave him to give him the opportunity to have a child with someone who could make one with him, unlike her. Lissy recalled, almost verbatim, the conversation she'd had with Claire doing her best to persuade her that Xander wouldn't think like that, it was her he loved. She didn't like having that memory, but was it one she could, or should share?

'That was an awfully long pause,' Bobbie said. She raised an enquiring eyebrow. 'Shall I go and make some tea and then you can tell? If you want to.'

'Please,' Lissy said.

That was the trouble with telling secrets – the teller felt better to be free of it but sometimes the secret was more than the hearer needed to know, to be responsible for the keeping of it.

'I don't know what to do with this room,' Lissy said when Bobbie came back with two steaming cups of tea and a plate with a couple of mince pies on it. That was another thing that Lissy couldn't ever imagine doing – going into someone else's kitchen and making tea, looking for something to eat. But it felt more than right seeing Bobbie do it.

'This room? How?'

'To decorate or not?'

The walls were painted a very soft shell pink. In the morning sun it was like being inside the petals of a dog-rose, Lissy had always thought. There was one very large mirror opposite the French doors that opened onto the small, front terrace, and just one small painting of a child – a little girl of about six with her dark hair in a plait down her back to her waist almost. Vonny had always said it reminded her of Lissy. In the painting the little girl was turning out a sandcastle from a bucket with the sea a cornflower blue in the background with petticoat frills of white foam at the water's edge. As well as the three couches and the single, large chair, there were small tables beside them all. In Vonny's day the tables had had books or newspapers on them, or an ornament or two – Vonny had loved ceramics – but Lissy had thought it all too cluttered; it didn't go with the plainness of the walls somehow and the unfussiness of the starched calico covers of the couches.

'So, you're thinking of keeping it, then?'

Lissy shrugged. Was she? It would be a huge change. She could, of course, sell her flat in Princesshay and commute to Exeter daily. It wasn't far. She could keep the practice on, maybe take on another senior partner so she'd have to go into the office less, but … was that what she really wanted? Now she'd spent Christmas making food for other people and not just herself as a diversion from a life she was fast coming to realise was less than satisfying, she knew there had to be change.

She took a mince pie off the plate and took a bite, swallowing it down with a couple of mouthfuls of tea.

'I'm thinking,' Lissy said, 'that this room could do with a couple of big paintings in it. Not hundreds of them so whatever the paintings are of get lost to the eye because it's just too much to take in, but something, well, monumental perhaps to go with the size of the room.'

'And I'm thinking that's a yes to my question about whether or not you're going to keep the house.'

'I think you're right,' Lissy laughed. 'Thanks for your input.'

'Sometimes it's good to run our ideas past other people. And a bit more input, whether or not you want it … you could commission something from Janey, yes? God only knows the poor woman could use the cash. She's said she's going to give me the painting she did of me at that art workshop but she bloody well isn't – I'm going to pay for it!'

'Whoa! Whoa!' Lissy laughed. 'I'll get myself out of the line of fire when that conversartion comes up because I think it might be important to Janey that you don't.'

'Maybe you're right,' Bobbie said. 'But we both know, you and me, that all this about paintings and redecoration and the like is just a diversion from telling me what it is you need to get off your chest.'

'When are you leaving?' Lissy laughed.

Not that she wanted Bobbie to leave right at that moment but it felt slightly uncomfortable that Bobbie seemed to be seeing inside her soul.

'Not until you tell,' Bobbie said, not at all put out by Lissy's remark.

'It's about Xander …'

'I thought it might be, you can't take your eyes off him. And if Janey and I weren't here you wouldn't be able to take your hands off him either.'

'Bobbie!' Lissy said. She really was irrepressible.

'Auntie Bobbie is waiting.'

'You take no prisoners.'

'Not usually. No.'

Lissy sighed.

'Well, it's not really Xander. It's Claire. Something she told me.' Lissy could still remember the feeling she'd got when Claire had told her because it had been so unexpected. How would she – Lissy – feel to be told she couldn't have a child, if that was what she wanted most in all the world?

'Which is?' Bobbie prompted.

'That she was about to leave Xander. She'd begun taking on more and more weekend classes so she didn't have to be at home with him. Something happened to change the dynamic between them.'

Should she be telling Bobbie any of this?

'Go on,' Bobbie said.

'They'd been for tests because a baby wasn't happening for them. You know how much that means to Xander because he said so a night or so ago, didn't he?'

'He did.'

'Well, the upshot is they were offered egg donation. Xander told me that, but Claire had also told me. The morning she was killed actually. She stopped on the dual carriageway to ring me. I did my best to dissuade her, but … well, we all know what happened then. I wish with all my heart now I'd been able to make her turn around and go back home. But then … '

'But then you wouldn't have Xander in your life as you do know,' Bobbie finished for her. 'Sometimes fate has different plans. What you've just told me is sad but you can't change what's happened. I think you know what you've got to do if you're going to move this relationship on a step. You can't keep it in. It'll fester. It'll spoil everything. You'll always have that knowledge and it will come to you in moments you don't want it to.'

'You mean like when we're making love?'

'Surely, you're not going to go that far!' Bobbie gave Lissy a mock-shocked look.

'No good closing the stable door after the horse has bolted,' Lissy laughed.

There was a knock on the door then

'Oh, they're back,' Lissy said. She got up to go and let them in.

'No time like the present,' Bobbie said. She swung her legs round off the couch and pulled herself to her feet and Lissy hoped she'd be able to be as lithe as Bobbie was when she was that age.

'I'm feeling a bit anxious about it now,' Lissy said. Together they were walking towards the hall.

'I'll take Janey upstairs,' Bobbie said. 'Clear the deck for you. I've got some things she might like to look through.'

'Thanks,' Lissy said.

They'd reached the door now and Lissy opened it. Her heart flipped deliciously at the sight of Xander.

'All present and correct,' he said.

'And just the girl I want to see,' Bobbie said. She reached out a hand to draw Janey into the house. 'I've laid out some things you might like, Janey. Can you come upstairs with me?'

'Now?' Janey said.

'Now.'

Lissy wanted to laugh because Bobbie very much did what it said on the tin, didn't she?

'Okay,' Janey said. Together she and Bobbie walked across the hall to the stairs.

Xander began to follow them.

'Xander …' Lissy began.

He turned back to look at her.

'Can it wait?' Xander said. 'I'm rather less than good to know right now. I am in dire need of a shower and a change of clothes. Skanky would describe how I am.' He put a finger and thumb, clothes peg fashion, over his nose, and Lissy laughed.

She could do skanky if it was Xander. But she could see, now she was looking at him properly, that his legs had white patches where the salt had dried on them, and there were also a couple of dry patches on his chin.

Xander put a hand up to run his fingers through his hair.

'Eurgh,' he said. 'See what I mean?'

Yes, Lissy saw – his hair was stiff with salt, but still she wouldn't have minded doing her best to tussle it up for him.

'Back in about ten,' Xander said.

'I'll be waiting,' Lissy said as Xander blew her a kiss and ran for the stairs.

Chapter 40

Janey

'All of it?' Janey said in disbelief.

Bobbie had laid out at least six outfits on her bed and Janey wondered for a moment if she'd walked into some sort of fashion shoot. Everything was colour-coordinated, laid out in darkening shades from the palest blue to the deepest indigo – like an artist's palette.

'All of it,' Bobbie said. 'I've been around long enough to know what looks good on people. And you do the blues better than I do. You might need to shorten the trouser ends or the hem of that dress,' she went on, pointing to a long-sleeved denim-coloured dress a bit like a seamless T-shirt only longer. 'So ... yours for the taking. You know, just in case when Xander and his heavies take you back to yours – or your ex-yours I should say – there's nothing there because your husband's cut it into strips and chucked it out of the bedroom window. It's been known.'

While once that thought might have scared her, Janey could only laugh at the vision of it now.

'Yeah,' she said. 'That did occur to me.'

'Is there anything you'd miss if that happens?'

'Not a lot. Underwear mostly. When the shops open tomorrow I'm going to have to go and get some.'

'And have you got anything to get it with?' Bobbie asked.

So direct. So Bobbie. No beating about the bush. Janey wished she could be a bit more like Bobbie and say what she meant which was something Janey had been afraid of doing for far too long.

'Not a lot. Xander and I walked back via a cashpoint and there's a bit more in my account than I thought. So good.'

'Not a fortune though?'

'No. £119 to be exact.'

'Not so good,' Bobbie said. She clapped her hands together. 'But not insurmountable. Nothing is.'

Bobbie picked up the denim-coloured dress and held it out towards Janey.

'Do you want to try it on?'

'Now?'

'Why not now? It's going to be our last meal here together later.'

'Our last meal,' Janey said. How sad was that. She'd be staying on but with Lissy back in Exeter most of the week it would just be her rattling around in the huge house when she wasn't in her room painting. She knew she wouldn't be able to stay at Strand House for ever and then she'd be on her own again – but that had been her choice. But right now, after the meals they'd eaten together and the confidences they'd shared she'd miss everyone. And badly. 'It's been a wonderful four days.'

'Hasn't it just! Perhaps I should have said our last meal this time around. I'm sure there will be other times now, if not here then somewhere.'

'I'll hang on to that thought,' Janey said.

'You do that,' Bobbie said. 'But right now I think we should make an effort for tonight's meal. Oh, God, sorry. Me and my big mouth again. That wasn't meant to suggest you don't make an effort, but …'

'It's okay,' Janey said, putting up a hand to stop Bobbie's flow. 'I know what you mean. Even with the stuff I left behind I couldn't hold a candle to you. Or Lissy for that matter.'

'Never judge yourself by anyone else, Janey,' Bobbie said. 'Now, go and try this on.' She pointed towards her en suite. 'Splash any of my perfume you see in there around. Tip coming up. Spray it in front of you in a zig zag fashion and then walk into it like you're walking through a cloud.'

'Isn't that a waste?' Janey said, taking the dress from Bobbie. It really was a glorious shade of faded denim. Already in her mind she was thinking about how she could replicate it in paint – it was exactly how the sea looked sometimes in winter under a pale sky.

'No laws against waste,' Bobbie said. 'Go.'

So Janey went. She came back out a few moments later and did a twirl for Bobbie. She was six years old again, and dressed for a party in a dress her mother had bought in a sale in Rockheys, with ribbons in her hair and shiny black patent shoes with a bar across. White socks.

'The butterfly is emerging,' Bobbie said. 'Now this.'

She picked up a pair of indigo, wide-legged trousers, and a cowl-necked jumper just a few shades lighter. Janey, getting into the spirit of the moment, took them. And so it went on – outfit after outfit tried on and paraded in front of Bobbie and she was told she was more beautiful than the time before in each one.

'The dress, I think. For dinner tonight,' Janey said.

'Perfect choice,' Bobbie told her.

'But I can't let you do this for me and give nothing back.'

'We don't give to receive, Janey,' Bobbie said. 'Or at least we shouldn't. In my opinion anyway. Always there will be those who have more to give and those who have less. Besides, it's not as if I've had to pay for all that stuff!' She waved an arm across the bed where the clothes she'd just given Janey were laid although not as neatly as they had been when Janey had come into the room. 'Manufacturer's freebies most of it.'

'I don't believe a word of it,' Janey laughed.

Bobbie was just trying to maker her feel better about taking it all, and they both knew it.

'Tax deductable expenses, then.'

'I don't believe that either!'

Bobbie pulled a wry face and tipped her head from side to side – it might be the truth, or it might not, the gesture said. She looked like one of those nodding dogs you still sometimes see on the parcel shelf of old cars driven by even older people, and Janey laughed. But she knew what she had to do now. She picked up the dress she'd chosen to wear to dinner tonight.

'Wait there. I'll go and put this on again. I'll be right back.'

It didn't take her long. She was back in no time, the painting she'd done of Bobbie at the art workshop in her arms, cradled like a baby. She'd worked on it back in her shed studio after that class – putting in shading, adding light on Bobbie's chiseled cheek bones, deepening the green of the velvet chair on which Bobbie had posed.

'Yours,' she said, walking back into Bobbie's room.

'Oh …'

'A gift. A Christmas gift.'

'Lissy said no gifts,' Bobbie said. 'That was the rule.'

'And you said yourself that rules are to be broken, so I'm breaking that one. For you.'

She held out the painting for Bobbie to take.

'Oh …' Bobbie said again. There were, Janey noticed, tears in her eyes. 'I know it's hardly modest of me to say so but, it's beautiful. Both, you know, the artwork and, well …'

'You,' Janey finished for her.

'That too!' Bobbie laughed, taking the painting from her. She held it out in front of her studying it. Then she went over to the dressing table and propped it up against the wall and stood back. 'Do you think I look better from a distance, though?'

Janey knew what she was getting at. She hadn't ironed out the lines besides Bobbie's eyes or the slight droop of Bobbie's very small breasts. A few liver spots on the backs of her hands had been put in too. She hadn't really known Bobbie very well then and she hadn't considered for a moment they'd meet again or be here spending Christmas together. It had been an artistic study, nothing more. All the same Janey was pleased that she'd captured the essence of Bobbie, her style and the almost balletic way she held herself.

'It's figurative portraiture,' Janey told her. 'But if you don't like it ...'

'I love it. I shall treasure it. Perhaps, now, with Oliver back in my life and three granddaughters who might look at it and be embarrassed beyond belief to see Grandma in the buff, it might be best not to hang it over my fireplace as had been my intention.'

'No, maybe not,' Janey laughed. 'I could do you another one for public exhibition.'

She'd been making sketches of them all – back in her room and from memory – over the holiday.

'For which I'll pay.'

'Something for the future,' Janey said.

Future? Had she really said that? Just four days ago she hadn't dared hope she'd have one and now she most definitely did. There was still lot to be got through – like a divorce for a start, and all the banking details and wills and all sorts of things couples do until they're not couples anymore – but Bobbie, Lissy, and Xander had shown her that she could. 'Shall we go down now? Lissy might need some help.'

Bobbie wagged a finger at her.

'Not yet. I've just heard Xander come out of his room. We'll give them a few minutes alone, shall we?'

And then Bobbie winked.

'What do you know that I don't?' Janey laughed.

'Now that, my lovely young friend, would be telling. Besides we can't go yet because it takes me an age to Polyfilla up my face.' Bobbie picked up a tube of something and snapped off the lid. 'Eyeliner. My trademark, along with my long silver hair – and God help anyone who calls it grey!'

'Eyeliner,' Janey said. She had a pot of tinted lip balm and that was about the sum of her make-up routine. And that was the way she liked it, but horses for courses and all that.

'Want some?' Bobbie said. She seemed to have finished expertly applying it and Janey was glad now she'd done the smokey eyelids and the eyeliner on Bobbie in the portrait. She'd thought at the time how incongruous it was that a nude model would be fully made up but now she'd got to know Bobbie better she could see the portrait just wouldn't have been the same without it – it gave it soul.

'Not at the moment, thanks,' Janey said. 'I'll just sit here and watch your masterclass. Just in case, you know, one day I do.'

Chapter 41

Xander

He came downstairs, fresh from his shower, smelling – he knew – a lot sweeter than he had when he and Janey had got back from a quick visit to check on Felix, who was fine but giving him the cold shoulder still for not being there, and a trip to a cashpoint for Janey to check on her finances.

He'd heard Janey and Bobbie laughing in Bobbie's room as he'd stepped out onto the landing just now.

Expecting Lissy to be in the kitchen preparing supper – so very effortlessly, with small, sure movements, that it seemed a miracle to Xander that such deliciousness arrived so quickly at the table - he went there first. No Lissy. He tried the dining room and then the sitting room. Perhaps she'd gone upstairs to change? He decided to check the laundry room but she wasn't there either. And then he heard her voice. Quite cross but as though she was trying to keep the volume down. With a bit of a wobble though. Who could she be talking to? And where?

There was a door on the opposite wall of the laundry room. He'd assumed it was a cupboard of sorts but he saw now that it was slightly ajar. Lissy sounded to him, as though someone was stressing her out for some reason. Well, not on his watch, they wouldn't be. He strode across the room, stopped at the door and listened. If she'd heard him then she'd know he was close and there for support.

'No, Cooper. Absolutely not. You haven't got a leg to stand ...'

Cooper. Lissy's ex-husband. She'd not talked about him to Xander much but he'd assumed that was because there wasn't a lot to say, apart from the fact he'd tried to claim a portion of Lissy's salary as part of the divorce settlement. Fat chance, mate, Xander thought, knowing he should go right now.

He heard her sigh as she was obviously being interrupted, and when he heard no answering comment from Cooper he guessed this was a phone call and that Cooper hadn't got into the house somehow and he wouldn't have to go in there and punch his lights out. Lissy had probably gone in there to take it so no one overheard. That old chestnut that eavesdroppers never hear good of themselves popped into his mind. His heart was racing though.

'Do what you like, Cooper,' he heard Lissy say. 'Solicitor, barrister, judge if you want. But I can save you the time because I've already found out my legal position in all this and Strand House and everything that comes with it is one hundred per cent legally mine. You are owed nothing. Got that? Nothing! Now sod off. I've got guests here and supper to cook ...'

That's my girl! Stand up to the bullying bastard! He expected Lissy to come out then and he began to move away as quietly as he could so she wouldn't know he'd been there but then he heard her sigh again.

She said, 'Yes, there is someone. Not that I have to have your permission.' Again, a little pause while Cooper was, presumably, saying something. 'You don't need to know his name. Then again, perhaps you do, and for the record he's worth ten of you. Xander. And before you ask, yes, I do think we have a future. So I ...'

Another exasperated sigh from Lissy and Xander wondered

why she didn't just put the phone down and then block his number as Janey had blocked Stuart's.

'I'll pretend you didn't say that,' Lissy said. Her voice was icy now. It had lost that slightly edgy, nervous tone. 'If I thought for a second Xander might be a golddigger, as you put it, I wouldn't have taken things as far as I have.' Lissy paused for breath and Cooper must have said something because then Lissy said. 'Oh, for God's sake Cooper, it might not be the news you want but get over it. Okay?'

It obviously wasn't okay because Xander could hear Cooper's very angry voice now although not the actual words.

'Well, since you ask, it started a long time ago. I wasn't unfaithful to you if that's what you're thinking. I kept those feelings very much to myself but I don't care who knows now. It's not a secret anymore. Goodbye!'

Xander heard the click as Lissy killed the call. It sounded almost like gunshot in his ears. So much for eavesdroppers not hearing good of themselves! He'd heard enough to melt an igloo, never mind the cockles of his heart.

Move, Xander, move before …

The door was flung open and Lissy stood there. She looked more beautiful in anger than Xander could ever have thought she would – tears were running down her face and she was pink with the emotion of dealing with the call. She ran her hands through her hair and then swiped at her tears with the back of her hand.

'You heard?' she said.

'Most of it,' Xander said. He held out his arms and Lissy walked into them. She placed the side of her head against his chest, tucking her head under his chin. What a fit! What a perfect fit! 'Not a Christmas present you needed or wanted that call, eh?'

'No. But it'll be the last. I've blocked him,' Lissy snuffled into him. 'Sorry, I'm soaking the very lovely shirt you've put on.'

'This old thing!' Xander joked. 'Soak away.' He wrapped Lissy more tightly in his arms and rocked her gently. 'What's that room you were in anyway? I assumed it was a cupboard door when I came in here before.'

Lissy pushed herself away from him a little.

'Come and look.'

Their hands linked and Lissy led the way.

It was a small room – only a little bigger than the en suite in Xander's room. A set of French doors looked out onto the back terrace. There was a wood-burner in the corner with a basket of logs beside it. Two bucket chairs, piled with cushions. It didn't seem to go with the 1930s look of the rest of the house somehow. Could he, he wondered, incorporate this into his plan for the L-shaped conservatory he'd drawn for Lissy? Hmm, something for the future he'd just heard Lissy say she wanted. Plenty of time, then, to ask that question.

'It's like a rabbit warren, this place,' Xander said. 'I had no idea this was here.'

'That's how Vonny always wanted it. It was her bolthole. She jokingly called it her library, even though she only had about a dozen books. It's where she went when she had guests. There seems to be more of her here than in the rest of the house. I cleared lots of her things away but I left this til last. Hardly room to swing a cat she always said but she loved the secretiveness of it. Do you understand?'

'And now it's helped you tell Cooper your secret? About me? About us?'

'I suppose it has. I hadn't thought of that, but yes, it has. I hope you didn't mind me saying?'

'How could I? That was all my birthdays and all my Christmases rolled into one. Besides, Lissy, I've got a cat. Not that I'm in the habit of swinging it.'

'Ha ha,' Lissy laughed. 'I know. Felix. I've been meaning to talk to you about him. Do you think, you know, at some time in the future, once we've sorted out our lives as they are now, that he'd be happy to move?'

'Move?' Xander said, knowing just what she meant – move to Strand House. But he'd tease her along. 'Move where?'

'Here, of course!' Lissy swung round to stand in front of him. 'Had that call gone on you'd have heard me say that, well, I'm sure you can guess the rest.'

'Yeah. So very perceptive of you to come to the conclusion that I'm not a golddigger, and …'

'Oh, shut up and give us a kiss,' Lissy giggled.

So, Xander did.

'Xander,' Lissy said, when they came up for breath, 'there's something I've got to tell you. Something I know which you need to know, too.'

Xander's heart started to plummet and his mouth went dry. 'Okay …'

'Something Claire told me. Just before she died.'

'Best tell,' Xander said. Whatever it was he wanted to know now.

'Claire told me she was leaving you. She wasn't happy with the egg donation option you'd been offered and she wanted to set you free to have a child with someone who could make one with you. We had that conversation the morning she died. I tried to dissuade her but we both know now that I didn't manage that. She said she'd found a flat to rent in Teignmouth …'

'Teignmouth,' Xander said. Claire had been spending a lot of time in Teignmouth. He'd assumed it was taking the fitness classes she ran but …

'Are you cross? That I've told you?'

'No.'

'Bobbie said keeping the secret would only fester inside me if I didn't tell you. You told me about the tests and I should have said that I already knew but I didn't. But I needed to tell you that I already knew. Are we still friends?'

For answer, Xander cupped Lissy's face in his hands, tilted her head up to face his. He bent down and kissed her, a pure sweet kiss.

'We're more than friends, Lissy. No going back for either of us now. No secrets.'

'No secrets,' Lissy said, kissing him. 'But there is something else. I don't know how I'd feel if I were to be told what Claire was told. I don't know if I can have a child or not ... '

'But you'd like one?'

Lissy nodded.

'But ... and this is all a bit hypothetical at the moment ... if we become a couple and I can't have a child, knowing now that you would love to be a dad, I would consider all options. God, this is getting a bit deep, isn't it?'

'Just scratching the surface, I'd say,' Xander said.

There didn't seem to be anything to add to that so Xander didn't. He kissed Lissy instead and she made it very obvious she was happy to be kissed.

'Cooee! Anyone home?' Bobbie's voice ringing out in the echo that was Lissy's kitchen, eventually parted them.

'We've been summoned,' Xander said, breaking the kiss.

'But we'll resume at a later hour.'

'I'll hold you to that!' Xander said.

Chapter 42

Lissy

'Boxing night supper,' Lissy said, placing a Le Creuset of pot-roasted venison in the centre of the table. Hardly traditional – because didn't people usually eat cold cuts for at least three days after the twenty-fifth of December? – but then this had hardly been a traditional Christmas for any of them. 'One of my *Blue Peter* moments.'

Everyone laughed, knowing exactly what she meant – one she'd made earlier. Which she had. She'd made it the night before leaving for Strand House back in her flat in Princesshay with venison bought from the Powderham Estate and then driven down with it, placing it in the freezer until it was time to give it its moment in the sun, as it were.

'Redcurrant sauce to go with it,' she said. 'Also a *Blue Peter* moment. Plates, Bobbie, please?'

Lissy had pre-carved the meat in the kitchen so it was just a matter then of serving it out.

'God, but that smells heavenly,' Bobbie said, as Lissy placed a very generous portion on a plate and Bobbie handed it to Janey. 'Do you think you could teach me to cook like this?'

'And me,' Janey said. 'I mean, take the mashed potato.' She reached for the pottery serving dish decorated with chickens that Lissy had bought in the market in Totnes. 'It's so fluffy, like a cloud. Or a rumpled-up duvet.'

'Now there's a description!' Lissy laughed. 'I think it would be a first if I were to describe mashed potato like a rumpled duvet. Not even Jamie Oliver's thought of that, I shouldn't think.'

She couldn't really take any credit for the mashed potato though because it was a melange of ideas gleaned from magazine cookery features or television programmes – potatoes, steamed, and then pressed through a sieve before adding single cream instead of milk before stirring in leeks softened in butter with a dash of lemon.

She carried on serving out the venison and everyone helped themselves to the carrots Lissy had roasted with garlic, thyme, rosemary, and sage. And the beans – French beans steamed briefly so that they still had a bit of crunch.

'I thought,' Xander said, 'a carrot was a carrot was a carrot. You know, peeled and pre-cut in a bag that you chuck in a saucepan and ...'

'Boiled to death!' Bobbie said.

There then followed a lively discussion of meals remembered from their childhood which had all been, pretty much – before the advent of celebrity chefs – over-cooked vegetables with over-cooked meat.

'Seriously, though ...' Janey said as they were all tucking into a deep lemon tart that contained six lemons and as many eggs and – Lissy knew – more cream than it was sensible to eat in a single sitting, but hey, this was Christmas. 'Seriously, I think you've got the makings of a business here, Lissy. You could run work-shops, a bit like that one we all met on, but not just cooking. How about painting, and maybe Bobbie giving people tutorials on how to throw their clothes together so they look like they've stepped off the front page of *Vogue* or something? This is—' Janey carried on, waving her arms around the hall which seemed to have become the place to eat in the house '—a healing house. Look what it's done for us all.'

Janey picked up her glass of wine and sipped.

'A healing house,' Lissy said. 'I like that.'

Janey was right, of course, because it had healed *her* being here with Vonny after her parents' acrimonious divorce. And there had been a weekend after Cooper had told her he wanted a divorce when she'd come down and Vonny had filled her with scones and jam and cream and let her cry and cry, holding her in her arms and saying nothing – no homilies about how it would for the best, and that everything would be all right. But maybe she knew she didn't have to say any of that because Lissy knew now, beyond doubt, that it was for the best and everything was going to be all right.

'Penny for them,' Xander said. Lissy felt his foot touch hers under the table.

'Worth far more than that,' she said. 'Every single one.'

'It's healed me,' Janey said. 'I know there's a way to go for me before I'm who I really am again but it's started the process.'

'Good,' Lissy said.

Bobbie was pushing a portion of tart around her plate as though wondering if she should eat it or not.

'Leave it if it's too much, Bobbie,' Lissy told her. 'I'm over-generous with my portions.'

'With everything I'd say,' Bobbie told her. 'You can't have known, Lissy, that Oliver was going to get in touch yesterday, but have it on record that I'm glad that call came when I was here, with you all. In this house. I agree with Janey, it is a healing house. And I am going to eat this last portion of tart if it's the last thing I ever do! Which I hope it won't be!'

'Oh, it won't,' Lissy said. 'I wonder,' she carried on, 'where we will all be one year from now?'

'Well,' Xander said, whippet-fast, 'I'm rather hoping I might be spending it here. Or with you in my cottage. I don't know that Felix will take kindly to me abandoning him two Christmases in a row.'

'We'll work on that,' Lissy said.

'I …' Janey said, draining the last of her wine and putting a hand over her glass when Xander went to fill it up for her. 'I want to have started selling my paintings. There's a gallery on Sands Road and I'm going in there just as soon as I can with some of my work. I'll need to get it framed and they do that as well. I'm going to ask if they'll sell them for me on commission. It will be a start.'

'And an online gallery,' Lissy said. 'You could have one of those as well.'

'A foot in both camps,' Xander agreed. 'Although it might help your case that I rowed for the Scouts with James who runs that gallery!'

'Not what you know but whom,' Bobbie said, sounding serious and Lissy thought she looked on the verge of tears. There was definitely a catch in her voice when she said, 'Different people come into our lives at different times for a different reason. And then sometimes they go out of them again.'

'Oliver, you mean,' Lissy said. There was no need to tiptoe around the issue because Bobbie didn't need that anymore.

'Oliver,' Bobbie said. She smiled at Lissy in a knowing sort of way and she wondered if Bobbie meant having Sebastian back in her life, too, although she wasn't going to mention him at the moment.

'Yes, Oliver,' Bobbie went on. 'But not just him. I've told Lissy, you two, but someone else has come back into my life. Or could be back in it. Sebastian. I searched for him on Facebook and sent him a Friend request. He answered with almost indecent haste, I have to say. I was more than flattered, and the old heart did more than a bit of a flutter, I can tell you.'

'Good,' Lissy said. 'Friending is a start.'

That's all she and Xander had been for years – friends, because Claire had been hers and he'd been married to her. Despite the memory of that almost-kiss that wouldn't die that's all they'd been. But not anymore.

'Yes,' Bobbie laughed, 'and there are two people not a million miles from me who've moved friendship on a notch, I'd say.'

'Too much information!' Janey laughed.

'Possibly,' Bobbie grinned. 'I won't go into details, but to answer your question, Lissy ... one year from now I like to think I might be spending my first ever Christmas with my son. And his family. If that's what they all want. Oliver went out of my life although never from my thoughts, but he's back now. Some don't come back, sadly.'

Bobbie leaned over and patted the back of Xander's hand.

'Like Claire, you mean,' Xander said. 'There were good times and then not so good times, but if we're sensible we hang onto the good and – as the Beatles had it back in the day – "with a little help from our friends" we let the not so good go. This house has definitely helped with that. And you, Lissy. Well, all of you. Shall we have a thoroughly narcisstic touch? A toast? To us?'

Instinctively all four reached for their glasses.

'Just a dribble, Janey,' Xander said, pouring in half an inch of the very excellent Rioja they'd all been drinking with the pot-roast venison. 'Can't have a toast without a drop of the hard stuff, can we?'

'To us!' they all shouted, all happy, all happily a little bit tipsy. And then they all chinked glasses and Lissy thought it sounded like bells tinkling somewhere in the distance. There came an echoing tinkle and all four of them looked up towards the chandelier that hung over the table, holding their breath as three crystal droplets flickered towards one another and back again, the sound melodic.

Claire? Vonny? Maybe Vonny's husband? A shiver of something Lissy didn't really believe in rippled up her spine and over her shoulders. Whatever it was that had made those crystal droplets move didn't matter.

'That,' she said to the others, 'is the magic of Christmas making its presence felt, I think.'

'We'll drink to that, then,' Xander said.

So they had another toast.

'I don't know that I want this to end,' Bobbie said, 'and there's me with a whole new, hopefully, wonderful life to me moving on to!'

'Come back,' Lissy said. 'Whenever you like.'

'Oh, I will. I'm going to take Janey up on her idea of a fashion workshop. So book me in for that, Lissy.'

'And my painting one,' Janey said.

'I'll do the cleaning,' Xander joked. 'And put the rubbish out.'

'You so will not!' Lissy said. And then it occurred to her – she was definitely going ahead with this idea, no more doubts, no more what ifs. She could hardly wait to get back to Exeter now and her practice and her flat and start putting both on the market.

The clock was creeping around to midnight. Christmas was almost over. Bobbie had rung Sam and he said he could do better than find someone to drive Bobbie to London in the morning, he'd do it himself. He also said his wife was due a few days away because she'd put up with him taxiing hither and thither the whole holiday so if it was all right with Bobbie she could sit in on the trip and then he'd only charge her half fare. Xander had been in touch with the lads who worked for him, and they, in turn, had been in touch with a couple of their rugby-playing mates so in the morning there'd be six of them going with Janey to fetch her computer and anything else she wanted to bring back to Strand House, and to sort out Janey's husband if needs be, although Xander had said he was pretty certain that the mere sight of them would frighten the coward half to death.

Lissy stood up. She waved an arm over the detritus of possibly the best meal she'd ever cooked and eaten.

'Ready for the fireworks?' she asked.

'Oh yes, I'd forgotten about the Boxing Night fireworks,' Xander said. 'Who sets them off?'

'No idea,' Lissy said. 'Someone in one of the big villas on the headland at Livermead has been doing it for as long as I can remember. We've got just about the best view of them here though. Shall we grab coats?'

It had definitely got colder as the evening had worn on and Lissy had increased the temperature of the central heating a little.

'Definitely,' Bobbie said. 'I've not watched fireworks in years but, well, it'll seem like a celebration.' She got up and fetched her coat, handing Janey hers.

Xander lifted Lissy's coat from its hook and held it out for Lissy to slip her arms into. Then he, very tenderly, did up the buttons for her – such a caring, loving gesture.

Then they all stepped outside, and Lissy pulled the door to behind them, leaving it ajar a little. They all huddled close together, arms around one another's shoulders – Janey, Lissy, Xander and Bobbie, all in a row.

Lissy heard the mantel clock in the dining room strike midnight, as fireworks filled the sky with colour and light and noise – every colour in the rainbow and a few more besides, and then a million, trillion gold and silver stars rained down.

'What a finale to a wonderful Christmas holiday!' Bobbie said.

Finale? Not yet. A few, wonderful snowflakes were fluttering down now, dancing and swirling in the light from the lamppost at the end of the cul-de-sac. Money couldn't have bought that, could it?

Snowflakes were blowing, soft as feathers, into their hair now.

'More perfect than perfect!' Janey said. 'Snow as well!'

'My parting gift to you all,' Lissy joked. 'Until the next time.'

'Until the next time!' they all chorused, and Lissy knew there *would* be a next time now their friendship had become even stronger, unbreakable even.

Yes, she thought, sometimes a rash decision can be the right one … for everyone.

One Year Later…

Bobbie

Another year, another Christmas. This year Bobbie is on her way to Sydney where she is going to spend Christmas and New Year with Oliver and his family. They all had a wonderful time together when Bobbie got back to London after her stay at Strand House. She'd never put Oliver up for adoption which made the getting to know one another, for them, easier. Her granddaughters couldn't get enough of looking through Bobbie's old press cuttings, and trying on her clothes, experimenting with her make-up. Oliver's wife was thrilled to have Bobbie for a mother-in-law, especially as Bobbie often passed on clothes she was given from shoots. They have all Skyped regularly and Bobbie feels she already knows the layout of Oliver's house and the bedroom that she and Sebastian will share when they get there. And that was another surprise, how easy it was for her and Sebastian to slip back into what they'd had when they'd first met. All it had taken was a Facebook search and a Friend Request and now here they were, back together. Thank God for today's technology Bobbie thinks, and says, often.

Janey

Janey still has to pinch herself to believe that she is living the life she has now. She is living in Xander's house now that he is up at Strand House with Lissy. She knows it's not for ever but it is for now and she couldn't be happier. Felix has elected to stay with her, it seems. Xander did take him with him, but every morning Felix was back again, having let himself in through the catflap and curled himself into a purring ball beside Janey on the bed.

Most days Janey walks over to the Port Light for coffee. She's become good friends with Ana – best friends even – who runs it and it feels good because Janey hasn't had a best friend before.

As promised, Xander introduced her to his friend, James, who runs the gallery and framing business, and while it is very early days for them – and Janey is not yet divorced although that is going ahead – it is good to have him in her life.

She went to stay with Bobbie in London for a whole month, filling God knows how many sketchbooks with drawings and little vignettes of London scenes – both the well-documented and the unknown. Beavering away, well into the night, on the top floor of Bobbie's mews house she painted a portrait of Bobbie and her son and his daughters, taken from a photograph Bobbie had on the mantelpiece in the dining room to say thank you for her friendship and for spoiling her something rotten during her stay.

This Christmas, Janey has invited her old neighbours, Annie and Fred, to spend Christmas Day with her. And Guinness, of course. They've kept her up to date with the goings on in her old home which is now on the market as part of Janey's divorce proceedings. Stuart has – so they told her – gone to stay with the floozy (as Fred called her) he brought home the previous Christmas. He no longer teaches at the local college. Janey no longer cares.

James will also be joining Janey, Annie and Fred, and Guinness for Christmas lunch. Janey and James have not yet shared a bed, although Janey thinks this could all change once he has driven Annie and Fred back to Totnes when Christmas Day is over to which end she has bought a new duvet set for the bed now she is earning enough money to do so. Life can only get better.

Lissy & Xander

The names now come joined together, said in the same breath as bread and cheese and the Queen and her handbag, Xander likes to joke. Their daughter, Freya Claire, was born on the 22nd September, which bears out the folk theory that more babies are born nine months after Christmas than at any other time of the year.

Lissy made Xander what was quite possibly the least romantic offer a woman could to a man and said she'd go through his accounts. She found more than a few ways where he could save money, so much so that he didn't have to let any of his men go and has actually taken on two more. Now that he has a focus in life again – Lissy and his daughter – he is much better about getting back to people when they call about jobs they would like him to quote for. His jobs book is full. He did, however, find time to build the conservatory for Lissy, and extend what Vonny had called her library and which Lissy and Xander now call the snug.

Lissy is yet to start running any courses at Strand House, but she will. She loves cooking even more now she has Xander and Freya Claire to cook for. She has begun devising menus for when she takes things to a more professional level in the future. She has never known a year fly so deliciously fast before because she was more than occupied selling her flat and business in Exeter and being pregnant.

It is Christmas Eve. Xander's mother will be joining them for lunch tomorrow and Xander's only sadness is that his father never got to meet his granddaughter. His mother is more than making up for his father's loss by showering Freya Claire with love and big Lego and at least a dozen teddies.

Lissy's mother has softened now she has a granddaughter and will be coming, with Mark, to stay in the New Year and meet Freya Claire. Lissy hopes this will go some way to improving relations with her mother but already their phone calls are becoming more frequent and less of a strain to them both. Bobbie told Lissy that a baby changes everything, and it seems she might be right.

'Déjà vu,' Xander says as Lissy climbs into his lorry, Freya Claire in her arms. They are heading for the Christmas Tree Farm.

Another Christmas at Strand House has begun …

Acknowledgements

I'll begin by thanking Gerri Gill for her gloriously glam and feel-good Facebook posts; they lifted my spirits on the darkest days and 'gave birth' to Bobbie to boot! Black and white rules, Gerri!

Marilyn Chapman is a not-yet-met-face-to-face friend but is the most supportive and encouraging of friends, nonetheless. Thanks, Maz.

And now to the two Js – Jennie and Jan, friends of long-standing. They listen to my moans, offer advice and praise or slap my wrists, whichever is needed. Thanks, girls – my life would be the poorer without you both.

Brixham Writers, as ever, are my anchor in a storm. Anne, Kate, John, Brenda, Margaret, Hannelore, Catherine, Ella, Michelle, Sandra, Ian, and not forgetting Carole in Spain who is always with us in spirit – you rock, one and all!

My very grateful thanks also to Charlotte and the team at HarperCollins for giving me this publishing opportunity.

And lastly, but by no means least, my love and thanks to my husband, Roger, who has been my personal barista and wine waiter in the making of this novel.

Dear Reader,

Thank you so much for taking the time to read this book – we hope you enjoyed it! If you did, we'd be so appreciative if you left a review.

Here at HQ Digital we are dedicated to publishing fiction that will keep you turning the pages into the early hours. We publish a variety of genres, from heartwarming romance, to thrilling crime and sweeping historical fiction.

To find out more about our books, enter competitions and discover exclusive content, please join our community of readers by following us at:

🐦 *@HQDigitalUK*

f *facebook.com/HQDigitalUK*

Are you a budding writer? We're also looking for authors to join the HQ Digital family!
Please submit your manuscript to:

HQDigital@harpercollins.co.uk.

Hope to hear from you soon!

ONE PLACE. MANY STORIES

Turn the page for an exclusive extract from
Summer at 23 The Strand...

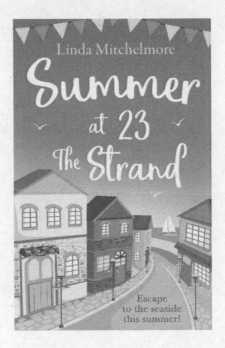

Chapter 1

Early May

Martha

'I'll just check your details.' The clerk behind the desk in the tourist office on the seafront spoke without looking up. Martha, peering out from under the rim of her black straw hat, held her breath. Would the woman detect a lie? A false address? Not a fictitious name as such but not the one the world knew her by? 'So, that's Martha Langford? Eighteen Staplethorpe Avenue, Brighton? Right? From one seaside resort to another, eh?'

'Yes to all that,' Martha said.

'Well, you'll just love it here in Hollacombe, I'm sure. A proper little home from home is how our guests describe Number 23. Here's the key. You'll find your chalet is about five hundred yards to your left as you leave this office. One double bedroom, one sitting room with sofabed cum galley kitchen, one loo with basin and shower. All breakages to be paid for. No barbecues on the wooden deck, I'm afraid, because the chalets are wooden. Fire risk, and all that. To be vacated a fortnight from today by 10 a.m. to give the cleaner time to turn it all around before the next occupants. The key with the luggage-label tag on it to be posted through the letterbox here if we're closed. Any problems—'

'I'll sort them,' Martha interrupted. The last thing she needed was to have to come back here and, possibly, have someone else turn up at Number 23 The Strand to sort out whatever problem she might have. Just standing here, listening to the clerk reciting what she must have recited hundreds of times before, was giving her goose bumps. The sooner she got out of here the better.

'Of course, this could be the last season this particular chalet is let because it's up for sale,' the clerk said as though Martha hadn't spoken. 'It's owned by the local authority at present, as are a couple of others and they need to cut costs, so they're up for sale too. The others are privately owned by locals who keep them for their own use at weekends and in the school holidays, although some do rent them out to holidaymakers. There's not been a lot of interest in Number 23 so far but it's early in the season. Any questions?' The clerk cocked her head to one side questioningly.

'Can't think of any,' Martha said, perhaps a bit too sharply, which is what happens when one's nerves are on end. She didn't want to be rude but she had to go.

Well, Martha thought, as she closed the door of the chalet behind her, what a lovely surprise. She'd glanced at the photos on the website when she'd booked, of course, but she hadn't studied it in much detail. It was bigger than she'd been expecting – more ski chalet than beach hut, perhaps a bit boutique hotel – and just as the lady in the tourist office had said, a little home from home. And so very clean. A nest. Martha felt the welcome of it wrap around her, warm her. The boarded walls were painted a soft shade of yellow, like vanilla custard, with a frieze of sten-cilled scallop shells in deep turquoise where the walls met the ceiling. Pretty, cotton curtains with blue and yellow sailboats hung at the windows in the double bedroom and living room. The cream, linen-covered sofabed was piled with large and squashy cushions in various shades of yellow and blue, and two small but matching armchairs had biscuit-coloured fleece throws draped over the arms, for colder days perhaps. The duvet on the double bed, covered in a turquoise, jacquard-style pattern, was thick and sumptuous, and the pillows large, plump and inviting.

'All very Eastern Seaboard,' Martha said out loud. 'I love it.'

Some of the tension she'd been carrying with her was beginning to seep away. Yes, she'd made the right decision coming here. It was as though this chalet had been waiting for her. She patted the duvet, her hand almost disappearing in its sumptuousness.

'And I could lie down on you right now,' she laughed, surprising herself with that laugh because she hadn't laughed for weeks now. But she couldn't flop down on it just yet. Martha drew her breath in and then let it all out again slowly, her shoulders dropping as she physically relaxed. Yes, it felt good here. It would give her space and time to rethink what she wanted to do with the rest of her life. But first, she just had to do something with her hair.

Martha had never done a home hair dye before. Ever since she'd been eleven years old and at stage school, her naturally blonde hair had always been professionally cut and coloured. And, of course, for filming she'd often worn wigs. It felt strange, but empowering, to be choosing a new hair colour without others calling the shots. So she'd chosen red; a sort of rosehip red with a bit of gloss to it to cover her natural blonde. The basin in the bijou bathroom – small but perfectly appointed the brochure had said, and so it was – looked as though a murder had been committed as Martha rinsed her hair one last time. Now to dry it. And then cut it. She pulled her hair high over her head and, with eyes closed, chopped straight across. When she opened her eyes again she had about eighteen inches of ponytail in her hand. Shaking her head to loosen her hair, she braved the mirror.

Not bad. Not bad at all. Next came the coloured contact lenses. Martha's eyes were the palest blue, bordering on turquoise, but she reckoned a redhead might have green eyes. So in went the onyx contacts.

'I hardly recognise myself,' Martha said, in a Scottish accent, light years away from her true Home Counties way of speaking. But that was the advantage of being an actress. She could become anyone from anywhere. And she had. Many, many, times. From stage work to period TV dramas, through a six-month stint on a 'soap', to Hollywood. But there was a downside – over the years so many other people had pulled her strings, as it were. So many that she felt she had almost lost the essence of who she was inside. Almost.

Her agent, Ralph Newcombe, had been furious when she'd decided to turn her back on it all.

'You cannot be serious!' he'd raged at her in his office that smelled of whisky and cigarettes, making Martha gag. Or rather making Serena Ross, as she was known to the world, gag. 'You are making me look an utter fool pulling out of this! I've worked my backside off getting you, not the lead role admittedly, but a not insignificant role in a Tom Marchant film. Bets were on that you'd get Best Supporting Actress at the Oscars. And you pull this stunt! I'll be surprised if you ever work again!'

That night, Martha had gone back to the flat the film company had provided and cried and cried and cried. No need for glycerine on her bottom lashes to bring on the tears. And then she'd called Tom and told him she wouldn't be coming back to the set. She'd been flattered by his attention, even though she'd known he was married with two small children – as did the rest of the world. Sitting close to him on breaks, sharing a burger or a salad, a *frisson* of excitement had fizzed through her. His invite to dinner after the day's filming had been tempting. So she'd gone. Just dinner, he'd said. And it had been. Although if she were honest with herself it wouldn't have taken much for their feelings to run over – perhaps not this time they had dinner, but definitely the next. Tom had felt it too.

'Taxi time,' he'd said, leaning across the table to give her hand a squeeze. 'The danger hour approacheth. Two people from out of town with hours to fill till morning.'

Tom had even called the taxi for her, walked with her to the door – just a little behind her with a hand in the small of her back. And that's when she'd been startled by a barrage of camera flashes and saw in rapid fast-forward how it would be if she were to enter a full-blown affair with Tom. She – and he – would be hounded.

Martha, not liking herself very much at that moment for what she'd been on the cusp of, had turned to Tom then.

'The danger hour is too dangerous for me,' she'd said. 'I'm not in the habit of breaking up marriages, despite the magic...'

'...between us,' Tom had finished for her.

Martha didn't think Tom was a serial adulterer, although she was under no illusion that she'd been the first to tempt him. For the two weeks they'd been thrown together, working on *Breaking Ice*, he'd showered her with gifts, in time-honoured Hollywood style – bespoke perfume and a designer handbag, Italian silk scarves and an amethyst pendant on a fine gold chain. She'd worn that pendant on her first – and last – dinner date with Tom. But she'd known in an instant, the camera flashes almost blinding her, that she hadn't been in love with him – merely in lust, feelings heightened and enhanced by the place and the setting and the fabulous clothes. There could be many Toms in the future if she stayed here among the beautiful people with money to spend and lavish lifestyles. Was that what she wanted?

And that was when she'd made her decision to end her contract on *Breaking Ice* and go home, back to the UK. And then... what?

Well, she had a fortnight to work out where her life was going, and a town she didn't know to explore. In front of her, there was the curve of a bay the colour of faded denim, flat as the proverbial pancake at that moment, and the sun was shining. First she'd need to find a supermarket of sorts to buy food, and maybe a bottle of wine, although she knew it was dangerous – very dangerous – to drink alone. Martha placed her four-inch heels in the cupboard in the bedroom, slid her feet into flip-flops, took a deep breath, and went out.

'Can I help you with that?'

A man's voice. A Scottish accent. To answer or not? With one foot on the bottom step of the wooden steps that led up to the deck of 23 The Strand, and her arms full of carrier bags and a lamp she'd picked up in a charity shop, Martha considered her options. If she answered, she'd need to drop the Scottish accent she'd been using for a couple of days and which was becoming second nature now, because this man was likely to ask where in Scotland she came from, and she only knew Edinburgh, Glasgow and Aberdeen, each of which had its own particular accent.

'I can manage, thanks. Only a few more steps,' she said. And then the newspaper that had been on top of one of the bags fell to the floor.

The man picked it up, shifting awkwardly as he rebalanced himself.

'Damned leg,' he said, rubbing a hip. He looked at the photo and the headline on the front page and then at Martha.

ACTRESS SERENA ROSS QUITS *BREAKING ICE*

The photo was one taken on the steps of the hotel as Tom had guided her to her taxi. There were, Martha knew, more photos of them both inside, cosied up in the restaurant, because she was wiser now and knew that the man in the corner hadn't been taking selfies but had been taking photographs of her and Tom.

'I'll take that,' she said. 'Thanks. The press scraping about in the gutter as per usual, I expect,' she added, with a nod to the front page of the newspaper.

'More than likely,' the man said. 'Don't shoot but... Hugh Fraser. Photographer. Currently on sick leave while my leg heals.'

Oh my God! What sort of a photographer, she wanted to know – paparazzi? – but she was afraid to ask. Her hat had slipped back over her head as she struggled with her bags. If he was paparazzi, would he recognise her? She might have changed her hair colour and be wearing coloured lenses, but her mouth was the same shape. Her nose. Her high cheekbones, for which she was known in the world of acting.

'I'm sorry about your leg,' she said, acting a calmness she didn't feel inside, although it was true she was sorry. 'What happened?'

'You know how, on TV, when you see photographers following a story in the street and they're running backwards and taking photos? Have you ever wondered if they fall over?'

Martha gulped. So he was paparazzi? What on earth was she doing keeping him here, engaging him in conversation?

'Yes, yes, I have.'

'Well, I did. Right over a low wall. Only it was an urban fox I was trying to film without scaring it off. Compound fracture. Hence my stay here for a couple of weeks to strengthen my muscles now the break's been sorted. Running on sand is good for that.'

'Oh!' Martha said, unable to stop the smile that crept to her lips as a cartoon strip of Hugh running backwards and going over the wall played in her head. 'Sorry. It's not funny, I know.'

'That's okay. Every one of my colleagues fell about laughing. And you are?'

'Martha Langford.'

'I'd shake your hand, Martha Langford, if you had one free for me to shake. How about I come over all macho and carry this newspaper up the steps for you?'

And then he did just that, but carefully and with a bit of a limp, Martha noticed.

Hugh took Martha's bags and parcels from her as she scrabbled in her pocket for the chalet key.

'I'm at Number 20.' He waved the newspaper in the direction of his chalet. 'Belongs to my parents, actually. Holiday home of sorts. I'd stop with them in their house back in Exeter but Mum would smother me to death with kindness. Much better I fend for myself a bit, get those muscles working again. Keep an eye open for the next big scoop, as it were.'

Martha shivered. She had no intention of being Hugh's next big scoop.

'Thanks,' she said. 'You know. For your help. Just put my bags on the deck. I can manage now. Things to do. Bye.'

With almost indecent haste she scooped her bags into her arms and grabbed the newspaper from him, pushed the door open with her knee, sidled in behind it and then closed it with a foot.

Hugh seemed like a nice bloke – the sort of bloke she'd be happy to spend time with in normal circumstances, because photographers could be useful to an actress. But her circumstances weren't normal, were they, if the papers were still carrying stories about her quitting *Breaking Ice*? And she wasn't entirely sure she still wanted to be an actress any more anyway. And what was more, she badly needed to get to know herself better before she even thought about making a new relationship with anyone. And could she trust Hugh not to be on his laptop right now letting the world know he knew where Serena Ross was holed up?

Martha kept a low profile for a few days, always on the lookout for Hugh in case he wanted to talk, or asked too many probing questions she didn't want to answer. She'd seen him running a couple of times a day, not fast and rather ungainly, as though he was still carrying pain from his broken leg. She'd also seen him look up at her chalet as he made his way back to his own. But the red sand of the beach and the soft shush as the sea met the shore with a petticoat frill of white foam was calling her. The only thing Martha was missing from her old life at the moment was the gym. There were probably more than a few gyms in the area but she didn't want to join one. Power walking and running could be just as good. She couldn't hide from the world for ever. Or from Hugh. She had to get out there.

Hugh always looked glowing and happy when he got back from a run. Martha badly needed some of that – glowing and happy. But running on the beach was tide-dependent so she bought a tide-table from the kiosk at the end of The Strand that also sold teas, coffees, ice creams and a few beach toys, so she could work out when Hugh might be running and when he might not. She simply couldn't risk, at the moment at least, that he might recognise her, although she had a gut feeling he already had. Only that morning she'd seen him swing his long legs – rather stiffly – over the sandstone wall and drop onto the beach, landing awkwardly, struggling to get his balance the way a duck might on a frozen pond. She ought not to have laughed. Hugh had looked up directly towards her chalet as though he had sensed her watching him. She'd ducked quickly behind the curtain, but the speed of her movement made the fabric flutter. Had he seen?

To run, Martha would need trainers and some leggings and a T-shirt, so she went out to buy everything along with a few groceries. And a newspaper. Back at her chalet she decided to take a mug of coffee and the newspaper down to the beach. She laid a towel on the sand and sat down.

Martha shivered, a double-page feature on the demise of Tom's marriage – TOM MARCHANT'S WIFE FILES FOR DIVORCE – falling open on her lap. Another actress, Amy Stevens, had been cited. Not her. So she'd been right – she hadn't been the first to turn Tom's head. And neither would Amy be the last. Martha felt relief wash over her that she hadn't entered a full-blown affair with Tom and that there had been little between them except animal attraction, a few small gifts and one dinner after filming.

'Was it something I said?'

Hugh. Standing above her on the steps that led to and from the beach. *Could he read the headline from there?*

Martha closed the newspaper with one deft movement. She did not look up.

'No.'

'But you've been avoiding me?'

'If that's what you think,' Martha said with a shrug.

'I like to think I'm thicker-skinned than that.'

Hugh jumped – rather awkwardly it had to be said – down onto the sand and sat beside her without being asked.

'You're not still letting that get to you, are you?' Hugh asked, tapping a finger on the newspaper in Martha's – now shaking – hands.

Oh my God. He knew, didn't he? He knew that, despite the red hair dye, the coloured contacts, the wide-brimmed hat, and her almost exclusion from normal life, she was really Serena Ross.

'You haven't written this, have you?' she asked, waving the newspaper at him. Sometimes it was better to graciously admit defeat than fight a corner she was never going to win. He would know by her answer that she'd guessed he knew.

'No. Of course not. I'm a photographer – wildlife and landscape mostly – not a fully paid-up member of the paparazzi. But I did recognise you. And I've read that particular newspaper this morning and I see Mr Marchant has moved on.'

'That's not a very flattering remark,' Martha said. He was making it sound as though she were totally dispensable, which, while it might be true in Tom Marchant's case, was doing nothing for her self-esteem.

'I'm not rushing to judge you. You're here for your own reasons and it's not for me to pry.'

'I'm not suggesting you are for one moment but... well... I'm a bit sensitive right now.'

'Yes, I can see how that might be. But if it helps, today's newspaper is tomorrow's fish and chip wrappings, as the saying has it.'

'If only,' Martha said with a mock-groan.

'True. But if you ask me – which I know you're not – you are far, far prettier than his, um, latest squeeze.'

'Well, thank you, kind sir,' Martha said, unable to stop a smile creeping to the corners of her mouth. 'I'll take that as a compliment.'

'Please do.'

Martha felt her smile widen.

'That's better. Cliché alert – you're even prettier when you smile.'

'Thank you again, kind sir.' Martha laughed. 'I know I've not done enough of it lately. But I'll need to go now. My coffee's gone cold and...'

'I could make you another,' Hugh said. He gave Martha a big grin, the strength of it rippling the skin beside his eyes. 'I'm in dire need of a coffee myself after my run. Stay right there,' he went on, wagging a finger playfully at her. 'I'll be right back.'

Before Martha could find breath to reply, Hugh had loped and limped his way back up the steps.

Martha considered simply getting up and going back to her own chalet, because although she didn't think Hugh was a controlling sort of man in any way, she didn't know him well enough to really judge. And it had felt as though it was an order he'd issued just now.

But she stayed. She was safe enough here on a public beach and, as far as she could tell, Hugh didn't have a camera of any sort with him. She folded up the newspaper and put it underneath her beach towel and waited.

Hugh was soon back. He'd put two mugs of black coffee, a

small jug of milk, some tubes of sugar and a packet of Hobnobs on a tray.

'Could you hang on to that while I sit back down?' he asked. 'Only I get a bit of a balance issue now and then from the leg and I wouldn't want to shower you with it.'

'Of course,' Martha said, reaching up to take the tray.

Hugh sat back down and took the tray from her.

'How do you take your poison?'

'Black, no sugar, thanks,' Martha said.

'Ah,' Hugh said, 'we have the same impeccable taste in coffee.'

'Indeed we do,' Martha said, accepting her coffee and holding it to her in both hands. How civilised this was, just yards from their chalets, nothing between them and the horizon except shell-strewn sand and some strings of seaweed left by the tide.

'I hope you don't mind,' Hugh said, 'but I've brought my phone. I don't take it with me when I'm out running in case it falls out of my pocket.' He placed the tray on the sand beside him and took out a top-of-the-range phone from the pocket of his shorts. 'So many interesting things in the sand to take photographs of.'

Martha heard her own sharp intake of breath, like a gunshot in her ears. Of course, people took pictures with phones as well as cameras, and phones could be so slim and so easy to hide. A shiver of unease wriggled between her shoulder blades.

'But no photos of you. Promise,' Hugh said. 'I think I could work out where your thought processes were going there!'

'More than likely.' Martha laughed nervously. She sipped at her coffee – very good coffee she was pleased and surprised to note. But she wanted the focus off her for the moment, so she asked: 'What sort of photographs do you take? And sell, presumably?'

'How long have you got?'

'Until I've finished this coffee?' Martha quipped – gosh, how good that felt, to make a joke.

'Right. Well. Best drink slowly! I do wildlife photography and sell it to book publishers and magazines. Newspapers. I take landscape photographs for the same outlets. Both here and abroad for all of that. Most of that is commissioned but I also sell to photo-banks and agencies, and I have no jurisdiction over where those photos go. When cash flow has been stagnant I've done engagement parties, weddings – both in the UK and exotic beach locations, local theatre productions, that sort of thing. Enough to be going on with?'

'Yes. Thank you,' Martha said. She had a feeling she knew what sort of photographs Hugh might take that went to photo-banks and agencies over which he didn't have, as he'd said, jurisdiction: photos of celebrities being where they ought not to have been, and with people they ought not to have been with. But it was only a feeling – she had no proof.

'And do you know something, Martha?' Hugh went on. 'I've had all-expenses-paid trips to Bali and Bondi Beach, various Greek Island beaches and countless places in Spain, and it's always puzzled me as to why people bother to go all that way when we have perfectly lovely beaches in this country. I mean, look at this one.'

Martha looked. Indeed it did look magnificent with the sun shining, the sea, as she looked out towards Torquay at one side of the bay and Brixham at the other, appeared as though someone had scattered a million diamonds over it. Seagulls dipped and dived on the thermals and a cormorant dived for fish, then reappeared a few seconds later some way from where it had gone down.

'On a day like today, yes,' Martha said. 'I suppose people go abroad for the guaranteed sunshine.'

'Ah!' Hugh said. 'Not always guaranteed, I'm afraid. A friend's wedding I covered in Bali was rained off completely – monsoon didn't come into it! I could set up some wonderful shots here. The bride, barefoot, with her skirt hoisted to her knees, dipping a toe in to test the water for a paddle, with the groom holding her firmly by the waist, his trousers rolled up over his calves, so she doesn't stumble.'

Goodness, what a romantic, Martha thought. Was there a significant woman in his life, she wondered, but wasn't going to ask. They were only ships passing in the night here, weren't they? Hugh was healing and she was, too, in a way.

'I say,' Hugh said, scooping up a handful of sand and shells and letting the sand sift through his fingers. 'Could I borrow a corner of your towel to photograph these? The stripes are sharp and the navy against the white of the shells will be a perfect backdrop.'

'Be my guest,' Martha said, and edged a little further away as Hugh moved towards her, making space for his photoshoot.

'What I'll do,' Hugh said, 'is lay the shells in a line down the navy stripes. See, some of them have little swirls of long-discarded egg cases encrusted on them. And this one has got a frond of seaweed so firmly attached to it it's going to take more than my strength to pull it off.'

'It's like a hat,' Martha said. 'Or a fascinator.'

'Exactly that. And this one is so perfect it's like one half of a pigeon's egg. And just as delicate.' Hugh handed the shell to Martha, placing it gently on her palm when she held out her hand to take it.

'Exquisite,' Martha said. And it was. She knew beaches were always covered in shells from which the living beings had long gone, but she'd never stopped to examine any of them in detail as Hugh was now.

She watched, in silence, as Hugh took photograph after photograph, so absorbed in what he was doing now that he didn't speak either. For Martha it was a comfortable silence.

'I'll photoshop them later,' Hugh said, holding his phone towards Martha. 'But you get the gist.'

Martha was surprised to find Hugh had taken at least twenty

photos of the shells against the backdrop of her beach towel. They were all of the same thing and yet they all looked different.

'I'd buy a card – a postcard or birthday card – with any one of these on it,' she said.

'Now, there's a thought! Never thought of doing cards or postcards. Thanks for the tip.'

Martha had finished her coffee, eaten one of Hugh's Hobnobs, and knew she ought to go. Besides, Hugh seemed to have run out of things to say now they had exhausted the subject of the shells.

And then Hugh surprised her.

'There's a fête on the green tomorrow. Two o'clock. Would you like to come?'

'A fête?' Martha's father had always termed the village fête 'a fête worse than death' but they'd always gone anyway, she and her parents, and bought things they didn't really need or want because they felt sorry for the stall-holders. She hadn't been to a fête in years.

'I know. Very old-fashioned things, but it's for a good cause. They hold two or three during the summer on the green the other side of the promenade and I usually go if I'm in the area. Please say you'll come.'

'I don't think I can,' Martha said. She knew she didn't have a good excuse if Hugh pressed the issue. It was beginning to feel like a date, this invite, and she wasn't ready to date yet.

'It's for a good cause.'

'From my childhood memories of fêtes, they usually are. The church roof or the Scouts' trip to summer camp or somesuch.'

'Neither of those,' Hugh said. 'This one's for the local hospice. It's where my brother spent his last few days.'

Martha hadn't expected that, but the actress in her made her hang on to her composure – a composure she didn't feel inside. Inside she felt crass, and gauche, and uncomfortable, as though Hugh had fed her his final line on purpose to test her reaction.

'I'm very sorry for your loss,' she said. 'But I still can't come. Now, if you'll excuse me…'

She got to her feet and pulled at a corner of her beach towel.

'Of course,' Hugh said, standing up, although it took a second or two for him to get his balance because of his bad leg. 'Thanks for the loan of the beach towel.'

'And for the coffee and biscuits,' Martha responded, pulling the towel towards her.

It was only as she got halfway up the steps that she realised she'd left her newspaper on the sand where it had been underneath the beach towel. Well, she wasn't going back for it now.

But when she got to the door of her chalet and glanced round, she saw Hugh had made it to the top of the steps and was dropping her newspaper in a litter bin. The kindness of his action in getting rid of something about which she had been upset earlier brought a lump to Martha's throat. He really was such a good and kind man, wasn't he? But at the back of her mind was the thought that she couldn't be entirely sure if the invite to the fête had been because she was Martha Langford or… Serena Ross.

Martha tossed and turned all night. She'd been unforgivably rude walking off like that. Hugh had said his brother had died in the hospice and although she didn't know how old Hugh was, his brother couldn't have been very old either. Panic had made her behave the way she had and she was going to have to get over that.

Martha took a mug of tea and a round of toast and marmalade out onto the deck at half past eight the next morning. She took one of the throws and draped it over her knees while she sat at the metal bistro table and waited for Hugh to emerge from his chalet for his morning run.

But there was no Hugh that morning. Martha waited until almost ten o'clock then went in search of him.

'Well, good morning. This is a nice surprise,' Hugh said, opening the door to her knock, as though the fact she'd rebuffed him the day before hadn't happened. He was in checked pyjama bottoms but naked from the waist up. And his feet were bare. His hair was damp and curling every which way as though he was fresh from the shower and she'd knocked and interrupted him just as he was about to put a comb through it.

'I've come to apologise for my appalling behaviour yesterday,' Martha said. 'I meant it when I said I was truly sorry to hear about your brother's death, but I was rude to rush off the way I did without asking you about it. I'm sorry.'

'Apology accepted,' Hugh said. 'After Harris – that was my brother's name, by the way – died there were people who crossed the street to avoid saying anything to me at all.'

'Oh God, that's awful. Sometimes people simply don't know what to say, I suppose, and say nothing rather than say the wrong thing. I've done it myself.'

'It's exactly that,' Hugh said. 'I'd ask you in but this is serious bachelor-pad land at the moment. I'm going to have to give it a thorough going over before I hand it back to my parents.'

Martha tried to peek around him to test the truth of his statement but his not inconsiderable body was blocking her view.

'I can be messy on occasion,' she said. 'As more than a few flatmates have mentioned! But, well, I just came to say I'm truly sorry for how I reacted and if you want to talk to me about Harris, I'll be happy to listen. But I'll go now.'

'Okay. As you see, I'm hours behind. But how do you feel about joining me for a spot of lunch later? The Shoreline does a mean burger, and lots of interesting fish, and salads for the diet-conscious. Do you know it?'

'Give me a rough direction.'

'Halfway between here and the harbour. Keep going in a straight line. You can't miss it. It's got fantastic views.'

'I think I know where you mean.'

'Good. Harris and I used to eat there in the holidays. I could tell you about him.'

'I'd like that, Hugh,' Martha said.

'So would I. So, can I ask you to meet me there?' Hugh asked. 'About one o'clock?'

'Of course,' Martha said. She hadn't planned her day beyond apologising to Hugh, but now she had a lunch date – was it really a date so early in the acquaintance? – she thought she might get into her newly purchased running kit and go for a run. It might help to clear her head. 'I'll look forward to it.'

'Me too, Martha Langford,' Hugh said with a grin.

He was letting her know it was as Martha he was wanting to get to know her, not just because she was also known as Serena Ross, wasn't he? Martha's heart lifted a little.

Martha was early, only about fifteen minutes, but she decided to go on in and find a table.

Oh! Another surprise because there were full-length windows on three sides, the ceiling was very high with Raffles-style fans, and the whole place was filled with light. Outside there was a small balcony along two sides. Tables and chairs were set up outside but Martha decided it wasn't quite warm enough to sit out, although a few people were.

She chose a table for two, by the window facing the sea. The restaurant was built over the road, closed for the summer to traffic, and with the tide high it was as though she was sitting in the prow of a ship. She hadn't expected that – it was almost like being on a cruise in the Mediterranean if she allowed her imagination to run away with her. She picked up the menu. Lots to choose from. Was Hugh going to offer to pay or should she suggest they go Dutch. If they went Dutch it would be easier to say, 'Well, that was nice, but I don't think we have a future together.'

Red snapper or crab? Quinoa salad or pesto pasta?

'Penny for them,' Hugh said.

'They might cost a little bit more than that.' Martha laughed, looking up into his smiling face.

Hugh laid a hand of greeting, briefly, on Martha's shoulder and sat down opposite. 'Thanks for coming.'

'I'm glad to be here and, seeing as I had my first ever run this morning after I left you, I'm rather hungry.'

'Really? The first? Ever?'

'Yep. Although I've been guilty of being a bit of a gym bunny in my time, and daily dance lessons when I was at stage school.'

Talking about this now, it was starting to feel as though it was all in the past for her. Was it? Could it be?

'Did you like it? The run, I mean.'

'I'll let you know tomorrow what opinion my calves have on that,' she said, laughing.

'It gets easier,' Hugh said. 'As most things do.'

And the smile on his face seemed to freeze, and although he was looking at Martha it was as though he was also looking inside himself.

'Do you want to talk about Harris before we eat? You said earlier you used to come here with him so it can't be easy being here with someone who isn't your brother. We could just order a drink and talk? I'm not going to die of hunger if we postpone lunch for a while.'

'I didn't have you down as a mind-reader,' Hugh said. 'But yes, I was thinking about Harris. I imagined for a moment that he was going to come marching in, tell me it was my turn to buy the drinks – he always said that, even though I bought far more rounds than he ever did.'

'And you wish you could be buying that round now?'

A waiter arrived at their table. 'What can I get you?' he asked.

'Just a drink for the moment for me,' Martha said. 'We'll eat later. Okay with that, Hugh?'

'Fine, fine,' Hugh said. 'I'll have a pint of local ale. And you, Martha?'

'Prosecco if you have it,' Martha said.

'We sure do. Won't be a moment.'

'That was inordinately kind,' Hugh said. 'To realise I was struggling a bit there. I seemed to have lost all power of thought and speech for a second.'

'We all need a bit of help and understanding sometimes,' Martha said. 'Tell me about Harris.'

'It'll be easier if I show you.' He took out his phone from his jeans pocket. 'I've got hundreds on here. I'll spare you the baby brother photos.' He looked up from scrolling through and smiled at Martha.

'I can probably live without seeing those,' she said, doing her utmost to lighten what was, to Hugh, a difficult moment. 'What did he do?'

'Sports teacher. With a bit of English on the side. Rugby was his game, although he was pretty good at just about everything he tried – tennis, cricket, water sports of every description. Here. That's a good one.'

Hugh handed the phone to Martha, and a good-looking chap, with hair fairer than Hugh's and a big, rugby player's frame, smiled out at her. Despite the physical differences, she could see the likeness between the brothers.

'How did he die?' Martha asked, handing back the phone.

'Leukaemia,' Hugh said. 'He responded to treatment at first and we all held our breath with hope, but then it just stopped working for him and he shrunk before our eyes. It was swift in the end.'

The waiter came back with their drinks then.

'Can you come back in about half an hour, mate?' Hugh said.

'Sure can. Enjoy your drinks.'

'Nice bloke,' Hugh said. 'But I think it's plainer than day that we're not enjoying much at the moment.'

'It can't be easy for you,' Martha said. 'But I'm not sad I'm here. How long ago did Harris die?'

310

'Just over two years. It's still a bit raw. It's why I try to go to as many of those fêtes as I can and help them raise a bit of money so others can get the care Harris did. Although what I'm going to do with yet another teddy bear won on the tombola I don't know!'

'Offload it to a charity shop?' She was feeling guilty now that she hadn't gone along with Hugh, but there was no point saying so. Hugh just needed to talk. About himself. About Harris.

'I could. But a stupid part of me thinks Harris wants me to have the stupid things. They're tactile. Look… sorry, Martha, I know I'm being less than a thrilling lunch companion. I can be a right miserable sod at times. It's why I've been known to drink myself stupid more often than was good for my liver, although I'm over that bit now. It's why I turned into a bit of a recluse, turned down commissions. And it's why my long-term relationship broke down. Violins time, eh?'

Martha had a feeling that, with this remark, he was subtly letting her know he was unattached at the moment.

'What was she called? Your long-term girlfriend? If you don't mind telling me?'

'No. I don't mind. Abby. Abigail. Losing her was like losing Harris all over again but time has healed me more quickly there. And I realise now she could have been more understanding. Harris had only been gone three months when she walked out. And so, here I am, trying to put all the pieces of my life back together, along with my broken leg. Doing my best to live again. But I'm being a right bloke, aren't I, talking about me all the time?'

'I did ask you to,' Martha said. 'And besides, you must know a fair bit about me if you've ever watched TV or been to the cinema. Or read the newspapers.'

'Yeah, that must suck at times, too, having every bit of your private life splashed across the media.'

'It does. But I don't have to take it any more.' The restaurant

311

was beginning to fill up now and people had come to sit at tables either side of Martha and Hugh. She couldn't risk anyone over-hearing what she was saying. 'Shall we order now?'

'Good idea,' Hugh said.

'And then we can think, perhaps, of something we can do that will put our respective lives back on track.'

Running, it seemed, was the activity that suited them both. Hugh ran on the beach at least three times a day, while Martha preferred to run along the promenade, but only twice a day. If they saw one another in the distance they waved, but Hugh hadn't issued another invite to lunch, or dinner. And Martha wasn't entirely sure she wanted another invite because she still wasn't entirely convinced Hugh wouldn't suddenly send photos of her to some agency. She'd told her parents she was staying with a friend until the hullabaloo had died down, and that she was fine, and would call them soon. Friends texted her and left voicemails but she didn't reply to them either, having told anyone who needed to know the same story she'd told her parents. Sometimes she saw Hugh on the beach, bending to photograph something lying in the sand, or focusing on some-thing out at sea. A couple of times she'd got that feeling a person gets when someone is looking at them and she'd turned to look up at the headland above the chalets, and Hugh had been there. There was a wonderfully panoramic view of the bay from up there and he'd probably been taking landscape, or seascape, shots. He'd obviously seen her, because he'd waved to her as she turned.

But here was Hugh now, walking towards Martha's chalet where she was sitting on the deck, hat on to shield the low light from her eyes, reading in the late-afternoon sunshine.

He had a bottle of wine in one hand, and two glasses hanging from the fingers of the other.

'I hope you don't mind,' Hugh said, walking up the steps of

Number 23. 'But my motto these days is never to drink alone, and I fancied a drink, so I hope I can persuade you to join me.'

'Is the sun below the yardarm?' Martha said, smiling.

'It is somewhere in the world.' Hugh laughed back. He set the bottle and glasses down on the patio table and took a corkscrew from his jeans pocket. 'So, can I pour?'

'You can,' Martha said. 'I might have some nibbles to go with that – some crisps and savoury crackers, and two or three varieties of cheese.'

'Sounds divine,' Hugh said.

Hugh had poured her a very full glass of wine when she got back with the nibbles.

'To you,' Hugh said, handing the wine to her.

'Cheers,' they said as one, chinking glasses.

'I've come to thank you,' Hugh said.

'For what?'

'For having lunch with me the other day. I'd never have been able to go in there had you not been waiting for me. I was hiding behind a pillar waiting for you and watched you go in. But now I've faced my demons and I've been in there alone. Just coffee and cake, but I did it. I sat where we sat having lunch and, really, it was fine.'

'I don't know what to say,' Martha said, cradling her glass in her hands. 'Unless it's that I was happy to join you, and I'm glad you've faced that particular demon.'

'We'll drink to that then,' Hugh said, holding his glass out towards Martha to clink again.

'Onwards for us both!' Martha said, holding her glass high as Hugh reached over to touch it with his. 'I don't know if you've noticed but when I've been running I haven't worn my hat. And my hair's been tied back at the nape of my neck.'

'And no one came up and accused you of anything? Not that anything you may or may not have done is anyone else's business.'

'No. No one. I think there might have been two or three people

313

who recognised me because, when people do, a sort of disbelief that it could be me running towards them, or in the queue for an ice cream, comes over their face like a veil. And then, when I've gone, they whisper to their companion, only often it's louder than a whisper and I catch my name on the breeze... Serena Ross.'

'Be careful who you pretend to be or you might forget who you are.'

'Gosh, that's a very profound statement,' Martha said.

'Not mine, I'm afraid. I'm quoting, only I've forgotten who for the moment. Is that how it's been for you for a while? With the acting name, I mean.'

Martha nodded. 'I see that now. These past few days have been good. Since you showed me the shells on the beach and pointed things out to me, I'm seeing more, if that makes sense.'

'Perfect sense. And 'seeing more' is my cue to come in with a suggestion. My mission here is twofold. There was the chance to share a bottle of wine, of course, but it was also to tell you there's a small boat that does wildlife trips, coast-hugging. It leaves from the harbour early. Would you like to join me? Can you do early?'

'Ah, so you've noticed I don't emerge for my run until after coffee time?'

'I have. Would eight o'clock at the harbour be too early? The carrot here is that there'll more than likely be dolphins off Berry Head.'

'Really?'

'The boat leaving at eight bit, or the dolphins bit?'

'I can do early if I'm going to see dolphins.'

'You're on,' Hugh said. 'My treat.'

Martha was up at six o'clock the next morning. Hugh had said it might be an idea to wear a jacket with a hood if she had one with her, and a scarf, because it was still only May and, while the forecast was good, it could be a lot colder on the water than it was sitting on the decks of their chalets in the shelter of the cliff behind them.

He'd said it in a very non-bossy way as though he really was concerned she might get chilled.

Hugh had said he'd call for her at seven and they could walk over to the harbour. But when she looked out to see if he was on his way she saw he was on the beach, his phone/camera to his eye, back to the sea, photographing the chalets on The Strand.

Why was he doing that? Was he waiting for her to open the door so he could get a shot of her coming out? Was she being paranoid? Whichever, a ripple of unease snaked its way up her spine and out over her shoulders, and she shivered.

But just as Hugh had faced his demons by going into The Shoreline on his own without his brother, so she would have to face the fact that not every lens aimed her way was going to be for evil ends.

Martha reached for her coat, scarf and shoulder bag and went out. Hugh slid his phone back into his pocket and walked to greet her.

'Gorgeous morning for it, Martha,' he said. 'I don't think you'll regret this.'

'I hope not,' Martha said. 'I've usually got pretty good sea legs.' And then she decided to let Hugh know she'd seen him photographing her chalet. 'What were you taking photographs of just now?'

'The chalets. And yours in particular.'

'Why?' Martha said. She didn't know whether she wanted to go and see dolphins any more.

'Because there was a peregrine falcon hovering above it. I think it must have seen a piece of cockle or something a seagull had dropped. I'll show you if you like.'

'Please.'

'We'll need to get going if we're going to catch that boat,

though.' Hugh placed an arm under Martha's elbow and steered her round in the direction of the harbour. 'I'll find the best shots and show you as we go along.'

And he did, but still Martha was uneasy.

'Have you ever seen the film *Roman Holiday*?' Martha asked.

'Yep. Dozens of times. It's my mother's favourite. After Harris died she curled up on the couch watching it on a loop for months. I watched with her more times than I can count. So, I think, reading between the lines here, that you're saying I'm not the Gregory Peck character who gets to kiss the iconic Audrey Hepburn character, but that I'm… the photographer?'

'But you haven't taken any photos of me that you're going to present to me, as happened in the film, when my fortnight of escapism here is over?'

'Nope. But then, photographers don't, for the most part, have to sit in a darkroom developing stuff these days. There are no negatives to blackmail people with. Anything unwanted is deleted with a swipe of a finger. 'But back to *Roman Holiday*… Audrey Hepburn's character, Princess Ann, and the journalist, Joe Bradley, as played by Gregory Peck, were never going to get together, were they? Even though they did share just the one kiss,' Hugh went on. 'See how well I know this film!'

'And the Princess Ann character was never going to get it together with the photographer?' Martha smiled.

'Irving Radovich, as played by Eddie Albert. Who never got to kiss Audrey Hepburn, although, as I said, Gregory Peck did. And what a kiss! What fantastic on-screen chemistry those two had, eh? And off-screen for all we know.'

They'd reached the end of the beach now, and would have to get back on to the promenade to make their way to the harbour. Hugh, with his long legs, stepped on to the prom and held a hand out to help Martha up.

Hugh was looking at Martha, a gentle smile playing about his lips. He ran his tongue around them as though they had suddenly gone dry with nerves. She had the feeling he would very much like to kiss her. And much to her surprise, Martha found she wanted very much to kiss him too. In all her twenty-seven years she'd never kissed anyone who hadn't been involved in the world of acting. But would that be wise? Could their worlds knit together happily? Would they?

'Well,' Hugh said, breaking the spell that seemed to have been cast over them both. 'The boat and the dolphins wait for no man. Come on.'

'You weren't joking when you said it was a small boat.' Martha laughed. 'I've been in bigger baths in the States!'

'I'll have to take your word for that!' Hugh grinned.

They were sitting in the stern, just seven other passengers seated onboard. And two crew. *Tea and coffee available on request* was written on a scrap of paper pinned to the cockpit and Martha wondered where it could possibly be made in such a small space – and how, given the boat rocked as the captain spun it round to point out to sea. But then the sea seemed to flatten out as though it had been ironed and they were sailing over a sheet of satin.

'Cormorants,' Hugh said. 'Fairy Cove.'

Just yards out of the harbour and Martha had seen her first cormorant up close, standing on a rock a few yards from the shoreline of a fairy-sized cove. How large they seemed so close up, how glossy and rather elegant-looking with their small heads and slender bodies.

'And the gulls are just waking up in their cliff roosting places,' Hugh said, pointing up at the red sandstone cliff. 'And terns.'

'It's a bit of a day of firsts for me already,' Martha said. 'I mean, do we ever really look at cormorants and seagulls and terns in the normal course of events?' She never had – they were just there, seagulls being a nuisance much of the time, but from the boat they looked as though they'd just come through a washing machine on a white wash, they were so bright in the early-morning light.

'Well, I do,' Hugh laughed. 'They can be my bread and butter, seagulls. Thank God for photo memory cards these days because I can take literally thousands of images and then discard what I don't want. Forgive me if I ignore you for a moment, but there's loads I want to take pictures of.'

'Snap away,' Martha told him.

The captain was giving a running commentary about the area and the wildlife and Martha was happy to let his words wash over her as her eyes drank in the view. Hugh kept standing up to take pictures, then sitting down again, touching her on the arm now and then, gently but briefly, to ask if she was okay, and was she warm enough.

And then, there they were. As the boat rounded Berry Head, there were the dolphins. The captain shut down the throttle so that there was only the shush of the sea and the rumble of the motor as they all stood, as though choreographed, watching the dolphins jump and dive. No one spoke. A woman on the port side put her hands to her mouth and her eyes went wide with wonder as though she couldn't quite believe what she was seeing. Martha tried to count them… seven, eight, nine… but couldn't be sure she wasn't counting the same ones twice. As the boat rocked gently on the current, and everyone seemed to instantly find their sea legs, the dolphins came nearer. Martha had the urge to reach out and touch one, they were so close.

Martha lost track of time. She'd heard how seeing dolphins could be an almost religious experience and now she knew it to be true. Never would she have thought she could see them here, off the Devon coast, and in May, and in the company of a man she'd only just met. They were so free, so joyous, the way they leapt and then disappeared beneath the water again only to surface a few yards further away to make the same manoeuvre all over again. And it was then that Martha knew she had never had that freedom. Her life in acting had been scripted by her mother for the most part. Yes, she'd had a gift for acting – and dancing and singing – but had she only been living the life her mother had wanted for herself? She had spent two-thirds of her life living in what she now realised was a rather cloistered world.

Although it had been Martha who had run out on her acting life, it had taken meeting Hugh to show her the beauty in the real world.

'Thank you for bringing me, Hugh,' she said, sitting back down, quite giddy with emotion now.

'It's been my pleasure.'

The dolphins were moving further away now. Still rising from the water but not as high as they had been.

'I'll hold this experience to me for ever, I think,' Martha said.

'Me too. And we could,' Hugh said, 'make a few more before your fortnight's up. If that's okay with you, Miss Martha Langford.'

There it was again – Hugh's use of her real name, not her stage name. He liked her because of who she was, not what she was.

'We could,' Martha said. 'And I think we should.'

So they did. They still ran each day, but separately, because Martha was never going to be able to keep up, running on sand, with Hugh. But they always met for coffee, at one of the many cafés along the seafront, or back at Martha's chalet, taking their drinks down onto the beach to drink if the tide was out, burying their bare feet in the sand, and letting the sand trickle through their fingers as they talked and shared aspects of their past lives. In the evenings they wandered up into the town to find a restaurant or pub for supper. They even had a hilarious hour in the Penny Arcade playing the gaming machines – winning sometimes, losing sometimes. A bit like life, Martha thought, although she thought she might be on a winning streak now she'd met Hugh.

Hugh had taken Martha's arm in a gallant way and linked it through his to cross roads, but they didn't hold hands. Or kiss.

On Martha's last night, sitting on the deck of 23 The Strand, Hugh uncorked a bottle of champagne he said he'd had cooling in his fridge, along with a plate of deli nibbles Martha had a feeling he'd bought for just such an occasion.

'Glasses out,' Hugh said, indicating the frothing champagne and the need to get it into glasses before it frothed all over the deck.

'Yes, sir!' Martha laughed, holding out the champagne glasses towards him.

When they were filled to the brim, she handed one to Hugh.

'A toast,' he said. 'To you. For helping me with my grief over Harris. So, to you.'

Martha gulped back tears, then took a sip of champagne.

'And to you,' she said, clinking glasses. 'And to legs and hearts that will mend, given time.'

'That too,' Hugh said, tapping Martha's glass again.

'What will you do now?'

'Photography, of course. I've a fancy for photographing the oceans of the world, running on the world's beaches. I've got an idea for a TV series running around in my head – 90 Mile Beach, Bondi Beach. Woolacombe in North Devon, even. It doesn't have to be a big beach or a famous one. The concept is I'd run with a well-known personality and we'd look at the geography and wildlife around us, and put the world to rights as we ran. What do you think?'

I think it's a rotten idea. I want you to stay in my life, not go running off with some random person you might fall in love with on a tropical beach. Was he telling her this was the end of their friendship? Or was he putting the ball in her court, giving her an 'out' if she wanted it?

'Sounds good,' Martha said.

'Once more with feeling,' Hugh laughed.

'Sounds *really, really* good.'

'That's better. A seven out of ten that time. And you?' Hugh asked.

'I've not made any firm plans yet. I quite fancy stage work again. It's all too easy to iron out mistakes while filming for TV or the cinema. The money would be less but I've got enough to live on for a while. Then again, there's an idea buzzing about in my head like a mosquito that I could train to teach drama. Not at a stage school but in an ordinary comprehensive perhaps.'

'Go for it,' Hugh said. 'You've got a beautiful speaking voice. Well, a beautiful everything actually.'

'That's a lovely thing to hear,' Martha said. 'And?'

'And what?' Hugh swirled the stem of his glass in his fingers. He looked down at the table, up at the sky, out to sea. His eyes settled on Martha for a second and she saw his Adam's apple going up and down.

He was struggling for the right thing to say, wasn't he?

'To our respective futures?' Hugh said eventually.

'I think we both know that isn't what I meant. And I do believe, Hugh, you're blushing.'

Martha prised Hugh's glass gently from him and placed it on the tiny table between them.

'I was taught in drama school that, in the right situation, more emotion, more feeling, more truth can be conveyed by what people *don't* say than by what they do. Action – and conversely inaction – really can speak louder than words sometimes.' Then she cupped Hugh's face in her hands and kissed him. Just a gentle kiss but she let it linger.

'Wow! Is that how they teach you to kiss in stage school?'

'Nope. That one came from the heart.'

And then Hugh kissed her back.

It was that old cliché of fireworks and music playing for Martha.

'And so did that. But back to our futures… I like live theatre,' Hugh said. 'Can I come and watch?'

'Of course. And I've decided a bit of running on the world's beaches is something I'd quite like too.'

'So, we've rewritten the end of *Roman Holiday*.' Hugh kissed her again.

'Get a room already!' someone shouted from the prom.

'Your cabin or mine?' Martha asked as Hugh released her from the kiss.

Martha wrapped the amethyst necklace Tom Marchant had given her in tissue paper and slid it into an envelope. She had no need of it any more but it might be just the thing someone else might love and cherish. On the outside of the envelope she wrote her message:

Dear next occupant,

I've had the most interesting and wonderful fortnight at 23 The Strand. Life-changing even. I hope you have a wonderful time too. I leave you this gift, which I hope you'll enjoy wearing or will give to someone you think would like it. It might be fun if you could leave some little thing as a welcome gift for the next occupant but that's by no means obligatory.

Best wishes

Martha

P.S. Formerly known as Serena Ross

The next book from Linda Mitchelmore,
The Little B & B at Cove End,
is coming in summer 2019!